GREEN PLANETS

Green

ECOLOGY AND SCIENCE FICTION

Planets

Edited by Gerry Canavan and

Kim Stanley Robinson

WESLEYAN UNIVERSITY PRESS   MIDDLETOWN, CONNECTICUT

Wesleyan University Press

Middletown CT 06459

www.wesleyan.edu/wespress

© 2014 Wesleyan University Press

All rights reserved

Manufactured in the United States of America

Designed by Mindy Basinger Hill

Typeset in Calluna Pro

Wesleyan University Press is a member of the Green Press

Initiative. The paper used in this book meets their minimum

requirement for recycled paper.

Hardcover ISBN: 978-0-8195-7426-8

Paperback ISBN: 978-0-8195-7427-5

Ebook ISBN: 978-0-8195-7428-2

Library of Congress Cataloging-in-Publication Data

available on request.

5   4   3   2   1

Title page and part title art: Brian Kinney | shutterstock.com

FOR THE FUTURE

CONTENTS

As its title suggests, this volume was first inspired by Mark Bould and China Miéville's *Red Planets: Marxism and Science Fiction*. But where that book focused primarily on the long-standing connection between science fiction and political leftism, *Green Planets* takes up instead the genre's relationship with ecology, environmentalism, and the emerging interdisciplinary conversation variously called ecocriticism, environmental philosophy, and the ecological humanities.

The oxymoronic combination of "science" and "fiction" in the term "science fiction" suggests in miniature the internal tension that drives analysis of the genre. Is science fiction primarily "science" (knowledge, fact, truth), or is it primarily "fiction" (whimsy, fantasy, lie)? Does the genre offer a predictive window into the world of a future that is soon to come, or does it instead merely reflect the assumptions, anxieties, and cultural preoccupations of its own immediate present? It's little wonder that for decades many writers and critics of science fiction have chosen to eschew the name "science fiction" entirely, preferring "speculative fiction" or (even more commonly) the ambiguous shorthand "SF" as a means of avoiding the problem of the "science" on which the genre is nominally based. In fact almost none of the fantastic, otherworldly tropes most closely associated with SF in the popular imagination are "scientific" in any meaningful sense; the physical laws of reality, as far as anyone can tell, prohibit all the best-loved plot devices, from hyperdrives to mutant superpowers to time travel to perpetual motion machines. Despite frequent pretensions to the contrary from fans and promoters of the genre, the popular designation of a text as SF still typically registers not its careful fidelity to current scientific understanding but rather the extremity of its deviation from what science tells us is true.

And yet, despite all the necessary caveats and disavowals, it cannot be denied that we find ourselves living in science fictional times. Waiting in a doctor's office for the results of a genetic test that will tell her the true story of her own future, using a cheap handheld device that can in seconds wirelessly access a vast digital archive of all human knowledge, a person can effortlessly browse all the latest apocalyptic predictions about mankind's radical destabilization of the planet's climate and the concurrent mass extinction of its animal and plant life in between breaking news reports about the latest catastrophic flood, drought, or oil spill. As noted SF author William Gibson once put it: "Today, the sort of thing we used to think in science fiction has colonized the rest of our reality."[1] It's true that cars still don't fly—but they have started to drive themselves.

Nowhere is the science fictionalization of the present clearer than in contemporary considerations of humanity's interaction with its environment, which frequently deploys the language and logic of SF to narrativize the dire implications of ecological science for the future. Fairfield Osborn's *Our Plundered Planet,* published in 1948, briefly paused its ecological critique to wonder if perhaps there aren't humanoids somewhere else in the universe treating their planet better than we treat ours; two years later Norbert Weiner, the father of cybernetics, took stock of energy scarcity and entropic breakdown to unhappily declare us "shipwrecked passengers on a doomed planet" in his *The Human Use of Human Beings*.[2] Paul Crutzen's recent assertion of the Anthropocene—a proposed post-Holocene "epoch" that posits that the multiple impacts of human civilization on the planet will be visible in the geologic record—takes up the cosmic viewpoint native to SF to imagine the future scientists who will uncover the scant evidence of our existence on a long-deserted, post-human Earth; in *Man the Hunter,* from 1969, Richard B. Lee and Irven DeVore deployed the same imaginative frame to consider the "interplanetary archaeologists" of the future, from whose perspective "the origin of agriculture and thermonuclear destruction will appear as essentially simultaneous."[3] Rachel Carson, who jump-started the contemporary environmental movement with her stirring denunciation of chemical pesticides, famously chose to begin her book not with some detached presentation of the facts at hand but with a science fictional parable, "A Fable for Tomorrow," about the inhabitants of a small town "somewhere in America" whose hubris destroys paradise.[4] The "Spaceship Earth" metaphor for discussing resource scarcity and sustainability has become so naturalized that most completely forget its origins in SF. Even now, contemporary debates over the reality of climate change and the urgent need for renewable forms of energy production still frequently break down into accusations that one party or the other is dabbling in "science fiction," not "science fact"; implicit in this petty sniping is the concession that it is increasingly hard for us to tell the difference between the two. In many ways—and many of them quite disturbing—SF looks less and less like "fiction" at all, and something more like the thin edge of the future as it breaks into the present.

The authors of *Green Planets: Ecology and Science Fiction* share this foundational assumption that science fictional ways of thinking have something useful to teach us about the way the contemporary moment thinks about nature and the world. In this respect it is the latest entry in a long tradition of sf criticism inaugurated by Darko Suvin in his 1972 article "On the Poetics of the Science Fiction Genre," which announced sf's importance as the "literature of cognitive estrangement."[5] Here Suvin recasts that apparently hopeless contradiction between science/cognition and fiction/estrangement in much more positive terms: the *estrangement* of sf is an incredibly flexible artistic tool for disorienting and defamiliarizing the conditions of everyday life, opening up the mind to previously unimagined possibilities, while *cognition* functions as the reality principle that keeps our imaginations honest. The alienated view-from-outside offered by cognitive estrangement allows us to examine ourselves and our institutions in new (and rarely flattering) light; sf distances us from the contemporary world-system only to return us to it, as aliens, so that we can see it with fresh eyes. For Suvin, and for the generation of sf critics that followed, sf is thus at its core always about utopia: the dream of another world that wasn't just a hopeless fantasy, a glimpse of the better history that could actually be ours, if we would only choose to build it. Even the dystopian nightmares and secular apocalypses that so dominate contemporary sf point us, by negative example, in the direction of utopia: *whatever else you do, don't do this....*

Two decades ago, in the introduction to a collection of ecotopian fictions called *Future Primitive,* my coeditor Kim Stanley Robinson offered up a succinct description of the crisis facing the human race in our moment of technological modernity: "We are gaining great powers at the very moment that our destruction of our environment is becoming ruinous. We are in a race to invent and practice a sustainable mode of life before catastrophe strikes us."[6] Our civilization, Robinson goes on, consequently finds itself today in the throes of an incomprehensibly vast project of "rethinking the future," a Herculean and vertiginous task that links political environmental movements and radical animal-rights activists to politicians to venture capitalists to organic farmers to freelance inventors to biologists to physicists to chemists to economists to ecofeminists to philosophers to literary critics to writers of sf. Indeed, the recognition of the immense planetary scale of ecological crisis, and the shocking inadequacy of our response thus far, extends the Suvinian interest in cognitive estrangement and utopian dreaming across the entirety of politics and culture today—now the prerequisite for our collective survival. The future has gone bad; we need a new one.

For over a century the thought experiments of sf have been probing our possible futures, providing an archive of the imagination where science, story, and political struggle can converge and cross-pollinate. The ambition of *Green Planets* is to trace key moments in this vital and ongoing conversation.

Gerry Canavan

Notes

1. Mavis Linnemann, "William Gibson Overdrive," Phawker.com (August 15, 2007), http://www.phawker.com/2007/08/15/coming-atraction-william-gibson-qa/.

2. Fairfield Osborn, *Our Plundered Planet* (Boston: Little, Brown, 1948), quoted in Eric C. Otto, *Green Speculations: Science Fiction and Transformative Environmentalism* (Columbus: Ohio State University Press), 7–8; Norbert Weiner, *The Human Use of Human Beings* (New York: Da Capo Press, 1950), 40.

3. Richard B. Lee and Irven DeVore, eds., *Man the Hunter* (Chicago: Transaction, 1969), 3.

4. Rachel Carson, *Silent Spring* (1962; New York: Houghton Mifflin, 2002), 2–3.

5. Darko Suvin, "On the Poetics of the Science Fiction Genre," *College English* 34, no. 3 (1972): 372–82 (372).

6. Kim Stanley Robinson, ed., *Future Primitive: The New Ecotopias* (New York: Tor Books, 1994): 10–11.

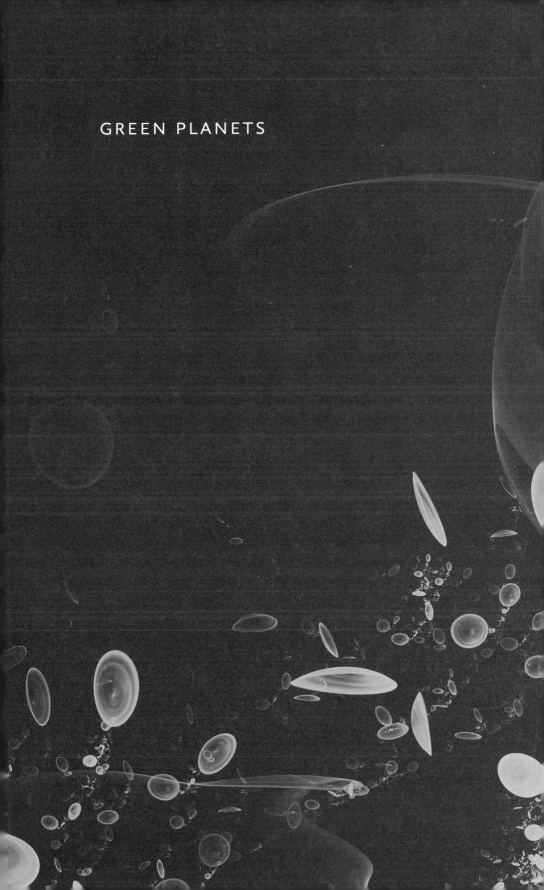

GREEN PLANETS

Introduction

If This Goes On

GERRY CANAVAN

And it is now that our two paths cross.
Both simultaneously recognise his Anti-type:
    that I am an Arcadian, that he is a Utopian.
He notes, with contempt, my Aquarian belly:
    I note, with alarm, his Scorpion's mouth.
He would like to see me cleaning latrines: I would
    like to see him removed to some other planet.

W. H. Auden, "Vespers" (Part 5 of *Horae Canonicae*)

Borrowing his categories from Auden, Samuel R. Delany has written that two ideological positions are available to us in modernity, each one carrying either a positive or a negative charge. One can imagine oneself to be the citizen of a marvelous New Jerusalem, the "technological super city where everything is clean, and all problems have been solved by the beneficent application of science"—or else one can be a partisan of Arcadia, "that wonderful place where everyone eats natural foods and no machine larger than one person can fix in an hour is allowed in. Throughout Arcadia the breezes blow, the rains are gentle, the birds sing, and the brooks gurgle." Each position in turn implies its dark opposite. The flip side of the Good City is the Bad City, the Brave New World, where fascist bureaucrats have crushed the soul of the human, machines have replaced work and love, and smog blocks out the stars; the other side of the Edenic Good Country is the Land of the Flies, where the nostalgic reverie of an imagined rural past is replaced instead by a reversal of progress and an unhappy return to the nightmare of history: floods, wars, famine, disease, superstition, rape, murder, death.[1]

These loyalties shape our political and aesthetic judgments. The person whose temperament draws her to the New Jerusalem, Delany goes on to say, will tend to see every Arcadia as a Land of the Flies, while the person who longs for Arcadia will see in every city street and every shiny new gadget the nascent seeds of a Brave New World. What seems at first to be a purely spatial matter (*in what sort of place would you rather live?*) turns out in this way to be as much about temporality and political projection (*what sort of world are we making for ourselves?*). Delany's four categories imply speculation about the kind of future we are building and what life will be like for us when it arrives. In this respect Delany's schema is of a piece with the dialectic between "thrill and dread," between utopia and apocalypse, that Marshall Berman says in *All That Is Solid Melts into Air* defines "modernity" as such: "To be modern is to find ourselves in an environment that promises us adventure, power, joy, growth, transformation of ourselves and the world—and, at the same time, that threatens to destroy everything we have, everything we know, everything we are."[2] Though Berman pays little attention to the emergence of SF in that work, his description of modernity as the knife's edge between utopia and apocalypse nevertheless usefully doubles as a succinct description for virtually every SF narrative ever conceived. And little wonder: SF emerges as a recognizable cultural genre out of the same conditions of technological modernity that generated literary and artistic modernism at the dawn of the twentieth century, with the ecstatic techno-optimistic anticipation of *Amazing Stories* founder Hugo Gernsback matched always by the unending cavalcade of disaster, catastrophe, and out-and-out apocalypse that Everett and Richard F. Bleiler, in their massive index to the SF of the period, group under the single evocative heading "Things Go Wrong."[3] Indeed, the persistence (and continued popularity) of SF into the contemporary moment can perhaps be thought of as the last, vital vestige of the original modernist project: from dazzling architectural cityscapes and off-world colonies to superweapons run amuck and catastrophic climate change, from Marinetti's worship of progress, technology, and speed to Kafka's deep and abiding suspicion of the project of modernity as such, SF extends the overawing directive to "make it new" to the farthest reaches of time and space.

Delany argues that the dialectics between city and country and between utopia and apocalypse that generate our New Jerusalems, Arcadias, Brave New Worlds, and Lands of the Flies are crucially operative in basically all SF. Thus the pastoral Arcadia of Wells's Eloi in *The Time Machine* (1895) is revealed to require the Brave New World of the Morlocks as its true material base, just as Huxley's *Brave New World* (1932) requires for its own continuation the preservation of an Arcadian "Reservation" as an internal safety valve. In *1984* (1949) the Arcadian refuge has always already been corrupted by totalitarianism, with secret microphones hidden in the flowers and trees. In a host of post-apocalyptic nuclear and zombie fictions from during and after the Cold War, a hopeless and wretched Land of the Flies is imagined as the only possible alternative to the New Jerusalem/Brave New World of American-style consumer capitalism and the national security state; in *Soylent Green* (1973), *Silent Running* (1972), and dozens of other 1970s and post-1970s environmental disaster narratives, we find capitalism hurtling hopelessly toward a final Land of the Flies anyway, as the bitter consequence of its insistence on ceaseless innovation and endless expansion on a finite and limited globe. Ernest Callenbach's influential *Ecotopia* (1975) articulates in that moment of crisis the possibility of a New Jerusalem that *is* an Arcadia, precisely through the Pacific Northwest's imagined secession from a United States that is rapidly collapsing into both a fascist Brave New World and starvation-ridden Land of the Flies. And even in something like the children's film WALL-E (2008) we find tomorrow's desolate Brave New World of plastic trash and consumer junk can still be recovered as an Arcadia, if only because our robots are smart enough to love nature more than we do.

It is only in postmodernity, Delany goes on to say, that new ideological forms are generated at the interstices of the first four. The first of these is the Junk City—the dysfunctional New Jerusalem in slow-motion breakdown, where the glittering spires haven't been cleaned in quite a while, where the gas stations have all run out of gas, and where nothing works quite the way it did when it was new. The positive side of Junk City is an ecstatic vision of improvisational recombinative urban chaos, "the Lo Teks living in the geodesic superstructure above Nighttown in Gibson's 'Johnny Mnemonic,'" to borrow Delany's example, or perhaps something like a fix-it shop in the ruins of today's Detroit. The other hybrid position is the ruined countryside, toxified by runoff from the cities and factories, which we need not even to turn to SF to imagine; we sadly have enough of these places in the real world as it is. And the flip side of the ruined countryside, its positive charge, is the unexpectedly sublime vision of decadent beauty that Delany calls the Culture of the Afternoon—the way a sunset, shining splendidly through the smog, glistens off the antifreeze.[4]

▶ ▶ ▶

Among other things, the shift from the modern to the postmodern as articulated by Delany registers a loss of political-historical agency in favor of a sense of doomed inevitability. The science fictional "Fable for Tomorrow" that opens Rachel Carson's *Silent Spring* (1962), we might note, tells of an Arcadia "in the heart of America where all life seemed to live in harmony with its surroundings" that is corrupted and destroyed by the introduction of chemical poisons that slowly kill all life in the area. But "No witchcraft, no enemy action had silenced the rebirth of new life in this stricken world. The people had done it themselves"—and thus *we*, reading *Silent Spring* before the final disaster, might yet choose to do otherwise.[5] Similarly, in the nuclear apocalypses that dominated the Cold War imagination of the future, agency is retained always in the spirit of an urgent but still-timely warning; living in the present, rather than the scorched and radioactive future, we can choose not to build the last bomb, and choose not to push the button that will launch it. The haunting UNLESS that punctuates the end of Dr. Seuss's *The Lorax* (1971) captures well the sense of hope that is retained even in the most dire jeremiads, which presume that politics and indeed revolution are still possible, that we might still collectively choose to leave the world better than we found it.

For Fredric Jameson, it is also this loss of faith in the possibilities of political and social transformation—the evacuation of futurity that Francis Fukuyama famously called "the end of history"[6]—that marks the shift from modernity to postmodernity. The incapacity for the imagination of alternatives to global capitalism has been frequently encapsulated by Jameson's well-known, oft-misquoted observation from *The Seeds of Time* that "it seems to be easier for us today to imagine the thoroughgoing deterioration of the earth and of nature than the breakdown of late capitalism."[7] Back when we were modern, we believed real change was possible; now that we are postmodern, we are certain it is not.

Shifts in the dominant vision of ecological apocalypse between the modern and postmodern periods reflect this paradigm shift in our relationship to futurity. The superweapons of early twentieth-century SF—and their terrible actualization in the nuclear bomb—threatened to unpredictably explode at any moment in the future, destroying all we have, and transforming the planet into a radioactive cinder. Thus the urgent need in the present, expressed in so much leftist SF of the period, to oppose more bombs, more wars. But, as *Green Planets* contributor Timothy Morton has noted, the temporality of climate change, the characteristic planetary apocalypse of our postmodern moment, is rather different: "Global warming is like a very slow nuclear explosion that nobody even notices is happening. . . . That's the horrifying thing about it: it's like my childhood nightmares came true, even before I was born."[8] In the unhappy geological epoch of the Anthropocene—the name scientists have proposed for the moment human activities begin to be recognizable in the geological record, the moment visiting aliens or the future's *Cockroach sapiens* will be able to see scrawled in their studies of ice cores and tree rings that *humanity wuz here*[9]—the climate has always already been changed. The current, massive disruptions in global climate, that is to say, have been caused by the cumulative carbon release of generations of people who were long dead before the problem was even identified, as well as by ongoing release from the immense networks of energy, production, and distribution that were built and developed in the open landscape of free and unrestricted carbon release—networks on which contemporary civilization now undeniably depends, but which nobody yet has any idea how to replicate in the absence of carbon-burning fossil fuels. As Benjamin Kunkel has wittily noted: "The nightmare, in good nightmare fashion, has something absurd and nearly inescapable about it: either we will begin running out of oil, or we won't."[10] That is: either we have Peak Oil, and the entire world suffers a tumultuous, uncontrolled transition to post-cheap-oil economics, or else there is still plenty of oil left for us to permanently destroy the global climate through continued excess carbon emissions.

Despite the urgency of these increasingly undeniable ecological constraints placed upon human activity, however, late capitalism remains a mode of production that insists (culturally) and depends (structurally) on limitless expansion and permanent growth without end: into the former colonial periphery, into the peasant countryside, through oil derricks into the deepest crevices of the earth, and, then, in futurological imaginings, to orbital space stations, lunar cities, Martian settlements, asteroid belt mining colonies, sleeper ships to Alpha Centauri, and on and on. It is a process of growth whose end we can simply not conceive. "The Earth got used up," begins the intro to several episodes of Joss Whedon's western-in-space *Firefly* (2002), "so we moved out and terraformed a whole new galaxy of Earths."[11] It sounds so easy! But from a scientific standpoint the other planets in the solar system are simply too inhospitable, and the distances between solar systems far too great, for the fantasy of unlimited expansion to ever actually be achievable.

Moreover, putting aside the sheer impossibility of this persistent trope of capitalist ideology—the basic mathematical impossibility of economic growth that *literally* never ends—we should find that narratives of space colonization dialectically reinscribe the very horizon of material deprivation and ultimate limit that they are meant to relieve. "Escape" from Earth actually only constrains you all the tighter, in miniature Earths smaller and more fragile than even the one you left. In his essay "The Economics of the Coming Spaceship Earth," discussed in Sabine Höhler's chapter of *Green Planets*, Kenneth E. Boulding (the cofounder of the Society for the Advancement of General Systems Theory[12]) notes this reality as he characterizes the "critical moment" of the mid-twentieth century as a transition from a "cowboy economy" to a "spaceman economy":

> For the sake of picturesqueness, I am tempted to call the open economy the "cowboy economy," the cowboy being symbolic of the illimitable plains and also associated with reckless, exploitative, romantic, and violent behavior, which is characteristic of open societies. The closed economy of the future might similarly be called the "spaceman" economy, in which the earth has become a single spaceship, without unlimited reservoirs of anything, either for extraction or for pollution, and in which, therefore, man must find his place in a cyclical ecological system which is capable of continuous reproduction of material form even though it cannot escape having inputs of energy.[13]

The echo of Frederick Jackson Turner's 1893 "frontier thesis" is unmistakable; a once-open, once-free horizon of expansive possibility, which previously drove American history, has now slammed forever shut.

In the cowboy economy, consumption is an unalloyed good; if there are infinite reserves of everything (or abundant resources so inexhaustible as to be effectively infinite), the health of an economy is logically predicated on the expansion of consumption. But on a spaceship economy, governed by scarcity, reserves must always be tightly controlled, requiring a reevaluation of the basic principles of economics:

> By contrast, in the spaceman economy, throughput is by no means a desideratum, and is indeed to be regarded as something to be minimized rather than maximized. The essential measure of the success of the economy is not production and consumption at all, but the nature, extent, quality, and complexity of the total capital stock, including in this the state of the human bodies and minds included in the system. In the spaceman economy, what we are primarily concerned with is stock maintenance, and any technological change which results in the maintenance of a given total stock with a lessened throughput (that is, less production and consumption) is clearly a gain. This idea that both production and consumption are bad things rather than good things is very strange to economists, who

have been obsessed with tile income-flow concepts to the exclusion, almost, of capital-stock concepts.[14]

This central insight—an ecological one—makes visible certain contradictions that were programmatically obscured by the "space empire" fictions so popular in the Golden Age of SF. In stark contrast to the untold riches and total freedom they are imagined to provide, distant space colonies—whether on inhospitable moons or orbiting far-flung planets—are in fact necessarily markers of deep, abiding, and permanent scarcity, requiring, for any hope of survival, careful planning and rigorous management, without any waste of resources. From an earthbound perspective, the colonization of space appears wildly expansive, a "New Frontier" that opens up the entire universe to human experience and exploitation—but from a perspective inside one of these spaceships or colonies, life is a state of fragile and even hellish enclosure, at constant risk of either deadly shortages or deadly exposure to the void outside.

Asimov, of all SF writers, confronts this paradox in a late work, *Robots and Empire* (1985), which sees one of its robot heroes (operating under the self-generated "Zeroth" Law of Robots[15]) deliberately and permanently poison Earth's crust with radioactive contaminants in order to force humans off their otherwise paradisal home world. Earth is already perfect for us, the robot R. Giskard reasons—too perfect. The only way to get human beings off the planet and out into the universe (where, scattered across hundreds of worlds, the species will finally be safe from any local planetary disaster) is to destroy Earth altogether: "The removal of Earth as a large crowded world would remove a mystique I have already felt to be dangerous and would help the Settlers. They will streak outward into the Galaxy at a pace that will double and redouble and—without Earth to look back to always, without Earth to set up as a God of the past—they will establish a Galactic Empire. It was necessary for us to make that possible."[16] Taken in the context of the rest of Asimov's immense shared universe, the intended conclusion for the reader is that this robot indeed made the correct decision to poison the planet and kill all nonhuman life on Earth.[17]

The use of interstellar travel and space colonization as a metaphor for understanding and reimagining questions of material/ecological limit is well-trod ground in SF, in works ranging from Brian Aldiss's *Non-Stop* (*Starship* in the United States) (1951) to Robert Heinlein's *The Moon Is a Harsh Mistress* (1961)—which popularized the ecologically sound proverb "There ain't no such thing as a free lunch"—to my coeditor Kim Stanley Robinson's own unapologetically utopian *Mars* trilogy (1990s). It is even, in somewhat sublimated form, the kernel structuring Stephen King's recent horror blockbuster, *Under the Dome* (2009), in which an impenetrable barrier suddenly isolates Chester's Mill, Maine, from the rest of the outside world, leading to immediate resource scarcity, social breakdown, and violent chaos. As King told popeaters.com:

> From the very beginning, I saw it as a chance to write about the serious ecological problems that we face in the world today. The fact is we all live under the dome. We have this little blue world that we've all seen from outer space, and it appears like that's about all there is. It's a natural allegorical situation, without whamming the reader over the head with it. . . . But I love the idea about isolating these people, addressing the questions that we face. We're a blue planet in a corner of the galaxy, and for all the satellites and probes and Hubble pictures, we haven't seen evidence of anyone else. There's nothing like ours. We have to conclude we're on our own, and we have to deal with it. We're under the dome. All of us.[18]

As King suggests, and as Ursula Heise has described in more detail, in the 1960s and 1970s these questions of limit crystallize around a particular series of science fictional visual images that, while familiar and perhaps unremarkable today, were revelatory and even shattering in their moment: Soviet and especially NASA images of Earth as viewed from space, chief among them the "Earthrise" photograph obtained by the *Apollo 8* crew in 1968 and the "Blue Marble" photograph taken by the *Apollo 17* crew in 1972. (To Heise's list we might add the "Pale Blue Dot" photograph taken by *Voyager 1* in 1990, in which a six-billion-kilometer-distant Earth is but a single pixel, barely visible against a field of total darkness.) The wide circulation of these "blue planet" images, Heise writes, represents Earth as an immanent and immediately graspable totality, in which all differences between race, class, gender, nation, ideology, and ecosystem have been completely smoothed away: "Set against a black background like a precious jewel in a case of velvet, the planet here appears as a single entity, united, limited, and delicately beautiful."[19]

But the utopian possibilities encoded in this reading of the photo—*we are all one species on this pale blue dot*, we are all in this together—can just as quickly give way to the brutally apocalyptic. This is, after all, Al Gore's anxious use of the "Pale Blue Dot" photo in his climate change documentary *An Inconvenient Truth* (2006): "You see that pale, blue dot? That's us. Everything that has ever happened in all of human history has happened on that pixel. All the triumphs and all the tragedies, all the wars, all the famines, all the major advances. . . . It's our only home. And that is what is at stake: our ability to live on planet Earth, to have a future as a civilization."[20] In this reading "Spaceship Earth" quickly becomes not our paradise, but our prison—we are all of us trapped here, waiting to be killed either by cosmic accident or our own folly. Indeed, I would suggest that post-1970s recognition of this unhappy ultimate limitation on the future growth of wealth may do much to explain the cultural importance of cyberpunk in the 1980s and 1990s and speculation about a technological "Singularity" in the 2000s, as both at their core offer an alternative scheme for getting outside scarcity and precariousness—simply leave the material world altogether, by entering the computer. In virtual space, with no resource consumption or excess pollution to worry about, we can all be as rich as we want for as long as we want (or so the fantasy goes).

The more we learn, the smaller Earth seems—much too small, far too delicate, to encompass all our lavish dreams of inexhaustible, techno-futuristic wealth. And yet, forty years since a human being last set foot on the moon, we are increasingly just as certain that there is nowhere else for us to go. Thus ecological discourse, both in and outside SF, both during and after the 1970s, becomes characterized by a claustrophobic sense of impending ecological limit, the creeping terror that technological modernity, and its consumer lifestyle, may in fact have no future at all. Chad Harbach in *n + 1* captures well the material origins of this sense of dread:

> America and the fossil-fuel economy grew up together; our triumphant history is the triumphant history of these fuels. We entrusted to them (slowly at first, and with increasing enthusiasm) the work of growing our food, moving our bodies, and building our homes, tools, and furniture—they freed us for thought and entertainment, and created our ideas of freedom. These ideas of freedom, in turn, have created our existential framework, within which one fear dwarfs all others: the fear of economic slowdown (less growth), backed by deeper fears of stagnation (no growth) and, unthinkably, contraction (anti-growth). America does have a deeply ingrained, morally coercive politics based in a fear that must never be realized, and this is it. To fail to grow—to fail to grow ever faster—has become synonymous with utter collapse, both of our economy and our ideals.[21]

In a recent essay in *Harper's*, Wendell Berry makes much the same point, describing U.S. energy policy as a "Faustian economics" predicated on a "fantasy of limitlessness" that, when put under threat, produces claustrophobia and dread.[22] Dipesh Chakrabarty, drawing from Timothy Mitchell, has in turn suggested that we might extend this analysis even further, across the whole of post-Enlightenment liberal democracy: "The mansion of modern freedoms stands on an ever-expanding base of fossil-fuel use."[23] In this sense limit and apocalypse can be thought, in the ideology of American-style capitalism at least, to be nearly synonymous—indeed, the end of the liberal subject as such.

Few cultural documents depict this moment of anxious confrontation with limit more vividly than the opening sequence of the overpopulation disaster film *Soylent Green* (1973), which depicts a miniature history of America. We begin with a quiet classical piano score over a sepia-tinted montage depicting nineteenth-century settlement of the American West, in which the wide-open natural spaces of the frontier seem to dwarf their human inhabitants. But soon something begins to change. Suddenly there are too many people in the frame, then far too many people; cars and then airplanes begin to appear; cities grow huge. New instruments enter the musical track: trumpets, trombones, saxophones; the cacophony begins to speed. Now humans are dwarfed not by nature but by the ceaseless replication of their own consumer goods—replicating the logic of the assembly line, the screen becomes filled with countless identical cars. We see jammed highways, overflowing landfills, smog-emitting power plants, flashes of war, riots, pollution, and graves. The sequence goes on and on, using vertical pans to give the sense of terrible accumulation, of a pile climbing higher and higher and higher. Finally, we reach the end—the music slows back to its original piano score, combined with an out-of-harmony synthesizer, over a few sepia-tinted images of that same natural world in ruin, now filled with trash. The end of the sequence locates this site of ruin in the future; New York, 2022, population forty million. But of course these nightmarish images are all photographs from the present: the disaster has already happened, it's already too late.[24]

Thus we frequently find, in the Junk Cities and Cultures of the Afternoon that characterize the most contemporary sense of our collective ecological future, a sense that there is nothing left to do but somehow accommodate ourselves as best we can to ongoing and effectively permanent catastrophe. In *Nausicaä of the Valley of the Wind* (1984), a widely loved ecological anime from Japanese filmmaker Hayao Miyazaki, the eras of both green forests and global capitalism are in the distant past, lost in the mists of thousands of years. The legacy of our time—the legacy of a final war called the Seven Days of Fire—is a snarl of toxic jungles and mutant insects, in the gaps of which scattered human beings still struggle to survive. Paolo Bacigalupi's stories of the future (discussed by Eric C. Otto in his chapter in this volume) frequently see their quasi-human and nonhuman protagonists exploring polluted, toxic landscapes in search of new types of beauty (if any are possible) in a world where unchecked capitalism has completely destroyed nature. And in John Brunner's utterly apocalyptic *The Sheep Look Up* (1972)—the best of 1970s ecological SF, if only because it so unflinchingly shows us the worst—even this consolation is denied us as a parade of manmade environmental horrors poisons every aspect of our lives, where Things Go Wrong, and Wronger, and Wronger Still, but nothing ever changes.

The logical endpoint of such narratives generates a final position of the imagination located beyond even Delany's proposed Junk Cities and Cultures of the Afternoon: the Quiet Earth, a planet that is devoid of human life entirely. The negative charge of the Quiet Earth is the elegiac fantasy of an entirely dead planet—a murdered planet—in which the human species has left behind nothing but ruin before finally killing even itself. Margaret Atwood evokes this vision of a Quiet Earth in a short flash fiction (written for the *Guardian* during the 2009 Copenhagen climate summit) called "Time Capsule Found on the Dead Planet," which finds a human race whose apex of development was the twentieth-century creations of deserts and death. (In the face of this final extinction even her apocalyptic novel *Oryx and Crake*, written six years earlier, seems somehow upbeat.) In a spirit of mourning and loss, the speaker of the piece addresses him- or herself to the unknown aliens who have come, millennia hence, to bear witness to our vanishing: "You who have come here from some distant world, to this dry lakeshore and this cairn, and to this cylinder of brass, in which on the last day of all our recorded days I place our final words: Pray for us, who once, too, thought we could fly."[25]

Atwood's blighted vision of a ruined world recalls—and transforms—Percy Bysshe Shelley's 1818 poem "Ozymandias" as an anticipatory memory of Earth's barren future. In the desert of a "distant land" stands the toppled monument to the arrogant king of a lost civilization that believed both he and it to be immortal. But only the head and legs remain; all else has turned to dust. "Lone and level sands" stretch "round the decay of that colossal wreck"; the thriving cities and once-verdant landscapes of Ozymandias's empire have been utterly erased by a totalizing desertification that, in the present moment, inevitably suggests the bleak endpoint of global climate change. Look upon our works, ye Mighty, and despair. Nothing beside remains.[26] "When we contemplate ruins," Christopher Woodward writes, "we contemplate our own future";[27] the apocalypse is thereby transformed into a memory, an event that is yet to come but which has also somehow, paradoxically, already happened.

The positive side of the Quiet Earth retains at least some small sense of hope, though for other life forms, not for us. As Imre Szeman and Brent Bellamy show in their *Green Planets* chapter on recent depictions of nonhuman Earths in such productions as *Life after People* (2008) and *The World Without Us* (2007), such texts frequently suggest that the elimination of human beings can *itself* be thought of as a kind of misanthropic ecotopia; without us, at least, the dogs and the trees and the birds and the bees can go on living. In the Kenyan short SF film *Pumzi* (2010), directed by Wanuri Kahiu, the allegorical stakes are these explicitly; after a devastating series of water wars and droughts, the human race has been driven underground, clinging to every drop of water that can be wrung from sweaty T-shirts or recovered from the condensation on bathroom mirrors. The world outside the bunker is totally dead. But our scientist hero, Asha (meaning "hope" in Sanskrit, "life" in Swahili), discovers a plant seed that she believes can still germinate; stealing into the forbidden world outside, Asha sacrifices first her meager water ration and ultimately her own life to nourish the world's last, and first, tree. A shift to the sublime, God's-eye perspective of time-lapse photography shows the slow return of life to the desert after years, decades, centuries—Asha's corpse nourishing its roots. If it's us or them, the film suggests, perhaps we should choose them.[28]

▶ ▶ ▶

But perhaps we can pull ourselves back from this brink. "We have to accept," Slavoj Žižek has recently written, "that, at the level of possibilities, our future is doomed, that the catastrophe will take place, that it is our destiny—and then, against the background of this acceptance, mobilize ourselves to perform the act that will change destiny itself and thereby insert a new possibility into the past."[29] The bizarre time-travel logic of this notion suggests the visions of ecological apocalypse might have some radical political potential after all. If capitalism has always been, in K. William Kapp's memorable formulation, "an economy of unpaid costs,"[30] then the growing recognition that the bill is coming due can represent a kind of nascent revolutionary consciousness. Looking through the lens of the apocalypse—skipping ahead, that is, to the end of the story—we can see capitalism more clearly, without the distortions of ideology, complacency, and reaction that ordinarily cloud our view. And then we might, even now, act. As Octavia E. Butler once wrote of her novel of neoliberal deprivation and devastating ecological collapse, *Parable of the Sower* (1993), "Sometime ago I read some place that Robert A. Heinlein had these three categories of science-fiction stories: The what-if category; the if-only category; and the if-this-goes-on category. And I liked the idea. So this is definitely an if-this-goes-on story. And if it's true, if it's anywhere near true, we're all in trouble."[31] Perhaps the true fantasy of apocalypse then is not so much that we will be destroyed but that *something might intervene in time to force us to change*—apocalypse in its original, biblical sense, from the Greek ἀποκάλυψις, connoting not a final end but an unveiling: *revelation*. The fantasy of apocalypse is here unveiled as itself a mode of critique, a crying out for change.

At the core of James Cameron's *Avatar* (2009)—whatever else we might have to say about the film's lavish visual spectacle and its troubling politics of race, gender, disability, and indigeneity—is the fantasy that a typical American might somehow be *transformed*: put into another body, located in another social-historical context, capable of living a different sort of life. The desire for this transformation is so strong that it leads even the film's domestic audiences to root against what is essentially the U.S. military as it invades the planet Pandora looking to seize control of its valuable resources for the benefit of a desperate, dying Earth—with our hero leading the resistance and successfully forcing the imperialists off the planet. And his reward for all this in the end is to be permanently transferred into the body of the big-O Other—to, in essence, not have to be an eco-imperialist any longer.[32] Little wonder, perhaps, that despite the anxiety over the film's clear evocation of Orientalist and white-savior fantasies like Pocahontas and *Dances with Wolves* that has dominated its reception in the Western academy, *Avatar* has frequently been embraced by indigenous activists in the Global South, who see in it a science fictional reflection of their own struggles.

A similar miracle takes place at the end of little-seen box-office flop *Daybreakers* (also from 2009), which makes literal the metaphor famously employed by Karl Marx: "Capital is dead labour, that, vampire-like, only lives by sucking living labour, and lives the more, the more labour it sucks."[33] Ten years after a viral outbreak that has turned the national elite into vampires, in *Daybreakers'* 2019 there are no longer enough humans left to feed America's insatiable desire for blood. Vampires who go without blood for too long are transformed into monstrous "subsiders" that attack anything that moves; as the film opens, the subsider epidemic is just reaching the suburbs. Coffee shops advertise that they "still sell 20% blood," while "blood riots" rock the Third World. All efforts at an energy substitute are stalled. America has reached Peak Blood.

The solution here is again personal transformation: it turns out that through controlled exposure to the sun, vampires can be cured. But the "cured" vampires cannot be revampirized; in fact their blood itself now contains the cure, turning any vampire who drinks from them into a cured human as well. What is being imagined is a kind of viral enlightenment operating through an epidemiological social network—friend to friend, relative to relative, coworker to coworker—that has the power to slowly transform a society of vampire-consumers back into human beings once again.[34]

The active fantasy in both these narratives, and in dozens of others across the field of ecological SF, is salvific: that the nightmare of exploitation, and our own complicity in these practices, might somehow be stopped, despite our inability to change. As Kierkegaard put it, in an epigram sometimes invoked by Darko Suvin: "We literally do not want to be what we are."[35] (Since U.S. consumerism is so often framed as an addiction, the ecological state of grace imagined by these films may well be thought of as something like AA's "Higher Power.") The task before us then would seem to be to transform that dream wish into waking act, to find ways to nourish and sustain the drive to change even in a world of ordinary, nonmiraculous causation, transforming Reagan and Thatcher's slogan that "there is no alternative to capitalism" to Suvin and Jameson's that "there is no alternative—to utopia."[36] "Someone once said that it is easier to imagine the end of the world than to imagine the end of capitalism," Jameson writes:

> We can now revise that and witness the attempt to imagine capitalism by way of imagining the end of the world.
>
> But I think it would be better to characterize all this in terms of History, a History that we cannot imagine except as ending, and whose future seems to be nothing but a monotonous repetition of what is already here. The problem is then how to locate radical difference; how to jumpstart the sense of history so that it begins again to transmit feeble signals of time, of otherness, of change, of Utopia. The problem to be solved is that of breaking out of the windless present of the postmodern back into real historical time, and a history made by human beings.[37]

How then to imagine a history in which modernity's ongoing destruction of nature does not itself carry the weight of an immutable law of nature? Where might we even begin?

One interesting, if complicated, attempt to do depict an alternative mode of history comes somewhat unexpectedly during the credit sequence of a recent

children's film, Disney's *WALL-E*. Here we see precisely the difficulty of imagining an equitable and sustainable future history made by human beings—what
my coeditor, borrowing from Australian agriculturists Bill Mollison and David
Holmgren, has elsewhere called a "permaculture"[38]—in the intriguing credit
montage that follows the film's abrupt happy ending. As in Atwood's "Time
Capsule," the logic of interstellar expansion and space empire has been reversed:
here, the janitorial robot WALL-E has brought the morbidly obese Americans of
the future *back* to the Earth they once ruined, and robot and human together
begin the process of rehabilitating the global ecology the humans completely
destroyed. The extremely earnest Peter Gabriel song playing over the sequence,
"Down to Earth," points our attention to this reversal of the usual direction of
progress: "Did you feel you were tricked / By the future you picked?" Instead of
a future "high in the sky" where "all those rules don't apply," the lyrics offer us
snow, rivers, birds, trees, and "land that will be looked after."

Recalling the looping cyclical repetitions of history of Marx's *18th Brumaire of
Louis Bonaparte*, this attempt to imagine and represent a non-apocalyptic, non-
disastrous future is not (and perhaps cannot be) depicted narratively. Instead,
it is represented through a montage showing some aspect of the new historical
situation through some artistic medium of the past—the sort of artistic media
Pixar might consider its own computer-generated practice to have superseded,
from cave paintings to Monet's watercolors—blessedly cutting off with the landscape art of Vincent van Gogh in, one supposes, an attempt to avoid having to
unhappily endure all the many disasters of the twentieth century a second time.
(Precisely this fantasy is, after all, at the core of the recent steampunk movement
in SF, which similarly offers us the thrills of advanced technology without the
constraints, limits, and existential horrors that historically came alongside it.)

The paradox inherent in *WALL-E*'s visualization of ecotopia is clear: it sidesteps
the question of how the generally hopeless ecological situation the film depicts
(a hyperbolic, super-exaggerated version of the very quagmire we find ourselves
in) could ever actually get any better, finding recourse instead in a nostalgia that
imagines this better future as a replication of the very path that led us into the
disaster in the first place. But at the same time the bizarre cognitive estrangement of the montage—the historical juxtapositions, the anachronistic presence
of robots at every stage, the culmination of history in a new permaculture that is
shown to take its roots from van Gogh's famous workboot—prevents this from
being the merely nostalgic or bad utopian fantasy of a "return to nature" that
it might initially appear to be. In foregrounding the impossibility of imagining

historical difference, while insisting at the same time on the vital necessity of doing so, WALL-E pushes us unexpectedly in the direction of utopia, forcing us to think about what the radical singularity of that historical break might entail. It deploys the meager imaginative tools we have at hand to refashion the fixed reality of Joyce's "nightmare of history"[39] as it actually happened into the fresh possibility of a new history, still open and unfixed, and somehow done right this time. History, for a few scant minutes at least, becomes unmoored; things, after all, might yet be otherwise.[40]

The utopian potentiality implied—and, often, made possible—by apocalyptic critique is the necessary critical move to rescue us from a diagnosis of the world situation that would otherwise appear utterly hopeless. In his contribution to Mark Bould and China Miéville's *Red Planets: Marxism and Science Fiction*, the collection that inspired this volume, Carl Freedman identifies as a central disjuncture in Marxist thought the distinction between deflationary and inflationary modes of critique. But, as Freedman shows, deflation and inflation necessarily function as a dialectic. The cold calculus of deflation—"the attempt to destroy all illusions necessary or useful to the preservation of class society in general and of capitalism in particular"—is predicated on the baseline moral recognition that the injustice, deprivation, and suffering that is being described *ought not exist*; and the soaring utopian heights of inflation can only surpass mere wishful thinking when they arise out of a historical-scientific understanding of capitalist reality as it now exists.[41] Ecocritique, like the cognitive estrangements of SF, and like the leftist project as a whole, necessarily operates along this same dialectic of deflation and inflation. And, like these other modes, ecocritique requires both deflation and inflation to stay vital. This is why the impulse toward the miserable, deflationary naming of all the various ongoing ecological catastrophes is always matched (if only in negative) by an inflationary, futurological impulse toward the better world that might yet be. Here utopia and apocalypse unexpectedly collapse into one another—they are each disguised versions of a single imaginative leap into futurity.

The essays in *Green Planets* are predicated on the proposition that two hundred years of SF can help us collectively "think" this leap into futurity in the context of the epochal mass-extinction event called the Anthropocene (which the literary theorists more simply call "modernity"). SF is our culture's vast, shared, polyvocal archive of the possible; from techno-utopias to apocalypses to ecotopian *fortunate falls*, it is the transmedia genre of SF that has first attempted to articulate the sorts of systemic global changes that are imminent, or already happening, and begins to imagine what our transformed planet might eventually be like for those who will come to live on it. Especially taken in the context of escalating ecological catastrophe, in which each new season seems to bring with it some new and heretofore-unseen spectacular disaster, my coeditor's well-known declaration that in the contemporary moment "the world has become a science fiction novel" has never seemed more true or more frightening.[42] Indeed, such a notion suggests both politics and "realism" are now *always* "inside" science fiction, insofar as the world, as we experience its vertiginous technological and ecological flux, now more closely resembles SF than it does any historical realism. In this sense perhaps even ecological critique as such can productively be thought of as a kind of science fiction, as it uses the same tools of cognition and extrapolation to project the conditions of a possible future—whether good or bad, ecotopian or apocalyptic—in hopes of transforming politics in the present.

In that spirit, the thirteen chapters in this book explore thirteen such transformations, divided into three sections. In Part I, "Arcadias and New Jerusalems," four critics explore and deconstruct utopian visions of ecological futures. In "Extinction, Extermination, and the Ecological Optimism of H. G. Wells," Christina Alt foregrounds the unexpected use of extermination imagery and mass extinction in Wells's *Men Like Gods* as a marker of *utopian* potentiality—tokening a human race now fully in control of its powers and of the planet. In "Evolution and Apocalypse in the Golden Age," Michael Page traces a fraught dialogue between optimism and pessimism across such classic SF works as Laurence Manning's *The Man Who Awoke* (1933), Clifford Simak's *City* series (1940s), Ward Moore's *Greener Than You Think* (1947), and George R. Stewart's *Earth Abides* (1949). In his contribution, Gib Prettyman critiques the historic inability of Marxist critics to fully appreciate Ursula K. Le Guin's utopian philosophical interest in Daoism, and considers the opportunities made possible by this way of thinking for an ecological leftism that goes beyond economic socialism. Finally, Rob Latham takes up both Le Guin's *The Word for World Is Forest* (novella 1972, novel 1976) and Thomas Disch's *The Genocides* (1965) to unpack the critique of exterminative and genocidal fantasy as presented in key texts of the New Wave movement in 1960s and 1970s SF.

Part II, "Brave New Worlds and Lands of the Flies," turns to much more catastrophic imaginings of both the future of the environment and the people who live in it. In "'The Real Problem of a Spaceship Is Its People': Spaceship Earth as Ecological Science Fiction," Sabine Höhler reads the ubiquitous "Spaceship

Earth" metaphor of contemporary ecological discourse as itself SF, and unpacks the political consequences of this figuration, tracking the way its use trends toward neoliberal calls for austerity, "lifeboat ethics," and the "case against helping the poor." Andrew Milner's "The Sea and Eternal Summer: An Australian Apocalypse" and Adeline Johns-Putra's "Care, Gender, and the Climate-Changed Future: Maggie Gee's *The Ice People*" take up two very different approaches to the present's paradigmatic vision of generational ecological disaster, climate change, both of which deploy the retrospective viewpoint of the people of the future to speak to people in the present. Milner's chapter also considers the unique role Australia plays in the global imaginary, both in and outside SF, while Johns-Putra's consideration of Gee's novel draws connections to the larger field of feminist and ecofeminist writing (Atwood, Lessing, Winterson) with which that novel is in conversation. Elzette Steenkamp's reading of recent South African SF in "Future Ecologies, Current Crisis," which traces figurations of gender, race, and indigeneity through Jane Rosenthal's novel *Souvenir* (2004) and Neill Blomkamp's film *District 9* (2009), looks to apocalyptic futurity as a *novum* that reveals for us the absolute interdependence of self, other, and environment in the present, as well as suggests new possibilities for what it means to be "human" at all. Finally, drawing from such works as Douglas Coupland's *Girlfriend in a Coma* (1998), Margaret Atwood's *Oryx and Crake* (2003), and China Miéville's *Kraken* (2010), Christopher Palmer closes the section with a sustained consideration of how the tragic valence of the apocalyptic imaginary gives way to a more comic sensibility in an era when the many catastrophes and disasters have become so well-rehearsed as to have all already happened.

The final section of the text, "Quiet Earths, Junk Cities, and the Cultures of the Afternoon," considers both recent figurations of postmodern (and posthuman) hybrid landscapes, as well as the new ways of thinking that such visions suggest. Eric Otto's "The Rain Feels New" explores the Cultures of the Afternoon presented in the short fictions of Paolo Bacigalupi, arguing that despite the despair that seems to permeate these works, they nonetheless maintain a utopian political charge. In "Life after People: Science Faction and Ecological Futures," Brent Bellamy and Imre Szeman take up a new subgenre of apocalyptic fantasy they call "science faction": Quiet Earth visions of a world totally emptied of people, in which our cities are left to rust, degrade, and rot. Bellamy and Szeman argue that texts like *Life after People* and its ilk, despite their popularity and their nominal focus on important environmental questions, in fact do little to provoke a genuine or effective ecological politics. In "Pandora's Box:

Avatar, Ecology, Thought"—putting to one side the political questions about capitalism and globalization raised by the plot of the film in favor of interrogating its ontological grounding—Timothy Morton reads *Avatar* against the grain as a philosophical treatise about worlding and worldlessness, and the strange strangers of Earth's biosphere who surround us both in similarity and in radical difference. The Na'vi become refigured here not as a vision of some imagined primitivist past, but as a figure for what a genuinely postmodern *future* might entail. Finally, using Stanislaw Lem and Greg Egan as her companion theorists, Melody Jue suggests in "Churning Up the Depths: Nonhuman Ecologies of Metaphor in *Solaris* and 'Oceanic'" that we might be able to draw new modes of cognition, and new frames for theory, by thinking about the inversion and interplay of surfaces and depths at work in ocean environments.

An interview with my coeditor—"Still, I'm Reluctant to Call This Pessimism"—serves as an afterword for the volume, exploring not only the central place of the environment in Robinson's fiction but also the varied uses of science, religion, crisis, capitalism, human and nonhuman life, optimism, pessimism, apocalypse, and ecotopia in the wide constellation of texts that is ecological sf.

Notes

The editors would like to thank the network of writers, readers, editors, colleagues, interlocutors, friends, and spouses whose generosity and support made the completion of this work possible, as well as offer our most extravagant special thanks to Mark Bould and China Miéville for allowing us to build upon their very good idea.

W. H. Auden, "Vespers," in *Collected Shorter Poems: 1927–1957* (London: Faber and Faber, 1966), 333.

1. Samuel R. Delany, "On Triton and Other Matters," *Science Fiction Studies* 17, no. 3 (November 1990), http://www.depauw.edu/sfs/interviews/delany52interview.htm. Delany also discusses these ideas in "Critical Methods/Speculative Fiction," repr. in *The Jewel-Hinged Jaw: Notes on the Language of Science Fiction* (New York: Berkley, 1977), 119–31.

2. Marshall Berman, *All That Is Solid Melts into Air: The Experience of Modernity* (New York: Penguin Books, 1988), 13.

3. Everett Bleiler and Richard Bleiler, *Science-Fiction: The Gernsback Years* (Kent, OH: Kent State University Press, 1998), xv.

4. Delany, "Triton."

5. Rachel Carson, *Silent Spring* (New York: Houghton Mifflin, 2002), 2–3.

6. Francis Fukuyama, "The End of History?" *National Interest* 16 (Summer 1989): 3–18.

7. Fredric Jameson, *The Seeds of Time* (New York: Columbia University Press, 1994), xii.

8. Timothy Morton, Kathy Rudy, and the Polygraph Collective, "On Ecology: A Roundtable Discussion with Timothy Morton and Kathy Rudy," *Polygraph* 22 (2010): 234.

9. See Paul J. Crutzen, "Geology of Mankind," *Nature* 415 (January 2002): 23.

10. Benjamin Kunkel, "The Politics of Fear, Part II: How Many of Us?" *n+1* (March 18, 2008), http://nplusonemag.com/politics-fear-part-ii-how-many-us.

11. Joss Whedon, *Firefly* (Fox, 2002). This version of the opening narration opened several episodes in the middle part of the first and only season.

12. Systems theory's reliance on feedback as a structuring principle links it closely with later developments in ecology.

13. Kenneth E. Boulding, "The Economics of the Coming Spaceship Earth," repr. in *The Environmental Debate: A Documentary History, with Timeline, Glossary, and Appendices*, ed. Peninah Neimark and Peter Rhoades Mott (Amenia, NY: Grey House, 2010), 209.

14. Ibid., 210.

15. "A robot may not harm humanity, or, by inaction, allow humanity to come to harm." The derivation of the "Zeroth Law" allows the robots to effectively ignore all the "Three Law" safeguards humans had installed to protect themselves from their creations, and ultimately leads to the establishment of a cabal of immortal robots that secretly orchestrates the coming millennia of future history, in accordance with what they determine to be humanity's best interests.

16. Isaac Asimov, *Robots and Empire* (New York: Del Ray Books, 1985), 467.

17. Ecology returns again at the end of the series in a somewhat unexpected form in Asimov's *Foundation's Edge* (1982) and *Foundation and Earth* (1986), set several millennia after *Robots and Empire*. Here, an aging R. Daneel Olivaw (the other of the two robots, the one who did not poison Earth's crust but who endorsed the decision in retrospect) offers a representative of the Foundation a choice between a Second Galactic Empire or a "Galaxia," a galaxy-wide, deep-ecological communal mind. This character chooses Galaxia—a souped-up Gaia theory on an interplanetary scale—for an unexpected reason: he paranoiacally determines that the extinction of individuality in favor of group consciousness will make for the best possible military defense if any hostile aliens attempt to invade our galaxy, neatly linking environmentalist concerns with the needs of the national security state.

18. Stephen King, "Video Interview: Stephen King on *Under the Dome*," Popeaters.com (October 27, 2009), http://www.popeater.com/2009/10/27/stephen-king-under-the-dome -interview/.

19. Ursula Heise, *Sense of Place and Sense of Planet: The Environmental Imagination of the Global* (New York: Oxford University Press, 2008), 22.

20. *An Inconvenient Truth*, directed by Davis Guggenheim (2006; Los Angeles: Paramount, 2006), DVD.

21. Chad Harbach, "The Politics of Fear, Part III: Business as Usual," *n + 1* (December 4, 2007), http://nplusonemag.com/politics-fear-part-iii-business-usual.

22. Wendell Berry, "Faustian Economics: Hell Hath No Limits," *Harper's*, May 2008, 36.

23. Dipesh Chakrabarty, "The Climate of History: Four Theses," *Critical Inquiry* 35 (Winter 2009): 197–222 (208). See also Timothy Mitchell, *Carbon Democracy: Political Power in the Age of Oil* (London: Verso, 2011).

24. *Soylent Green*, directed by Richard Fleischer (1973; New York: Warner Home Video, 2003).

25. Margaret Atwood, "Time Capsule Found on the Dead Planet," *Guardian*, September 25, 2009, http://www.guardian.co.uk/books/2009/sep/26/margaret-atwood-mini-science-fiction.

26. Percy Bysshe Shelley, "Ozymandias," in *The Norton Anthology of English Literature*, vol. 2 (New York: W. W. Norton, 2006), 768.

27. Christopher Woodward, *In Ruins: A Journey through History, Art, and Literature* (New York: Random House, 2003).

28. "Pumzi," directed by Wanuri Kahiu, *Africa First: Volume One* (2010; New York: Focus Features, 2011), DVD.

29. Slavoj Žižek, *First as Tragedy, Then as Farce* (London: Verso, 2009), 151.

30. K. William Kapp, *The Social Costs of Private Enterprise* (New York: Schocken Books, 1971), 231.

31. Octavia E. Butler, "'Devil Girl from Mars': Why I Write Science Fiction" (MIT Communications Forum, 1998), http://web.mit.edu/comm-forum/papers/butler.html.

32. *Avatar*, directed by James Cameron (2009; Los Angeles: Twentieth Century Fox, 2010), DVD.

33. Karl Marx, *Capital*, vol. 1 (New York: Penguin Books, 1976), 342.

34. *Daybreakers*, directed by Michael Spierig and Peter Spierig (2009; Santa Monica, CA: Lionsgate, 2010), DVD.

35. Quoted in Darko Suvin, *Defined by a Hollow*, Ralahine Utopian Studies, vol. 6 (New York: Peter Lang, 2010), 218.

36. Ibid., 11.

37. Fredric Jameson, "Future City," *New Left Review* 21 (May–June 2003), http://newleftreview.org/?view=2449.

38. "Permaculture suggests a certain kind of obvious human goal, which is that future generations will have at least as good a place to live as what we have now." Geoff Manaugh, "Comparative Planetology: An Interview with Kim Stanley Robinson," BLDGBLOG (2007), http://bldgblog.blogspot.com/2007/12/comparative-planetology-interview-with.html.

39. James Joyce, *Ulysses* (New York: Vintage, 1990), 34.

40. *WALL-E*, directed by Andrew Stanton (2008; Burbank, CA: Disney-Pixar, 2008), DVD.

41. Carl Freedman, "Marxism, Cinema, and Some Dialectics of Science Fiction and Film Noir," in *Red Planets: Marxism and Science Fiction*, ed. Mark Bould and China Miéville (Middletown, CT: Wesleyan University Press, 2009), 66–82 (72).

42. Alison Flood, "Kim Stanley Robinson: Science Fiction's Realist," *Guardian*, November 11, 2009, http://www.guardian.co.uk/books/2009/nov/10/kim-stanley-robinson-science-fiction-realist.

ARCADIAS AND

NEW JERUSALEMS

1

Extinction, Extermination, and the Ecological Optimism of H. G. Wells

CHRISTINA ALT

Over the course of his long writing career H. G. Wells passed through alternating periods of optimism and pessimism in his views of humanity, science, and the future of the earth. In his late-Victorian works of scientific romance, he reveals a pessimistic attitude arising in part from evolutionary ideas circulating at the time. In *The Time Machine* he expresses anxieties over devolution; in *The Island of Doctor Moreau* he warns of the dangers of scientific overreaching and suggests the ineffectuality of human attempts to intervene in evolutionary processes; and in *The War of the Worlds* he challenges assumptions of human primacy and dominance by introducing a threat to humanity in the form of a highly evolved Martian competitor. These works taken together convey a sense of human beings existing at the mercy of natural processes beyond their control. However, as the twentieth century began, Wells found reason for new optimism, as evidenced by works such as *Anticipations*, *A Modern Utopia*, and *Men Like Gods*. One factor contributing to this modern optimism was the emergence of new scientific disciplines that promised to provide new ways of understanding and intervening in natural processes. Ecology was one of these emerging disciplines; however, perhaps unexpectedly, given current popular conceptions of ecology, in the early twentieth century the optimism engendered by the growing understanding of the relationships between organisms and their environments manifested primarily as a new confidence—even arrogance—in humanity's ability to exert control over the natural world. In fact, Wells's use of ecological ideas in his early twentieth-century works of SF suggests that in the early stages of its development as a discipline, ecology helped to restore the confidence in human dominance that had been unsettled by evolution's revelation of humanity's animal origins.

To illustrate this claim, I will compare the attitudes and actions toward the natural world depicted in Wells's late-Victorian novel *The War of the Worlds*, published in 1898, with those represented in his early twentieth-century novel *Men Like Gods*, published in 1923. These two novels are useful texts to consider in an exploration of Wells's changing views of science and nature because they center on similar scenarios. In both novels, terrestrial human beings encounter a more advanced species or culture that possesses greater scientific knowledge and technological skill than they themselves; in both novels, the advanced culture endeavors to exert control over the natural world through the management or extermination of other life forms; and in both novels, a struggle between the terrestrial human beings and the alien culture ensues and is ultimately decided in a contest between nature (in the form of disease germs) and biological science. However, despite the similar scenarios considered in these two novels, the resolutions that they offer differ dramatically, registering the shift in attitude that Wells underwent in the intervening quarter century.

THE WAR OF THE WORLDS

The War of the Worlds famously describes the invasion of Earth in the closing years of the nineteenth century by a highly evolved and technologically advanced Martian species seeking a new planet to colonize as their own more distant planet grows cold. The Martians plan to first subdue human beings by force, destroying their homes and decimating their population, and then to cultivate the human species as a form of livestock and a food source. The threat to human dominance posed by the arrival of the Martians causes the human narrator of the tale to experience "a sense of dethronement, a persuasion that I was no longer a master, but an animal among the animals, under the Martian heel. With us it would be as with them, to lurk and watch, to run and hide; the fear and empire of man had passed away."[1] *The War of the Worlds* thus dramatizes the ways in which the promulgation of evolutionary ideas in the Victorian period stripped humans of their sense of special status as beings deliberately set above the rest of creation, leading them to recognize themselves as animals and, moreover, as animals subject to competition for their place in the hierarchy of nature and for their survival as a species. In an extension of this argument, Wells's allusion to the obliteration of the indigenous people of Tasmania by European invaders alongside his references to the extinction of numerous animal species brought about by European exploration and colonization demonstrates that the history of imperialism, although typically driven by one human group's belief in its superiority over others, ultimately refutes rather than confirms human exceptionalism and highlights human beings' vulnerability to extinction.

Human beings are accorded little agency in *The War of the Worlds*. Wells stresses that in encounters with the Martians, both individual people and larger human groups survive largely by chance. The artilleryman that the narrator befriends is saved from the heat ray that kills the rest of his regiment only because his horse stumbles in a rabbit hole and throws him just as the alien weapon is fired.[2] London is saved from immediate destruction not by human defenses but by the Martians' decision to wait for the arrival of the rest of their invasion party before moving on the city. The narrator states that it is only "by a miracle" that he escapes the Martians in their tripods, and he speaks of feeling overwhelmed by "the immensity of the night and space and nature, [and] my own feebleness and anguish."[3] It is not any special capacity or insight that saves individuals and communities, but only luck and the unintended effects of the Martians' own decisions and strategies.

This lack of human agency extends to the final contest between the inhabitants of Earth and the Martian invaders, a contest in which human beings play no conscious or deliberate role. Unlike the majority of alien invasion narratives that were to follow Wells's novel, *The War of the Worlds* does not culminate in a heroic confrontation between human beings and aliens in which the invaders are repulsed by the brave and ingenious actions of human beings. In *The War of the Worlds* humanity and the Earth are saved from conquest not by human knowledge, might, heroism, or ingenuity but rather by the unanticipated susceptibility of Martian organisms to earthly bacteria. It is nature, not science, that is decisive in this battle; human beings play no active role in their own salvation.

The defeat of the Martians by earthly bacteria indicates that the Martians are not entirely in control of their destiny either. Wells suggests that, subsequent to the Martians' failure to establish themselves on Earth, they may have launched a more successful invasion of Venus; nevertheless, the novel as a whole makes clear that scientific knowledge and technological power cannot guarantee the survival of a species, and that even the most advanced species has only limited agency in the face of the natural world and the physical laws that govern it.

Reflecting their sudden experience of dethronement by the Martians, human beings are repeatedly compared to animals in *The War of the Worlds*. Wells's chosen animal analogies overtly signal the diminishment of human beings, but they also operate more subtly to unsettle the hierarchy of value from which these diminishing allusions take their meaning—with the result that what might otherwise constitute the wholly diminishing equation of a "higher" species with a "lower" one instead suggests a fundamental troubling of the boundaries between the high and the low. Wells repeatedly likens people fleeing from Martian attacks to ants, whether to suggest that human beings are so insignificant as to be beneath the notice of the invaders or to stress the fact that the Martians at times destroy targets randomly out of a "mere wantonness of power."[4] However, the descriptions of ants that he offers do not simply serve as an image of powerlessness and insignificance. The narrator's companion the artilleryman declares: "The ants build their cities, live their lives, have wars, revolutions, until the men want them out of the way, and then they go out of the way. That's what we are now—just ants."[5] The artilleryman's intended point is that humans, like ants, live at the mercy of other, more powerful species, but his account of the social life of ants also functions as a reminder that ants are themselves highly complex social organisms.

This is not the only comparison that Wells makes between human beings and social insects. The narrator likens the Martians' use of a stifling black vapor to suffocate any creature that stands in the way of their progress to "smok[ing] out a wasps' nest," and elsewhere he ponders the extent of the Martians' understanding of human beings, wondering, "Did they grasp that we in our millions were organized, disciplined, working together? Or did they interpret our spurts of fire, the sudden stinging of our shells, our steady investment of their encampment, as we should the furious unanimity of onslaught in a disturbed hive of bees?"[6] This analogy is perplexing, for by the nineteenth century the highly complex and cooperative behavior of bees, wasps, and other social insects was common knowledge, thanks to the work of naturalists such as François Huber and John Lubbock. The bee is therefore a strange choice for a model of random, disorganized behavior, leading one to question whether Wells's choice of analogy is intended to suggest that the Martians' underestimation of human beings' level of organization and cooperation is paralleled by human beings' underestimation of other species.

The most dramatically dehumanizing of all Wells's animal analogies in *The War of the Worlds* is the comparison that opens the novel: "No one would have believed in the last years of the nineteenth century that this world was being watched keenly and closely by intelligences greater than man's and yet as mortal as his own; that as men busied themselves about their various concerns they were scrutinized and studied, perhaps almost as narrowly as a man with a microscope might scrutinize the transient creatures that swarm and multiply in a drop of water."[7] This opening comparison of human beings to microscopic organisms suggests the radically reduced significance, the puniness and negligibility of human beings when viewed from an extra-planetary perspective; however, this analogy also fundamentally destabilizes notions of hierarchy, for it foreshadows from the very first sentence of the novel the ultimate downfall of the Martian invaders owing to their susceptibility to terrestrial bacteria. Within this radically diminishing analogy, then, is a hint that the most seemingly negligible of species have crucial roles to play and that the accepted hierarchy of higher and lower forms of life is an inaccurate measure of worth or power. Thus, although *The War of the Worlds* initially appears to dethrone human beings only to set up the Martians in their place, its depiction of the seemingly indomitable Martians as vulnerable to seemingly lowly bacteria fundamentally destabilizes conventional notions of dominance and hierarchy.

In addition to the animal metaphors that demean human beings through comparison with lower creatures while simultaneously challenging the categories of high and low, the experience of invasion and subjugation by another species leads the narrator to develop a new perspective on nature. The newly subjugated position of human beings causes the narrator to identify with other animals, to empathize with the creatures over whom human beings had previously asserted unreflecting dominance. Watching the progress of the "mechanical colossi of the Martian tripods," the narrator begins to imaginatively enter into the mental and emotional perspective of other species, "to ask myself" as he puts it, "for the first time in my life how an ironclad or a steam engine would seem to an intelligent lower animal."[8] Emerging later from hiding to find the town of Sheen in ruins around him and already overgrown with Martian vegetation, the narrator experiences "an emotion beyond the common range of men, yet one that the poor brutes that we dominate know only too well. I felt as a rabbit might feel returning to his burrow and suddenly confronted by the work of a dozen busy natives digging the foundations of a house."[9] The narrator extends his sense of fellow feeling even to animals commonly viewed as vermin, reflecting, "I, who had talked with God, crept out of the house like a rat leaving its hiding place—a creature scarcely larger, an inferior animal, a thing that for any passing whim of our masters might be hunted and killed. . . . Surely, if we have learned nothing else, this war has taught us pity—pity for those witless souls that suffer our domination."[10] *The War of the Worlds* is thus underpinned by an idealization of sympathy.

The War of the Worlds expresses a distinctly fin de siècle, evolution-induced anxiety about the future of human dominance, the power of technology, and the long-term survival of the species and the planet. However, its evolutionary pessimism is tempered by the emergence of a new experience of empathy across species boundaries. In *The War of the Worlds*, humans experience what it is to be treated as pests to be exterminated or livestock to be exploited, and while this experience results in a sense of diminishment or dethronement, it also leads to a compensatory empathy for and identification with the animal.

EARLY ECOLOGY AND HUMAN AGENCY

In the quarter century between the publication of *The War of the Worlds* and *Men Like Gods*, a number of new trends in biological research emerged. These included the early stages of the development of genetics, arising from the rediscovery of Gregor Mendel's work on inherited characteristics, and a new focus on animal behavior, which gained institutional recognition as the science of ethology. Of particular relevance to Wells's shifting attitudes toward nature and science was the emergence of ecology in Britain in the early decades of the twentieth century. One of the most significant figures in the transmission of ecological ideas and the establishment of ecology as an institutionalized discipline in Britain was the botanist A. G. Tansley. Tansley was the driving force behind the formation in 1904 of the Central Committee for the Survey of British Vegetation, which conducted the first ecological survey of the British Isles; he was the first president of the British Ecological Society, founded in 1913, and in the same year he helped to establish the *Journal of Ecology*, which he also edited for many years. Tansley's views of biology, the ways in which it should be studied and the ends to which it should be applied, are thus clearly relevant to an understanding of early ecology in Britain.

Tansley's views are perhaps best expressed in the article "The Reconstruction of Elementary Botanical Teaching," published in the *New Phytologist* in December 1917. This article expressed the grievances and aspirations of the rising generation of botanists. There were five signatories to this article, but perhaps because Tansley was the founder and editor of the *New Phytologist*, the article was widely viewed as Tansley's brainchild, so much so that it became known informally as the "Tansley Manifesto." Recent scholarship by historians of science A. D. Boney and Peder Anker on the controversy surrounding the manifesto demonstrates convincingly that Tansley was not alone in holding the views expressed in the article, but the name stuck nonetheless.[11] In this article, Tansley and his associates argued that the study and teaching of botany was too narrowly focused on morphological work and excluded important emerging areas of study. They declared that "botany in this country is still largely dominated by the morphological tradition, founded on the attempt to trace the phylogenetic relationships of plants, which began as the result of the general acceptance of the doctrine of descent. . . . Plant physiology is relegated in most cases to a subordinate place. . . . The newer studies of ecology and of genetics play a very small part in the curriculum. The result is that the student's introduction to the study of plant life is unbalanced and has a definite morphological bias."[12] This morphological bias troubled Tansley and his colleagues not simply because it resulted in a general lack of breadth in biological teaching and research but also and more particularly because morphological work that focused on tracing phylogenetic relationships was to a great extent an academic study with very few practical applications. While commending British morphologists for having "worthily upheld the loftiest traditions of pure science," Tansley and his colleagues contended that excessive focus on the "tracing out of an obscure phylogeny . . . is sterile and leads to little but further refinements of itself . . . because it has no outlets on practical life."[13] Tansley and his associates wished to focus instead on the solution of practical problems and on "the part which plants play or can be made to play in the economy of the world."[14] Ecology struck early twentieth-century botanists as an ideal example of a scientific discipline with close connections to practical life. Speaking of ecology, Tansley and his colleagues state that "here we have the scientific bases of agriculture, of forestry, of the economic utilization of waste lands, of the use of plants in coast protection, of every industry in which man grows plants, or employs plants which grow spontaneously, for specific purposes, for his own use or for the use of his animals."[15] The emphasis on the value of the new discipline of ecology to humanity's use and management of natural resources is unmistakable.

The emphasis on the practical usefulness of ecological work to human life continued to dominate the rhetoric of ecology throughout the interwar period. Julian Huxley summarized the outlook of the time in his introduction to Charles Elton's *Animal Ecology* (1927) with his assertion that ecology was "destined to a great future" because it offered a means of assuming "control of wild life in the interest of man's food supply and prosperity" and would ultimately make it possible for man to "assert his predominance" over "his cold-blooded rivals, the plant pest and, most of all, the insect."[16] Elton himself, speaking in a series of radio broadcasts on ecology in the early 1930s, declared that "scientists are engaged on this absorbing adventure of finding out how these [natural] systems work—both for the interest of the search and in order to obtain the best deal that is possible for humanity."[17]

In justifying their call for greater attention to practical science, Tansley and his colleagues argued that "science—especially experimental science—increases our power of doing things."[18] Practical and applied sciences such as ecology and genetics—as these disciplines are represented in the Tansley Manifesto—are thus valuable because they increase human agency. Applied sciences such as these are promoted as a solution to the late-Victorian sense of the powerlessness of human beings in the face of natural forces that is so effectively communicated in *The War of the Worlds*.

Having briefly summarized the perspective and preoccupations of early twentieth-century ecologists, I turn now to Wells's 1923 novel *Men Like Gods* to trace the ways in which both the rise of ecology and early twentieth-century biologists' preoccupation with practical, applied work that would increase the human power of "doing things" are reflected in Wells's work of modern utopian SF.

MEN LIKE GODS

In *Men Like Gods*, the novel's central character, Mr. Barnstaple, finds himself transported, along with a motley collection of 1920s Londoners, to a planet where "life has evidently evolved under almost exactly parallel conditions to those of our own evolution" but which is judged to be several thousand years ahead of Earth in its development.[19] In this Utopian world of the future, Barnstaple and his fellow travelers encounter a human society, far superior to their own in scientific knowledge, that has applied its understanding and skills to the task of assuming control over natural systems and regulating nature for human benefit.

The Utopians recount that one of the first initiatives set in motion following the creation of a Utopian world-state was the implementation of

> the long-cherished ideal of a systematic extermination of tiresome and
> mischievous species. A careful inquiry was made into the harmfulness and the
> possibility of eliminating the house-fly, for example, wasps and hornets, various
> species of mice and rats, rabbits, stinging nettles. Ten thousand species, from
> disease-germ to rhinoceros and hyena, were put upon their trial. Every species

was given an advocate. Of each it was asked: What good is it? What harm does it do? How can it be extirpated? What else may go if it goes? Is it worth while wiping it out of existence? Or can it be mitigated and retained?[20]

This trial scenario, in which human beings assume the authority to pass the "verdict" of "death final and complete" upon other species, suggests that a species' right to exist is determined primarily if not solely by its usefulness and appeal to human beings in their capacity as the planet's dominant species.[21]

As a result of this inquisition, "there had been a great cleansing of the world from noxious insects, from weeds and vermin and hostile beasts."[22] Some large predators such as the wolf and hyena had been systematically hunted out of existence, while others such as the leopard and the bear had been "combed and cleaned, [and] reduced to a milk dietary" or "converted to vegetarianism."[23] Rats, mice, and "the untidier sorts of small bird" had been eliminated.[24] An extended campaign against various species of insects had led to an "enormous deliberate reduction of insect life in Utopia," and all native disease germs had likewise been eradicated.[25] Troublesome or useless plants had been either disposed of or refashioned through breeding and hybridization into plants of practical or aesthetic value to human beings.

Reflecting the growing understanding of the importance and complexity of ecological relationships at the time of the novel's composition, Wells has the Utopian Urthred declare that "the question of what else would go if a certain species went was one of the most subtle that Utopia had to face."[26] However, this awareness of ecological relationships does not deter the Utopians in their systematic engineering of extinctions; rather, it is seen as providing the knowledge necessary to *successfully carry out* the desired exterminations. Thus, the Utopians note that the aforementioned "enormous deliberate reduction of insect life in Utopia . . . had seriously affected every sort of creature that was directly or indirectly dependent upon insect life"; insectivorous birds such as swallows and flycatchers, for example, "had become extremely rare," but this concomitant loss is viewed as acceptable collateral damage by the Utopians.[27]

Wells employs Barnstaple, a simultaneously idealistic and discouraged writer for a liberal London newspaper, as his authorial stand-in within the novel and as his principal respondent to the attitudes and undertakings of the Utopians. From the first, Barnstaple shows himself to be receptive to the extreme environmental management practiced by the Utopians. As a self-professed "expert and observant mower of lawns," he shows himself to be supportive of artificially cultivated and maintained environments.[28] He rhapsodizes about "the beauty of a world subdued" and approvingly describes the "whole land" of Utopia as being "like a garden, with every natural tendency to beauty seized upon and developed and every innate ugliness corrected and overcome."[29]

In commending the Utopians' active pursuit of a program of mass extinction, their achievement of "a world where ill-bred weeds . . . had ceased to thrust and fight amidst the flowers and where leopards void of feline malice looked out with friendly eyes upon the passer-by," Barnstaple suggests Wells's tacit endorsement of an exterminatory and controlling approach to nature.[30] Barnstaple reflects: "How peaceful was the Utopian air in comparison with the tormented atmosphere of Earth. Here there was no yelping and howling of tired or irritated dogs, no braying, bellowing, squealing and distressful outcries of uneasy beasts, . . . the tiresome and ugly noises of many an unpleasant creature were heard no more. . . . The air which had once been a mud of felted noises was now—a purified silence."[31] The contrast between Wells's approving description of the peaceful silence resulting from engineered extinctions and Rachel Carson's warning vision of a silent spring four decades later illustrates a crucial difference in perspective between early twentieth-century ecology and ecology as it came to be conceived in the latter half of the twentieth century.[32]

The Utopians' manipulation and regulation of their natural environment demonstrates their scientific prowess. In *The War of the Worlds*, scientific knowledge and technological skill were not enough to ensure victory for the Martians, but *Men Like Gods* restages the contest between nature and the scientific knowledge of an advanced civilization, this time with a different outcome. Shortly after the arrival of the human beings from 1920s London in Utopia, it becomes apparent that they have unwittingly introduced earthly germs to Utopia and that these germs have the potential to cause deadly plagues among the Utopians, who, having long ago eradicated all the harmful germs of their own planet, have no natural immunity to these or any other diseases. In an inverted repetition of the alien invasion scenario from Wells's earlier novel, the more belligerent members of the Earthling party regard their fortuitous biological advantage as a weapon to be employed in the seizure of this newfound planet. Ultimately, however, the Earthlings' hopes for conquest by way of disease are disappointed. The Utopians successfully isolate the disease germs introduced by earthly humans and through vaccination neutralize the threat that they pose. The disease bacteria that function as the unexpected agents of humanity's salvation in *The War of the Worlds* become in *Men Like Gods* mere "poisons" that serve no useful purpose and cannot withstand Utopian science.[33]

In *The War of the Worlds*, humans and Martians alike exist at the mercy of natural forces on both the microscopic and macroscopic level, beset on one scale by disease germs and on another by the cooling of the sun and planetary climate change. In *Men Like Gods*, however, the Utopians are no longer constrained by these forces but are instead masters of them. First hypothetically and then practically, Wells raises the possibility of limits to the Utopians' power, only to dismiss this possibility: surveying the order of Utopia, Barnstaple asks, "Might not some great shock or some phase of confusion still be possible to this immense order? . . . Might not the unforeseen be still lying in wait for this race? . . . No! It was inconceivable. The achievement of this world was too calmly great and assured."[34] Barnstaple's confidence in the indomitability of the Utopians is subsequently confirmed when, confronted by the beginnings of a potentially global epidemic, "the science and organization of Utopia had taken the danger by the throat and banished it."[35] Wells likewise presents the Utopians as masters of natural forces on a macroscopic level. When Barnstaple asks a Utopian scientist if his people do not fear, as the people of Earth fear, "that at last there must be an end to life because our sun and planets are cooling," the Utopian responds, "Perish! We have hardly begun! . . . Before us lies knowledge, endlessly, and we may take and take, and as we take, grow."[36] By this, Barnstaple is convinced that the Utopians, and by extension the future inhabitants of Earth, will one day "lift their daring to the stars" and thus escape the end that must eventually await all life on a slowly cooling planet.[37]

The Utopian conviction that scientific mastery of nature and physical laws makes it possible for humanity to permanently escape extinction promotes an attitude toward other organisms wholly different from that depicted in *The War of the Worlds*. In Wells's earlier novel, human beings' recognition of their animal condition and their sense that all organisms face the threats of competition, subjugation, and extinction led to a sense of identification and sympathy with the nonhuman world. In *Men Like Gods*, however, the idea of extinction or subjugation as a shared threat is replaced by an assurance that by taking control of nature for themselves and meting out extinction to *other* species as they see fit, human beings can ensure their own survival (and dominance) as a species. The sense of identification and sympathy with other species suggested in the earlier novel is replaced by a divisive, dismissive, and hierarchical attitude that aims to elevate human beings above the natural world and results in a program of calculated control and extermination.

This divisive and dismissive attitude is made apparent not only through the practical program of control and eradication to which organisms are subjected in *Men Like Gods* but also through the metaphorical use of animals in the novel. Animals categorized as pests and targeted for extermination are employed as embodiments of the qualities that Utopians wish to eradicate from their society. The Utopian Urthred states, "The gnawing vigour of the rat, . . . the craving pursuit of the wolf, the mechanical persistence of wasp and fly and disease germ, have gone out of our world. . . . We have obliterated that much of life's devouring forces. And lost nothing worth having."[38] As a convert to Utopian values, Barnstaple similarly expresses his disgust with earthly society through a series of animal comparisons. He criticizes the "parasitic host of priests" that governs earthly morality, compares the squabbles of his fellow travelers to "a dog-fight on a sinking ship," scorns an Earth woman in his traveling party as "an unintelligent beauty-cow," denounces the "trampling folly" of Earth's political leaders, and declares that "the aggressive conqueror, the grabbing financier, the shoving business man, he hated as he hated wasps, rats, hyenas, sharks, fleas, nettles and the like."[39] He asserts that were he to tell the people of Earth of his experiences in Utopia, "They would not believe it. . . . They would bray like asses at me and bark like dogs! . . . So they must sit among their weeds and excrement, scratching and nodding sagely at one another, . . . sure that mankind stank, stinks, and must always stink, that stinking is very pleasant indeed, and that there is nothing new under the sun."[40] The attribution of animal characteristics to human beings in *Men Like Gods* is wholly disparaging, tempered by no redeeming sympathy with the animal. To align oneself with the animal here is to reject the possibility of progress and to associate oneself with stupidity, violence, and filth.

These derogatory animal analogies culminate in Barnstaple's expression of something akin to revulsion for the human inhabitants of his own time and place, whom he describes as "that detestable crawling mass of un-featured, infected human beings."[41] Barnstaple can envision only two possible outcomes to the standoff between the Earthlings and the Utopians: "Either the Utopians would prove themselves altogether the stronger and the wiser and he and all his fellow pirates would be crushed and killed like vermin, or the desperate ambitions of Mr. Catskill [the British war secretary] would be realized and they would become a spreading sore in the fair body of this noble civilization."[42] Whatever the outcome, the Earthling party consistently appears pestilent and pernicious to Barnstaple. Whereas in *The War of the Worlds* the narrator's experience of being treated as an expendable or exploitable creature causes him to accord new value to other animals, in *Men Like Gods* Barnstaple's comparison of human beings to despised animals leads him to suggest that human beings too warrant extermination if they impede or endanger progress. While human vulnerability promotes identification and sympathy with the animal, knowledge and power engender a dispassionate, impersonal, and controlling attitude toward nature that in turn promotes a dangerous disregard for human life. Thus, unexpectedly, Wells's "pessimistic" early novel produces an impulse toward cross-species identification, while his more "optimistic" later novel produces a fantasy of total control through exterminative violence that is predicated upon anthropocentrism and human exceptionalism.

The contrasting resolutions to comparable scenarios presented in *The War of the Worlds* and *Men Like Gods* suggest that the early twentieth century's growing understanding of the interrelationships between organisms and their environment produced a new sense of power over nature that countered evolutionary anxieties regarding the dethronement of human beings but also potentially diminished the sympathy with the nonhuman that this sense of dethronement had made possible. This shift is made most evident through the contrasting perspectives on extinction that Wells's two novels offer. Between the publication of *The War of the Worlds* and of *Men Like Gods*, extinction, in Wells's mind, went from being feared as a threat to human survival to being viewed as a phenomenon to be harnessed by human beings so that they might decide for themselves the composition of "nature." Subsequent works of sf seem inclined to move away from the exterminatory optimism of Wells's early twentieth-century novel. Olaf Stapledon's *Last and First Men* (1930), for example, depicts the extermination of the indigenous species of other planets as the inhabitants of Earth spread outward through the solar system, but the book offers no explicit commendation (or condemnation) of this process. C. S. Lewis's subsequent *Space Trilogy* (1938–45) vehemently denounces from a Christian theological perspective such human presumption. Wells's *Men Like Gods* preserves a historical moment in which ecological knowledge was seen as a means of increasing human beings' ability to use and control nature and thus suggests the complex and variable aims, affiliations, and justifications of ecology over the course of its development as a discipline.

Notes

1. H. G. Wells, *The War of the Worlds* (Cherrybrook, NSW: Horizon, 2009), 169–70.
2. Ibid., 62.
3. Ibid., 34.
4. Ibid., 74–75, 202.

5. Ibid., 178.

6. Ibid., 104, 100.

7. Ibid., 1.

8. Ibid., 61.

9. Ibid., 169.

10. Ibid., 175.

11. A. D. Boney, "The 'Tansley Manifesto' Affair," *New Phytologist* 118, no. 1 (1991): 3–21, and Peder Anker, *Imperial Ecology: Environmental Order in the British Empire, 1895–1945* (Cambridge, MA: Harvard University Press, 2001).

12. Frederick Frost Blackman et al., "The Reconstruction of Elementary Botanical Teaching," *New Phytologist* 16, no. 10 (1917): 242.

13. Ibid., 246, 243.

14. Ibid., 243.

15. Ibid., 247.

16. Julian Huxley, introduction to *Animal Ecology* by Charles Elton (Chicago: University of Chicago Press, 2001), xiv, xv, xiv.

17. Charles Elton, *Exploring the Animal World* (London: George Allen & Unwin, 1933), 66.

18. Blackman et al., "Reconstruction," 249.

19. H. G. Wells, *Men Like Gods* (New York: Macmillan, 1923), 51.

20. Ibid., 92.

21. Ibid.

22. Ibid.

23. Ibid., 94.

24. Ibid., 165.

25. Ibid., 92.

26. Ibid., 93.

27. Ibid., 91, 93.

28. Ibid., 17.

29. Ibid., 260, 170.

30. Ibid., 34.

31. Ibid., 307.

32. It is possible to exaggerate the gap between Wells's view and Carson's. In *Silent Spring*, Carson sought to promote awareness of the dangers of the synthetic chemical pesticides used to eliminate pest species, but she did not reject the notion of pest control altogether. She asserted the importance of eliminating insect disease vectors such as malaria-bearing mosquitoes, and her condemnation of the overuse of synthetic pesticides such as DDT arose in part from the fact that the overuse of these chemicals allowed species to develop a resistance to these substances, which jeopardized future efforts to fight insects. Nevertheless, she recommends interference in natural processes only in extreme cases, stating, "All this is not to say that there is no insect problem and no need of control. I am saying, rather, that control must be geared to realities, not to mythical situations, and that the methods employed must be such that they do not destroy us along with the insects" (Rachel Carson, *Silent Spring* [New York: Houghton Mifflin, 2002], 9).

33. Ibid., 198.
34. Ibid., 173–74.
35. Ibid., 252.
36. Ibid., 301, 303.
37. Ibid., 314–15.
38. Ibid., 104–5.
39. Ibid., 168, 195, 230, 230, 205.
40. Ibid., 308.
41. Ibid., 285.
42. Ibid., 204.

2

Evolution and Apocalypse
in the Golden Age

MICHAEL PAGE

In the 1974 anthology *Before the Golden Age*, Isaac Asimov writes of *The Man Who Awoke* series of stories by Laurence Manning: "In the 1970s, everyone is aware of, and achingly involved in, the energy crisis. Manning was aware of it forty years ago, and because he was, I was, and so, I'm sure, were many thoughtful young science fiction readers."[1] At the time of Asimov's writing, ecology as a topic in the cultural conversation and in SF was on an upswing. Books like Paul Ehrlich's *The Population Bomb*, Gordon Rattary Taylor's *The Biological Time Bomb*, Roberto Vacca's *The Coming Dark Age*, Frank Herbert's *New World or No World*, and the Club of Rome's *The Limits to Growth* were reaching wide audiences. In SF, several anthologies focused on ecological issues, including Fred Pohl's *Nightmare Age*, Tom Disch's *The Ruins of Earth*, Terry Carr's *Dream's Edge*, Harry Harrison's *The Year 2000*, and Roger Elwood and Virginia Kidd's *The Wounded Planet*—as did numerous novels, notably Ursula Le Guin's *The Word for World Is Forest*, Frank Herbert's *Hellstrom's Hive*, Philip Wylie's *The End of the Dream*, John Brunner's *The Sheep Look Up*, and films like *Soylent Green*, *Silent Running*, *Logan's Run*, *Phase IV*, and *Zardoz*. Carr remarks in the introduction to *Dream's Edge* that "concern for the problems and prospects of our earthly environment come naturally to writers and readers of science fiction—it is as intrinsic to the genre as knowledge of physics, chemistry, the workings of politics and human psychology."[2] Herbert similarly writes in the introduction to *The Wounded Planet* that ecology was the "hot gospel blasting at us from all sides . . . ecology as a phenomenon reflects a genuine underlying malaise. . . . The species knows its travail. This shines through every bit of ecological science fiction I have ever read."[3] For Herbert, SF writers and ecologists are fellow travelers.

It has been nearly forty more years since Asimov made these remarks, and the ecological crisis ("energy" and otherwise) is now forty years further up the line. We seem to be in another upswing, both in SF and the wider culture. Ecological SF is particularly "hot" right now, if some of the most recent titles are any indication: Paolo Bacigalupi's *The Drowned Cities*, Tobias Buckell's *Arctic Rising*, Rob Ziegler's *Seed*, and Kim Stanley Robinson's *2312*, all released in the first few months of 2012 alone. Yet ecological issues have always been present in SF, integral to the background of the futures (human triumphant, apocalyptic, or otherwise) that SF writers imagine. Ecology is necessary for extra-planetary world building, according to Brian Stableford,[4] as the classic examples of Herbert's *Dune* and Le Guin's *The Left Hand of Darkness* attest. But it is just as central to any future-Earth scenario: what would future-Earth SF be without depictions of our planet either as degraded by the rampant waste and consumption of the twentieth and twenty-first centuries, or else as technologically sophisticated futures that have solved (or at least learned to manage) the crises precipitated by our era? Thus, almost all SF is foundationally ecological in nature.

Just as SF is inherently ecologically oriented, so too is much SF criticism. In the years since Brian Stableford remarked that ecocriticism "tended to ignore SF,"[5] many "ecocritics" outside of SF have begun to explore SF texts, including such critical writers as Stacey Alaimo, Lawrence Buell, Ursula Heise, Timothy Morton, and Patrick Murphy.[6] Indeed, ecocriticism and SF criticism have much common ground and seem to be beginning to merge. SF and SF criticism have much to offer the ecocritical movement.

Certainly, the concerns of mainstream ecocriticism have important affinities with SF and SF criticism. Cheryll Glotfelty's observation in the introduction to *The Ecocriticism Reader* that "most ecocritical work shares a common motivation: the troubling awareness that we have reached the age of environmental limits, a time when the consequences of human actions are damaging the planet's basic life support systems"[7] is compatible with the study of SF. Arguably, SF is the genre of literature best suited to probing these environmental limits. Ecocritic Glen A. Love goes so far as to say that "environmental and population pressures inevitably and increasingly support the position that any literary criticism that purports to deal with social and physical reality will encompass ecological considerations."[8] We could push this one step further and say *any literature*. SF is an ideal venue for the type of engagement with biological and ecological issues that Glotfelty and Love call for here. If science fiction writers are inherently ecological writers, by extension science fiction critics are necessarily ecocritics in one way or another. Ecocritic Lawrence Buell, who works considerably outside SF, recognizes this centrality of SF to ecocriticism: "For half a century science fiction has taken a keen, if not consistent interest in ecology, in planetary endangerment, in environmental ethics, in humankind's relation to the nonhuman world. . . . No genre potentially matches up with a planetary level of thinking 'environment' better than science fiction does."[9]

The science fiction writers of the genre's golden age, like Asimov, who read the early issues of *Amazing*, *Astounding*, and *Wonder* were introduced to ecological issues in various ways in the often crude but insightful stories of the era. In his monumental catalog of the early magazine stories, *The Gernsback Years*, Everett Bleiler lists over sixty stories under the heading "Earth, future geography" alone that have some degree of ecological content.[10] Granted, most of this is the extrapolated background setting for what is often a crudely executed adventure story, but it is that very setting that is so crucial to the contemplation of futures built upon the consequences of present actions or the extrapolation of future alternatives. By the time Asimov's generation came of age, this ecological awareness had become so embedded into the discourse of sf that it was virtually invisible, assumed by the reader to be part of the scenario of the typical sf story.

Here I consider four exemplary works of ecological sf from that golden age: Laurence Manning's *The Man Who Awoke* stories, published in consecutive issues of *Wonder Stories* in 1933 and later put in book form in 1975; Clifford Simak's *City* series, published in John W. Campbell's *Astounding* throughout the mid-40s;[11] Ward Moore's *Greener Than You Think* (1947); and George R. Stewart's *Earth Abides*, which, though written outside the generic sf discourse, has nonetheless become a genre classic since its publication in 1949. These four books participate in the two major modes of ecological thought as it appears in sf: the evolutionary and the apocalyptic.

EVOLUTION

Let's first consider the evolutionary mode. Evolution is paradigmatic in sf, as it is in science itself.[12] Istvan Csicsery-Ronay Jr. notes that "looking at the corpus of sf in the twentieth century, we see veritable schoolbook applications of evolutionary ideas."[13] Both Manning's *The Man Who Awoke* and Simak's *City* exemplify the evolutionary mode of ecological sf. I would argue, however, that though there is much commonality between *The Man Who Awoke* and *City*, they engage with evolutionary ecological thought in rather different registers. As Norman Winters, the hero of *The Man Who Awoke*, awakens beyond the pastoral "forest society" of the nearer future, and technology reasserts itself, Manning's evolutionary mode becomes a saga of humanity's technological development leading to universal mastery, much in the manner of Stapledon's *Last and First Men*. In *City*, though technology is ubiquitous in the background that makes the doggish utopia possible (unlimited atomic power and the guiding hand of Jenkins and other Asimovian robots that serve the dogs), Simak nevertheless emphasizes an antitechnological pastoral register.

The overall trajectory of *The Man Who Awoke* stories traces a progressive evolutionary model in which humanity follows its "destiny" and masters the larger universe. This brand of evolutionism has its origins in the evolutionary controversies of the mid-nineteenth century. Though Darwin made no special place for humanity in the evolutionary saga theorized in *The Origin of Species*, many alternative evolutionary theories did.[14] In his late essay, "Evolution and Ethics," T. H. Huxley, though firmly committed to the Darwinian evolutionary model in which all species must inevitably succumb to extinction, nevertheless suggested that human intelligence made possible an "ethical process," what we call culture, from which we can collectively act within the universe to make it, at least for a time, a more sustainable and equitable place for us and the larger biosphere. This perspective greatly influenced H. G. Wells, the single most important influence on early American magazine SF,[15] and much of Wells's science fiction explores the implications of Huxley's argument, as does the science fiction of Olaf Stapledon, clear influences on Manning's stories.

The Man Who Awoke is one Norman Winters, a wealthy banker from the twentieth century who desires to see what the future will bring, and uses his wealth to create a sleep chamber that will allow him to awake in the far future. An obvious progenitor is Rip Van Winkle, but there are more immediate echoes in Edward Bellamy's *Looking Backward*, W. H. Hudson's *A Crystal Age*, and Wells's *When the Sleeper Wakes* (which had been reprinted in *Amazing Stories Quarterly* in 1928). In the first story, titled "The Forest People" in the book version, Winters awakes three thousand years in the future, when the ruins of New York City are buried in a verdant forest landscape. He encounters a culture adapted to a forest economy, with no farming, manufacturing, or other practices of industrialization, much like that in *A Crystal Age* or William Morris's *News from Nowhere*. Sustainability is practiced much in the manner of Ernest Callenbach's later *Ecotopia*, and humans live in balance with the rest of nature. Bleiler calls this "a world that might be considered an ecological extremist's ideal."[16] This ecologically centered society was evolved because of the consumption and waste of much of Earth's natural resources during Winters's era, referred to as the "age of Waste." The Chief Forester voices a pointed indictment of our era:

The height of the false civilization of Waste! Fossil plants were ruthlessly burned in furnaces to provide heat; petroleum was consumed by the billion barrels; cheap metal cars were built and thrown away to rust after a few years' use; men crowded into ill-ventilated villages of a million inhabitants—some historians say several million. . . . For what should we thank the humans of three thousand years ago? For exhausting the coal supplies of the world? For leaving us no petroleum for our chemical factories? For destroying the forests on whole mountain ranges and letting the soil erode into the valleys?[17]

But the Forest culture is not utopia. A growing discontent among the youth who are not allowed to step forth and create their own communities without careful population strictures and environmental management is emerging. Winters is captured by this underground movement and commiserates: "I understand you have a very poor opinion of my own times, due to our possibly unwise consumption of natural resources. Even then we had men who warned us against our course of action, but we acted in the belief that when oil and coal were gone mankind would produce some new fuel to take their place."[18] Catalyzed by Winters's presence, the youth revolt, throwing their society into chaos; Winters must retreat to his bunker with the hope of finding utopia further in the future.

Taken by itself, this story fits well within the pastoral ecological mode, as an indictment of present ecological transgressions. But Manning's intention was not to end Winters's journey at this early period. Winters exits his chamber four more times and encounters various stages of human cultural, technological, and ecological evolution. At first glance the remaining stories might be left out of an ecological analysis, but each is crucial in its own right. In "Master of the Brain," Winters emerges five thousand more years in the future and encounters a dystopian technological society, probably derived from Fritz Lang's *Metropolis*. The energy crisis of the Forest period has been solved, and technology has again triumphed. The "Brain," a vast computer, controls all human activity. Humans indulge in controlled pleasure palaces, but no longer have any sense of self: "Here was material to delight his historian's soul—the very kind of future civilization that dreamers and prophets had imagined back in the twentieth century—a thrilling vista of wonders and a consummation of the mechanical evolution."[19] Once again, Winters's presence facilitates a revolt, and he returns to his bunker. His evolutionary trajectory continues as he goes seven thousand years further in the third story, "The City of Sleep," where "the climate had long since changed"[20] and people now escape into what amounts to permanent virtual reality. The previous pattern again asserts itself, with Winters providing a solution to the future's crisis, facilitating another change in the human social order. When Winters next awakens in another five thousand years in "The Individualists," the problems he helped solve in "The City of Sleep" have led to a culture of sparse human population, where everyone is devoted to the pursuit of personal scientific interests. However, the society is out of balance, with each individual trying to best his fellows, leading to single combat using gigantic robotic machines, like those in *The War of the Worlds*. In the final story, "The Elixir," Winters emerges in AD 25,000, where immortality has been achieved and humanity explores the galaxy in search of the meaning of existence. The final chapter within this story, "The Search for Infinite," brings Winters to the ultimate understanding of universal existence and makes overtures to a grand finale for human evolution into beings of pure energy. With this finale Manning achieves one of the central themes of SF, depicting an extraordinary vision of technological, evolutionary fulfillment.

Simak takes an alternative evolutionary view in *City* (which ranks among the highest achievements from the golden age of Campbell's *Astounding*), emphasizing the pastoral over the technological and making for a more pointed ecological fable, though ultimately he comes to a similar conclusion as Manning. Though humanity is the focus of the first several stories in the collection, our species eventually disappears from the scene, becoming a myth for our dog inheritors. Here Simak is more consistent with a Darwinian evolutionary paradigm, which gives no special seat to the human species, though the dogs' evolutionary process is a result of human manipulation via genetic engineering and legacy technology (the robot guardians, the unlimited energy). By removing humanity from the picture, Simak is able to explore an ecological alternative to the world-destroying technological practices of contemporary humanity.

The first tale, "City," tells of the dissolution of cities and the movement of humanity to a rural existence. The dogs find the very concept of the city unfathomable; doggish economists and sociologists regard it as "an impossible structure, not only from the economic standpoint, but from the sociological and psychological as well."[21] With the establishment of atomic power and hydroponics there is no longer need for urban centers or farms, reflections of the ideal of the technological future that was at the time being packaged in *Popular Mechanics* and similar publications.[22] This in turn allows for the dispersal of families out of cities to rural acreages where they live in pastoral tranquillity. Improved transportation via "the family plane and helicopter" make travel easier and convenient and thus facilitate this new pastoral cultural formation. The story introduces the first in the line of Websters (notice the similarity to Manning's Winters), John J. Webster, who is among the last to abandon the city. Ironically, the city becomes a sanctuary for displaced farmers who have moved into the abandoned houses after their farms have collapsed. Simak here illustrates the economic and social fallout that any new cultural formation will necessitate.

The second tale, "Huddling Place," set in the second decade of the twenty-second century, involves Dr. Thomas Webster, John J.'s grandson. By now humanity has fully adapted to the rural, isolated life. But it comes with a cost. Contact with Martians has taken place, and Thomas Webster, an expert in Martian brain physiology, is close friends with Juwain, a Martian philosopher on the verge of an insight that will alter the consciousness of both human and Martian. They communicate regularly through televisor technology that anticipates today's Internet. Service robots take care of most human needs, leading to further isolation: "For what need was there to go anywhere? It all was here. By simply twirling a dial one could talk face to face with anyone one wished, could go, by sense, if not in body, anywhere one wished. Could attend theater or hear a concert or browse in a library half-way around the world. Could transact business one might need to transact without rising from one's chair."[23] Webster suffers from acute agoraphobia, and when Juwain requires an emergency brain operation that only Webster is qualified to do, Webster is unable to overcome his fears and take the trip to Mars. As a consequence of Webster's inaction, Juwain dies. The implication is that Juwain's discovery would have led humanity to a more balanced, ecologically sound existence, and thus opened the door for universal fulfillment. Thus Simak explores the possible consequences of isolated existence facilitated by technologies—technologies, it is worth noting, that are now commonplace.

The next three tales—"Census," "Desertion," and "Paradise"—show humanity's gradual migration to Jupiter and transformation into another form, which is condemned as a retreat from the universal fulfillment implied by Juwain's lost insight. The interstitial material for "Paradise" is important. The dog editor writes:

Bit by bit, as the legend unfolds, the reader gets a more accurate picture of the human race. By degrees, one gains the conviction that here is a race which can be little more that pure fantasy. It is not the kind of race which could rise from humble beginnings to the culture with which it is gifted in these tales. Its equipment is too poor. So far its lack of stability has become apparent. Its preoccupation with a mechanical civilization rather than with a culture based on some of the sounder, more worthwhile concepts of life indicates a lack of basic character.[24]

With the sixth tale, "Hobbies," humanity has mostly abandoned Earth, leaving it to the dogs. The dogs live, as the previous story suggested, in a pastoral paradise. In the prefatory note to "Hobbies," the editor raises the question: "If Man had taken a different path, might he not, in time to come, have been as great as Dog?"[25] This is an important subtle critique, not only mocking anthropocentric narratives of evolutionary history but suggesting that the dogs' pastoral social order is a viable alternative to the mechanistic civilization of twentieth-century technological man. Ironically, however, the dogs are embedded in a technological civilization left them by humanity. Robots serve as their "hands" and caretakers. Yet this allows the dogs to maintain their doggishness and pursue a balanced (innocent?) existence. The dogs have formed what Jenkins calls "a civilization based on the brotherhood of animals—on the psychic understanding and perhaps eventual communication and intercourse of interlocking worlds. A civilization of the mind and of understanding . . . a groping after truth, and the groping is in a direction that man passed by without a glance."[26] In his recent book, *The Ecological Thought*, Timothy Morton argues that, "the ecological thought *is interconnectedness* in the fullest and deepest sense."[27] Simak here said much the same thing seventy years earlier. This animal society is realized in the seventh tale, "Aesop," where the robot Jenkins becomes the teacher and storyteller for the dogs and their animal brethren, who are now completely free of humanity. The interrelation of all animals is again a central topic: "Man never thought of one great animal society, never dreamed of skunk and coon and bear going down the road of life together, planning with one another, helping one another—setting aside all natural differences."[28] However, harmony is soon lost when a fox kills a chicken. A crisis ensues, but is curtailed from a threat from the outside, from another dimension, and the dogs must leave Earth for a parallel world, leaving it to mutated ants. The interstitial prefaces throughout *City* suggest the dog utopia is restored in this alternate world.

Brian Aldiss notes the significance of *City* for investigating "new relationships among living things,"[29] while Thomas Clareson calls it the key work of "criticism of modern urban-industrial society,"[30] observing that "not one of Simak's immediate contemporaries condemned Western society so harshly; no one consigned humanity to oblivion. . . . He created a credible, nonhuman world capable of sustaining metaphors regarding the human condition."³¹ This critique of technological society specifically conveys a pastoral emphasis, as Darko Suvin has pointed out. According to Suvin, the pastoral's "imaginary framework of a world without money-economy, state apparatus, and depersonalizing urbanization allows it to isolate, as in a laboratory, two human motivations: erotics and power-hunger."³² Simak himself said in a later interview: "At the time I wrote *City* I felt there were other, greater values than those we find in technology. . . . The city is an anachronism we'd be better off without."³³ Yet despite Simak's seeming indictment of technology, it should be stressed that the doggish utopia is only possible because of the technological innovations of humankind that have been left to them: sustainable and unlimited power, robot servants, and the very ability to speak and thus to tell tales. As Jill Milling observes, "Though Simak's fables appear to constitute a simple indictment of human destructiveness, the irony provided by the frame narrative and by the qualified resolutions of conflicts in this episodic narrative creates a moral ambiguity characteristic of many science fiction tales."³⁴

Like Manning, Simak takes a broad evolutionary perspective, but with an alternative trajectory: emphasizing balance and harmony in nature rather than technological development, and shifting the lens from humankind to other species. Simak is usually identified as SF's most rural, pastoral writer, and some critics have disparaged his later work as too conservative and overly sentimental. But in *City*, Simak offers an alternative critique to the urban, techno-futurism of much SF and much SF criticism, and it remains an important moment in ecological SF.

APOCALYPSE

The second major mode of ecological thought in SF is the apocalyptic, which generally involves a widespread destruction of human civilization, but which also often works on a small-scale level of destruction of an insular group or ecosystem. While much SF explores the notion of human evolutionary progress, many stories examine the consequences of human destructiveness and species annihilation. The apocalyptic mode in SF is central to the early development of the genre, from Cousin de Grainville's technological, Christian apocalypse *The Last Man* to the secular apocalypses of Mary Shelley—the micro-apocalypse of *Frankenstein* and the macro of her own *The Last Man*. Wells, of course, introduced the evolutionary apocalypse in several of his quintessential scientific romances, such as *The Time Machine*, *The Island of Doctor Moreau*, *The War of the Worlds*, and *The Food of the Gods*. The apocalyptic tradition seems to me to break down into two modes: the pastoral-elegiac, which looks back upon a lost civilization but also often posits a new beginning; and the satiric-ironic, which imagines the end of humanity within the evolutionary saga and ironically reflects on human folly. To use Wells as a marker, we could, perhaps, consider *The Time Machine*, which is certainly the quintessential evolutionary SF story, as also the quintessential elegiac apocalypse for its meditation on the waning of the human species—whereas the insular apocalypse of *The Island of Doctor Moreau* or the near-miss Martian invasion of *The War of the Worlds* might both best fit within the satiric-ironic sub-mode. Gary K. Wolfe's five stages of action in the apocalyptic narrative are useful for considering both *Greener Than You Think* and *Earth Abides*: "(1) the experience or discovery of the cataclysm; (2) the journey through the wasteland created by the cataclysm; (3) settlement and establishment of a new community; (4) the re-emergence of the wilderness as antagonist; and (5) a final decisive battle or struggle to determine which values shall prevail in the new world."[35]

Ward Moore's *Greener Than You Think*, first published in 1947, is a consummate example of the satiric-ironic apocalypse, bringing into question humankind's ethic of scientific innovation, consumerism, capitalism, and power. It engages with the possible threats of bioengineering and what could possibly go wrong when we manipulate the environment. Following the dropping of the atomic bombs on Japan, SF was exploring the ecological implications of nuclear warfare; in *Greener Than You Think*, Moore showed that the coming doom might not come from the bomb, but from some other form of catastrophic technology. In his study of the secular apocalypse in literature, *Terminal Visions*, W. Warren Wagar calls the novel significant for depicting "the sense of man's helplessness before nature raging out of control."[36] Initially, it reads like Wells's *The Food of the Gods* (which starts as satire before shifting to Wells's utopian agenda) before echoing *The War of the Worlds*, then ending bitterly with no hope for humanity, let alone all other life, as the grass covers the entire planet. Much of the novel develops into a satire of contemporary politics, both at home and abroad, anticipating the follies of the Cold War. Since the tone is generally satiric and witty—as Sam Moskowitz put it, "told with broad catastrophic sweep"[37]—the black humor somewhat masks the fact that this novel is as dark in its implications as Thomas Disch's much more somber *The Genocides*.

In the novel an itinerant salesman, Albert Weener, interviews Josephine Francis, inventor of a process called the Metamorphizer that transforms the genetic structure of plants. Francis's hope is to increase the fecundity of the harvest, thus eliminating hunger and poverty: "It will change the face of the world, Weener. No more used-up areas, no more frantic scrambling for the few bits of naturally rich ground, no more struggle to get artificial fertilizers to worn-out soil in the face of ignorance and poverty. . . . Inoculate the plants with the Metamorphizer—and you have a crop fatter than Iowa's or the Ukraine's best. The whole world will teem with abundance."[38] Weener sees a moneymaking opportunity, and before Dr. Francis can finish her laboratory fail-safes, he applies the substance to a barren lawn in the San Fernando Valley. The sparse devil grass instantly begins to grow out of control, and Los Angeles is soon absorbed by an unrelenting patch of grass. Weener later comes face to face with the green colossus: "As I stood there with fascinated attention, the thing moved and kept on moving; not in one place, but in thousands, not in one direction, but toward all points of the compass. It writhed and twisted in nightmarish unease, expanding, extending, increasing; spreading, spreading, spreading. Its movement, by human standards, was slow, but it was so monstrous to see this great mass of verdure move at all that it appeared to be going with express speed, inexorably enveloping everything in its path."[39]

Dr. Francis is called before a congressional hearing by the "Committee to Investigate Dangerous Vegetation,"[40] and here Moore's political satire is at its finest. Francis works for a solution, but the grass spreads across the continent, and war soon breaks out between the United States and Russia as the grass begins to gain footholds around the globe. As the narrative continues, Weener invests in a food substitute, which becomes essential to survival as the grass ravages farmland, and he becomes a wealthy magnate. His abject acquisitiveness and brutal disregard for the victims of the disaster he has caused is a biting attack on industrial capitalism and the quest for power. Weener is certainly one of the most despicable lead characters in all of sf, but a fitting foil for Moore's satiric purposes. Eventually, as the entire planet is consumed by the grass, Dr. Francis's efforts to find an antidote have failed, and Weener, on his extravagant yacht, filled with nubile women, sails the ocean, until the grass begins to take hold there as well. The black comedy of the final line is devastating: "The Grass has found another seam in the deck."[41] Moore's satiric vision anticipates the ironic apocalypses of J. G. Ballard and forces us to take a stern look at contemporary values that threaten the very sustainability of our planet.

George R. Stewart's *Earth Abides* is an elegiac apocalypse depicting the end of the modern era when a disease strikes down all but a small fraction of the human population, leaving all other flora and fauna intact, until the lack of humanity begins to alter the ecosphere. It has been tremendously influential upon works such as Stephen King's *The Stand*, Kim Stanley Robinson's *The Wild Shore*, and David Brin's *The Postman*, among others—and, as Gary K. Wolfe notes, it is "one of the most fully realized accounts in all science fiction of a massive catastrophe and the evolution toward a new culture."[42] It is fairly obvious that Jack London's "The Scarlet Plague" looms behind *Earth Abides*; however, Wolfe notes that "the sources of the novel seem to lie less in the tradition of science fiction catastrophes than in Stewart's own abiding concern with natural forces which seem almost consciously directed against human society."[43] Prior to *Earth Abides*, Stewart's commercially and critically successful novels *Storm* (1941) and *Fire* (1948) examined natural forces acting beyond human control.

The central character, Isherwood "Ish" Williams, a young graduate student studying ecology, is isolated in the mountains when the plague strikes. Bitten by a rattlesnake, Ish comes down the trail to the nearest dwelling for help only to find it empty. He finds a newspaper that gives details of the catastrophe:

> The headlines told him what was most essential. The United States from coast
> to coast was overwhelmed by the attack of some new and unknown disease of
> unparalleled rapidity of spread, and fatality. Estimates for various cities, admit-
> tedly little more than guesses, indicated that between 25 percent and 35 percent
> of the population had already died. . . . In its symptoms the disease was like a kind
> of super-measles. No one was sure in what part of the world it had originated;
> aided by airplane travel, it had sprung up almost simultaneously in every center of
> civilization, outrunning all attempts at quarantine.[44]

As an ecologist and a student of nature, Ish has an observer's temperament, and thus, rather than panic and fall into despair, he determines to travel across the country to see the extent of the changes wrought upon humankind and the subsequent environmental consequences. This is indicative of what Wolfe posits as the "journey through the wasteland," where the protagonist must witness the aftermath of the catastrophe. As an ecologist, Ish is particularly well-suited to this role of witness: "Even though the curtain had been rung down on man, here was the opening of the greatest of all dramas for a student such as he. During thousands of years man had impressed himself upon the world. Now man was gone, certainly for a while, perhaps forever. Even if some survivors were left, they would be a long time in again obtaining supremacy. What would happen to the world and its creatures without man? *That* he was left to see!"[45] And what Ish discovers is that the ecology begins to change dramatically: the various animals and plants dependent upon and cultivated by humankind die out; they can only survive by humanity's stewardship; this includes such surprising creatures as rats and ants, both of which suffer massive die-offs because of overpopulation, since their populations aren't checked by human practices. This illustrates the extent to which humankind has shaped, shepherded, and cultivated the environment. Since all is interconnected, to eliminate humanity would fundamentally alter the ecology of the entire system. Ish realizes that new adaptations will occur and additional die-offs will open new niches; the evolutionary process begins to reassert itself throughout the biosphere.

As the novel progresses, Ish encounters other survivors and forges a relationship with an African American woman named Em. Returning to the West Coast, they form a community, raising families and adapting to change as the infrastructure of civilization begins to break down. Ish hopes to preserve some of the qualities of the lost era, but the children are adapting to another mode of existence. His hopes are shattered when a disease brought by an outsider into their community wipes out many, including his son Joey, who had showed a penchant for reading and contemplative thought. This signals the end of the old ways. In the final section, as Ish comes to the end of his life, he is dubbed the "Last American," and we poignantly witness the end of our era, though we are left with a rather melancholy promise of something new. Though *Earth Abides* has pastoral qualities much like Simak's, the tone of this apocalyptic novel is decidedly more elegiac, perhaps because it is not about the transformation of the species but about the end of modern civilization.

The apocalyptic environmentalism of Moore and Stewart warns us against ecological complacency and self-assured and unexamined species triumphalism. Both Moore and Stewart remind us that apocalypse might be just around the corner, as we eat up the planet, poison and degrade its biosystems, and put into jeopardy the continued sustainability of the human species, and most others. Though these apocalyptic narratives function within the same evolutionary paradigm as Manning's *The Man Who Awoke* and Simak's *City*, they leave us less assured that the ecological challenges ahead will be manageable, resolvable, or survivable. Although Manning and Simak show us in their evolutionary narratives that change itself is inevitable, they are far less pessimistic in their long-term vision of the evolutionary saga, whether universal fulfillment is achieved by human, canine, or some yet evolved species. The struggle between an apocalyptic pessimism and an evolutionary optimism is a defining characteristic of SF, and one of the reasons why these golden age ecological narratives, be they evolutionary or apocalyptic, are still relevant to the present. As Farah Mendlesohn has importantly noted, "Science fiction is less a genre . . . than an ongoing discussion," an "argument with the universe."[46] The combined argument of evolution and apocalypse, optimism and pessimism, has the potential to coalesce in the reader and facilitate transformational ecological thought. It is in that struggle between optimism and pessimism, dramatized by these narratives and others like them, that we can begin to do the critical work of ecological transformation.

Together, these four books not only show historically the engagement with ecological challenges by Golden Age SF writers, but they still offer valuable reflections and insights on ecological questions for today, as we edge closer to ecological crisis, and provide avenues for fresh ecological thinking, through the persistent struggle between optimism and pessimism. The importance of ecological thinking to our contemporary crisis is self-evident. SF provides us with a methodology to begin formulating alternatives. Lawrence Buell asks "whether planetary life will remain viable for most of the Earth's inhabitants without major changes in the way we live now."[47] Studying SF (and more broadly literature) using an ecological lens can perhaps better prepare us for impending environmental change. Glen Love points to a possible future for literary studies: "Literary studies today may find new purpose in redirecting human consciousness, through our teaching and scholarship, to a full consideration of our place in an undismissible but increasingly threatened natural world. Paradoxically, taking nature seriously in this way—embracing the social within the natural—may provide us with our best hope of recovering the disappearing social role of literary criticism."[48] Ecocritic Patrick Murphy concurs: "How might the long-term attitude of our students and other members of our culture toward environmental protection and restoration be affected by the teaching of works . . . that are devoted to nature and environmental topics? The ideas taught today can become the practice of tomorrow, but only if they are taught today."[49] This is a call for a more ecologically oriented literary criticism, a call for a deeper engagement with the literature that examines the human animal in the fullness of its environment—which is to say, a call for all of us to read, study, and teach SF.

Notes

1. Isaac Asimov, ed., *Before the Golden Age* (Garden City, NY: Doubleday, 1974), 344.
2. Terry Carr, ed., *Dream's Edge* (San Francisco: Sierra Club Books), 1.
3. Frank Herbert, introduction to *The Wounded Planet*, ed. Roger Elwood and Virginia Kidd (New York: Bantam, 1973), xi–xvii.

4. Brian Stableford, "Science Fiction and Ecology," in *A Companion to Science Fiction*, ed. David Seed (Oxford: Blackwell, 2005), 129.

5. Ibid., 140.

6. See Stacey Alaimo, *Bodily Natures: Science, Environment, and the Material Self* (Bloomington: Indiana University Press, 2010); Lawrence Buell, *The Future of Environmental Criticism* (Oxford: Blackwell, 2005); Ursula K. Heise, *Sense of Place and Sense of Planet: The Environmental Imagination of the Global* (Oxford: Oxford University Press, 2008); Timothy Morton, *The Ecological Thought* (Cambridge, MA: Harvard University Press, 2010); Patrick D. Murphy, *Ecocritical Explorations in Literary and Cultural Studies: Fences, Boundaries, and Fields* (Lanham, MD: Lexington Books, 2009).

7. Cheryll Glotfelty, "Introduction: Literary Studies in an Age of Environmental Crisis," in *The Ecocriticism Reader*, ed. Cheryll Glotfelty and Harold Fromm (Athens: University of Georgia Press, 1996), xx.

8. Glen A. Love, *Practical Ecocriticism: Literature, Biology, and the Environment* (Charlottesville: University of Virginia Press, 2003), 1.

9. Buell, *Future of Environmental Criticism*, 56–57.

10. Everett F. Bleiler and Richard Bleiler, *Science Fiction: The Gernsback Years* (Kent, OH: Kent State University Press, 1998), 634–35.

11. The last story, "The Simple Way" ("Trouble with Ants") appeared in *Fantastic Adventures* in 1951.

12. I have discussed this in my book *The Evolutionary Imagination from Erasmus Darwin to H. G. Wells: Science, Evolution, and Ecology* (Burlington, VT: Ashgate, 2012). See, among other studies, John J. Pierce, *When World Views Collide: A Study in Imagination and Evolution* (Westport, CT: Greenwood Press, 1989); Nicholas Ruddick, *The Fire in the Stone: Prehistoric Fiction from Charles Darwin to Jean M. Auel* (Middletown, CT: Wesleyan University Press, 2009); Istvan Csicsery-Ronay Jr., *The Seven Beauties of Science Fiction* (Middletown, CT: Wesleyan University Press, 2008). A good introduction to modern science is Peter J. Bowler and Iwan Rhys Morus, *Making Modern Science* (Chicago: University of Chicago Press, 2005).

13. Csicsery-Ronay Jr., *Seven Beauties*, 90.

14. See Michael Ruse's *The Evolution Wars* (Santa Barbara, CA: ABC–CLIO, 2000) and *Monad to Man: The Idea of Progress in Evolutionary Biology* (Cambridge, MA: Harvard University Press, 1996).

15. Wells's fiction appeared in every issue of *Amazing Stories* from its inception in April 1926 to August 1928.

16. Everett F. Bleiler, "Laurence Manning," in *Canadian Fantasy and Science-Fiction Writers*, ed. Douglas Ivison (Detroit: Gale, 2002), 181.

17. Laurence Manning, *The Man Who Awoke* (New York: Ballantine, 1975), 20–21.

18. Ibid., 25.

19. Ibid., 45.

20. Ibid., 71.

21. Clifford D. Simak, *City* (Garden City, NY: Doubleday, 1952), 1.

22. See Gregory Benford and the Editors of *Popular Mechanics*, eds., *The Wonderful Future That Never Was* (New York: Hearst Books, 2010).

23. Simak, *City*, 37.

24. Ibid., 96–97.

25. Ibid., 121.

26. Ibid., 151.

27. Morton, *Ecological Thought*, 7. Emphasis mine.

28. Simak, *City*, 166.

29. Brian W. Aldiss, *Trillion Year Spree: The History of Science Fiction* (New York: Atheneum, 1986), 225.

30. Thomas D. Clareson, *Understanding Contemporary American Science Fiction: The Formative Period (1926–1970)* (Columbia: University of South Carolina Press, 1990), 45.

31. Ibid., 48.

32. Darko Suvin, *Metamorphoses of Science Fiction* (New Haven, CT: Yale University Press, 1979), 9.

33. Quoted in Bruce Shaw, "Clifford Simak's *City* (1952): The Dogs' Critique (and Others')," *Extrapolation* 46, no. 4 (Winter 2005): 498.

34. Jill Milling, "The Ambiguous Animal: Evolution of the Beast-Man in Scientific Creation Myths," in *The Shape of the Fantastic*, ed. Oleana H. Saciuk (Westport, CT: Greenwood Press, 1990), 105.

35. Gary K. Wolfe, "The Remaking of Zero: Beginning at the End," In *The End of the World*, ed. Eric S. Rabkin, Martin H. Greenberg, and Joseph D. Olander (Carbondale: Southern Illinois University Press, 1983), 8.

36. W. Warren Wagar, *Terminal Visions: The Literature of Last Things* (Bloomington: Indiana University Press, 1982), 187.

37. Sam Moskowitz, *Seekers of Tomorrow* (Cleveland: World Publishing Co., 1966), 425.

38. Ward Moore, *Greener Than You Think* (New York: Crown, 1985), 3.

39. Ibid., 53.

40. Ibid., 90.

41. Ibid., 322.

42. Wolfe, "Remaking of Zero," 16.

43. Ibid., 16.

44. George R. Stewart, *Earth Abides* (Boston: Houghton Mifflin, 1976), 12–13.

45. Ibid., 24.

46. Farah Mendlesohn, "Introduction: Reading Science Fiction," in *The Cambridge Companion to Science Fiction*, ed. Edward James and Farah Mendlesohn (Cambridge: Cambridge University Press, 2003), 1–2.

47. Buell, *Future of Environmental Criticism*, vi.

48. Love, *Practical Ecocriticism*, 163–64

49. Murphy, *Ecocritical Explorations*, 4.

Daoism, Ecology, and World Reduction in Le Guin's Utopian Fictions

GIB PRETTYMAN

For scholars who approach Ursula K. Le Guin's fictions from the perspective of Marxist critical theory, ecology and Daoism can be problematic aspects of her work. In the effusion of Le Guin scholarship that coincided with the establishment of the journal *Science Fiction Studies* (SFS) in the early 1970s, critics were quick to identify characteristic subjects of "wholeness and balance" and to link them to her ecological concerns and the Daoist dynamic of yin and yang.[1] On the one hand, critical theorists saw in these subjects an inspiring awareness of systemic relationships, evocation of "non-capitalist habitats," and rejection of capitalist alienation, particularly given the publication of her overtly anarchist utopian novel *The Dispossessed* in 1974.[2] On the other hand, they found her "mythopoetic" invocations of balance to be wishful thinking and to imply that radical political action was misguided.[3] Sorting out this ambivalence was especially relevant to critical theorists in terms of assessing Le Guin's utopianism, which they regarded as a positive historical development and a key aspect of SF as a contemporary cultural genre.

Starting with the hugely influential work of Darko Suvin and Fredric Jameson, then, critical theorists have worked to highlight the radical energies of Le Guin's fictions while simultaneously downplaying politically troublesome aspects of her invocations of Daoism[4] and ecology. Although experimentation with non-Western spiritual traditions was a hallmark of the postwar counterculture, Daoism was (and remains) a poorly understood tradition for most critics. Both Suvin and Jameson viewed Daoism with distrust and dismissed it as politically misleading. Ecology, by comparison, represented a major cultural and historical issue in the early 1970s. As Peter Stillman notes, Le Guin was writing at the outset of the modern environmentalist movement, symbolized by the first Earth Day in 1970.[5] The field known as "deep ecology" was also coalescing at this time.

Rather than treating this issue directly, however, Suvin and Jameson interpreted Le Guin's ecological themes as fantasies that revealed the inescapable political contradictions of capitalism. In particular, Jameson described Le Guin's approach as "world reduction," which he saw as a fantasy of escaping from the history of capitalism. Reduced thus to the status of compensatory fantasies, neither Daoism nor ecology was engaged as a strategic framework in its own right. Indeed, serious doubts were suggested about Le Guin's use of both.

In the essay that follows, I revisit this under-explored ground between the concerns of critical theory and Le Guin's intellectual uses of ecology and Daoism. I argue that Le Guin's fictional explorations of ecological relationships do perform real political work on a cognitive and epistemological level by emphasizing a range of challenges to conventional egoistic perceptions. From this perspective, what Jameson identifies as world reduction can be seen to serve a cognitive and material purpose by focusing on the primary epistemological implication of ecology: namely, the historical necessity to reframe familiar assumptions of egoism and anthropocentrism.

I am not using "ego" here in its psychoanalytical meaning, but using it rather to indicate one's sense of being a separate, enduring, and self-centered actor in the world. This is the sense employed by eco-socialist Joel Kovel when he asserts in *The Enemy of Nature* that consumer capitalism is "the way of the Ego."[6] Ego, Kovel argues, is "the anti-ecocentric moment enshrined by Capital" and "the secret to the riddle of growth and the mania of consumption." From this perspective, global consumer capitalism constitutes the cultural, technological, institutional, and psychosocial apotheosis of egoism, turning natural self-interest into an imperative pseudo-subjectivity enforced by "the titanic power of the capitalist state and cultural apparatus."[7] It is the "enshrinement" of egocentrism that makes capitalism "the enemy of nature," Kovel argues. In a very real sense, the artificial environments that we have constructed around ourselves—everything from houses and cities to markets and media and virtual realities—are material manifestations of all-consuming egoism. Therefore, one can critique the ecological pathologies of global capitalism as "expressions of an impeded motion between inner and outer world."[8] Such an approach is at once psychological, philosophical, and material.

In describing capitalism as "the way of the Ego," Kovel formulates in socialist terms what critical traditions like Buddhism and Daoism have long asserted: that egoistic perceptions and institutions are inherently mistaken. Seen from sufficient distance, the egoistic "self" is clearly an unreliable category and even a kind of fiction, as everything about self-"identity" is in constant flux and ultimately proves to be transitory. Buddhist psychology points out that to act as though one were a fixed and enduring entity leads to certain characteristic problems such as egoistic "attachment"—trying to grasp and possesses things that are in fact always changing—which it asserts is a primary cause of human suffering. Similarly, Daoist philosophy emphasizes the enduring context of Dao (Tao)—the fundamental nature of things and processes of the world—over egoistic illusions and scholastic definitions. In addition to the illusion of fixed identity, another egoistic illusion is the sense of being distinct and separate from the rest of the world. Buddhism and Daoism therefore also explore methods for recognizing fundamental interconnections beneath the appearance of separate "forms."

Although these concerns of Eastern philosophy are often considered "mystical," their similarities to the fundamental insights of ecology are evident: both frameworks emphasize systemic processes and aim to critique egoistic illusions. And as Kovel's combination of ecology and socialism suggests, these concerns are arguably compatible with Marxist critique as well. Theoretically, all these frameworks could contribute toward cognitive reframing that would undermine capitalism and the way of the ego. As Kovel puts it, "Recognition of ourselves in nature and nature in ourselves" and "subjective as well as objective participation in ecosystems" are "the essential condition[s] for overcoming the domination of nature, and its pathologies of instrumental production and addictive consumption."[9]

Le Guin's fictions, I argue, work toward this "recognition of ourselves in nature" by using insights derived from Daoism and ecology to challenge familiar contexts of ego. Daoism and ecology are thus at the heart of her political vision, both as cognitive strategies and material limits. In order to explore these assertions, I first briefly detail how Suvin and Jameson approach Le Guin's Daoist ecology and consider the implications of the world reduction that Jameson sees in her work. Then I describe how Le Guin's utopian strategy, informed by Daoism, uses specific forms of world reduction to challenge egoistic assumptions. Finally, I consider the implications of Le Guin's strategy relative to that of critical theory and demonstrate how material limits to egoism represent a problem for critical theory as such.

ECOLOGY AS SYMPTOM

As befitting his influence on the field of SF in general, Darko Suvin helped to set the tone for reading Le Guin from the perspective of critical theory.[10] He greatly admired Le Guin's work, and famously consulted with Le Guin on the vision of *The Dispossessed*—though to what extent is unclear.[11] Suvin also edited the special issue of *Science Fiction Studies* (November 1975) devoted to Le Guin's work.[12] In his own contribution to that special issue, "Parables of De-alienation: Le Guin's Widdershins Dance," Suvin presented his basic solution to Le Guin's problematic valorization of Daoism and ecology by distinguishing between representations of "static balance" and "dynamic balance." Le Guin, he argued, maintained an active and dynamic vision, a "widdershins dance" of critical perceptions of the world, that was equivalent in many respects to the insights of Marxist critique.[13] This dynamic vision represented "the quest for and sketching of a new, collectivist system of no longer alienated human relationships, which arise out of the absolute necessity for overcoming an intolerable ethical, cosmic, political and physical alienation."[14] Suvin argued that Le Guin's work had matured from the comparatively simplistic and ahistorical "mythopoetics" of her "apprentice trilogy"—*Rocannon's World* (1966), *Planet of Exile* (1966), and *City of Illusions* (1967)—to the more complexly historical engagements in *The Dispossessed*.[15] He saw her utopianism as evidence that "the forces of de-alienation are on the rise in Le Guin's writing, parallel to what she (one hopes rightly) senses as the deep historical currents in the world."[16] He interpreted her newest utopian fiction at that point, "The New Atlantis" (1975), as further evidence of "the realistic, bitter-sweet Le Guinian ambiguity" and of the "clear and firm but richly and truthfully ambiguous Leftism" which "situates her at the node of possibly the central contemporary contradiction, that between capitalist alienation and the emerging classless de-alienation."[17]

In emphasizing Le Guin's work as an "SF of collective practice,"[18] Suvin strongly downplayed her Daoism. Rather than "a static balancing of two yin-and-yang-type alternatives, two principles or opposites (light-darkness, male-female, etc.) between which a middle Way of wisdom leads," Suvin argued, Le Guin's "ambiguities" are "in principle dynamic, and have through her evolution become more clearly and indubitably such." He saw Daoism as merely a superseded early interest, arguing that her thought had "evolved" through the Daoism of Laozi (Lao Tzu) to the anarchism of Kropotkin and Goodman, and claimed that "attempts to subsume her under Taoism" would be "not only doomed to failure but also retrospectively revealed as inadequate even for her earlier works."[19] He regarded Daoism as too simplistic and too mythical to be of use in accurately understanding the political implications of Le Guin's representations of "permanent revolution and evolution."[20]

Suvin did not similarly dismiss Le Guin's ecology, but he downplayed it as well. Despite noting capitalism's "intolerable ethical, cosmic, political and physical alienation," Suvin did not consider her ecological approach to cosmic and physical alienation at face value. Instead, he treated her ecological ideals primarily as metaphors of renewed collective relationships. His reading of "The New Atlantis," for example, paid no attention to Le Guin's early depiction of catastrophically raised sea levels resulting from the greenhouse effect. Likewise, his reading of *The Word for World Is Forest* emphasized psychical rather than physical alienation. For Suvin, "the forest which is the word for the world in the language of Selver's people" represents (like Daoism) "a static balance, a closed circle of unhistorical time."[21] Instead of considering Le Guin's concerns for material ecosystems, then, Suvin reads the novel in relation to "the all-pervading psychical eco-system of modern capitalism." Suvin treats Le Guin's ecological concerns as just another item in the list of grievances against capitalism and its social order, or as an analogy for properly political alienation, rather than an urgent historical framework in its own right.

Fredric Jameson shares Suvin's commitment to critiquing the fundamental political implications of texts using the frameworks of psychoanalysis and critical theory. Jameson insists that a text's subject matter and intended themes are not especially significant in their own right, but rather constitute evidence of the author's imaginative attempts to address contradictions in historical social structures. Suvin captures this idea succinctly in a later essay with an epigraph from Roland Barthes: "What is the meaning of a book? Not what it argues, but what it argues with."[22] Like Suvin, then, Jameson reads texts symptomatically, such that their overt content or details are analyzed for what they reveal of psychic processes—deep fears or hopes from our collective "political unconscious"—and in turn those psychic processes indicate distortions and contradictions of the existing political order. In a way, this involves reading texts negatively: watching for the symptomatic places where they necessarily fail, as opposed to treating their intended themes and chosen subjects as positive content in its own right. At the same time, however, symptomatic failures can reveal the enduring hopes of people in the face of political alienation. Jameson labels this enduring hope "the desire called Utopia."[23]

While Jameson addresses Le Guin's ecological ideals more explicitly than Suvin did, then, he similarly treats them primarily as symptomatic evidence of more familiar political issues. In his essay "World Reduction in Le Guin," which also appeared in the Le Guin issue of *SFS*, Jameson considered the political ambiguities that her Daoist-inspired focus on ecology represents from a Marxist perspective.[24] One of the major psychic processes that he identified in Le Guin's work was "world reduction." Pointing primarily to *The Left Hand of Darkness* (1969) and *The Dispossessed*, Jameson described Le Guin's world reduction as "a principle of systematic exclusion, a kind of surgical excision of empirical reality, something like a process of ontological attenuation in which the sheer teeming multiplicity of what exists, or what we call reality, is deliberately thinned and weeded out through an operation of radical abstractions and simplification."[25] The extremely cold and barren planet Gethen in *Left Hand of Darkness*, for example, represents "an experimental landscape in which our being-in-the-world is simplified to the extreme."[26] The moonscape of Annares in *The Dispossessed* is a similarly barren "experimental landscape," particularly given that it serves as the setting for imagining a utopian society.

Jameson saw mixed implications in Le Guin's world reduction. On the positive side, such simplification of our being-in-the-world tries to imagine away capitalism, and is therefore evidence of utopian desire. But clearly any resulting critique or alternative vision would be questionable to the extent that it is based on fantasized world reduction. From this perspective, as Jameson's term suggests, world reduction is largely a wished-for escape from the frustrating complexity of lived existence in the modern world. Jameson saw this wish in part as "a symbolic affirmation of the autonomy of the organism," but also as "a fantasy realization of some virtually total disengagement of the body from its environment or eco-system." It yields a situation, he argued, "in which our sensory links with the multiple and shifting perceptual fields around us are abstracted so radically as to vouchsafe, perhaps, some new glimpse as to the ultimate nature of human reality."[27] In other words, world reduction suggests both regrettably escapist and laudably utopian impulses. Although he referred to Le Guin's world reduction as an "experimental ecology," however, Jameson didn't explore its significance in terms of ecology per se.

The ambivalent significance of world reduction again indicates the problems that Le Guin's invocation of ecology and Daoism pose from the perspective of critical theory. To point toward ecological ideals or seek a glimpse of "the ultimate nature of reality" is a laudable reaction to political alienation, but it also seems escapist when considered in relation to the "all-pervading psychical eco-system" of global capitalism. From the perspective of critical theory, ecological ideals of balance or wholeness seem to be outside of history. This perception is only amplified when the source of the ecological ideals is an ancient and mystical system such as Daoism, which Jameson takes to be a key source of Le Guin's "anti-political, anti-activist stance."[28] Like Suvin, then, Jameson seeks to separate positive ideals and political longings from the particular frameworks of ecology and Daoism that Le Guin uses to formulate them.

At least in the case of ecology, this unwillingness to consider Le Guin's frameworks seems to be a significant shortcoming, given that ecological crises are an important historical context in their own right. And in terms of Daoism, Suvin's assessment also appears to be wrong in at least one respect: Le Guin in fact turned toward Daoism with even more vigor and subtlety in her later work, including her explicit utopian theorizing and her most experimental utopian work. Given these facts, there would seem to be room for critical theorists to engage more with Le Guin's ecological and Daoist frameworks in their own right.

By the same token, Jameson's insights reveal an important problem for critics who take Le Guin's ecology and Daoism seriously, because world reduction is clearly a perplexing technique for someone who supposedly values ecological insights. Ecology as a positive framework emphasizes qualities such as diversity, complexity, and systemic balance, whereas world reduction seems to ignore those factors, or actively to fantasize them away. Critics who admire Le Guin's ecological ideals, no less than critical theorists who distrust them, need to consider the relationships between her world reduction and her uses of Daoism and ecology.

YIN UTOPIANISM

Suvin and Jameson are certainly correct about capitalism as an all-pervading psychic ecosystem, and world reduction has remained characteristic in Le Guin's work, including her later utopian novels *Always Coming Home* (1985) and *The Telling* (2000). Thus the basics of their reading are not at issue: Le Guin does attempt to imagine capitalism away, and both the desire to escape and the severely limited ability to do so are symptomatic of our historical period. However, I maintain that Le Guin's Daoist ecology does more than simply confirm the basic diagnosis and the critical framework that interprets the symptoms. Insisting on an ecological perspective yields politically effective cognitive estrangement of the sort that Suvin posits for SF. Specifically, ecology involves two related cognitive processes: unlearning the egoistic and anthropocentric illusions that underlie the psychic ecosystem of capitalism, and learning the real limits that characterize the material ecosystem and circumscribe human culture. Seen this way, Le Guin's world reduction is not just an effort to fantasize capitalism away, but a strategic response to the worldview of capitalism—and Daoism provides an essential framework for conceptualizing that strategy.

This is basically the artistic and political strategy that Le Guin outlined in her 1982 lecture "A Non-Euclidean View of California as a Cold Place to Be," where she used the Daoist framework of yin and yang to contrast her utopianism with that of the Western tradition. "Yin" roughly signifies the dark, soft, passive, metaphorically "feminine" aspects of the universe, while "yang" is its bright, hard, aggressive, metaphorically "masculine" aspects. From Le Guin's perspective, "Utopia has been yang. In one way or the other, from Plato on, utopia has been the big yang motorcycle trip. Bright, dry, clear, strong, firm, active, aggressive, lineal, progressive, creative, expanding, advancing, and hot."[29] By contrast, Le Guin claimed that she was "trying to suggest, in an evasive, distrustful, untrustworthy fashion, and as obscurely as I can," that "our final loss of faith" in the "radiant sandcastle" that was the European and masculine utopian tradition might "enable our eyes to adjust to a dimmer light and in it perceive another kind of utopia"—a "yin utopia."[30]

Although she used the framework of yin and yang, it is important to notice that she saw her yin utopianism as a strategic counterweight rather than a mystical celebration of inevitable balance. In a response to the sfs special issue on her work, Le Guin noted that "all too often . . . I find the critic apparently persuaded that Yin and Yang are opposites, between which lies the straight, but safe, Way"—a conception of Daoism that she insists "is all wrong."[31] Her explicit theorizing in "Non-Euclidean" demonstrates instead how Daoism can be used to diagnose and combat imbalance. "Our civilization is now so intensely yang," Le Guin declares, "that any imagination of bettering its injustices or eluding its self-destructiveness must involve a reversal." Le Guin glosses her envisioned "reversal" by citing a passage from Laozi's *Daodejing* (Tao Te Ching):

The ten thousand things arise together
and I watch their return.
They return each to its root.
Returning to one's roots is known as stillness.
Returning to one's destiny is known as the constant.
Knowledge of the constant is known as discernment.
To ignore the constant
is to go wrong, and end in disorder.[32]

Le Guin didn't cite any translator for this rendering of the passage; presumably it is her own, derived from comparison of prominent translations.[33] Fifteen years later, in her own published translation of Laozi, Le Guin titled this passage "Returning to the Root" and rendered it in more natural and ecological language:

> The ten thousand things arise together;
> in their arising is their return.
> Now they flower,
> and flowering
> sink homeward,
> returning to the root.
>
> The return to the root
> is peace.
> Peace: to accept what must be,
> to know what endures.
> In that knowledge is wisdom.
> Without it, ruin, disorder.[34]

Here the confident subjectivity and intellectual abstractions of the earlier translation ("destiny," "discernment," "the constant") are almost completely replaced by analogies to impersonal natural processes, a hallmark of Daoist thought. The result is a series of fundamental ecological insights: recognizing the enduring relationships between all things, recognizing their endless impermanence, recognizing their fundamental properties, and recognizing the "wisdom" of this "knowledge" as opposed to anthropocentric and egoistic constructions of order. Using these insights, Le Guin's yin utopianism seeks to challenge ego-logical frameworks by appealing to ecological ones.

As it was for Daoists in the Warring States period of Chinese history, it is the "ruin" and "disorder" of existing social institutions that leads Le Guin to her strategy of envisioned simplification and "return." She argues for the need to compensate in the opposite direction from our "intensely yang" culture, and to undo the confident egoism that moves us farther and farther from "what endures." Paradoxically, then, Le Guin's yin utopia imagines not a "no place," but precisely a radical version of the here and now: "If utopia is a place that does not exist, then surely (as Lao Tzu would say) the way to get there is by the way that is not a way. And in that same vein, the nature of the utopia I am trying to describe is such that if it is to come, it must exist already."[35] In suggesting this paradoxical utopian strategy, Le Guin asserts that her intent "is not reactionary, nor even conservative, but simply subversive. It seems that the utopian imagination is trapped, like capitalism and industrialism and the human population, in a one-way future consisting only of growth. All I'm trying to do is figure out how to put a pig on the tracks."[36] Le Guin lumps capitalism, progressivism, utopianism, and Marxism together as manifestations of the prevailing egoistic orientation toward endless growth. Instead, she wants to emphasize a radical knowledge of place, of here and now. Both ecology and Daoism represent critical frameworks for this approach.

Such cognitive world reduction, or "return to the root," has become an increasingly significant aspect of our historical moment since 1975. No doubt, as Jameson suggests, it primarily reveals a desire to imagine away capitalism. However, it also represents the recognition of real limits and the real reductions that must eventually occur, one way or the other. In *Ecology as Politics*, published at the same time as the Le Guin issue of *SFS*, André Gorz notes that capitalism—specifically, what we would now call industrial capitalism—was confronting numerous concrete ecological limits. In the 1970s, oil shortages and pollution were the most evident examples of ecological limits. Kovel, writing at the turn of the twenty-first century, could point to a laundry list of devastating ecological statistics, including the encompassing crisis of global climate change. Now we can add physiological phenomena like the diabetes and obesity epidemics, which are essentially physiological limits on growth and consumption—points at which industrial "satisfaction" of appetites destroys the organism itself. Even the fictions and abstractions of postindustrial capitalism are reaching real limits, such as financial institutions that are "too big to fail" or digital "addictions" that unfit us for survival in the real world. In all these ways, assumptions of endless growth and ever-increasing consumption are, as Gorz said, encountering physical contradictions or "counterproductivities."[37] These are ecological limits of ego-logic, experienced from squarely within consumer culture (to say nothing of globalization's relentless effects on nonindustrialized peoples and cultures). To practice "ecological realism," Gorz insists, the point "is not to refrain from consuming more and more, but to consume less and less—there is no other way of conserving the available reserves for future generations."[38] Cognitively, "to understand and overcome such 'counterproductivities,' one has to break with economic rationality."[39] Le Guin, then, is expressing a basic ecological strategy of our times: trying to counteract the way of the ego.[40]

Le Guin's Daoism functions as a critical framework for this cognitive reframing away from ego-logic and toward eco-logic in ways that go well beyond the familiar distinction of yin and yang and the ideal "way" of Dao. The Daoism of Laozi and Zhuangzi (Chuang Tzu) is a philosophical worldview—not a set of canonical beliefs or scriptural revelations like the typical Western understanding of religions. Therefore, Daoism contributes to Le Guin's work not as beliefs to be affirmed, but as strategies to be pursued. Daoism's most important ecological strategies are challenging conventional knowledge and recognizing the intrinsic characteristics of things, both of which serve to reframe the way of the ego.

Daoism as a critical framework is fiercely critical of conventional knowledge, scholasticism, and intellectual "truths" that derive from confident imposition of anthropocentric values. Laozi's "wise soul"[41] is marked by humility, not as an ethical duty, but out of respect for the complexity of natural processes and in opposition to the dominant society, whose confident imposition of conventional "knowledge" creates injustices and imbalances. Like Gorz's ecology, Laozi explains the epistemological limits of "rationality" in terms of evident physical limits: "Brim-fill the bowl, / it'll spill over. / Keep sharpening the blade, / you'll soon blunt it."[42] In explaining her yin utopianism, Le Guin quotes Zhuangzi's insistence that "the best understanding . . . 'rests in what it cannot understand. If you do not understand this, then Heaven the Equalizer will destroy you.'"[43] To a large extent, ecological reframing means unlearning conventional perceptions that seem so fixed from the perspective of the way of the ego.

The Daoist framework of natural processes and fundamental qualities also reveals the enduring strength of what is apparently weak and how it can function as a corrective to existing social and political power. Le Guin has this aspect of Daoism in mind when she describes a yin utopia as "dark, wet, obscure, weak, yielding, passive, participatory, circular, cyclical, peaceful, nurturant, retreating, contracting, and cold."[44] Daoism teaches that what appear to be "weak" characteristics such as yielding can actually be powerful strategies, just as soft water wears away hard rock, or a useless tree survives the carpenter's ax, or the low valley is fertile. Again, this valorization of the "weak" is not simply an ethical or moral principle, but (like critical theory) an observation that claims to result from the fundamental qualities and relationships of things.

Indeed, in studying intrinsic characteristics, Daoism constitutes a theory of power. The book attributed to Laozi is known as the *Daodejing*, meaning the classic work (*jing*; Wade-Giles: *ching*) about *dao* and *de* (*te*). Critics who are un-familiar with Daoism tend to focus on Dao as the encompassing mystical ideal and on yin and yang as primary categories. However, Le Guin understands the importance of *de*, meaning the fundamental properties and powers of a thing, its "virtues" in the old sense of "characteristic qualities," as when we talk about the virtues of (say) a particular herb or type of wood. Unfortunately, *de* is often translated simply as "virtue" and thus garbled by the modern moralistic impli-cations of that word.[45] Le Guin's published version of the *Daodejing* translates the title as "A Book about the Way and the Power of the Way," so she effectively renders *de* as "power" of a specific kind. Le Guin's decision to translate it as "power" shows how she turns to Daoism as a strategy, not (as Jameson asserts) simply as abstract ethics. Another key aspect of Daoist challenges to the ego, then, is recognizing *de* and understanding "what must be" and "what endures," especially as counterweights to less enduring social and political forms of power.

Le Guin's fictions—and particularly her utopian fictions—employ these Dao-ist ecological frameworks in a variety of ways, all of which challenge the root issue of egoistic assumptions. Sometimes the Daoist frameworks go unnoticed because they mirror familiar SF techniques, such as when she uses satire to high-light egoism. Suvin notes the satire of self-deluded consumer hyperbole in "The New Atlantis," for example, where an authoritarian and commercial culture that is literally sinking under the weight of its environmental devastation consoles itself with preposterous advertising. The portrayal of Captain Davidson in *The Word for World Is Forest* is also a dark satire of monstrous male egoism, especially when compared to the mystical invocation of Selver and the dreamtime of the forest culture. A similar satire is evident in the portrayal of Dr. Haber in *The Lathe of Heaven*, with George Orr's oppositional humility rendered in explicitly Daoist terms. *The Dispossessed* satirizes the confident knowledge of Urrasti scientists through their equally confident pronouncements of "logical" sexism. *Always Coming Home* satirizes both the extinct "backwards-head" inhabitants of California and the monological culture of the Condor as counterpoints to the ecological ways of the Kesh. In *The Telling*, the governments of Earth and Aka are satires of fundamentalism and industrialism, respectively, and again serve to emphasize the reasonable "unreason" of the old ways. In all of these cases, satirical portrayals of egoism are contrasted with more humble cultural beliefs as a means of challenging the centrality of "logical" power.

While such satires are insightful, however, their heavy-handedness is likely to lead to defensive push-back and thus to fall short of the radical cognitive reframing envisioned by ecology and Daoism. One thinks, for example, of Thomas Disch's indignant reaction to the feminist sf of Le Guin and others; *Always Coming Home*, Disch argued, "requires nothing less ... than the abolition of Western civilization as we know it."[46] Similarly, the grossly pathological egoism of Captain Davidson or the ridiculous sexism of the Urrasti scientists could easily make a reader feel that she was not egoistic by comparison. Satire externalizes egoism in the form of an identifiable opposition, making it easy to dismiss as something that other people should stop doing. As Suvin observed, "unfortunately alienation within the all-pervading psychical eco-system of modern capitalism is not always so conveniently embodied in a malevolent Other."[47]

Another familiar technique that Le Guin uses to challenge egoism and conventional knowledge is the crisis. As Zhuangzi's admonition about "Heaven the Equalizer" indicates, ecological crisis and compensatory reversal are major indications of using overly egoistic "knowledge." "Heaven the Equalizer" is the same phrase that another translator rendered as "the Lathe of Heaven."[48] In both cases, the English word "heaven" gives it a theistic feel that obscures its essentially ecological significance: systemic relationships are a physical characteristic of any ecosystem, and thoughts and actions find physical limits there. Ecology emerged as an important framework in the '60s and '70s in response to the crises of pollution and natural resource depletion. Ecology, like healthy egoism or *Dao*, is not directly perceptible; only when things go wrong and a crisis arises do most people understand that they have lost the way.

Often Le Guin's crises focus on psychological or epistemological approaches to problems. In *City of Illusions*, Falk/Ramarren's crisis over his identity occurs on the epistemological level, for example, with the Daoist "Old Canon" and the Thoreauvian "New Canon" as his guides. The drought crisis in *The Dispossessed* serves to compare the *de* of collective cooperation for survival to the *de* of dog-eat-dog survival, thereby exploring the concrete borders between essential self-interest and collective cooperation. At other times, however, crisis serves to externalize the enemy in ways similar to satire. In *The Telling*, efforts to preserve the library at Silong involve combating an enemy that represents several contemporary spheres of power—state, corporation, media propaganda, economics—all combined into a single enemy. Like satire, then, invoking crisis risks implying that egoism is an external enemy, as opposed to confronting the everyday complexity of "normal" egoism.

Along with overt techniques such as satire and crises, Le Guin also challenges egoism and anthropocentric rationality in more subtle ways. One example of systematic challenge to ego is Le Guin's disciplinary reframing. As numerous critics have pointed out, Le Guin's protagonists are often anthropologists or ethnologists. As such, they struggle to understand unfamiliar cultures while also finding their own beliefs and assumptions estranged. A large part of the typical "development" of her anthropological characters is therefore unlearning or reframing of fundamental assumptions. Sometimes, as with the Handdara in *The Left Hand of Darkness*, an exotic belief in unlearning or unreason is described in mystical terms that echo Laozi. At other times—notably in *The Dispossessed* and *The Telling*—processes of unlearning are overtly political and realistically explored. In both cases, the substitution of anthropological frames for more familiar historical and political frames serves to model processes of unlearning and subtly emphasizes the transitory nature of human cultures and institutions.

Le Guin's attention to the "unreasonable" is another characteristic way in which her fictions work toward unlearning conventional knowledge. In *Always Coming Home*, for example, the Valley people don't distinguish between subjective time and "real" time. In the section "Time and the City," the narrator describes how the People of the Valley are baffled by "historical" questions. To Pandora's questions, the puzzled "Archivist" replies, "You talk all beginnings and ends, spring and ocean but no river." By comparison, we are told, the Valley "is all middle."[49] This lack of desire to impose rational narratives is contrasted with the hyper-rationalization of the Condor people, who "because [they] said that everything belonged to One [God], they forced themselves to think in twos: either this, or that." As a result, "They could not be among the Many."[50] Rigid monological or binary structures of thought, Le Guin suggests, are forms of fundamentalist thinking that interfere with properly ecological perception and healthy situation in the lived world.

The Telling also dramatizes healthy forms of unreason. Le Guin has indicated that "what happened to the practice and teaching of Taoism under Mao" served as inspiration for the novel.[51] Sutty, the novel's ethnographic heroine and utopian visitor, studies the Daoist-like traditional culture of Aka, which she labels "an ancient popular cosmology-philosophy-spiritual discipline."[52] She dismisses some of its beliefs and practices as "hocus pocus"—including such things as superstitious sign reading, numerology, bold claims of "supernal powers," and so forth. Sutty also dismisses "literal readings" or "fundamentalism . . . reducing thought to formula, replacing choice by obedience, these preachers turned the living word into dead law."[53] But along with the rational rejection of hocus pocus and fundamentalism, she finds that the humble traditional culture includes genuine and valuable forms of unreason. As one of the storytellers says, "What we do is unreasonable." The narrator explains, "[she] used that word often, unreasonable, in a literal sense: what cannot be understood by think-ing."[54] Compared with this obscure but naturalistic and life-affirming unreason, the ostensibly rational frameworks enforced by the Corporate State are brutal and pathetic and unreasonable in a bad sense: using bad reasoning, literalizing metaphors, creating fundamentalism. Here again, Le Guin's Daoist ecology produces utopianism that aspires to be a very reasonable form of unreasoning, as a challenge to economic rationalism and the way of the ego.

At its most radical, Le Guin's challenge to egoism involves challenging the uses of encompassing narratives in general. Most conspicuously, the structure of *Always Coming Home* demonstrates the refusal of encompassing narrative, undermining rational categories of identity and even the notion of individual human significance. The book has no central human protagonist; the closest thing is Stone Telling, whose story is largely about the transformations of her "identity" in relation to her surroundings and the course of time. The apparent subject of the book is the Valley culture, but the real subject is our process of trying to find a way "into" the Valley mind frame. Le Guin models this process in a very ecological and Daoist way in the chapter titled "Pandora, Worrying about What She Is Doing, Finds a Way into the Valley through the Scrub Oak," where she meditates on a scrub oak as a living representation of wilderness and on the mind's illusory desire to explain it. "Look how messy this wilderness is," Pandora thinks. The scrub oak in front of her "right here now" has "no overall shape," "isn't good for anything," and has "no center and no symmetry." The leaves seem "to obey some laws," but only "poorly." To consider it accurately is to realize that "the civilized mind's relation to it is imprecise, fortuitous, and full of risk," because "all the analogies run one direction, our direction."[55] This echoes a famous passage from Zhuangzi about an ugly old tree that endures because it is "useless."[56] Le Guin uses Pandora's meditation to illustrate both the difficulty of "understanding" the Valley and the illusory egoism of applying fixed rational frameworks to the lived complexity of nature. This is world reduction that forces the reader to feel an ecological framework by stripping away basic narrative and conceptual "analogies."

Always Coming Home's experiments with non-narrative epistemology chal-lenge not only the ego's perspective of an enduring consciousness but also the historian's sense of what is history and how human existence should be explained. As seen with the scrub oak, "Pandora" as authorial consciousness playfully challenges the conventional view of author as controlling will by confessing what is unknown and unknowable, by reinscribing herself in the text, and by embracing the world as "not accidentally but essentially messy."[57] She frequently stands in for the reader, pursuing our "hobby-horse" of seeking definite outlines of the "history" of the Kesh. Even more than the frameworks of archaeology and anthropology, non-narrative epistemology emphasizes the ephemeral reality of human categories and cultures. Unlike postmodernist challenges to authorship and narrative, however, Pandora's uncertainty points toward definite material insights about our egoistic uses of narrative and the real ecological processes that our master narratives help us to ignore.

Although *The Telling* lacks the narrative experimentation of *Always Coming Home*, it also explores the non-narrative (and ambiguously historical) situation of being all middle, as the title suggests. Again we see world reduction, as Sutty retreats from political complexity throughout the novel; she first flees dystopian fundamentalism on Earth and then the totalitarian industrialization of Dovza City until she arrives at the "backwoods" of Okzat-Ozkat and finally at the library at Silong, a virtual monastery in the mountains. The precious "telling" represented by the library entails a focus on the local, on small stories, on the process of telling stories as the human way to "tell the world," and on maintaining the enchantment of local life as opposed to the systematic disenchantment enforced by the world state. Sutty struggles to understand the telling and what it represents in rational terms, but discovers (like Pandora) that "a telling is not an explaining."[58]

However—unlike *Always Coming Home*—the novel's plot and form raise this lesson of "the telling" into a narrative whole: the power of the Ekumen, it is implied, trumps the Akan corporate state and finds a way to preserve the books. Ironically, this preservation of the library at Silong contradicts the impermanence that the worldview of the telling insists upon. *The Telling* explores the Daoist eco-logic of embracing unreason and avoiding confident narrative explanations, but it also presents a narrative that fantasizes a deus ex machina political victory. *Always Coming Home* is more radical in both form and content. At the archive maintained by one of the Kesh lodges, even preservation of cultural treasures is subordinated to the recognition of impermanence. As the Archivist explains, they have annual "destruction ceremonies," because "books are mortal. They die. A book is an act; it takes place in time, not just in space. It is not information, but relation." This living attitude is contrasted to (but also somewhat supplemented by) the inhuman "City of Mind," where the machine-logic goal is to keep "a copy of everything."[59] But while *The Telling* offers its readers narrative compensations that *Always Coming Home* does not, the utopian goals of the novels are similar: to challenge egoistic perceptions, including comprehensive narratives, in terms of ecological frameworks.

ECOLOGY AS LIMIT

Given the extent of Le Guin's deployment of yin utopianism, I would argue that Suvin and Jameson were mistaken to consider her Daoism an insignificant framework and to assume that it implies only static balance, ahistorical mysticism, and contemplative passivity. On the contrary, Daoism contributes to the dynamic balance that Suvin admired and to the cognitive effects that both theorists explore in their work on SF and utopia. Rather than being a mistaken framework, Le Guin's yin utopianism contributes strategically toward goals that are in many ways similar to those of critical theory. Indeed, both critics noted political affinities between their outlooks and Le Guin's work. Suvin argued that her "political position can be thought of as a radical critic and ally of socialism defending its duty to inherit the heretic democratic [and] civic traditions," and that her anarchism "can [either] be malevolently thought of as the furthest radical limit at which a disaffected petty-bourgeois intellectual may arrive, a leftist Transcendentalism, or benevolently as a personal, variant name for and way to a truly new libertarian socialism."[60] Jameson acknowledged similar possibilities for reading Le Guin's work as radical, noting that if it is "the massive commodity environment of late capitalism that has called up this particular literary and imaginative strategy" of world reduction, then it would "amount to a political stance as well."[61] Le Guin's Daoist ecology contributes as much to these political effects as any other cognitive framework. Within a historical period that dreams of endless growth despite mounting examples of ecological limits, both ecology and Daoism have the potential to provide critical cognitive reframing.

Of course, Suvin and Jameson were correct to think that Le Guin's ecological frames of reference represent challenges to the conventions and priorities of critical theory. As revealed by their cautious assessments of her work, frameworks that imagine forms of self-limitation are not generally appealing to critical theorists, who understandably associate them with the imposition of bourgeois morality and historical restrictions on freedom. They also regard any visions of materially reduced lifestyles to be ahistorical given the economic realities of industrial modernization and the ever-increasing complexity of late capitalism. Similarly, frameworks that emphasize philosophical changes (such as Le Guin's strategy of emphasizing eco-logic over ego-logic) strike critical theorists as a nonpolitical focus on thoughts and attitudes, as opposed to collective and material political action. These are important concerns when attempting to assess the real political effects of cultural texts in our ideologically and materially constrained world.

By the same token, however, the reluctance of Suvin and Jameson to consider Le Guin's ecological framework highlights how critical theory subtly relies on the industrial vision of endless growth. Ideologically, critical theory finds it hard to reconcile its view of freedom with any real limitations on individual desire or action, even while celebrating Le Guin's "radical disbelief in the individualist ideology."[62] Suvin himself suggested that the non-Marxist traditions that she draws on might provide a "precious antidote to socialism's contamination by the same alienating forces it has been fighting so bitterly in the last century—by power apparatuses and a pragmatic rationality that become ends instead of means." By comparison to critical theory's ideal of endless revolution, Le Guin's Daoist ecology asserts that real limits exist, that knowing those enduring limits and relationships is wisdom, and that "ruin and disorder" result from forgetting or ignoring the limits. Reading Le Guin's ecological concerns and world reduction primarily as symptomatic reaction ignores the real limits that the ecological framework raises.

Le Guin's characteristically optimistic narratives don't presume that wholeness and balance will occur, or examine how systemic world reduction would occur, but they do envision characters and cultures where the wisdom of "knowing what endures" can be practiced and tested. This yin utopianism combines the cognitive and material critique of critical theory with a radical form of world reduction that attempts to envision healthy limits on egoism. In both its cognitive and material aspects, her yin utopianism attempts to return us to the root. Challenging egoism is undoubtedly a utopian goal, given the psychosocial ecosystem of global consumer capitalism. But in a very real sense, the way of the ego is not the real ecosystem, and not what endures.

Notes

1. The phrase "wholeness and balance" comes from Douglas Barbour, "Wholeness and Balance in the Hainish Novels of Ursula K. Le Guin," *Science Fiction Studies* 1 (1974): 164–73. The seventh issue of *SFS* (vol. 2, no. 3, November 1975) was devoted entirely to Le Guin's work. In addition to Barbour's "Wholeness and Balance: An Addendum" (248–49), essays in

this special issue that referenced themes of balance included Donald F. Theall, "The Art of Social-Science Fiction: The Ambiguous Utopian Dialectics of Ursula K. Le Guin," 256–64; Ian Watson, "The Forest as Metaphor for Mind: 'The Word for World Is Forest' and 'Vaster Than Empires and More Slow,'" 231–37; and David L. Porter, "The Politics of Le Guin's Opus," 243–48.

2. The phrase "non-capitalist habitat" is from Darko Suvin, "Parables of De-Alienation: Le Guin's Widdershins Dance," 136. The essay was first published in *Science Fiction Studies* 2, no. 3 (November 1975): 265–74, and republished (among other places) in Suvin, *Positions and Presuppositions in Science Fiction* (Kent, OH: Kent State University Press, 1988), 134–50. My citations refer to the latter.

3. The term "mythopoetic" was widely applied to Le Guin's work; see for example Rafail Nudelman, "An Approach to the Structure of Le Guin's SF," trans. Alan G. Myers, *Science Fiction Studies* 2 (1975): 210–20.

4. I use the pinyin system of transliterating Chinese, which has become the international standard. Le Guin and most previous critics of her Daoism use the older Wade-Giles system, which transliterates the word as "Taoism." For details of the two see http://pinyin.info/index.html. To facilitate continuity with earlier scholarship, I provide the Wade-Giles equivalent in parentheses for terms that are different in pinyin.

5. Stillman, "*The Dispossessed* as Ecological Political Theory," in *The New Utopian Politics of Ursula K. Le Guin's "The Dispossessed,"* ed. Laurence Davis and Peter Stillman (Lanham, MD: Lexington Books, 2005), 55.

6. Joel Kovel, *The Enemy of Nature: The End of Capitalism or the End of the World?* (London: Zed Books, 2007), 233.

7. Ibid., 234.

8. Ibid., 233.

9. Ibid., 230.

10. Examples of prominent critical theorists whose work on Le Guin follows in the path of Suvin and Jameson would include Tom Moylan and Carl Freedman. China Miéville overtly questions Suvin's assumptions in "Cognition as Ideology: A Dialectic of SF Theory," his afterword to *Red Planets: Marxism and Science Fiction*, ed. Mark Bould and China Miéville (Middleton, CT: Wesleyan University Press, 2009), 231–48.

11. Le Guin and Suvin have given conflicting accounts of Suvin's involvement with and influence on *The Dispossessed*. Le Guin says that Suvin was the novel's "first reader and first critic" and influenced the ending of the book; see for example "A Response, by Ansible, from Tau Ceti," in Davis and Stillman, *New Utopian Politics*, 308. Suvin denies any major involvement; see "Cognition, Freedom, *The Dispossessed* as a Classic," in *Defined by a Hollow: Essays on Utopia, Science Fiction and Political Epistemology* (Oxford: Peter Lang, 2010), 513n.

12. *Science Fiction Studies* 2, no. 3 (November 1975).

13. Suvin, *Positions and Presuppositions*, 134.

14. Ibid., 135.

15. Ibid., 136.

16. Ibid., 143.

17. Ibid., 149.

18. Ibid., 138.

19. Ibid., 145. Porter's essay, in the same issue, made a similar point about Daoism as a temporary phase of Le Guin's work.

20. Ibid.

21. Ibid., 138.

22. Darko Suvin, "Afterword: With Sober, Estranged Eyes," in *Learning from Other Worlds: Estrangement, Cognition, and the Politics of Science Fiction and Utopia*, ed. Patrick Parrinder (Durham, NC: Duke University Press, 2001), 239.

23. See Part 1, "The Desire Called Utopia," in Fredric Jameson, *Archaeologies of the Future: The Desire Called Utopia and Other Science Fictions* (London: Verso, 2005), 1–233.

24. *Science Fiction Studies* 2, no. 3 (November 1975): 221–30. Jameson's essay was subsequently reprinted as "World Reduction in Le Guin: The Emergence of Utopian Narrative," in *Ursula K. Le Guin: Modern Critical Views*, ed. Harold Bloom (New York: Chelsea House, 1986), 57–70, and with its original title in Jameson's *Archaeologies of the Future*, 267–80. My references are to the latter.

25. Jameson, *Archaeologies of the Future*, 271.

26. Ibid., 269.

27. Ibid.

28. Ibid., 275. For example, Jameson notes the "Tao-like passivity" (275) of George Orr in *The Lathe of Heaven*—a reading he developed at length in "Progress versus Utopia, or, Can We Imagine the Future?" published in 1982 and republished in *Archaeologies of the Future*, 281–95.

29. Le Guin, *Dancing at the Edge of the World: Thoughts on Words, Women, Places* (New York: Harper & Row, 1989), 90.

30. Ibid., 88, 90.

31. Le Guin, "A Response to the Le Guin Issue," *Science Fiction Studies* 3, no. 1 (March 1976): 43–46.

32. Le Guin, *Dancing at the Edge of the World*, 90. Le Guin notes that the quoted passage is from bk. 2, chap. 38 of the *Daodejing*.

33. Le Guin had long been experimenting with her own translations of the *Daodejing*; see her introduction and "Notes" to her *Lao Tzu, Tao Te Ching: A Book about the Way and the Power of the Way* (Boston: Shambhala, 1998).

34. Le Guin, *Lao Tzu*, 22.

35. Le Guin, *Dancing at the Edge of the World*, 93.

36. Ibid., 85.

37. André Gorz, *Ecology as Politics*, trans. Patsy Vigderman and Jonathan Cloud (Boston: South End Press, 1980), 16.

38. Ibid., 13.

39. Ibid., 16.

40. Of course, this strategy is far from infallible. Gorz notes that "ecology, as a purely scientific discipline, does not necessarily imply the rejection of authoritarian, technofascist solutions" (17), and even the desire to break from capitalism and the way of the ego can

itself be easily commodified and rendered impotent. Ultimately, however, "ecological concerns are fundamental; they cannot be compromised or postponed" (20).

41. Le Guin, *Lao Tzu*, 110–11.

42. Ibid., 12.

43. Le Guin, *Dancing at the Edge of the World*, 92–93.

44. Ibid., 90.

45. For Le Guin's account of this translation decision see Le Guin, *Lao Tzu*, 110. On the philosophical implications of translating *de (te)*, see Alan Watts, "*Te*—Virtuality," in *Tao: The Watercourse Way* (New York: Pantheon, 1975), 106–22.

46. Quoted in Amy M. Clarke, *Ursula K. Le Guin's Journey to Post-Feminism* (Jefferson, NC: McFarland, 2010), 124.

47. Suvin, *Positions and Presuppositions*, 137.

48. For Le Guin's account of this see her *Dancing at the Edge of the World*, 93n, and *Lao Tzu*, 108.

49. Ursula K. Le Guin, *Always Coming Home* (New York: Harper & Row, 1985), 163.

50. Ibid., 352–53.

51. Quoted in Susan M. Bernardo and Graham J. Murphy, *Ursula K. Le Guin: A Critical Companion* (Westport, CT: Greenwood Press, 2006), 83.

52. Le Guin, *The Telling* (New York: Harcourt, 2000), 131.

53. Ibid., 132.

54. Ibid., 141.

55. Le Guin, *Always Coming Home*, 239–41.

56. For one version of the story see *The Book of Chuang Tzu*, trans. Martin Palmer with Elizabeth Breuilly (London: Arkana, 1996), 6.

57. Le Guin, *Always Coming Home*, 240.

58. Le Guin, *Telling*, 139. The "umyazu" or libraries are described on 128–29.

59. Le Guin, *Always Coming Home*, 314–15.

60. Suvin, *Positions and Presuppositions*, 147.

61. Jameson, *Archaeologies of the Future*, 278.

62. Suvin, *Positions and Presuppositions*, 148.

Biotic Invasions

Ecological Imperialism
in New Wave Science Fiction

ROB LATHAM

4

In an essay on H. G. Wells's *The War of the Worlds* (1898), Peter Fitting argues that tales of "first contact" within science fiction tend to recapitulate "the encounters of the European 'discovery' of the New World." They are thus, whether consciously or not, conquest narratives, though "usually not character-ized as . . . invasion[s]" because "written from the point of view of the invaders" who prefer euphemisms such as "exploration" to more aggressive or martial constructions of the encounter.[1] The accomplishment of Wells's novel, in Fit-ting's analysis, is to lay bare the power dynamics of this scenario by depicting a reversal of historical reality, with the imperial hub of late-Victorian London itself subjugated by "superior creatures who share none the less some of the characteristics of Earth's 'lower' species, a humiliation which is compounded by their apparent lack of interest in the humans as an intelligent species."[2] The irony of this switch of roles is not lost on Wells's narrator, who compares the fate of his fellow Londoners to those of the Tasmanians and even the dodoes, "entirely swept out of existence in a war of extermination waged by European immigrants."[3] Stephen Arata uses the term "reverse colonization" to describe this sort of story, in which the center of empire is besieged by fantastic creatures from its margins; as Brian Aldiss puts it, "Wells is saying, in effect, to his fellow English, 'Look, this is how it feels to be a primitive tribe, and to have a Western nation arriving to civilize you with Maxim guns!"[4]

Taking this general argument one step further, John Rieder claims that all manner of disaster stories within SF "might profitably be considered as the ob-verse of the celebratory narratives of exploration and discovery . . . that formed the Official Story of colonialism."[5] The sense of helplessness—geographic, eco-nomic, military, and so on—reinforced by catastrophe scenarios lays bare the underlying anxieties of hegemonic power, its inherent contingency and vulnerability, notwithstanding the purported inevitability of Western "progress." Moreover, disaster stories, by inverting existing power relations and displacing them into fantastic or futuristic milieux, expose the workings of imperialist ideology, the expedient fantasies that underpin the colonial enterprise—for example, "although the colonizer knows very well that colonized people are humans like himself, he acts as if they were parodic, grotesque imitations of humans instead,"[6] who may conveniently be dispossessed of land, property, and even life. The catastrophe story brings this logic of dispossession home to roost, shattering the surface calm of imperial hegemony and thrusting the colonizers themselves into a sudden chaos of destruction and transformation such as they have typically visited upon others. Narratives of invasion in particular are "heavily and consistently overdetermined by [their] reference to colonialism," allowing a potentially critical engagement with "the ideology of progress and its concomitant constructions of agency and destiny"[7]—that is, the triumphalist enshrinement of white Westerners at the apex of historical development and the demotion of all others to what anthropologist Eric Wolf calls a "people without history."[8]

Of course, to interpret most invasion stories of SF's pulp era as critical of Western progress requires reading against the grain, since their evident message is the fearlessness and ingenuity of Euro-American peoples when confronted by hostile forces. The magazine *Astounding Science Fiction*, during its 1940s golden age, operated under a philosophy that Brian Stableford and David Pringle identify as "human chauvinism," by the terms of which "humanity was destined to get the better of any and all alien species."[9] Editor John W. Campbell saw the extraterrestrial expansion of the human race not only as a logical extrapolation of the exploratory impulse of Western civilization but also explicitly as an outlet for martial aggression; as he remarked in a letter to A. E. Van Vogt, when "other planets are opened to colonization . . . we'll have peace on earth—and war in heaven!"[10] One of the few tales of successful "foreign" invasion published during *Astounding*'s heyday was Robert Heinlein's *Sixth Column* (1941), where the invaders are not aliens from space but a Pan-Asiatic horde that occupies the United States, only to be undermined and eventually defeated by an underground scientific elite masquerading as a popular religion; reverse colonization is thus foiled and the Westward trend of empire reaffirmed. *Sixth Column* is a forerunner of postwar tales of communist menace, such as Heinlein's own *The Puppet Masters* (1951), in which slug-like parasites seek to brainwash the U.S. citizenry but ultimately prove no match for the native resourcefulness and righteous rage of humankind: "They made the mistake of tangling with the toughest, meanest, deadliest, most unrelenting—and ablest—form of life in this section of space, a critter that can be killed but can't be tamed."[11]

The cinema of the 1950s was filled with similar scenarios of sinister alien infiltration and dogged human resistance that basically allegorized the U.S. struggle with global communism and usually ended with the defeat of the invaders. Yet close readings of these stories reveal a strong undercurrent of unease beneath the bland surface confidence in American values: for example, in *Invaders from Mars* (1953), as I have argued in a previous essay, "the paranoia about alien invasion and takeover may merely serve to deflect anxieties about how seamlessly militarist power has inscribed itself into the suburban American landscape."[12] Similar disquiets can be perceived in films that depict literal communist attacks and occupations, such as *Invasion U.S.A.* (1952), which is, as Cyndy Hendershot has shown, as much about fears of U.S. decadence and conformism as it is about Soviet perfidy.[13] In other words, even invasion stories that valorize human (that is, Western) cunning and bravery may be troubled by doubts regarding the susceptibility to external incursions, the lurking rot at the imperial core that permits such brazen raids from the periphery.

By contrast with American treatments of the theme, which were pugnacious in their refusal to succumb to invasion, postwar British disaster stories had a distinctly elegiac tone, a quality of wistful resignation in the face of imperial decline. As Roger Luckhurst points out, British tales of catastrophe had "always addressed disenchantment with the imperialist 'civilizing' mission," but 1950s versions, confronted with the ongoing collapse of the global empire, used the disaster plot as "a laboratory reconceiving English selfhood in response to traumatic depredations."[14] The popular novels of John Wyndham, such as *The Day of the Triffids* (1951) and *The Kraken Wakes* (1953), take refuge in pastoralist fantasy as Britain's cities are overrun by marauding invaders, the imperial hegemon shrinking to beleaguered individual (or small-communal) sanctuaries. Brian W. Aldiss has coined the term "cosy catastrophe" to describe these sorts of plots, a category in which some have also placed the early fiction of John Christopher, though here, as Aldiss says, "the catastrophe loses its cosiness and takes on an edge of terror."[15] In Christopher's *The Death of Grass* (1956) and *The World in Winter* (1962), there is no refuge from the crisis because the environment itself has grown hostile, stricken by a virus that kills off crops or the advent of a new ice age. The absence of an alien menace in these novels vitiates the possibility of heroic resistance, replacing it with an ethos of brute survivalism, whose long-term prospects are desperate and unpromising. The sense of imperial comeuppance is particularly strong in *World in Winter*, where Britons displaced by glacial expansion flee to Nigeria, only to be rudely treated by their former colonial subjects.

Christopher's novels welded the traditional British disaster story with an emergent trend of eco-catastrophe that gained strength during the 1960s. The master of this new genre was J. G. Ballard, whose quartet of novels—*The Wind from Nowhere* (1960), *The Drowned World* (1962), *The Drought* (1964), and *The Crystal World* (1966)—variously scoured the earth, inundated it, desiccated it, and (most curiously and perversely) immured it in a jewel-like crust. Throughout these works, the author appears fundamentally uninterested either in explaining the disasters (only *The Drought* posits a human cause: widespread pollution of the oceans) or in depicting valiant efforts to fend off their ravages. Instead, the protagonists struggle toward a private accommodation with the cataclysms, a psychic attunement to their radical reorderings of the environment; as Luckhurst argues, "the transformation of landscape marks the termination of rationally motivated instrumental consciousness."[16] In other words, the very mindset that produced imperial hegemony—the confidence in reason, disciplined deployment of techno-science, and posture of mastery—has eroded, replaced by a deracinated fatalism and an almost mystical embrace of its own antiquation.

For Fredric Jameson, Ballard's scenarios of "world-dissolution" amount to little more than the exhausted "imagination of a dying class—the cancelled future of a vanished colonial and imperial destiny [that] seeks to intoxicate itself with images of death."[17] Yet, while it is difficult to argue that Ballard's novels express a conscious politics—aside from the ironized libidinal commitments of a surrealism tinged with Freud—his influence over what came to be known as SF's "New Wave" helped foster an overtly anti-hegemonic strain of eco-disaster stories during the 1960s and early 1970s. The New Wave generally adopted an anti-technocratic bent that put it at odds with the technophilic optimism of Campbellian hard SF, openly questioning, if not the core values of scientific inquiry, then the larger social processes to which they had been conjoined in the service of state and corporate power.[18] This critique of technocracy gradually aligned itself with other ideological programs seeking to reform or revolutionize social relations, such as feminism, ecological activism, and postcolonial struggles, adopting a countercultural militancy that rejected pulp SF's quasi-imperialist vision of white men conquering the stars in the name of Western progress. While Ballard might not have embraced this polemical thrust, his subversive disaster stories, with their stark irrationalism and pointed mockery of techno-scientific ambitions, gave it a significant impetus as well as a potent model to follow.

Thomas M. Disch's 1965 novel *The Genocides* is definitely cast in the Ballard-ian mode, a positioning that drew the fire of critics opposed to the New Wave's ideological renovation of the field. Disch's novel, which depicts an Earth trans-formed by faceless aliens into an agricultural colony in which humans are mere pests awaiting extermination, became something of a political hot-potato within the genre. The most prominent advocate for the New Wave among American commentators, Algis Budrys, responding to a laudatory review of the book by Judith Merril, attacked the novel as "pretentious, inconsistent, and sopho-moric," an insult to "the school of science fiction which takes hope in science and in Man."[19] Contrasting it with Heinlein's latest effort, *The Moon Is a Harsh Mistress* (1966)—which depicts "strong personalities doing things about their situation," its hero a "practical man-of-all-work figure" who just keeps "plugging away"[20]—Budrys complains about Disch's "dumb, resigned victims" who simply wait passively to be destroyed.[21] Unlike the can-do heroism of Heinlein and his ilk, *The Genocides* is an "inertial" sf novel, modeled on the disaster stories of Ballard, wherein "characters who regard the physical universe as a mysteri-ous and arbitrary place, and who would not dream of trying to understand its actual laws," putter about listlessly in a suicidal haze.[22] As David Hartwell comments, Budrys clearly could not imagine a successful work of sf in which scientific knowledge is not "*a priori* adequate to solve whatever problem the plot poses"—even, in this case, when vastly superior alien technologies have seeded and irretrievably transformed the entire surface of the planet.[23]

In a curious aside, Budrys considers the possibility that Disch is rejecting the "Engineers-Can-Do-Anything school" of pulp sf,[24] in favor of an older, more satirical and pessimistic tradition that extends back to H. G. Wells; and he goes on to forecast an imaginary critical-historical study championing Ballard for "having singlehandedly returned the field to its main stem" following the pulp era's arguably naïve optimism.[25] Budrys's projected title for this volume, *Car-tography of Chaos*, seems precisely to acknowledge the entropic dissolution of the scientific modes of missionary imperialism accomplished by the New Wave disaster story, though Budrys doesn't really develop the point. Another review of the novel, by Brian Aldiss, made a more concerted effort to link Disch with a strain of visionary pessimism in the field. Decrying the "facile optimism" of American pulp sf, with its fantasies of a prodigal nature effortlessly exploited by a sagacious "scientocracy," Aldiss praises *The Genocides* for providing "an unadultered shot of pure bracing gloom." The effect, despite Disch's American provenance, is "curiously English," portraying a "dwindling community" confronting an "unbeatable problem . . . as credible a menace as I ever came on."[26] Aldiss never quite explains why this scenario should be viewed as particularly English, but he doubtless had in mind the Wyndham-Ballard school of postimperial melancholy, here transplanted to the United States.

And, indeed, that is the signal accomplishment of Disch's novel: to extrapolate the end-of-empire thematics of the postwar disaster story to a specifically American context. Certainly by the mid- to late 1960s, revisionist historians and left-wing political commentators such as William Appleman Williams, David Horowitz, Gabriel Kolko, and Harry Magdoff had begun to critique U.S. foreign policy during the Cold War as explicitly imperialist, driven by economic and military imperatives designed to enrich and expand the powers of a corporate elite.[27] While not suggesting that Disch was expressly aware of these thinkers, I do feel that his novel belongs within the general orbit of a New Wave critique of modern technocracy, scorning his country's nascent imperial aims with the same cold-eyed cynicism that Wells summoned to chasten his late-Victorian compatriots. Even more than Wells, Disch stresses the total indifference of the aliens to the monuments of human civilization, excrescent "artifacts" they are capable of wiping away as casually as a farmer uproots weeds; as one character bitterly muses: "It wounded his pride to think that his race, his species was being defeated with such apparent ease. What was worse, what he could not endure was the suspicion that it all meant nothing, that the process of their annihilation was something quite mechanical: that mankind's destroyers were not, in other words, fighting a war but merely spraying the garden."[28] Indeed, as this mundane metaphor suggests, Disch, in *The Genocides*, develops a powerful critique of what has subsequently come to be called, by environmental historians and activists, *ecological imperialism*.

As the discipline of ecology was consolidated during the postwar period, and especially as the concept of ecosystem as a functional totality of life processes gained widespread currency,[29] evolutionary biologists began to study the implications of the introduction of foreign flora and fauna into existing environments. The classic study in the field is Charles S. Elton's *The Ecology of Invasions by Animals and Plants*, first published in 1958 and still in widespread use in biology classrooms.[30] Elton considers such significant "biotic invasions" as the spread of the Japanese beetle throughout the northern United States and the incursion of sea lampreys into the Great Lakes region, theorizing their competition for resources with native species, their unsettlement of and integration into food chains, and the ramifying consequences of genetic mixing through subsequent generations. In order to convey the dramatic quality of these "great historical convulsions,"[31] Elton occasionally has recourse to SF texts to furnish illuminating models or metaphors, from Professor Challenger's discovery of a "lost world" of primordial life in Arthur Conan Doyle's 1912 novel,[32] to the uncontrollable dissemination of escaped laboratory animals in H. G. Wells's 1904 novel *Food of the Gods*.[33] As the latter example suggests, the study of biotic invasions cannot ignore the important role of human agency; as Elton comments, "One of the primary reasons for the spread and establishment of species has been quite simply the movement around the world by man of plants, especially those brought for crops or garden ornament or forestry."[34] He even addresses the history of colonial expansion in a chapter considering the impact on the ecosystems of remote islands of Captain Cook's voyages during the late eighteenth century.[35]

During the 1970s and '80s, environmental historians began to extrapolate some of the insights of ecosystems theory to explain the consequences of major migrations of human populations. William McNeill's *Plagues and Peoples* (1976), which examines the role of disease in shaping historical encounters between cultures, meticulously shows, in a chapter entitled "Transatlantic Exchanges," how the European conquest of the Americas was facilitated by the "biological vulnerability" of Amerindian groups to foreign pathogens, especially smallpox.[36] Rather than attributing the success of New World colonization to superior technology and culture alone, works such as McNeill's—and William Cronon's *Changes in the Land* (1983), which examines the environmental impact of the introduction of European livestock and agricultural practices in colonial New England[37]—anatomized the role, intended and unintended, of biotic transfers in conferring an advantage in the competition between native peoples and foreign invaders. As Alfred Crosby summarizes in his landmark work of synthesis, *Ecological Imperialism* (1986), "the Europeans had to disassemble an existing ecosystem before they could have one that accorded with their needs," with the outcome at times resembling "a toy that has been played with too roughly by a thoughtless colossus."[38] In this new colonial history, the influence of Christianity and gunpowder pales beside the proliferating synergy of microbes and weeds, deforestation and domestication. In Alan Taylor's words, "the remaking of the Americas was a team effort by a set of interdependent species led and partially managed (but never fully controlled) by European people."[39]

While Disch could certainly not have known this body of work when he wrote *The Genocides*, there is ample evidence that he was always deeply interested in ecological issues and in linking this concern with the developing New Wave critique of American technocracy. In 1971, Disch edited a major anthology of eco-catastrophe stories, *The Ruins of Earth*, complaining in his introduction that "too often science fiction has given its implicit moral sanction" to wholesale transformations in the environment without concern for the consequences. This introduction, entitled "On Saving the World," stands as one of the strongest statements of an ecological awareness within the New Wave assault on traditional SF:

> The very form of the so-called "hard-core" s-f saga, in which a single quasi-techno-logical problem is presented and then solved, encourages [a] peculiar tunnel vision and singleness of focus that is the antithesis of an "ecological" consciousness in which cause-and-effect would be regarded as a web rather than as a single-strand chain. The heroes of these earlier tales often behave in ways uncannily reminis-cent of psychotics' case histories: personal relationships (as between the crew members of a spaceship) can be chillingly lacking in affect. These human robots inhabited landscapes that mirrored their own alienation.

SF, in short, had for too long been an uncritical cheerleader for the social en-gineering of nature emanating from a narrow technocratic mind-set and was only now beginning to shake free of this imperialistic delusion. Disch went on to celebrate the early novels of Ballard, especially *The Drought*, as prophetic visions of how a violated nature might take revenge on its heedless exploiters. Budrys was thus correct to infer in *The Genocides* a viewpoint inimical to "the school of science fiction which takes hope in science and in Man"—though instead of "hope," Disch would have said "the faith, usually unquestioning, in a future in which Technology provides, unstintingly and without visible dif-ficulty, for man's needs."[40]

The Genocides is set in 1979, seven years after shadowy aliens have converted the planet into an agricultural preserve devoted to growing six-hundred-foot-high trees with leaves "the size of billboards."[41] Pushing up through concrete, shouldering aside buildings, and growing at an incredible rate, the trees have destroyed Earth's cities and thoroughly colonized its rural areas. The story fo-cuses on a group of farmers, located in northern Minnesota, who free up arable land by bleeding sap from the alien plants, which eventually kills them and thus conserves a tiny clearing amid the planet-wide canopy. In this clearing, they maintain a plot of corn, which in turn supports a small livestock population. Unfortunately, the aliens—"bored agribusinessmen," as Hartwell calls them, whose cultivation processes are entirely automated[42]—have finally taken notice of these human remnants, sending out flame-throwing drones *"adequate for the extermination of such mammalian life as they are likely to encounter,"* as one of their interoffice memos blandly puts it.[43] The drones incinerate the farm community, sending a handful of desperate survivors into the trees' hollow root system, where they subsist on the sugary fruit of the plants that grows underground. Murderous squabblings thin their ranks, which are further diminished by the arrival of mechanical harvesters that vacuum up the mature fruit. At the end, six ragged human scarecrows stagger across the scoured landscape, which has been burned clean by the harvesters, as the spores of "the second planting" begin to take root.[44]

Hartwell's reference to agribusiness is quite appropriate since, at one level, the novel is a powerful critique of techno-scientific methods for accelerating and amplifying natural processes of cultivation. This mechanized agriculture amounts to the systematic "rape of a planet" that has far-reaching consequences.[45] A hybrid crop designed in alien labs, the trees are brilliantly efficient machines of growth, but their burgeoning comes at the expense of the overall ecology. Since they don't shed their leaves, no compost accumulates, so the topsoil rapidly withers to dust. Their greedy consumption of carbon dioxide is quickly cooling the planet, making the winters brutally severe. And their monopolization of resources has systematically killed off higher species: the "balance of nature had been so thoroughly upset that even animals one would not think threatened had joined the ever-mounting ranks of the extinct."[46] An offhand allusion indicates the novel's critical perspective: as winter recedes and no birds emerge to herald the new season, the narrator grimly comments, "it was a silent spring"[47]—thus referencing Rachel Carson's classic 1962 critique of the deadly effects of agribusiness methods on the environment.[48] Unfortunately, human beings don't have the luxury of being absentee landlords of the planet, as Disch's aliens are, and so must directly suffer the long-term consequences of this ecological tinkering.

Disch's title, *The Genocides*, thus refers on one level to humanity's imminent self-extinction through ecological mismanagement, a snuffing out the narrator comments on at the end with Wellsian detachment:

Nature is prodigal. Of a hundred seedlings only one or two would survive; of a hundred species, only one or two.

Not, however, man.[49]

On another level, the novel allegorizes the biotic invasion of the New World, which resulted in the wholesale destruction of native cultures and ways of life. Like the Europeans in America, the aliens reconfigure the existing ecosystem to satisfy their own needs, at first ignoring the original inhabitants and then, when their methods of cultivation come into competition, brutally eliminating them. Yet, as in the histories of ecological imperialism described above, the most effective genocidal technique by far is the environmental transformation wrought by the invaders, which literally makes indigenous modes of agriculture impossible. As William Cronon points out, "European perceptions of what constituted a proper use of the environment . . . reinforced what became a European ideology of conquest": whereas Amerindians generally favored mobile settlements and subsistence agriculture supplemented by hunting, the colonists preferred fixed habitats, organized animal husbandry, and surplus crop production for purposes of trade.[50] The latter system required widespread deforestation, which killed off deer populations on which the natives were dependent, and the cultivation of large tracts of land, now conceived as permanent property rather than an open bounty. Disch's novel shows the consequences of such an arrangement from the Amerindian perspective, as the humans are confronted by literally alien biota maintained by superior technology and policed by ruthless violence.

Disch's jaundiced view of European supremacy in the New World is underlined by the most viciously satirical scene in the book, a Thanksgiving Day celebration. Following the incineration of their cattle by the alien machines, the community has lost its main source of protein. To promote harmony among a population grown restive and contentious, the governing patriarch decides to proceed with the occasion, serving up sausages prepared from the bodies of a group of urban marauders the community has recently slain. "Necessity might have been some justification. There was ample precedent (the Donner party, the wreck of the *Medusa*)." But the patriarch's goal in enforcing this communal cannibalism is more sinister and jingoistic: to unite the group in a "complex bond," a "sacrament" that transmutes the squalid act into patriotic solidarity. And so the others sit there, chewing desultorily, bickering with one another, and growing drunk on liquor fermented from the sap of the alien trees. As their resident scientist drily comments, "Survival is a matter of ecology. . . . Ecology is the way the different plants and animals live together. That is to say—who eats whom."[51] This pathetic remnant of European colonization, enjoying a hallowed holiday feast that sentimentally commemorates its triumph, is reduced to feeding on their erstwhile countrymen in order to survive. Reinforcing this sarcastic portrait of collapsed American hegemony, Disch dates the aliens' extermination order *4 July* 1979, with the projected completion of the project 2 February 1980—Groundhog Day, now the harbinger of an eternal winter for the human race.[52] Watching Duluth go up in flames kindled by the alien drones, one of the characters waves and snickers, "goodbye, Western Civilization."[53]

While ecological extrapolation was not new to SF in 1965—indeed, Frank Herbert's *Dune*, serialized in *Analog* magazine during 1963–64, probably did more than any other single book to bring ecological awareness into the center of the genre—Disch's *The Genocides* gave the topic a sharp polemical edge through its arraignment of traditional SF's complaisant scientism. Techno-scientific development, in the novel, is not a cure-all for the problems posed, but is itself the problem: the faceless alien technocrats, armed with a battery of sophisticated machines, show a casual contempt not only for natural balance but for human life itself. The besieged community Disch portrays has as much chance against this monolithic apparatus as Third World farmers have against Western agribusiness enterprises; their small-scale agrarian revolt, pitched against the environmental monopoly of the trees, fails as miserably as, say, the Guatemalan revolution against the United Fruit Company in the 1950s. Disch's novel points the way toward more politicized engagements with ecological issues in SF, such as John Brunner's *Stand on Zanzibar* (1968) and *The Sheep Look Up* (1972); as Michael Stern observes of the latter novel, "the relation of the US to the rest of the earth's societies . . . takes the form of a total but undeclared ecological war"[54]—an invasion less of Western biota than of industrial pollution, resource extraction, and neocolonial "development" projects. During the early 1970s, the genre witnessed not only a handful of theme anthologies devoted to these issues—including, alongside Disch's *Ruins of Earth*, Rob Sauer's *Voyages: Scenarios for a Ship Called Earth* (1971) and Roger Elwood and Virginia Kidd's *Saving Worlds* (1973)—but even fanzines with an environmentalist agenda, such as Susan Glicksohn's short-lived *Aspidistra*. In the balance of this essay, though, I will focus on a second major New Wave text that specifically treats ecological imperialism in the terms outlined above: Ursula K. Le Guin's short novel *The Word for World Is Forest* (1972).[55]

In many ways, Le Guin's novel reads like an inversion of *The Genocides*: rather than the victims of biotic invasion, Earth people are the invaders, and rather than seeding a host of trees, they lay waste to a vast forest on the planet Athshe. Le Guin quite calculatedly draws parallels between the exploration of space and the history of Western colonialism: despite the existence of "Ecological Protocols" governing interaction with alien biospheres, largely designed to keep other worlds from being reduced to the "desert of cement" bereft of animal life that the Earth itself has become,[56] the colonists on Athshe behave exactly like classic imperialists, renaming the planet "New Tahiti," conscripting its humanoid population into forced labor camps, and systematically extracting its riches, especially lumber. The tale's main villain, Captain Davidson, captures the mindset perfectly: contemptuous of the natives as lazy "creechies" yet lusting after their women; eager to command the landscape as proof of his manhood and cultural superiority, seeing in the endless vistas of trees only a "meaningless" expanse of wasted resources, rather than the richly meaningful cultural world it is for the native inhabitants. He has nothing but scorn for the "bleeding-heart" attitudes of the expedition's token ecologist and anthropologist, viewing the situation in basically military terms: "You've got to play on the winning side or else you lose. And it's Man that wins, every time. The old Conquistador."[57] Whereas in Disch the motives of the alien invaders remain obscure, Le Guin provides, in Davidson, a scathing portrait of overweening racist machismo as the root impulse supporting projects of imperial domination. While the effect is perhaps to overly psychologize the colonial relationship, de-emphasizing crucial political-economic imperatives, her treatment does infuse a strong ecofeminist consciousness into the traditional invasion scenario.[58]

Still, the tale did have an essentially political origin; Le Guin has indicated that the military-ecological rape of Vietnam by U.S. forces is what impelled her writing: "It was becoming clear that the ethic which approved the defoliation of forests and the murder of noncombatants in the name of 'peace' was only a corollary of the ethic which permits the despoliation of natural resources for private profit or the GNP, and the murder of the creatures of the Earth in the name of 'man.'"[59] Thus, we see Davidson and his renegade band decimating creechie villages in classic counterinsurgency fashion, "dropping firejelly cans and watch[ing] them run around and burn,"[60] while the Athsheans adopt guerrilla tactics as the only effective resistance. These blatant historical connections have led to complaints by some critics that the story is overly tendentious and moralizing,[61] yet as Ian Watson points out, the plot is broadly allegorical and can symbolize any number of instances of ecological imperialism, including "the genocide of the Guyaki Indians of Paraguay, or the genocide and deforestation along the Trans-Amazon Highway in Brazil, or even the general destruction of rain-forest habitats from Indonesia to Costa Rica."[62] William Cronon has shown how deforestation was a major factor in the reconfiguration of New World biota by European colonists: an ecological habitat to which the natives had adapted themselves was systematically culled to serve a new "mosaic" of settlement; and, like Captain Davidson and his comrades, the "colonists themselves understood what they were doing wholly in positive terms, not as 'deforestation,' but as 'the progress of cultivation'"[63]—even though the effects were often pernicious, ranging from topsoil erosion, to increased flooding, to the spread of marshes with their attendant diseases. The callous quality of the transformations wrought by the colonists, their lack of concern for enduring consequences, in both the historical record and in Le Guin's story, suggest the heedless alien genocide depicted with such casual savagery in Disch's novel.

A key difference between Le Guin's work and Disch's, however, is that, by the early 1970s, a quite developed discourse regarding the effects of ecological devastation, and a growingly militant environmentalist movement, had risen up to assert the "rights" of nature and native peoples over against the needs of Western neocolonialism. Generally guided by an ethic of "responsibility" and governed by a concern for long-term "sustainability," this movement was propelled by a conviction that the ongoing exploitation of nature augured nothing short of a catastrophe for the planet—"ecocide," according to the title of a 1971 collection of essays.[64] The Club of Rome's best-selling study *The Limits to Growth*, published in the same year as Le Guin's novel, argued that current levels of resource depletion were likely to lead to major socioeconomic crises in the relatively near future.[65] *The Word for World Is Forest* reflects these anxieties in its depiction of a home planet literally bereft of foliage, dependent on alien jungles to satisfy its appetite for "clean sawn planks, more prized on Earth than gold."[66]

In terms of the ethics of interaction with other species, positions ranged from John Passmore's view, in *Man's Responsibility for Nature* (1974), that human life is the basic standard of value in terms of which all potential violence against animals or plants must be gauged, to more radical arguments for the recognition and inclusion of nonhuman beings, such as Peter Singer's brief for *Animal Liberation* (1975).[67] An interesting text with relevance to Le Guin's story is legal scholar Christopher Stone's 1971 essay "Should Trees Have Standing?" Written as an intervention in a lawsuit pitting the Sierra Club against the Disney Corporation's efforts to build a resort in California's Sierra Nevada range, Stone's essay was groundbreaking in its attempt to define legal "'injury' not merely in human terms but with regard to nature. . . . Stone argued in all seriousness that trout and herons and cottonwood trees should be thought of as the injured parties in a water-pollution case," and not simply the people who might be deprived of clean water or the opportunity to enjoy a pristine landscape.[68] The impulse to protect trees in particular, not merely from their human uses but intrinsically, for themselves, formed a significant impulse of the environmental movement, as the deployment of the term "green" as a political rallying cry suggests.[69] On the one hand, this impulse may merely express a sentimental romanticization of nature, one that has too readily led to the disparagement of environmentalists as "tree huggers" (an identification facilitated, for example, by the dedication to an anthology commemorating the first Earth Day celebration: "to the tree from which this book is made"[70]); on the other hand, if pursued with intellectual rigor, such an attitude could lead to a conceptualization of "nature" not as an anthropocentric tool or an essentialist "other," but as a socially constructed reality with important dimensions of agency and autonomy.[71]

Le Guin's abiding humanism, however, makes it difficult for her to articulate an ethic of rights that does not inhere ultimately in human subjects. While the novel fudges the issue by essentially identifying the Athsheans with their habitat—like the forest, they are peaceful, close-knit, and actually green—the effect is to naturalize their culture and to see the violence committed against them as an environmental desecration. The forest *is* their world, as the title indicates, and alterations to it are alterations to them; by the end, they have, like the trees, learned violence and been scarred by the knowledge. They have been "changed, radically, from the *root*" by "an infection, a foreign plague."[72] The model of moral relation Le Guin finally defends is not surprising, given the central bond in her celebrated novel *The Left Hand of Darkness* (1969): a friendship, despite differences, between sentient humanoids. The novel's anthropologist-hero, Lyubov, is everything Captain Davidson is not: empathetic toward the Athsheans and comfortable in the enveloping forest, fondly protective of their mutual innocence and dignity.[73] Not only does this depiction bear a lingering noble-savage Romanticism,[74] but it leaves open the question of whether the denuding and strip-mining of an uninhabited planet would be ethically acceptable. If the forest were not *someone's* indigenous world, would it then be ripe for the picking? Can ecological imperialism only be committed against human subjects or their fictional surrogates?

Le Guin's attitude toward techno-science and its role in colonial conquest is also more ambivalent than in previous New Wave eco-catastrophes. Unlike Disch's *The Genocides*, in which advanced science is exclusively an agency of domination—and unlike ecocritics such as Lynn White, whose influential 1967 essay "The Historical Roots of Our Ecological Crisis" indicts Europe's "superior technology" that permitted its "small, mutually hostile nations [to] spill out over all the rest of the world, conquering, looting, and colonizing"[75]—Le Guin draws a distinction (a quite reasonable one, in my view) between military-industrial technologies designed for violent purposes, whether warfare or resource extraction, and *communication* technologies that allow for the exchange of ideas and information. In the novel, the arrival on the planet of an *ansible*—an interstellar radio that permits instantaneous messaging, despite the decades-long time lag of space travel—is the mechanism that alerts the new League of Worlds to the violation of Ecological Protocols and leads to the termination of the colonial administration and the eventual economic quarantining of the planet. Similarly, in the present day, communications media such as the Internet have facilitated the worldwide dissemination of data about serious ecological problems, such as global warming,[76] and computer simulation software has been used to model ecosystem interactions, such as (to cite a relevant example) the growth and decline of forest areas.[77] Le Guin, to her credit, resists the assumption, common to some New Wave texts, that Western techno-science itself has been irreparably contaminated by its conscription for technocratic-imperialist ends.

In his environmental history of the twentieth century, J. R. McNeill summarizes recent biotic invasions and concludes with a prognostication: "In the twenty-first century, the pace of invasions is not likely to slacken, and new genetically engineered organisms may also occasionally achieve ecological release and fashion dramas of their own."[78] If they do, one can be certain that sf writers will be there to chronicle the results, and to craft powerful moral allegories out of them. While they will doubtless draw upon the compelling example of major New Wave precursors, it is likely that their treatments of the topic will cleave closer to Le Guin's ethical-political ambivalence than to Disch's neo-Wellsian despair.

Notes

1. Peter Fitting, "Estranged Invaders: *The War of the Worlds*," in *Learning from Other Worlds: Estrangement, Cognition, and the Politics of Science Fiction and Utopia*, ed. Patrick Parrinder (Liverpool: Liverpool University Press, 2000), 127–45 (127).

2. Ibid., 130–31.

3. H. G. Wells, *The War of the Worlds*, in *Seven Science Fiction Novels of H. G. Wells* (New York: Dover, n.d.), 307–453 (311).

4. Stephen D. Arata, "The Occidental Tourist: *Dracula* and the Anxiety of Reverse Colonization," *Victorian Studies* 33, no. 4 (1990): 621–45; Brian W. Aldiss, *Trillion Year Spree: The History of Science Fiction*, with David Wingrove (New York: Avon, 1988), 120–21.

5. John Rieder, "Science Fiction, Colonialism, and the Plot of Invasion," *Extrapolation* 46, no. 3 (2005): 373–94 (376).

6. Ibid.

7. Ibid., 378.

8. Eric R. Wolf, *Europe and the People without History* (Berkeley: University of California Press, 1982).

9. Brian Stableford and David Pringle, "Invasion," in *The Encyclopedia of Science Fiction*, ed. Peter Nicholls and John Clute (New York: St. Martin's Press, 1993), 623–25 (624).

10. John W. Campbell Jr., letter to A. E. Van Vogt, March 3, 1945, in *The John W. Campbell Letters*, vol. 1, ed. Perry A. Chapdelaine Sr., Tony Chapdelaine, and George Hay (Franklin, TN: AC Projects, 1985), 49–55 (55).

11. Robert A. Heinlein, *The Puppet Masters*, rev. ed. (New York: Del Rey, 1990), 338. For a reading of the novel as an allegory of Cold War conflicts, see H. Bruce Franklin, *Robert A. Heinlein: America as Science Fiction* (New York: Oxford University Press, 1980), 98–101.

12. Rob Latham, "Subterranean Suburbia: Underneath the Smalltown Myth in the Two Version of *Invaders from Mars*," *Science-Fiction Studies* 22, no. 2 (1995): 198–208 (201). For a discussion of the 1956 film *Invasion of the Body Snatchers* that links it with Wells's and Heinlein's novels, see David Seed, "Alien Invasions by Body Snatchers and Related Creatures," in *Modern Gothic: A Reader*, ed. Victor Sage and Allen L. Smith (Manchester: Manchester University Press, 1996), 152–70.

13. Cyndy Hendershot, "Anti-Communism and Ambivalence in *Red Planet Mars*, *Invasion U.S.A.*, and *The Beast of Yucca Flats*," *Science Fiction Studies* 28, no. 2 (2001): 246–60.

14. Roger Luckhurst, *Science Fiction* (Cambridge, UK: Polity, 2005), 131–32.

15. Aldiss, *Trillion Year Spree*, 255. For an alternative take on Wyndham's work, which defends him as a more subversive writer than Aldiss allows, see Rowland Wymer, "How 'Safe' is John Wyndham? A Closer Look at His Work, with Particular Reference to *The Crysalids*," *Foundation* 55 (1992): 25–36.

16. Roger Luckhurst, *"The Angle between Two Walls": The Fiction of J. G. Ballard* (New York: St. Martin's Press, 1997), 53.

17. Fredric Jameson, "Progress versus Utopia; or, Can We Imagine the Future?" *Science-Fiction Studies* 9, no. 2 (1982): 147–58 (152).

18. For an overview of the New Wave movement, see my "The New Wave," in *A Companion to Science Fiction*, ed. David Seed (Oxford: Blackwell, 2005), 202–16. See also Luckhurst, *Science Fiction*, 141–95.

19. Algis Budrys, "Galaxy Bookshelf," *Galaxy* 25, no. 2 (1966): 125–33 (130).

20. Ibid., 127.

21. Ibid., 130.

22. Ibid., 128.

23. David Hartwell, introduction in *The Genocides* by Thomas M. Disch (Boston: Gregg Press, 1978), v–xv (xiv).

24. Budrys, "Galaxy Bookshelf," 129.

25. Ibid., 131.

26. Brian W. Aldiss, "Book Fare," sf *Impulse* 1, no. 11 (1967): 51–54 (51–53).

27. See, for example, William Appleman Williams, *The Tragedy of American Diplomacy*, rev. ed. (New York: Delta, 1962); David Horowitz, *The Free World Colossus: A Critique of American Foreign Policy in the Cold War* (New York: Hill & Wang, 1965); Gabriel Kolko, *The Politics of War: The World and United States Foreign Policy, 1943–1945* (New York: Vintage, 1968); and Harry Magdoff, *The Age of Imperialism: The Economics of US Foreign Policy* (New York: Modern Reader Paperbacks, 1969).

28. Thomas M. Disch, *The Genocides* (New York: Pocket, 1979), 104.

29. See Frank B. Golley, *A History of the Ecosystem Concept in Ecology: More Than the Sum of the Parts* (New Haven, CT: Yale University Press, 1996).

30. Charles S. Elton, *The Ecology of Invasions by Animals and Plants* (London: Chapman and Hall, 1972).

31. Ibid., 31.

32. Ibid., 31–32.

33. Ibid., 109.

34. Ibid., 51.

35. Ibid., 77–93.

36. William H. McNeill, *Plagues and Peoples* (Garden City, NY: Anchor Books, 1976), 177.

37. William Cronon, *Changes in the Land: Indians, Colonists, and the Ecology of New England* (New York: Hill & Wang, 1983).

38. Alfred W. Crosby, *Ecological Imperialism: The Biological Expansion of Europe, 900–1900* (Cambridge: Cambridge University Press, 1986), 279.

39. Alan Taylor, *American Colonies* (New York: Viking, 2001), 47.

40. Thomas M. Disch, "Introduction: On Saving the World," in *The Ruins of Earth: An Anthology of Stories of the Immediate Future*, ed. Disch (New York: G. P. Putnam's Sons, 1971), 1–7 (5).

41. Ibid.

42. Hartwell, xiv.

43. Disch, *Genocides*, 49, emphasis in original.

44. Ibid., 206.

45. Ibid.

46. Ibid., 26.

47. Ibid., 169.

48. The publication of *Silent Spring* is generally seen as the catalytic event that spawned the modern environmental movement: see Victor B. Scheffer, *The Shaping of Environmentalism in America* (Seattle: University of Washington Press, 1991), 119–21, and John McCormick, *The Global Environmental Movement*, 2nd ed. (New York: John Wiley & Sons, 1995), 65–67.

49. Disch, *Genocides*, 208.

50. Cronon, *Changes in the Land*, 53.

51. Disch, *Genocides*, 78–79.

52. Ibid., 11. Emphasis mine.

53. Ibid., 51.

54. Michael Stern, "From Technique to Critique: Knowledge and Human Interests in Brunner's *Stand on Zanzibar, The Jagged Orbit*, and *The Sheep Look Up*," *Science-Fiction Studies* 3, no. 2 (1976): 112–30. See also Neal Bukeavich, "'Are We Adopting the Right Measures to Cope?': Ecocrisis in John Brunner's *Stand on Zanzibar*," *Science Fiction Studies* 29, no. 1 (2002): 53–70, and, for a review of ecological themes in post-1960s SF, Patrick D. Murphy, "The Non-Alibi of Alien Scapes: SF and Ecocriticism," in *Beyond Nature Writing: Expanding the Boundaries of Ecocriticism*, ed. Karla Armbruster and Kathleen R. Wallace (Charlottesville: University Press of Virginia, 2001), 263–78.

55. Ursula K. Le Guin, "The Word for World Is Forest," in *Again, Dangerous Visions*, ed. Harlan Ellison (Garden City, NY: Doubleday, 1972), 32–117.

56. Ibid., 34.

57. Ibid., 35.

58. For a discussion of Le Guin's ecofeminism, see Patrick D. Murphy, *Literature, Nature, Other: Ecofeminist Critiques* (Albany: SUNY Press, 1995), 111–21.

59. Ursula K. Le Guin, "Introduction to *The Word for World Is Forest*," in *The Language of the Night: Essays on Fantasy and Science Fiction*, by Le Guin, ed. Susan Wood (New York: Perigee, 1979), 149–54 (151).

60. Le Guin, "Word," 73.

61. In her essay "Discovering Worlds: The Fiction of Ursula K. Le Guin" (in *Ursula K. Le Guin: Modern Critical Views*, ed. Harold Bloom [New York: Chelsea House, 1986] 183–209), Susan Wood complains that the author was "unfortunately [not] successful in avoiding the limitations of moral outrage at contemporary problems" (186–87). In the afterword to the novel published in *Again, Dangerous Visions* (117–18), Le Guin herself acknowledged that she is "not very fond of moralistic tales, for they often lack charity. I hope this one does not" (118).

62. Ian Watson, "The Forest as Metaphor for Mind: *The Word for World Is Forest* and 'Vaster Than Empires and More Slow,'" in Bloom, *Ursula K. Le Guin*, 47–55 (48).

63. Cronon, *Changes in the Land*, 124.

64. Clifton Fadiman and Jean White, *Ecocide—and Thoughts toward Survival* (Santa Barbara, CA: Center for the Study of Democratic Institutions, 1971). For a contemporaneous history, see Carroll Pursell, ed., *From Conservation to Ecology: The Development of Environmental Concern* (New York: Thomas Y. Crowell, 1973).

65. Among the many versions of this text is Donella H. Meadows et al., *The Limits to Growth: A Report for the Club of Rome's Project on the Predicament of Mankind* (New York: Universe Books, 1974).

66. Le Guin, "Word," 35.

67. Though both these works were published after Le Guin's novel, the issues they treated were widely debated during the late 1960s and early 1970s. For an excellent

overview of these debates, see Roderick Frazier Nash, *The Rights of Nature: A History of Environmental Ethics* (Madison: University of Wisconsin Press, 1989).

68. Ibid., 129. He goes on: "Fines would be assessed and collected (by guardians) on behalf of these creatures and used to restore their habitat or create an alternative to the one destroyed."

69. On the emergence of Green activism, see McCormick, *Global Environmental Movement*, 203–24.

70. National Staff of Environmental Action, eds., *Earth Day—The Beginning: A Guide for Survival* (New York: Pocket, 1970), v. On the origins of Earth Day, see Scheffer, *Shaping of Environmentalism*, 124–25.

71. For a critique of essentialist views of nature, see Jeffrey C. Ellis, "On the Search for a Root Cause: Essentialist Tendencies in Environmental Discourse," in *Uncommon Ground: Rethinking the Human Place in Nature*, ed. William Cronon (New York: W. W. Norton, 1995), 256–68. Major theoretical/historical studies of nature as a social construction are Neil Evernden, *The Social Creation of Nature* (Baltimore: Johns Hopkins University Press, 1992), and Carolyn Merchant, *Reinventing Eden: The Fate of Nature in Western Culture* (New York: Routledge, 2004).

72. Le Guin, "Word," 86. Emphasis mine.

73. On Lyubov in relation to other similar figures in Le Guin's work, see Karen Sinclair, "The Hero as Anthropologist," in *Ursula K. Le Guin: Voyager to Inner Lands and to Outer Space*, ed. Joe De Bolt (Port Washington, NY: Kennikat Press, 1979), 50–65.

74. On Romantic imagery in the novel, especially the anthropomorphizing evocation of the forest as "a metaphor for the landscape of consciousness," see Peter S. Alterman, "Ursula K. Le Guin: Damsel with a Dulcimer," in *Ursula K. Le Guin*, ed. Joseph D. Olander and Martin Harry Greenberg (New York: Taplinger, 1979), 64–76 (65).

75. Lynn White Jr., "The Historical Roots of Our Ecological Crisis," in *Politics and Environment: A Reader in Ecological Crisis*, ed. Walt Anderson (Pacific Palisades, CA: Goodyear, 1970), 338–49 (342). On the influence of White's essay, see Nash, *Rights of Nature*, 88–96.

76. See, for example, Climate Ark's continuously updated "Climate Change and Global Warming" website at http://www.climateark.org (accessed May 22, 2012).

77. See T. F. H. Allan, Joseph A. Tainter, and Thomas W. Hoekstra, *Supply-Side Sustainability* (New York: Columbia University Press, 2003), 259–61.

78. J. R. McNeill, *Something New under the Sun: An Environmental History of the Twentieth-Century World* (New York: W. W. Norton, 2000), 262.

BRAVE NEW WORLDS
AND LANDS OF THE FLIES

2

"The Real Problem of a Spaceship Is Its People"

Spaceship Earth as Ecological Science Fiction

SABINE HÖHLER

5

My fellow citizens: It is with a heavy heart that I bring you the findings
of the council. After deliberating in continuous sessions for the last four
months in unceasing efforts to find a solution to the devastating problem
of overpopulation threatening to destroy what remains of our planet, the
World Federation Council has considered and rejected all halfway measures
advanced by the various regional scientific congresses. We have also rejected
proposals for selective euthanasia and mass sterilization. Knowing the
sacrifices that our decision will entail, the World Council has nevertheless
reached a unanimous decision. I quote: "Because it has been agreed by the
nations of the world that the earth can no longer sustain a continuously
increasing population, as of today, the first of January, we join with all
other nations of the world in the following edict: childbearing is herewith
forbidden." To bear a child shall be the greatest of crime, punishable by
death. Women now pregnant will report to local hospitals for registration.
I earnestly request your cooperation in this effort to ensure the last hope
for survival of the human race.

zpg: *Zero Population Growth*

zpg, released in 1971, deals with the rigid measures for population
control that a densely populated Earth might require in the future. In the effort
to ensure the survival of the human race the World Council rules that having
children will be strictly illegal for the coming thirty years. Set in a thickly polluted American metropolis, the movie tells the story of the young white couple
Russ and Carol, who, upset with having to make do with a surrogate robot

baby, secretly give birth to a child, whom they hide carefully from friends and neighbors. However, the young family is discovered by a neighboring couple, itself with a strong desire for a child. A fight about proprietary rights results in blackmail and betrayal, and finally in the disclosure of the child to the authorities. The family is arrested, their elimination imminent.[1]

Around 1970, scenarios of population growth and restrictions on reproduction were explored not only in works of fiction. "ZPG—Zero Population Growth" was also the name of a US activist group founded in 1968 to raise public awareness of the "population problem." The group sought to confront the white American middle class with its lifestyle of using up far more than its global share of natural resources and adding more than its share to environmental pollution. ZPG meant to secure a birth rate of 2.2 to achieve a desired replacement rate of 1:1 and to thereby realize the dream of a numerically stable population—zero population growth. The initial mission was to encourage citizens to reduce family size: "Stop at Two," "Stop Heir Pollution," and "Control Your Local Stork" were some of ZPG's slogans advertised on bumper stickers, flyers, and posters, in public service announcements, magazines, and organized protest marches. ZPG also founded its own "Population Education Department" that produced classroom texts, and a video titled *World Population* that was used as an educational tool in public exhibitions, museums, and zoos. The organization did not confine its actions to showing movies and handing out condoms. It also urged changes in population policy and abortion legislation, and it opened vasectomy clinics.[2]

Among ZPG's founding members was the biologist Paul Ehrlich, whose popular book *The Population Bomb* (1968) briefly boosted group membership to more than thirty thousand in its first year.[3] Drawing on his studies of animal populations, Ehrlich warned about the impending destructive "explosion" of the human world populace. He became one of the founders of population ecology, which emerged from population biology by extending the realm of the natural sciences to the study of human societies in relation to their environments.[4] As the historian Matthew Connelly aptly put it, "Political problems were assumed to be biological in origin, potentially affecting the whole species."[5]

The "natural laws" of population growth leveled individual and social differences. People were aggregated into comparable numerical entities to make them "accountable": commensurable for the sake of statistics and responsible for their reproductive behavior. The ecological and governmental calculus of allocating contested earthly living space along the lines and divides of biological, ecological, and economical eligibility of human beings and populations warrant more research, to which I have contributed elsewhere.[6] This chapter, however, attends to the thin line between science fact and science fiction in population ecologists' accounts.

THE SCIENCE AND THE FICTION
OF POPULATION GROWTH

In the late 1960s and early 1970s the perceived "population problem" was neither about science nor about fiction only. Both ecological science and ecological fiction invented truisms about too many people sharing too little space and about how overpopulation would soon destroy what remained of planet Earth. "Ecocide" through unprecedented population increase, environmental degradation, and resource exploitation became the subject of numerous popular works of science. Ecologists employed alarming images of exponential growth of industrial pollution, the resource consumption of the rising world economy, or of sheer human numbers within the recently discovered limits of Earth as a "small planet."[7]

To understand the popularity of population ecology around 1970, its science fictional elements need to be taken seriously.[8] Population ecologists shared with science fiction writers similar sweeping concerns, like the "survival of the human race," and similar narrative strategies, like shifting present observations to other times and spaces. As Connelly observes, the actors "seeking support for campaigns to control world population continually pointed to the future because they could not actually prove that it had caused any particular crisis or emergency" in the present time.[9]

Moreover, population ecologists were poignantly prophetic about the future of *all* of humanity on the global scale. They corroborated their planetary predictions with scientific references to Malthusian and Darwinian evolutionary theories of natural selection and differential reproduction. Numerical approaches to social and political problems were supplemented by forthright deliberations on technical fixes. Suggestions of selective euthanasia and mass sterilization were not limited to works of SF but were also openly discussed in ecological publications. And finally, population ecologists proved to be genuine science fiction writers when toying with new forms of supranational governments and "new ways in which the world might be divided and united"[10] to allocate planetary living space and resources. How many people could the world support, who should live, who should decide, and how—these were the questions population ecologists concerned themselves with.[11]

I will focus on the work of Garrett Hardin (1925–2003), an American biologist and professor of human ecology at the University of California at Santa Barbara. Hardin was a prolific and provocative writer. His philosophy of reproductive restraints was highly contested during his lifetime and remained so after his death. Most notorious perhaps are his writings on the access to common resources and on reproductive responsibility, summarized in his 1972 book *Exploring New Ethics for Survival: The Voyage of the Spaceship Beagle*.[12] This book provides a case of ecological SF through its blending of analytic approach with fictional narrative. Drawing on the traditions of science fiction literature and film, Hardin asks his readers to suspend their disbelief in a near apocalyptic future. He sets his story on a spaceship, providing a perfect stage to a fast-motion recapture of humankind's history and impending doom as the population exceeds the "carrying capacity" of its finite environment.

Hardin defines carrying capacity as a measure of the maximum exploitation an environment will permit, without diminution, into the indefinite future. In terms of nature's revenues, Hardin states: "The carrying capacity is the level of exploitation that will yield the maximum return, in the long run."[13] In terms of population pressure, carrying capacity defines the maximum number of a species that an environment can support indefinitely without reducing its ability to support the same number in the future. The problem of a limited ecological carrying capacity, on Earth as in any other contained environment, came along with the question of how to dispense with the increasing "surplus" of human beings and entire human populations.[14]

The spaceship *Beagle* literally embodies this problem. To Hardin the *Beagle* serves neither as a device to explore new worlds and encounter alien life forms nor as part of a powerful fleet in interstellar war or as an exit technology to transport earthly nature to outer space and terraform new planets. Rather, the intergenerational spaceship serves as a metaphor and a model of human life in a finite environment.[15] Hardin's narrative resonates with recurring references to the ship in contemporary environmental discourse. Ehrlich repeatedly spoke of the "good ship Earth" on the verge of sinking.[16] The United Nations conference on the Human Environment in Stockholm in 1972 fashioned the One Boat concept, the thought that all of humanity shared a common fate within absolute limits.[17] From the voyages of discovery to the Space Age, the ship had been a reservoir of collective memory and imagination in Western culture. The ship harbored the congregation or family of mankind and was a figure of hope, shelter, and survival.

In the following sections I will explore three aspects of the *Beagle*'s voyage that were central to Hardin's new ethics for the survival of the human race: first, the conservation and replication of earthly achievements and failures, presenting the *Beagle* as ark and archive; second, the circulation and allocation of limited resources and living space, featuring the *Beagle* as a spaceship or technologically sustained metabolism; and third, the demands of its carrying capacity on the eligibility of its passengers for a place aboard, turning the *Beagle* into a lifeboat. I will close with Hardin's "lifeboat ethics," a selective ethics, which imagines a shipwreck situation to determine who should survive the global ecological crisis. Taking a strictly scientific approach to lifeboat capacity, Hardin saw traditional ethical considerations unhinged by necessity. His ethics for survival is thus perhaps the most striking work of science fiction produced in the 1970s.

CONSERVATION AND REPLICATION:
THE *BEAGLE* AS ARK AND ARCHIVE

Reflecting his analytical plot, each of the three parts of Hardin's book opens with a report from the *Beagle*'s journey. The reports describe practical features of life aboard: embarkation and first problems of environmental effluence; reproductive responsibility and regulatory mechanisms installed; and soaring overpopulation and ensuing drastic measures. The first part also explains the *Beagle*'s mission, begun in Hardin's own lifetime. "When people realized that Earth would be destroyed someday, they decided that they had to do something about it. Obviously the thing to do was to make a big spaceship, fill it with people, and blast it off towards other stars to look for a planet to settle on."[18] The U.S. government sent out the *Beagle* on a journey of 480 years to Alpha Centauri (the name of *Beagle* as homage to the change of humankind's place in the world brought about by Charles Darwin, and to the Americans' love of dogs). The ship measures three kilometers in diameter and harbors one thousand people; it is equipped with artificial gravity and with a plastic sky, nice family apartments, and TV. Apart from the lack of automobiles, the *Beagle* is "just like home."[19]

The mission also experiments with the Marxist critique that capitalism requires (wasteful) expansion to sustain itself. The spaceship is designed as a test case for a steady-state society. Nevertheless it soon turns out that the mission itself is an emission: the selected emissaries are on their way to emitting the

American way of life to the entire universe. Start-up businesses cause the first environmental problems on board when they begin swiftly depleting resources and polluting public goods like air and water. On a micro-scale, the predicament of supporting free enterprise and private profit on the one hand and acknowledging public demands on the other unfolds at an extremely accelerated pace. Within the perfect enclosure of the spaceship, the American spirit of industrialization and the capitalist economy and consumer cycle literally run up against the wall.

The *Beagle* is an archive that goes beyond the miniature worlds that authors like Jules Verne have furnished in such works as *20,000 Leagues under the Sea* (1870), in which the submarine *Nautilus* keeps a library of twelve thousand volumes, a collection of art and music, and a museum at the traveler's disposal. While Verne's nineteenth-century vessels were encyclopedic collections of humankind's knowledge and technology, the *Beagle* not only contains but replicates humankind's evolutionary successes and failures on a small scale. The *Beagle* represents the primal archive, the inventory of the life on Earth: the ark. Philosopher Peter Sloterdijk has analyzed the ark as the perfect example of the "ontology of enclosed space."[20] *Ark*, from the Latin *arca*, means case or compartment. According to Sloterdijk, the ark denotes an artificial interior space, a "swimming endosphere" that provides the only possible environment for its inhabitants.[21] In Hardin's account the spaceship makes a finite insular habitat; material, informational, or energetic exchanges with its environment are not possible. The *Beagle* is a closed system.

As the ship represents Earth, Earth itself turns into a ship, an exceptional site where life is at stake.[22] Hardin reminds his readers of the revolutionary change in perception brought about with the first pictures of Earth from space: "We must feel in our bones the inescapable truth that we live on a spaceship."[23] Hardin quotes Adlai E. Stevenson, U.S. ambassador to the United Nations, who in 1965 took up this image in his appeal to the international community. Stevenson referred to Earth as "a little spaceship" on which humankind traveled together as passengers, "dependent on its vulnerable reserves of air and soil."[24] In 1966, the English economist and political scientist Barbara Ward in her book *Spaceship Earth* pointed to the "remarkable combination of security and vulnerability" that humanity in the Cold War era found itself in.[25] The spaceship became an allegory for the need of a new balance of power between the continents, of wealth between North and South, and of understanding and tolerance in a world of economic interdependence and potential nuclear destruction.

Spaceship Earth also reconciled seemingly opposing ideals of sufficiency and efficiency in environmentalist thought. In a programmatic lecture, "The Economics of the Coming Spaceship Earth," given in 1966, the American economist Kenneth E. Boulding chose the spaceship as a metaphor to promote the "closed earth of the future," suggesting to foreclose the wasteful "cowboy economy" of the past for a frugal "spaceman economy."[26] The spaceship was his model of a self-contained cyclical economical and ecological system capable of continuous material reproduction. The American architect Richard Buckminster Fuller in his *Operating Manual for Spaceship Earth* (1969) used the spaceship as a metaphor of an intricate cybernetic machine to be expertly run by science and technology. Fuller summoned the engineering elite to take control of an earthly environment in bad repair.[27] He propagated the optimistic view that ecologically smart design and resource-efficient technologies would take the modern ideals into the future.[28]

Hardin endorsed Boulding's model of spaceman sufficiency but did not concern himself with the technological details of life support. Instead he pointed to an aspect that neither Boulding nor Fuller had addressed: "The real problem of a spaceship is its people."[29] Next to the question of government, the long-term changes brought about by generational succession had to be handled. In part two of his book we learn that the creators of the *Beagle* came up with the solution of eternal life for a tiny part of the population. The spaceship society is divided into "civilized man" (a category excluding women) and "procreative man" (this one including women). This arrangement allows Hardin to experiment with what he deems most valuable in human populations: culture or the development of ideas on the one hand, and evolution through natural selection on the other.

The "Argotes" form an all-male insular community of twelve who secretly monitor the common "Quotions." The Argotes are the custodians of the past; they were selected for their qualities of the mind, to act as trustees of civilization. To maintain the stability of intelligence and ideas, the Argotes do not reproduce biologically, and they are conveniently free of emotions and desire. The Argotes reproduce culturally by going through a cycle of perpetual youth to oppose the aging of the mind, "like pushing RESET on a computer."[30] The Quotions were selected for their fine biological qualities and then left to the basic processes of aging and mortality, sexual selection, reproduction, and mutation. They are subjected to chaotic nature, which develops human DNA but also threatens long-evolved cultural ideas and values from each generation to the next. The *Beagle*'s plan is to wait and see whether the Argotes or the Quotions will eventually prove more suited to colonizing a new planet.

Through decades and centuries the Argotes have been watching the Quotions divide and multiply and suffer all the major societal conflicts, which, as the records show, people on Earth also fought through. Repeatedly, the liberal ideals of freedom and competition clash with the sustainability ideal of freedom and responsibility. From these conflicts Hardin construes his major argument. After Darwin, he claims, a society can trust neither the individual conscience nor the appeal to individual responsibility. In a community favoring freedom and responsibility in using common resources, there will always be one who just favors freedom and takes more than his share. In a commons, or a "system of voluntary restraint," gains will be privatized while losses are socialized. Solidarity and altruism have no place in his philosophy, which excludes collective or socialist forms of joint property and joint property management: "Freedom in a commons brings ruin to all."[31]

For this point Hardin exploits his legendary *Science* article of 1968, "The Tragedy of the Commons," in which he attacked the allegedly prevailing practice that common earthly resources like forests, air, and oceans could freely be used and overused.[32] The scarcity and contamination of any commonly owned and used natural resource, so his argument goes, will inevitably increase, since it will eventually be exploited within a limited world. Hardin bases his justification on the biological principle of natural selection as he understood it: man is an "egoistic animal," and as "the descendant of an unbroken line of ancestors who survived because they were sufficiently egoistic," man will naturally attempt to secure and maximize his own advantage.[33] Ultimately the conscientious people will go extinct in favor of the ruthless and egoistic. According to Hardin the system of the commons can only work in a limitless world or in a world in which the carrying capacity has not yet been reached. "But it cannot work in a world that is reaching its limits, in which the decisions being made overstress the carrying capacity of the environment—in a word, in the world of a spaceship."[34]

To Hardin the Hobbesian nature of man must also preclude common access to procreation. Like many of his colleagues, Hardin built his assumptions on the Malthusian principle that humans will naturally breed and populations will increase geometrically or exponentially, while resource supply will grow arithmetically or in linear fashion only.[35] Natural selection, so thought Hardin, will favor *Homo progenitivus* ("reproductive man") at the expense of *Homo con-tracipiens* ("contracepting man").[36] When defining Spaceship Earth, Barbara Ward had warned that in "such a close community, there must be rules for survival."[37] Hardin claimed that a spaceship's mission was to reconcile freedom with coercion. He postulated "the necessity of coercion for all—*mutual coercion, mutually agreed upon*,"[38] a freedom collectively delimited and controlled through law.

ELIGIBILITY AND SELECTION: THE *BEAGLE* AS LIFEBOAT

Dystopic visions of a population-resource-environment predicament are explored in other works of SF around 1970. Frequently the city takes the place of the spaceship to signify the closed world. Sufficiency and efficiency aspects of closure feature both in artificially balanced societies and in conditions of "overpopulation." The movie *Logan's Run* (1976) presents a world in perfect ecological equilibrium. Three hundred years into the future, "the survivors of war, overpopulation and pollution live in a domed city, sealed away from the forgotten world outside. Here, in an ecologically balanced world, mankind lives only for pleasure, freed by the servo-mechanisms which provide everything." To maintain the equilibrium a mastermind computer executes an efficient scheme of population control. While the citizens believe in their chance of "renewal" at the age of thirty through competing in the spectacle of "Carrousel," the central feedback system behind the scenes keeps the total number of human lives stable according to a strict "one for one" rule: "One is terminated, one is born. Simple, logical, perfect. You have a better system?"[39]

Soylent Green (1973), a movie set in the year 2022, explores an alternative but no less "sustainable" path. New York City is thickly polluted; its population is forty million. Congestion, poverty, hunger, and corruption dominate the city. A merciless police force keeps the masses in control, clearing human surplus away with huge power shovels and garbage trucks. Governmental euthanasia facilities are running day and night. Director Richard Fleischer explores the excesses of a world applying Boulding's spaceship solution of the closed circulatory system to human mass. The single company that controls food production and distribution, the Soylent Corporation, devises a most efficient scheme in which dead bodies are recycled to organic material and reintegrated into the food chain.[40]

"There is a sense in which all these movies are in complicity with the abhorrent."[41] Susan Sontag's view from 1965 on disaster fiction also applies to the fiction of population disaster of the 1970s. But clearly the different works of fiction also presented different perceptions of what the disaster of overpopulation consists of, what it entails, and for whom. Undoubtedly, many works of SF, by exploring a variety of disastrous conditions and effects, have approached the "population problem" in a more thorough and differentiated way than many population scientists have.

Let us return then to the *Beagle*, which meanwhile also witnesses a gigantic population increase. In part three of Hardin's book the spaceship has traveled far beyond Alpha Centauri, as it turned out that the planet was "no good."[42] As hundreds of years stretched into thousands, the spaceship's population increased to twelve million people (naturally, all Quotions; there are still only twelve Argotes). The chapter with the evocative title "Freedom's Harvest" explains that several hundred years earlier, a massive conflict on matters of reproduction was decided in favor of the individual and inseparable right and freedom to reproduce. The pro-creation faction prevailed over the "Trustful Fellowship for Zero Population Growth" that believed in family planning and demanded to "Stop at Two." Predictably this group was heavily attacked for its insinuated ideas of policing and genocide.[43]

The Argotes rationalize this development by applying simple calculus on the grounds that "every reproductively isolated group potentially multiplies in exponential fashion."[44] Hardin draws on the Darwinian principle of differential reproduction to describe how one part of the spaceship's population ruthlessly outbred the other. As the right to breed selected for fertility, overcrowding selected for the tolerance of crowding—to the effect that literally no space on board is left for movement and action. The identical calculus had been applied to Earth in the twentieth century. Repeating the title phrase from authors Edward A. Ross (1927) and Karl Sax (1955), Hardin argues that, taking the 1970 rate of population growth of 2 percent, there would be "standing room only" on all the land areas, with a population of 8.27 x 1014, within six hundred years.[45] Converting the entire mass of Earth to human flesh would result in 1.33 x 1023 people, achieved in only 1,557 years. Hardin acknowledges that these thought experiments of converting masses might seem ridiculous: "The real point of the mathematical exercise (so often missed) is to compel choice."[46]

On the *Beagle* the Argotes choose to reduce the population drastically. In god-like fashion they force the Quotions to pick one out of three biblical scourges: famine, war, or pestilence. The Quotions opt for the disease, and the *Beagle* is once again sparsely populated. Hardin admits that sweeping death might lend itself as a solution to earthly problems in the form of an unintended consequence, but not as a political deliberation. To compel choice, politics needs to generate a "fundamental extension in morality." Hardin contests Adam Smith's "invisible hand" symbolizing the belief in the self-regulating capabilities of a market, state, or population, and in rational individual decisions for the greater good. To "close the commons" in breeding, Hardin claims, the society will have to abandon the "present policy of *laissez-faire* in reproduction."[47] Among other "corrective feedbacks" he suggests abandoning the welfare state, which promotes "overbreeding," and abolishing the 1967 United Nations Universal Declaration of Human Rights, which instituted the family as the natural and fundamental unit of society. Hardin essentially repeats a view he expressed in 1970: that of parenthood being not a right but a privilege to be granted to responsible parents only.[48]

Clearly, Ehrlich's Good Ship Earth was not an inclusive vehicle that emphasized commonality. Arks may seem egalitarian, but they are not free from power relations, and they do not strive for completeness. Even the biblical ark sorted its species into separate classes of purity, ruling out the unclean.[49] Sloterdijk has pointed to the selectivity that characterizes all ark narratives. In all stories of the ark, he reminds us, the choice of the few is declared a holy necessity, and salvation is found only by those who have acquired one of the few boarding passes to the exclusive vehicle.[50] Arks are discriminatory technologies; they combine the imperative of resource sufficiency with selective strategies and efficient rules of allocating resources to their occupants. In their most exclusive form arks become lifeboats.

LIFEBOAT ETHICS

The so-called population problem was never simply about "too many," to quote a 1969 book by the Swedish food scientist Georg Borgstrom.[51] It was not primarily the absolute number of the world's population, reaching three billion by the 1960s, that alarmed his contemporaries. Rather, population ecologists pointed to the disastrous effects of some parts of world population outbreeding others. Respectively, Hardin's aim was not to realize the *maximum* population that the nineteenth-century British philosopher and social reformer Jeremy Bentham might have had in mind when formulating his goal of "the greatest good for the greatest number."[52] Hardin aimed to achieve the *optimum* population, proportionately and responsibly composed and numerically safely below Earth's carrying capacity.

Hardin formulated his "Lifeboat Ethics" in the mid 1970s.[53] He abandoned the idea of Spaceship Earth, criticizing that it presupposed a powerful captain on its bridge to take a decision. Viewing Earth as a lifeboat prescribed rules of selection independent from Darwin's biology and from the (possibly fatal) choices of a steering elite. Survival on a lifeboat depended solely on its carrying capacity: the number of occupants in relation to the amount of provisions, their economic allocation, and the disposal of deadweight. The lifeboat enforced new criteria of eligibility: its physics determined its ethics.[54] Hardin himself took on a god-like authority when framing the basic law of the lifeboat in the Old Testament formula *Thou shalt not*: "Thou shalt not exceed the carrying capacity" became his quasi-biblical commandment of ecological correctness.[55]

On the ethical basis of Earth presenting a lifeboat Hardin made his "Case against Helping the Poor." He argued against the "fundamental error of the ethics of sharing" in international aid programs and urged wealthy nations to close their doors to acts of charity like immigration and food aid to the poor. The population of poor countries, his argument went, would simply "convert extra food into extra babies."[56] The optimum world population, able to survive on the planetary lifeboat, would have to be reached via a Darwinian process of selection that reflected a nation's "fitness." Fitness he defines according to orthodox liberal logic of achieved economic prosperity, and so determines that top nations or groups should be rewarded while communities not able to cleverly economize be punished. Hardin's disposition of human lives entirely ignores the historical roots of disparities of wealth through colonial exploitation and postcolonial power relations. Socially and historically developed problems he describes as biological in origin and individual in character. All the while, the good cause he claims to support deflects from the genocidal logics that inform his judgment.

EXIT STRATEGY

The concluding chapter of Hardin's book follows the Argotes preparing their return to Earth. The *Beagle*'s nuclear energy pack has been used up. Besides, after five thousand years of the ship's journeying through space, three young women have discovered the entrance into the Argotes' hiding place. Following the Eve principle of spoiling any sophisticated mission, the intruders have turned what began as a rational endeavor into a luxury cruise. The women introduced sex and brought genetic variety to the Argotes, meanwhile great-grandmothering a new population of Argotes. The price of sex has been mortality. Fourteen people are left in the secret hub of the ship, and essentially nothing distinguishes them from the Quotions outside.

The shuttle to Earth can carry twenty people. The Argotes discuss the question of who may go, displaying the ultimate lifeboat predicament. Should they draw lots? Should they give up their place voluntarily to one of the Quotions? In the end, the fourteen Argotes enter the shuttle, leaving six seats empty—for the safety factor—and leaving behind the millions of Quotions blissfully ignorant of their fate of certain death. This passage clearly exhibits the deeper meaning and consequence of Hardin's ethics for survival. Lifeboat ethics is not about an absolute morality that binds every human being in the same way at all times and all places. Lifeboat ethics calls for a situational morality. The truly knowledgeable and responsible will not take in more people than their lifeboat's carrying capacity allows for.

At least one question remains unanswered: Where will the lifeboat go? After the *Beagle*'s voyage of thousands of years, the state of planet Earth is utterly unknown. The last message arrived twenty years after the *Beagle* left; it is very probable that the Earth fell victim to nuclear destruction. Can this be a return home? Hardin leaves this part of the story untold—perhaps to him this is where true science fiction begins. As a population ecologist he takes no interest in visions of terraforming new planets and reinventing paradise. Hardin is engaged solely with numerical aggregates of living beings and with the distribution of countable resources and measurable living space. Noticeably, with his focus so narrow, there are things that escape him, first of all the insight that his science has been fiction all along.

Hardin misses out on the reflection that the science of ecology has been constructing the closed worlds it describes. The movie *ZPG: Zero Population Growth* I began this text with explores how an escape from philosophies of sufficiency and efficiency in the spaceship, the ark, and the lifeboat might be performed. By way of the junk-littered canals beneath the city, the couple Russ and Carol with their newborn can flee the state authorities in a tiny rubber dinghy. This lifeboat is not designed as an economic container but as a makeshift rescue vehicle. It takes the family to an abandoned beach, a former radioactive zone where they set out to make a new start. The wasteland serves as a metaphor of what may lie beyond the realm of rigid population control: an open wilderness, deserted and anything but pure, but also unrestrained and free to inhabit in new ways. This is not a return. The story presents the ship as an exit strategy to claim an environment that is not within but *outside* the confines of ecology.

Notes

1. *ZPG: Zero Population Growth*, dir. Michael Campus (2008; Los Angeles: Paramount, 1971), DVD. The epigraph for this chapter quotes from the opening sequence.

2. The Population Connection, "30 Years of ZPG," [ZPG] *Reporter*, December 1998, 12–19, http://www.populationconnection.org/site/DocServer/1219thirtyyears.pdf?docID=261.

3. Ibid. According to the article about the history of the organization between 1968 and 1998, "the years between 1969 and 1972 saw the membership of ZPG briefly blossom to more than 35,000 members" (13).

4. See Paul R. Ehrlich, *The Population Bomb* (1968; New York: Ballantine, 1969).

5. Matthew Connelly, "To Inherit the Earth: Imagining World Population, from the Yellow Peril to the Population Bomb," *Journal of Global History* 1, no. 3 (2006): 300. For more-encompassing treatment, see Matthew Connelly, *Fatal Misconception: The Struggle to Control World Population* (Cambridge, MA: Belknap Press of Harvard University Press, 2008). On population models and laws see Sharon E. Kingsland, *Modeling Nature: Episodes in the History of Population Ecology* (1985; Chicago: University of Chicago Press, 1995).

6. Sabine Höhler, "The Law of Growth: How Ecology Accounted for World Population in the 20th Century," *Distinktion: Scandinavian Journal of Social Theory* 14 (2007): 45–64.

7. Next to Ehrlich's *Population Bomb* the best known are perhaps Fairfield Osborn, *Our Plundered Planet* (1948; Boston: Little, Brown, 1950); Fairfield Osborn, *The Limits of the Earth* (Boston: Little, Brown, 1953); Fairfield Osborn, *Our Crowded Planet: Essays on the Pressures of Population* (Garden City, NY: Doubleday, 1962); Karl Sax, *Standing Room Only: The World's Exploding Population* (1955; Boston: Beacon Press, 1960), *Standing Room Only: The Challenge of Overpopulation*); Georg Borgstrom, *Too Many: A Study of Earth's Biological Limitations* (New York: Macmillan, 1969); Michael Hamilton, ed., *This Little Planet* (New York: Scribner, 1970). The 1972 study *The Limits to Growth* developed future scenarios termed the "behavior modes of the population-capital system." Donella H. Meadows et al., *The Limits to Growth: A Report for the Club of Rome's Project on the Predicament of Mankind* (New York: Universe Books, 1972), 91–92.

8. Science fiction is too broad a genre to be defined uniformly or conclusively. See Vivian Sobchack, *Screening Space: The American Science Fiction Film* (1987; New Brunswick, NJ: Rutgers University Press, 1997), chap. 1, "The Limits of the Genre," 17–63.

9. Connelly, "To Inherit the Earth," 314.

10. Ibid., 301.

11. J. H. Fremlin, "How Many People Can the World Support?" *New Scientist* 415 (1964): 285–87.

12. Garrett Hardin, *Exploring New Ethics for Survival: The Voyage of the Spaceship Beagle* (New York: Viking Press, 1972).

13. Ibid., 114.

14. Ehrlich repeatedly speaks of "human surplus": see *Population Bomb*, 167. See also Sabine Höhler, "'Carrying Capacity'—the Moral Economy of the 'Coming Spaceship Earth,'" *Atenea: A Bilingual Journal of the Humanities and Social Sciences* 26, no. 1 (2006): 59–74.

15. A number of twentieth-century science fiction writers have set their stories on "interstellar arks," self-contained generation spaceships on their way to distant worlds, to explore how societies evolve in closed environments, from Robert A. Heinlein's *Orphans of the Sky* (1941) to Brian Aldiss's *Non-Stop/Starship* (1958), to more recent works like Molly Gloss's *The Dazzle of Day* (1997).

16. "It is obvious that we cannot exist unaffected by the fate of our fellows on the other end of the good ship Earth. If their end of the ship sinks, we shall at the very least have to put up with the spectacle of their drowning and listen to their screams." Ehrlich, *Population Bomb*, 132.

17. Rafael M. Salas, *International Population Assistance: The First Decade; A Look at the Concepts and Politics Which Have Guided the UNFPA in Its First Ten Years* (New York: Pergamon Press, 1979), 125.

18. Hardin, *Exploring New Ethics for Survival*, 92.

19. Ibid., 12.

20. Peter Sloterdijk, *Sphären* (Frankfurt am Main: Suhrkamp, 1998–2004), vol. 2, *Globen (Makrosphärologie)* (1999), chap. 3: "Archen, Stadtmauern, Weltgrenzen, Immunsysteme. Zur Ontologie des ummauerten Raumes," 251–64. Translations are mine.

21. Ibid., 252.

22. "The earth is a spaceship." Hardin, *Exploring New Ethics for Survival*, 16.

23. Ibid.

24. Ibid., 17.

25. Barbara Ward, *Spaceship Earth* (New York: Columbia University Press, 1966), 15. On the figure of Spaceship Earth in environmental discourse see Sabine Höhler, "'Spaceship Earth': Envisioning Human Habitats in the Environmental Age," *Bulletin of the German Historical Institute* 42 (2008): 65–85; Sabine Höhler, "The Environment as a Life Support System: The Case of Biosphere 2," *History and Technology* 26, no. 1 (2010): 39–58.

26. Kenneth E. Boulding, "The Economics of the Coming Spaceship Earth," in *Environmental Quality in a Growing Economy*, Essays from the Sixth RFF Forum on Environmental Quality held in Washington, D.C., March 8 and 9, 1966, ed. Henry Jarrett (Baltimore: Johns Hopkins University Press, 1966), 9. Hardin recommends Boulding's vision; Hardin, *Exploring New Ethics for Survival*, 242.

27. Richard Buckminster Fuller, *Operating Manual for Spaceship Earth* (New York: E. P. Dutton & Co., 1971; originally published by Southern Illinois University Press, 1969). See also Peder Anker, "Buckminster Fuller as Captain of Spaceship Earth," *Minerva* 45, no. 4 (2007): 417–34.

28. These views were two early versions of the programmatic term "sustainable development" emerging in the late 1980s. World Commission on Environment and Development (Chairman Gro Harlem Brundtland), *Our Common Future* (Oxford: Oxford University Press, 1987).

29. Hardin, *Exploring New Ethics for Survival*, 92.

30. Ibid., 96.

31. Ibid., 118.

32. Garrett Hardin, "The Tragedy of the Commons," *Science* 162 (1968): 1243–48.

33. Hardin, *Exploring New Ethics for Survival*, 102.

34. Ibid., 118.

35. Thomas Malthus, *An Essay on the Principle of Population, as It Affects the Future Improvement of Society with Remarks on the Speculations of Mr. Godwin, M. Condorcet, and Other Writers* (London, 1798). On mid-twentieth-century Neo-Malthusianism see Björn-Ola

Linnér, *The Return of Malthus: Environmentalism and Post-war Population-Resource Crises* (Leverburgh, Isle of Harris, UK: White Horse Press, 2003); Paul Neurath, *From Malthus to the Club of Rome and Back: Problems of Limits to Growth, Population Control, and Migrations* (Armonk, NY: M. E. Sharpe, 1994).

36. Hardin, "Tragedy of the Commons," 1246.

37. Ward, *Spaceship Earth*, vii.

38. Hardin, *Exploring New Ethics for Survival*, 130. Emphasis in original.

39. *Logan's Run*, dir. Michael Anderson (2007; New York: Warner Bros. / Metro-Goldwyn-Mayer, 1976), DVD. I quote from the written prologue introducing the film and from one of its opening dialogues. The movie is based on the novel *Logan's Run* written by William F. Nolan and George Clayton Johnson (New York: Dial Press, 1967).

40. *Soylent Green*, dir. Richard Fleischer, Warner Bros./Metro-Goldwyn-Mayer, 1973). The screenplay is based on a novel by Harry Harrison titled *Make Room! Make Room!* (with an introduction by Paul R. Ehrlich) (1966; New York: Berkley, 1973).

41. Susan Sontag, "The Imagination of Disaster" [1965], in *The Science Fiction Film Reader*, ed. Gregg Rickman (New York: Limelight Editions, 2004), 113.

42. Hardin, *Exploring New Ethics for Survival*, 163.

43. Ibid., 157–59.

44. Ibid., 159.

45. Ibid., 172. Edward A. Ross, *Standing Room Only?* (New York: Century, 1927); Sax, *Standing Room Only* (1955). See also Höhler, "Law of Growth."

46. Hardin, *Exploring New Ethics for Survival*, 174.

47. Hardin, "Tragedy of the Commons," 1248, 1244.

48. Garrett Hardin, "Editorial: Parenthood: Right or Privilege?" *Science* 169 (1970): 427.

49. In a short story titled "The Stowaway," Julian Barnes has aptly summarized the themes of authority, order, and classification associated with the Ark (Old Testament, Genesis 1: 6–9). Julian Barnes, *A History of the World in 10½ Chapters* (1989; New York: Vintage, 1990), chap. 1: "The Stowaway," 1–30. An anonymous woodworm reports, "I was never chosen. In fact, like several other species, I was specifically not chosen."

50. Sloterdijk, 260–61.

51. Borgstrom, *Too Many* (1969). See also Höhler, "Law of Growth."

52. Hardin, "Tragedy of the Commons," 1244.

53. Garrett Hardin, "Lifeboat Ethics: The Case against Helping the Poor," *Psychology Today* 8, no. 4 (1974): 38–43, 123–26. On Hardin's problematic premises see Petter Næss, "Live and Let Die: The Tragedy of Hardin's Social Darwinism," *Journal of Environmental Policy & Planning* 6, no. 1 (2004): 19–34.

54. Garrett Hardin, "Ethical Implications of Carrying Capacity," in *Managing the Commons*, ed. Hardin (San Francisco: Freeman, 1977), 112–25.

55. Garrett Hardin, "Carrying Capacity as an Ethical Concept," in *Lifeboat Ethics: The Moral Dilemmas of World Hunger*, ed. George R. Lucas Jr. et al. (New York: Harper & Row, 1976), 134.

56. Garrett Hardin, "Living on a Lifeboat," *BioScience* 24, no. 10 (1974): 564.

The Sea and Eternal Summer

An Australian Apocalypse

ANDREW MILNER

6

Despite the international success of individual writers like Greg Egan and of individual novels like Nevil Shute's *On the Beach*,[1] Australian SF remains essentially peripheral to the wider contours of the genre. Yet there is a long history of what Adam Roberts describes as "works that located utopias and satirical dystopias on the opposite side of the globe,"[2] that is, in Australia. The earliest example he gives is Joseph Hall's 1605 *Mundus alter et idem sive Terra Australis ante hac semper incognita lustrata* (A world other and the same, or the land of Australia until now unknown), the last, Nicolas Edme Restif de la Bretonne's 1781 *La découverte australe par une homme-volant* (The discovery of Australia by a flying man).[3] Lyman Tower Sargent's bibliography begins slightly later, with Peter Heglin's 1667 *An Appendix to the Former Work, Endeavouring a Discovery of the Unknown Parts of the World. Especially of Terra Australis Incognita, or the Southern Continent*, and proceeds to list something like three hundred "Australian" print utopias and dystopias published during the period 1667–1999.[4]

There are yet others overlooked by even Sargent and Roberts: neither mention Denis Veiras's *L'histoire des Sévarambes*, for example, first published in part in English in 1675, in whole in French in 1679.[5] European writers made very extensive use of Australia as a site for utopian imaginings well before the continent's conquest, exploration, and colonization; even Marx's *Capital* ends its first volume with an unexpected vision of Australia as an open frontier beyond capital's grasp.[6] There are two reasons for this, the one obvious, the other less so. First, Australia remained one of very few real-world *terrae incognitae* available for appropriation by European fantasy as late as the second half of the nineteenth century. And second, although Australia is conventionally described as a continent, it is also in fact an island,[7] possessed of all the properties of self-containment and isolation that have proven so helpful to the authors of utopia ever since Thomas More.

Most of the earlier Australian utopian fictions took the form of an imaginary voyage narrated by travelers on their return home. Such imaginings became increasingly implausible as European explorers brought back increasingly detailed accounts of Australia's climate, topography, and people. The utopias were therefore progressively relocated farther into the interior, until the realities of inland exploration eventually proved equally disappointing. Thereafter, in Australia as elsewhere, utopias were increasingly superseded by future-fictional "uchronias." Robyn Walton cites Robert Ellis Dudgeon's *Colymbia*, published in 1873, as the first Australian SF utopia,[8] although Joseph Fraser's *Melbourne and Mars* is probably better known.[9] In Australia, again as elsewhere, as the twentieth century proceeded utopias were also increasingly displaced by dystopias. The best-known Australian examples are almost certainly Shute's *On the Beach*, a nuclear doomsday novel, and George Turner's *The Sea and Summer*, one of the first novels to explore the fictional possibilities of the effects of global warming. Both make powerful, albeit often scientifically implausible, use of Australia's self-contained isolation.

Much SF has been both deliberately intended by its authors and deliberately received by its readers as value-relevant. Some, but not all, science fiction consists in future stories; and some, but not all, is concerned either to advocate what its authors and readers see as desirable possible futures or to urge against what they see as undesirable ones. In short, the future story can be used as a kind of futurology. Science fiction of this kind is intended to be politically or morally effective—that is, to be socially useful. "We badly need a literature of considered ideas," Turner himself argued in 1990: "Science fiction could be a useful tool for serious consideration, on the level of the non-specialist reader, of a future rushing on us at unstoppable speed."[10] Three years earlier, in the "Postscript" to *The Sea and Summer*, he had written, "We *talk* of leaving a better world to our children, but in fact do little more than rub along with day-to-day problems and hope that the long-range catastrophes will never happen." This novel, he explained, "is about the possible cost of complacency."[11]

Much radical SF scholarship exhibits a certain antipathy to dystopia, essentially on the grounds that it tends, in Fredric Jameson's phrase, "to denounce and . . . warn against Utopian programs."[12] But many dystopias, including some of those most disliked by Jameson, actually function as implicitly utopian warnings rather than as "anti-utopias" in the strict sense of the term. This is true, I would argue, for *On the Beach* and *The Sea and Summer*. Writing in the Australian newspaper *The Age* in January 2008, Peter Christoff, the then–vice president of the Australian Conservation Foundation, observed that *On the Beach* had "helped catalyse the 1960s anti-nuclear movement." Comparing the threat of nuclear war in the 1950s with that of global warming in the early twenty-first century, he warned that "we are . . . suffering from a radical failure of imagination." When Christoff connected *On the Beach* to climate change, he did so precisely to urge the need for a parallel contemporary effort to imagine the unimaginable. "These are distressing, some will argue apocalyptic, imaginings," he admits, "but without them, we cannot undertake the very substantial efforts required to minimize the chances of their being realised."[13] *The Sea and Summer*, it seems to me, had attempted more or less exactly this two decades previously.

THE NOVEL WITHIN THE NOVEL

Turner was born in Melbourne in 1916 and published the first of five non-SF novels in 1959. He began reviewing genre fiction for *The Age* during the 1970s, produced his first SF novel, *Beloved Son*, in 1978, which was followed by sequels in 1981 and 1983,[14] and by the time of his death in 1997 had become in effect the genre's Australian elder statesman. Four other SF novels of his were published between 1987 and 1994 and a collection of SF short stories in 1990, and two posthumous works, an unfinished novella, *And Now Time Doth Waste Me,* in 1998, and the novel *Down There in Darkness* in 1999.[15] All were essentially exercises in futurology, all preoccupied with the ethics of sociopolitical action, all distinctively Australian in tenor. By far the most critically successful was *The Sea and Summer*, which in 1988 won both the Commonwealth Writers' Prize Best Book Award for the South East Asia and South Pacific Region and the Arthur C. Clarke Award for best SF novel published in Britain (the previous year's Clarke Award had gone to Margaret Atwood for *The Handmaid's Tale*). In 1985 Turner had published a short story, "The Fittest,"[16] in which he first began to explore the possible effects of global warming on his home city. He quickly expanded this story into a full-length novel that was published in 1987 in Britain as *The Sea and Summer* and as *Drowning Towers* in the United States.[17]

Like *On the Beach*, *The Sea and Summer* is set mainly in and around Melbourne, a vividly described place, terrifyingly transformed into the utterly unfamiliar. The novel is organized into a core narrative, comprising two parts set in the mid-twenty-first century, and a frame narrative, comprising three shorter parts set a thousand years later among "the Autumn People" of the "New City," located in what are today the Dandenong Ranges to the east of Melbourne.[18] The core narrative deals with the immediate future of our "Greenhouse Culture," the frame narrative with the retrospective reactions to it of a slowly cooling world. The latter depicts a utopian future society, which uses submarine archaeology to explore the drowned remains of the "Old City," but which is also simultaneously aware of the imminence of a "Long Winter" that might well last a hundred thousand years. The novel opens by introducing the frame narrative's three main characters: Marin, a part-time student and enthusiastic Christian, who pilots the power craft used to explore the drowned city; his great-aunt, Professor Lenna Wilson, an expert on the collapse of the Greenhouse Culture in Australia, who teaches history at the university; and Andra Andrasson, a visiting actor-playwright from Sydney, researching the twenty-first century as possible material for a play.[19] Together they explore the remains of the substantially submerged "Tower Twenty-three" (6–11) and investigate the ruins of the only twentieth-century "Enclave" never to have flooded (93–96), debating their meaning both on-site and at the university.

The core narrative takes the form of a novel within the novel, also titled *The Sea and Summer*, written by Lenna as a "Historical Reconstruction" of the thirty-first century's real past (15). In form it is polyphonic, tracing the development of the Greenhouse Culture through a set of memoirs and diary extracts written during the years 2044–61 by six main protagonists: Alison Conway, Francis Conway, Teddy Conway, Nola Parkes, Captain Nikopoulos, and Arthur Derrick. The only silent voice is that of the Tower Boss, Billy Kovacs, the novel's central character and also, perhaps, its central enigma, the remains of whose flat Lenna and Andra explore (9). This core narrative is counter-chronological, beginning and ending in 2061, but moving through the 2040s and '50s as it proceeds. The sections set in 2061 might therefore be considered a frame within the frame. In the first of these, Alison recalls her own childish delight in play on the beach at Elwood, from the vantage point of what we will later learn to be the last year of her life. She wistfully concludes: "The ageing woman has what the child desired—the sea and eternal summer" (20). In the second, her son Francis records his intermittent diary entries from the period February 2056 to March 2061, concluding with that for March 20: "Mum is dead. . . . Once, she said very forcefully, 'I've had a *good* life, Francis. So full.' Full, I thought, of what would have been avoided in a saner world. . . . Billy came in later, but by then she was rambling about the past, about summertime and the glistening sea" (311).

Professor Wilson's historical reconstruction depicts the twenty-first century as a world of mass unemployment and social polarization, where rising sea levels have resulted in the inundation of the city's bay-side suburbs. As it opens, the poor "Swill" already live in high-rise tower blocks, the lower floors of which are progressively submerged; the wealthier "Sweet" live in suburbia on higher ground; the "Fringe" subsist in the zones between. In 2033 a third of Australia has been set aside for Asian population relocation; by 2041 the global population has reached ten billion, and the cost of iceberg tows and desaliniza-tion projects has brought the economy close to bankruptcy (29, 21, 30). On his sixth birthday in 2041, Francis and his nine-year-old brother, Teddy, are taken by their parents, Fred and Alison, to see the sea. What they find is a concrete wall "stretching out of sight in both directions." Francis's mother surprises him, however, by explaining, "This is Elwood and there was a beach here once. I used to paddle here. Then the water came up and there were the storm years and the pollution, and the water became too filthy." "It must be terrible over there in Newport when the river floods," she continues. "A high tide covers the ground levels of the tenements" (23–24). In 2044 Fred is laid off and commits suicide, leaving Allie and the boys to move to Newport (30–34). There they meet Billy Kovacs, who becomes Alison's lover, Francis's mentor, and the reader's guide to the social geography of an Australian dystopia.

In adolescence both Teddy and Francis abandon their mother in pursuit of upward social mobility, although both will eventually be returned "home." For Teddy, mobility comes through formal education, leading to Police Intelligence Recruit School (48–49) and thence to a career as a police intelligence officer. For Francis, it comes by way of an unusual aptitude for mental arithmetic, leading to a career as a "cally that spouts answers without using a key or chip" (57), for illicit business deals. Each acquires an appropriate sponsor: for Teddy, "Nick" Nikopoulos, a captain in Police Intelligence (113); for Francis, Mrs. Nola Parkes, the owner of a small import-export firm, who, after the collapse of the money economy, directs the state sub-department performing essentially the same function (72). Alison and the boys tell their own stories, Nikopoulos and Parkes retell the stories from different vantage points, and eventually these are all contextualized by Derrick, a senior state official with a quite literal power of life or death over the other characters (291). "Why don't you all go home?" he tells them. "We're finished here" (301).

The novel is at its most compelling in its representations of the everyday horror of life in the drowning towers, and of the sheer ferocity of status con-sciousness within a class structure mutating into a caste system. Both are recur-rent motifs in both the frame and core narratives, although in the latter they invariably prove more telling because more experientially grounded. There is a terrible poignancy, for example, to Francis's diary entries for February 11, 2056: "Five years back in the Fringe and resigned to it. Not reconciled, never that. What a hopeless, helpless lot the Swill are" (306). And March 22, 2057: "Three times this month the water has raced through the house. Sea water, salt and cold. We pay now for our great-grandparents' refusal to admit that tomorrow would eventually come" (306–7).

In the novel's final subplot, Captain Nikopoulos, Billy Kovacs, and Teddy discover that Mrs. Parkes and Francis are unwittingly involved in a state-sponsored conspiracy to "cull" the Swill, by means of a highly addictive "chewey" designed to produce infertility. "A State that strikes its own," Nola Parkes protests, "at random, for experiment, is past hope" (303). Arthur Derrick's response is directed at Turner's twentieth-century readers as much as at Parkes herself: "Nola, idealism was for the last century, when there was still time . . . we're down to more primitive needs. The sea will rise, the cities will grind to a halt and the people will desert them. . . . The State has no time to concern itself with moral quibbles" (304).

THE FUTURE AND THE FUTUROLOGY

The debates among the Autumn People in the frame narrative are clearly designed to make meaningful sense of the Greenhouse Culture. For Marin, its meaning is straightforward and simple: "They were wicked—they . . . ruined the world for all who came after . . . they *denied* history" (6). Lenna, however, conceives of their distant ancestors more sympathetically, as victims of the unintended consequences of their own collective action. "In the twentieth and twenty-first centuries," she tells Andra, "the entire planet stood with its fingers plugging dykes of its own creation until the sea washed over their muddled status quo. Literally" (13). Andra's own underlying response is incomprehension. Attempting to grapple with the social inequalities of the Greenhouse era, he can only ask: "*How did this division arise? Why no revolution?*" (16). Lenna suggests the answer might lie in the "rise of the Tower Bosses" to run "small states within the State." This allowed the poor "a measure of contentment," she explains, "by letting them run their own affairs." Moreover, she continues, the Political Security executive was also able "to convince the Tower Bosses that only a condition of status quo could preserve a collapsing civilization" (93). Ultimately, however, Andra remains as uncomprehending as ever and, after "three years and a dozen attempts," abandons his play (315).

A primary effect of this frame narrative is to blunt the force of dystopian inevitability driving the core narrative. "We're very well equipped to endure a million years of cold," Lenna tells Andra. . . . We have knowledge and we have the Forward Planning Centres. We'll make the change smoothly" (12–13). A secondary effect, however, is to suggest how little control humanity can actually exercise over its destiny. "It is history that makes *us*," Andra observes in his closing letter to Lenna. "The Greenhouse years should have shown that plainly; the Long Winter will render it inescapable" (315). Much the same is true of the frame within the frame when it moves forward into the late 2050s. For here we learn how Teddy, Nikopoulos, and Kovacs, and eventually even Francis and Derrick, become involved in an attempt by the "New Men" to organize the Swill in preparation "for the dark years coming" (310). The crisis will not be averted, we know from the thirty-first century, but "little human glimpses *do* help," Lenna will conclude, "if only in confirming our confidence in steadfast courage" (316).

The least persuasive aspect of the novel is in its understanding of how the crisis developed. In the "Postscript" Turner identifies six "major matters" of futurological concern: population growth, food shortage, mass unemployment, financial collapse, nuclear war, and the greenhouse effect, only one of which—nuclear war—fails to feature in the novel, because it seemed to him increasingly unlikely in any foreseeable future (98, 317–18). Empirically, Turner's predictions have often proven surprisingly close to the mark. In the novel, world population reaches ten billion during the early 2040s (21); according to the 2010 biennial revision of the United Nations *World Population Prospects*, it will reach between 8 billion (low projection) and 10.5 billion (high projection) by 2050.[20] In the novel, "two-thirds of the world starves" by 2045 (158). This might have seemed hopelessly pessimistic during the 1980s and 1990s, when world hunger rates were persistently trending downward. But the numbers of hungry people increased from 825 million people in 1995–97 to 857 million in 2000–2002, 873 million in 2004–6, and were projected to reach a historic high of 1.02 billion, or a sixth of the world's population, by the end of the decade.[21]

In the novel, the Australian and world unemployment rate has reached 90 percent by 2041 (25). Again, this must have seemed an extraordinarily gloomy prognosis on the book's first publication, as indeed it still is for Australia, where the unemployment rate was as low as 5.4 percent early in 2013.[22] But the situation is very different across much of the European Union, where Spain has an unemployment rate of 27.2 percent, Greece 27 percent, Portugal 17.7 percent, Ireland 14.7 percent, and France 10.7 percent.[23] Moreover, youth unemployment rates are higher still: in the fourth quarter of 2012, the figure was 57.9 percent for Greece, 55.2 percent for Spain, 38.4 percent for Portugal, 36.9 percent for Italy, 29.4 percent for Ireland, 25.4 percent for France, and 20.7 percent for the United Kingdom.[24]

In the novel, the financial crisis that bespeaks the collapse of the international monetary system comes in the 2040s; in reality, something like it almost certainly began during the Global Financial Crisis of 2007-12. In the novel, there have been no nuclear wars, but the "armaments factories" nonetheless continue "belching out weapons . . . for a war nobody dared start . . . and an industry nobody dared stop" (71); in reality, we have indeed been spared nuclear war, but nonetheless, as of January 2011, eight states possessed between them about 20,530 nuclear warheads, 5,000 ready for use and 2,000 on high operational alert.[25] In the novel, average temperatures have risen by 4½ degrees Celsius (8.1 degrees Fahrenheit) and sea levels by 30 centimeters (almost 12 inches) between 1990 and 2041 (74-75); the current projections of the Intergovernmental Panel on Climate Change are less dramatic, pointing to temperature increases of between 1.1 and 6.4 degrees Celsius (2-11.5 degrees Fahrenheit) between 1980-99 and 2090-99 and rises in sea level of between 18 and 59 centimeters (7-23 inches).[26] But there is near-consensus among climate scientists that current levels of atmospheric greenhouse gas are sufficient to alter global weather patterns to disastrous effect and also strong evidence that recent increases in extreme weather events, such as heat waves and flooding, are related to climate change.[27] The experience of Hurricane Katrina in 2005 and Hurricane Sandy in 2012 tends to confirm these suspicions.

Nonetheless, neither Turner nor his characters have any sense of which, if any, of these processes is the driver of the catastrophic crisis that overcame the Greenhouse Culture. One suspects his own answer might well have been essentially Malthusian. Mine, by contrast, would be Marxian; that is, that all six—including the nuclear arms race, if not nuclear war itself—are likely outcomes, within a world of finite resources, of any system of unregulated competitive capital accumulation akin to that sketched in *The Communist Manifesto* and analyzed in detail in *Capital*.[28] No doubt, the days are long gone when one could take a creative writer to task simply for being insufficiently Marxist. One might, however, still object to the implausibility of a thousand years of hindsight failing to provide the history profession with any generally accepted account of so significant an event as the collapse of an entire social order.

This isn't entirely fair: Professor Wilson has, in fact, written a five-thousand-page *Preliminary Survey of Factors Affecting the Collapse of the Greenhouse Culture in Australia* (13). But she decides to offer Andra her fictionalized account because Andra lacks the "general historical and technical grounding" necessary to understand the longer work (14). Three years later he still appears not to have read her *Survey*. So we do not know what, ultimately, drove the system into crisis. We do, however, know how Turner thought it could best be avoided—that is, by rational planning based on scientific advice. The epigraph to the novel, repeated in the "Postscript," is taken from Sir Macfarlane Burnet, the Australian virologist, immunologist, and public policy activist, who won the Nobel Prize for Medicine in 1960: "We must plan for five years ahead and twenty years and a hundred years" (317). Lenna Wilson gives Andra Andrasson essentially cognate advice: "Keep up as well as you can with the scientific information and you could be able to think usefully if the time for action should arrive. Otherwise, live as suits you. Be like the Swill, aware but unworried" (99).

The obvious question to ask is why, when faced with the incontrovertible evidence of impending catastrophe, not only the Swill, but also the Sweet, the Fringers, and the state, should have failed to plan adequately. The novel is clear that science had indeed sounded warnings. "As I understand it," Andra observes to Lenna, "*they* knew what was coming. . . . Yet they did nothing about it." "They fell into destruction," she replies, "because they *could* do nothing about it; they had started a sequence which had to run its course in unbalancing the climate" (13). What neither she nor Turner adequately explain, however, is *why* they were unable to do anything about it, why they had started this sequence, and why it had to run its course. Logically, the answer can only be that some social power prevented them from acting on the scientific advice.

Yet Turner is at pains to insist that his fictional Australian elites were essentially well motivated. As Marin tells Andra, "The idea was not oppression but preservation. The Sweet, educated and by and large the most competent sector of the population . . . were necessary to administer the State. With the collapse of trade and . . . industry the Swill became a burden on the economy, easier and cheaper to support if . . . concentrated into small areas" (91). When Derrick, the most senior representative of Turner's Australian state, defends the cull to Nola, he does so in similarly benevolent terms: "If there has to be a cull—and you know damned well that sooner or later there has to be—let's at least learn to do it with a minimum of suffering for the culled" (297). How could an elite so well educated, so competent, so concerned to minimize suffering—in short, so much like the one Macfarlane Burnet had hoped for—have failed to prevent such preventable catastrophe? The answer must be that it, in turn, had been confronted by social powers more powerful and also less rational than itself. No doubt, there are a range of possible candidates available in the real world, but none within the novel. The competition between global capitalist corporations fits the bill rather nicely, however, as explanation for this peculiar combination of historically unprecedented power with historically unprecedented irrationality.

Which leads me, finally, to the linked questions of Turner's representations of the state and of Australian insularity. The novel is clear that, when the world financial system collapses, the nation state takes over the administration of the economy. So Francis Conway recalls that "I was fifteen when the money system collapsed worldwide. That, in a single sentence, records the passing of . . . private-sector capitalism. . . . The commercial Sweet had spent months preparing for the changeover. . . . With forgetful speed it became *convenient* to present an allocation card at a State Distribution Store" (71). This is also the moment at which Mrs. Parkes's import-export company becomes a government sub-department. At one level, Turner is very astute here, recognizing the way conventional Left-versus-Right disputes over public-versus-private ownership actually obscure the more fundamental continuities in management and structure that persisted, in both Western and Eastern Europe, through both the socializations of the 1940s and '50s and the privatizations of the 1980s and '90s. But at another level, he ignores the likelihood that truly global corporations might not be as readily devolved into state subsidiaries as are national firms. No matter how convenient the fictional device of insularity might be to utopian writers, one is left wondering what had happened to the international parent companies, to the World Bank, the International Monetary Fund, the General Agreement on Tariffs and Trade, the United States Federal Reserve Bank, the European Central Bank, the People's Bank of China, and so on. Did the economy simply wither away, much as Engels had imagined the state might?[29] It seems unlikely.

Turner's *The Sea and Summer* is clearly not the game-changing climate change dystopia for which Christoff might have hoped. It has been out of print for over a decade, and unlike *On the Beach* it has never been adapted for film, television, or radio. As Verity Burgmann and Hans Baer recently observed: "*The Sea and Summer* is an extraordinarily well-crafted and gripping novel that received international awards and critical acclaim but has not received the popular attention it deserves."[30] Its reissue early in 2013, as the first Australian title to be included in Gollancz's list of "sf Masterworks," is thus especially to be welcomed. It has its flaws, no doubt, not least an underlying failure to acknowledge the deep contradictions between the emancipatory potential of scientific research and the political economy of late capitalism. Nonetheless, Turner's novel is long overdue positive critical reevaluation, and hopefully this essay will make some small contribution to that effect. I for one have very selfish reasons to hope so, for I live in Elwood, only a few minutes' walk from the beach where Alison Conway used to play as a little girl.

Notes

1. Nevil Shute, *On the Beach* (London: Heinemann, 1957).

2. Adam Roberts, *The History of Science Fiction* (Basingstoke, UK: Palgrave Macmillan, 2005), 56.

3. Ibid., 56–57, 85–86.

4. Lyman Tower Sargent, "Australian Utopian Literature: An Annotated, Chronological Bibliography, 1667–1999," *Utopian Studies* 10, no. 2 (1999): 138–73.

5. Denis Veiras, *L'histoire des Sévarambes*, ed. A. Rosenberg (1679; Paris: Champion, 2001); Denis Veiras, *The History of the Sevarambians: A Utopian Novel*, ed. J. C. Laursen and C. Masroori (1679; New York: SUNY Press, 2006).

6. Karl Marx, *Capital: A Critique of Political Economy*, vol. 1, trans. Samuel Moore and Edward Aveling (1867; London: Lawrence and Wishart, 1970), 768.

7. This is not true for North America or South America, Europe or Asia or Africa. Of the six commonly recognized inhabited continents, only Australia is truly an island.

8. Robyn Walton, "Utopian and Dystopian Impulses in Australia," *Overland* 173 (2003): 7.

9. Joseph Fraser, *Melbourne and Mars: My Mysterious Life on Two Planets; Extracts from the Diary of a Melbourne Merchant* (Melbourne: E. W. Cole, 1889).

10. George Turner, "Envoi," in *A Pursuit of Miracles: Eight Stories* (Adelaide: Aphelion Publications, 1990), 209.

11. George Turner, *The Sea and Summer* (London: Faber and Faber, 1987), 318.

12. Fredric Jameson, *Archaeologies of the Future: The Desire Called Utopia and Other Science Fictions* (London: Verso, 2005), 199.

13. Peter Christoff, "The End of the World as We Know It," *The Age*, January 15, 2008, 13.

14. George Turner, *Beloved Son* (London: Faber and Faber, 1978); George Turner, *Vaneglory* (London: Faber and Faber, 1981); George Turner, *Yesterday's Men* (London: Faber and Faber, 1983).

15. Turner, *Sea and Summer*; George Turner, *Brainchild* (New York: William Morrow, 1991); George Turner, *The Destiny Makers* (New York: William Morrow, 1993); George Turner, *Genetic Soldier* (New York: William Morrow, 1994); Turner, *Pursuit of Miracles*; George Turner, "And Now Time Doth Waste Me," in *Dreaming Down-Under*, ed. Jack Dann and Janeen Webb (Sydney: Voyager, 1998); George Turner, *Down There in Darkness* (New York: Tor Books, 1999).

16. George Turner, "The Fittest," in *Urban Fantasies*, ed. David King and Russell Blackford (Melbourne: Ebony Books, 1985).

17. George Turner, *Drowning Towers* (New York: Arbor House, 1987).

18. Turner, *Sea and Summer*, 3–16, 87–100, 315–16.

19. Ibid., 3–6. All subsequent references will be given in the text.

20. United Nations, Department of Economic and Social Affairs, Population Division, *World Population Prospects, the 2010 Revision* (New York: United Nations, 2010), http://esa .un.org/wpp/Other-Information/faq.htm#q3.

21. Food and Agricultural Organization of the United Nations, More People Than Ever Are Victims of Hunger, press release (Rome: FAO Media Centre, 2008), 1.

22. Turner would almost certainly have been surprised by how easily Australia withstood the global financial crisis that began in late 2007 (to date, it is the only OECD country to have escaped recession), as also by the probable cause: the long-term restructuring of Australian trade relationships away from America and Europe and toward China and India.

23. "List of Countries by Unemployment Rate," Wikipedia, http://en.wikipedia.org/wiki /List_of_countries_by_unemployment_rate (last accessed May 22, 2013).

24. European Commission, *Unemployment Statistics* (Luxembourg: Eurostat, 2012), http://epp.eurostat.ec.europa.eu/statistics_explained/index.php/Unemployment_statistics (last accessed May 22, 2013).

25. Stockholm Institute for Peace Research, *SIPRI Yearbook 2011: Armaments, Disarmaments and International Security* (Oxford: Oxford University Press, 2011), 319–20.

26. "Summary for Policymakers," *Climate Change 2007: The Physical Science Basis; Contribution of Working Group 1 to the Fourth Assessment Report of the Intergovernmental Panel on Climate Change*, ed. S. Solomon, D. Qin, M. Manning, Z. Chen, M. Marquis, K. B. Averyt, M. Tignor, and H. L. Miller (Cambridge: Cambridge University Press, 2007), 13.

27. Gabriele C. Hegerl, Francis W. Zwiers, Pascale Braconnot, Nathan P. Gillett, Yong Luo, Jose A. Marengo Orsini, Neville Nicholls, Joyce E. Penner, and Peter A. Stott, "Understanding and Attributing Climate Change" in Soloman et al., *Climate Change 2007*, 727; Stephen H. Schneider, Serguei Semenov, Anand Patwardhan, Ian Burton, Chris H. Magadza, Michael Oppenheimer, A. Barrie Pittock, Atiq Rahman, Joel B. Smith, Avelino Suarez, and Farhana Yamin, "Assessing Key Vulnerabilities and the Risk from Climate Change," in *Climate Change 2007: Impacts, Adaptation and Vulnerability; Contribution of Working Group 11 to the Fourth Assessment Report of the Intergovernmental Panel on Climate Change*, ed. Martin Parry, Osvaldo Canziani, Jean Palutikof, Paul van der Linden, and Clair Hanson (Cambridge: Cambridge University Press, 2007), 796.

28. Karl Marx and Friedrich Engels, *The Communist Manifesto*, trans. Samuel Moore (1848; Harmondsworth: Penguin, 1967), 80–90; Marx, *Capital*, vol. 1, 612–48; Karl Marx, *Capital: A Critique of Political Economy*, vol. 3, ed. Frederick Engels (1894; London: Lawrence and Wishart, 1972), 211–31.

29. Frederick Engels, *Anti-Dühring: Herr Eugen Dühring's Revolution in Science* (1878; Moscow: Foreign Languages Publishing House, 1959), 387.

30. Verity Burgmann and Hans A. Baer, *Climate Politics and the Climate Movement in Australia* (Melbourne: Melbourne University Press, 2012), 37.

Care, Gender, and the Climate-Changed Future

Maggie Gee's The Ice People

ADELINE JOHNS-PUTRA

Anthropogenic climate change, global warming, the sixth mass extinction event—whatever we want to call it—is now fixed in the science fiction imaginary: witness the recent success of Paolo Bacigalupi's *The Windup Girl* (2010) and consider Kim Stanley Robinson's near-future depiction of abrupt climate change in the *Science and the Capital* trilogy (2004, 2005, 2007).[1] Perhaps just as noteworthy is the recent spate of novels about future climate-changed worlds by authors who are not usually identified with sf. This includes writers of so-called "literary" fiction on both sides of the Atlantic: Margaret Atwood, T. C. Boyle, Cormac McCarthy, Will Self, and Jeanette Winterson.[2] Doris Lessing's return to futuristic world-building in her "Ifrik" novels is worth considering in this vein.[3] So too is British novelist Maggie Gee, and the environmental catastrophe she depicts in her novel *The Ice People* (1998).[4]

I will take as a critical given the idea that novels constitute spaces in which to explore inner life as it relates to the outer world of social appearance and action. The specific case of the climate change dystopian novel is no different. These dystopian visions consider the lived experience of climate change, and attempt to refract through the personal the almost incomprehensible scale of this global ecological crisis. They attempt, too, to adapt the conventions of the novel form—the insistently concrete questions of setting, character, and plot—to the notoriously abstract nature of climate change. Climate change, remarks philosopher of science Sheila Jasanoff, is "everywhere and nowhere"—everywhere because it is a global problem that has become a mainstay of our collective cultural life, but nowhere because it is knowable and solvable only at a remove, through the mediation of science and the machinery of politics.[5] In response to these representational contradictions, the climate change dystopia constructs a vision of the future in which ecological crisis can be denied no longer and a consideration of its causes and possible solutions delayed no further. More often than not, in such novels, humankind's culpability in a climate-changed world, as well as our potential for change, become part of the psychological texture of the narrative.

In their assessment of humanity's collective hubris, such novels imply that we simply have not cared enough, and that the way forward lies in caring more. Many climate change dystopias offer object lessons in environmentalist empathy, suggesting that—quite simply—love will let us save, survive, or escape an ecologically degraded planet. Where SF has conventionally reveled in techno-logical world-building, these novels push the dark, dystopian side of science to the extreme, and insist on care and love as its only viable alternative. In Lessing's *Mara and Dann* (1999) and its sequel *The Story of General Dann and Mara's Daughter, Griot and the Snow Dog* (2006), the eponymous sister and brother are a study in affective contrast: compassionate, motherly Mara is able to overcome the traumas of climate refugeeism, while emotionally blunted Dann finds only psychological dead ends. In Winterson's *The Stone Gods* (2008), we find three interlocked time-shifting stories; each pits an environmentally and emotion-ally attuned protagonist called Billie (or Billy) against a world of technological brutality. The novel's refrain that "Love is an intervention" is confirmed when the last Billie finds happiness in death, a moment that facilitates a return to her long-sought-for mother.[6] Both Lessing and Winterson offer up eco-fables of a sort, but even in more considered assessments of environmental disaster, loving care provides the moral. In Atwood's dystopia-turned-apocalypse, *Oryx and Crake* (2003), life on Earth has been genetically engineered and ecologically exploited beyond recognition. Crake, a gifted scientist who decides to destroy humankind to save the planet, is therefore both villain and savior. His ultra-rational, anti-emotional solution effectively places the notion of environmental care under watch, even while science is taken to task.[7] Atwood returns, however, to the notion of care as optimal response in her characterization of Toby in the companion novel *The Year of the Flood* (2009), which narrates the experiences of a group of female survivors of Crake's apocalypse. Life for the women in both pre-apocalyptic dystopia and post-apocalyptic devastation is a matter of surviving a violent male-dominated techno-capitalistic society, and only Toby's successful application of the teachings of a fringe eco-cult secures the women's survival.

Obviously, that "care" is the answer to rampant scientism and ecological cri-sis is not a new idea and is certainly not restricted to the contemporary novel.

Indeed, it seems so apparently plain that a concept such as "earthcare," put forward by Carolyn Merchant in the 1990s, seems hardly to need explanation. Merchant states her position unequivocally: "Humans, who have the power to destroy nonhuman nature and potentially themselves through science and technology, must exercise care and restraint by allowing nature's beings the freedom to continue to exist."[8] Yet Merchant's seemingly commonsense assumptions about how we should care more and destroy less skim over some difficult territory, and the same could be said for countless other environmentalist calls to care. Questions need to be asked—questions about who does the caring and who or what is cared for; about who gets to make these decisions; about what models of human-to-human care might be invoked in the process (friendship, kinship, marriage, parenthood, and so on); about the gender dynamics of our models of care; and, finally, about the efficacy of care in and of itself as an ethical, psychological, and political position. Such questions need to be asked, then, of the contemporary climate change dystopian novel.

The context for this chapter is the emergence of care in the climate change dystopia as an appropriate response to technologically driven ecological crisis. I first interrogate the notion that care per se represents a useful environmentalist ethic and then investigate the vexed gender dynamics of care. This discussion provides a basis for reading Gee's novel as a rare example of a climate change dystopia that actively evaluates the environmentalist ethic of care and its use as a counterpoint to a debased notion of techno-scientism. Ultimately, my contention is that the now ubiquitous celebration of care is deceptively simple, and that—in a time of ecological crisis—it warrants a close reading.

WHY CARE? WHO CARES?

By "care" I mean a feeling—translated into an ethos—of concern for and consideration of the needs of others, whether human or nonhuman. I certainly do not intend to suggest that an attitude of care is an inherently immoral or unethical stance to take, but I do wish to encourage a cautious approach to care, particularly when it is taken for granted as an ideal environmentalist outlook and its relationship to prior models of care insufficiently attended to. Perhaps another way to put this is that there is a need to complement care with thoughtfulness in both senses of the word, as a considerate and a considered response. This complicates any simple idea of care as pure or "natural" feeling versus science and technology as the product of ratiocinative reasoning.

Being thoughtful about environmentalist care means attending not just to what is said but to what is not said about it. What is often effaced is any distinction between what it means to care for humans and what it means to care for the nonhuman environment, even as it would seem that an admirable ethos of reciprocity and empathy is being celebrated. Such an elision occurs, for example, when Merchant defines earthcare as a "partnership ethic" that "means that both women and men can enter into mutual relationships with each other and the planet independently of gender."[9] When examined closely, the human other and the (nonhuman?) planet sit uneasily together on this list of potential partners. To what extent can one's relationship with another human be compared to, aligned with, perhaps mapped onto, one's relationship with the planet, homogeneously invoked? While generally positive, environmentalist relationship ethics such as Merchant's are more than a little presumptuous about speaking for "the planet" and all it betokens. The moment the planet (or the environment, or nature) is construed as a subject, it is subjectified, whether we like it or not.[10] Further, such discursive constructions as the planet or the environment conjure up suitably vague subjects, connoting a vast nonhuman and human collective. While appealingly inclusive on the one hand, the lack of specificity in these constructions render them all the more appropriable by the (human) initiator of that construction on the other. Needless to say, nature cannot speak for itself. The same may be said for rhetorical moves to equate care for the planet with care for tomorrow: what is concealed is the unevenness of the power dynamic between present and future, in addition to that between human and nonhuman. Worth considering here is political scientist John Barry's suggestion that constitutional democracies establish an ecological contract between citizens and state to safeguard the welfare of "both non-humans and future human descendants." In a parenthetical but utterly pivotal remark, Barry qualifies his conceptualization of these "moral subjects"; they are, he notes, "worthy of moral consideration but not morally responsible agents."[11] The imbalance that allocates responsibility, voice, initiative, and, of course, *care* to one side and not the other is all-important: it is an imbalance of power.

Perhaps care always conceals power imbalance. Care must always be contextualized, the circumstances of both agent and object of care always attended to. For relationships of care risk exploiting either or both carer and cared-for; the role of carer is often maintained within the norms of self-sacrifice, and, equally, that of cared-for easily defined by powerlessness. As Chris J. Cuomo reminds us, "Caring can be damaging to the carer if she neglects other responsibilities, including those she has to herself, by caring for another," while "caring for someone can be damaging to the object of care, who might be better off, or a better person, if she cares for herself."[12] Further, the narrow focus that care places on the dynamic of carer and cared-for has a distorting effect not only within this relationship but between this relationship and others. For Joan C. Tronto, parochialism ranks alongside paternalism as the "two primary dangers of care as a political ideal": "Those who are enmeshed in ongoing, continuing, relationships of care are likely to see the caring relationships that they are engaged in, and which they know best, as the most important."[13] What is often forgotten, then, is the way in which relations of care are imbricated within complex power plays, which need to be interrogated before promoting these as a model for political action.

These problems intensify when, as so often happens in environmentalist discourse, the caring relationship is intentionally aligned with gender roles. The deliberate gendering of the environmentalist ethic of care is best expressed as "ecomaternalism," that is, the biologically deterministic construction of women as mothers and the subsequent alignment of them with the nonhuman environment under the signs of fertility and nurture.[14] In the wide-ranging discourse of ecomaternalism, "nature" and "woman" share everything from caring responsibilities for all species, to the status of victimhood at the hands of apparently masculinist technologies, to an exclusive relationship akin to a mother-daughter bond.[15] The climate change dystopias I have briefly considered all invoke this commonplace of public and environmentalist discourse: motherhood confers a sense of environmentalist wisdom (for Lessing's Mara), becomes a nostalgic sign of what the world has lost (for Winterson's Billie), or is denied by *man*kind's exploitative impulse (for Atwood's Toby).

Ecomaternalism's assumption that core characteristics of womanhood parallel the core characteristics of "nature" is really a long-standing tenet of ecofeminism.[16] In the earliest "spiritual" manifestos of the ecofeminist movement, women are exhorted to celebrate a special relationship with nature, usually based on descriptions of early matriarchal religions. This relationship is underpinned by a shared capacity for connectedness—ecological interrelatedness and women's apparently natural and ancient empathy for others are somehow the same thing.[17] Meanwhile, later ecofeminist writing, which tends to couch the discussion not in spiritual terms but in political or cultural contexts, insists on a structural link between women and nature, the product of patriarchal degradation.[18] The focus is thus on "standpoints."[19] As Mary Mellor explains, "Women, because of their structural disadvantage, can see the dynamics of the relationship between humanity and nature more clearly than can (relatively) privileged men."[20] Despite differences across the ecofeminist spectrum, then, the movement has tended to be united in its emphasis on a woman-nature affinity. This affinity is grounded in the notion of care, whether as a "natural" compassion or a sociopolitical effect of exploitation. Thus heavily invested in the enduring cultural-feminist notion of an "ethic of care," the critical wisdom of ecofeminism and ecomaternalism is that women are continually psychologically conditioned to care, as girls, as wives, and, most of all, as mothers; this is what makes them more environmentally conscientious.[21]

The idea of a woman-nature affinity is deeply problematic, and its problems must be considered in any evaluation of ecomaternalist care as both the ground and the manifestation of this affinity. For one thing, the idea reiterates a centuries-old version of the link between women and nature as a stereotype of the female as less-than-human.[22] In a not entirely straightforward tactic of reappropriation, ecofeminism attempts to combat what it sees as the blanket domination of women and nature with the very logic of that domination. For another thing, the insistence on an unmediated woman-nature link has opened ecofeminism up to the dreaded charge of essentialism, or—to use Cuomo's more accurate phrase—"false universalization," that is, a simplistically unified construction of femaleness and female experience.[23] Certainly, it is easy to poke holes in the spiritual ecofeminist version of the woman-nature affinity, given that this relationship is never rigorously analyzed. Yet even the more stringent "standpoint" arguments of ecofeminism display a relatively unnuanced identity politics. Where an informed or learned understanding of the environment is seen as a fundamental part of the female standpoint, this can in turn be troped as an empathetic trait automatically shared by all women. Ariel Salleh, for example, posits that "the actuality of caring for the concrete needs of others gives rise to a morality of relatedness among ordinary women, and this sense of kinship seems to extend to the natural world." Although Salleh insists that her brand of ecofeminism "does not set up a static ontological prioritization of 'woman,'" she presents a vision of "women's exploitation," "women's oppression," and "women's lives," all monolithically conceptualized. In other words, political ecofeminism does not always evade the risk of falsely universalizing female experience as environmental care. One might say that sociological, rather than biological, essentialism is essentialism nonetheless.[24]

Sweeping remarks about immanent states of being or universal standpoints tend to distract from a more useful understanding of the ecofeminist construction of the woman-nature affinity as a set of political choices. Indeed, not just the logical inconsistencies of the ecofeminist position but the fact that these are often concealed or brushed aside in ecofeminist writing should alert us to the extent to which this has been a tactical move (and, it must be said, a reasonably successful one at that). Rather than an ontological fait accompli brought about by women's natural or material conditions, the ecomaternalist ethic of care is worth considering as an ideological decision made in response to global society's prevailing narrative of technological progress. Such an idea informs the critique of ecomaternalist care mounted by Catriona Sandilands. Attacking what she sees as the identity politics of care at the heart of "motherhood environmentalism," Sandilands proposes as an alternative "a recognition of the impossibility of identity."[25] That is, identity, particularly in a political sense, is only ever forged in the ironic gap between the idea of identity and the knowledge of the contingency of that idea. Sandilands goes as far as to advocate a "strategic essentialism" for ecofeminism, based on the knowledge that neither "woman" nor "nature" possesses any stability as a concept.[26] In suggesting that identity is partial and provisional, and that much is to be gained from an ironic assumption of identity (or identities), Sandilands builds on Donna Haraway's cyborg feminism and its celebration of technology for enabling an identity-less world.[27] Sandilands, however, is concerned with ironic play not just as liberating but as politically productive of action and change. An ironic ecofeminism enables the assumption of ecomaternalist identity in order to elicit sympathy from others, say, or to inspire them to action, but always with the awareness that such a performance is equivalent to—not expressive of—identity.

A critical—or, one should say, thoughtful—perspective on ecomaternalism, described here in the terms provided by Sandilands, resituates care from being a fundamental element of female "identity" to a portable and contestable component of an ideological stance. Such a perspective enhances a reading of Maggie Gee's The Ice People and, particularly, its departure from the ecomaternalist ethos that underpins so many other eco-dystopian novels. In her fictional account of gender politics in a climate-changing, technologically driven world, Gee destabilizes the ethic of care, not just as a female prerogative in the face of masculinist scientism but as an ideal environmentalist response in and of itself.

Gee's first novel, *Dying, in Other Words*, appeared in 1981, and was followed by eleven more novels and, most recently, an autobiography. Critically acclaimed from the outset, Gee nevertheless remained relatively underrated until the 2002 publication of *The White Family*, a searching narrative about racial prejudice in contemporary England. Described by one scholar as a "compassionate humanist feminist," Gee displays in her work an interest in the tenuousness of middle-class life, investigating the impact on individuals—usually networks of family and friends—when what is taken for granted in political, social, or environmental terms is somehow lost.[28] Disaster is often enacted stylistically and structurally too: catastrophes occur as interruptions to Gee's normally realist style, for example, in the black pages and bird-shaped visual poetry that represent nuclear holocaust in *The Burning Book* (1983) and in the montage of disconnected paragraphs after London is deluged in *The Flood* (2005).[29] Gee's oeuvre is also characterized by its interrogations of gender inequity beyond simple equations of masculinist oppression and female triumph. In 1995, around the time of writing *The Ice People*, Gee remarked on the "black and white" tendency of "women's fiction": "I think it's too obvious to be a woman, and a feminist woman, writing about nice women and horrid men, which is a lot of what's going on, isn't it?"[30] *The Ice People*, then, is characteristic of Gee's fiction in its exploration of "average" family life devastated by environmental, social, and political change. In other ways, however, it is a one-off. It is so far the only one of Gee's books definable as SF, set in a future world whose technologies are described in detail.[31] Moreover, it departs, quite intentionally, from her regular cast of characters, the intricate network of people that radiates outward from the White family and that tends to recur in her novels.[32] *The Ice People* thus focuses tightly on a single nuclear family unit, its psychological dramas serving as cause, effect, and even microcosm of national and global crisis.

The novel is set in the middle of the twenty-first century, when global warming suddenly experiences a rapid reversal: the world enters an ice age, and anthropogenic climate change is countered by an even more destructive "natural" climate phenomenon. Much of the novel, however, is told in flashback, as Saul, the first-person narrator, looks back on a life that spans the onset and development of one environmental crisis and then another.

Saul is born in London in 2005, at the start of what will become known as "the Tropical Time" (16). By his teens and twenties, global warming has reached its height, but this is a time during which young men and women—feeling all the invincibility of youth—revel in, rather than worry about, climatic conditions. Along with climate change, the world has also experienced dramatic social breakdown—epidemics of diseases such as Ebola and mutant HIVs have just about shut down entire governments, including Britain's. However, the younger generation's response to all this is a kind of apathy. The twentieth-century battle of the sexes has given way to mutual antagonism and a trend for gender segregation, or "segging" (23)—it has become fashionable for young men and women simply to avoid each other. Such a society is recognizable as the logical outcome of the kind of masculinist-scientist-capitalist complex in extremis detailed in other climate change dystopias; this is a world very like the worlds described by Atwood and Winterson. The biosphere has been irretrievably damaged, medical tinkering in the form of antibiotics has produced resistant strains of killer diseases, and an unrestrained profit motive only further encourages social, political, and environmental dysfunction.

Granting the similarities to other climate change dystopias, however, there is a crucial difference with Gee's novel. This lies, in part, in Saul's status as a narrator; specifically, it lies in authorial manipulation of narrator unreliability, producing an interpretive—and gendered—irony. Intelligent, likable Saul is made all the more sympathetic by his first-person perspective. The reader is initially drawn into the novel as one is drawn into the typical science fiction dystopia, through empathy with the protagonist as outsider: he or she is "like us," and together we negotiate the brave new world of the text. It is difficult not to identify with Saul as he falls in love and settles down in an "old-fashioned," "twentieth-century" kind of way (28). However, Saul's seemingly commonsense description of his society is strikingly unreflective of the gender dynamics at play. He describes segging but cannot understand it. He cannot see, for example, that it is motivated by women, as a backlash against what they perceive to be the gender inequalities that still predominate in twenty-first-century life. Thus, it is Saul's wife, Sarah, who provides us with an alternative insight into segging. Employed as part of a state initiative to combat segging and to improve falling fertility rates, she teaches teenagers how to fall in love and finds that, while boys are receptive enough to the idea of "having women to love and support them," girls are "not all that excited about developing their nurturing sides" (36). The girls' concerns center on care as power imbalance: "I want to look after kids. . . . But why should I want to look after a man? They're not babies" (36). Sarah's attempts to explain the girls' perspective to Saul actually provokes an example of such imbalance:

"They're quite thoughtful, when you listen to them. I think they have a point about housework, too."

"But you enjoy it," I said. "Partly because you're so good at it. Your food always looks so beautiful. I mean, you turn that side of things into pure pleasure. I wish those girls could see what you do."

She didn't smile, but nodded slowly. "It takes a lot of time, though, Saul, you know."

"Time well spent," I said, kissing her. (37)

Sarah's concerns and Saul's response only clarify the inequities of care in traditional male-female relations so familiar to twentieth-century feminism: it is not just that the woman's conventional role is to provide care, but care is too often neither returned nor adequately rewarded.

The novel's analysis of gender relations occurs alongside its depiction of increasing environmental chaos. First, the breakdown of Saul and Sarah's marriage is reflective of a global gender conflict: as Sarah and many women like her turn militant in their separatism, men like Saul become more resentful of women, more insistent on cultivating what they see as masculine traits, and, yet, more desiring of conventionally feminine care and attention. Then, the world descends into an ice age, and the trajectory of anthropogenic climate change is abruptly reversed. It is not just that Saul and Sarah's battle of the sexes is part of an all-out war; it is significant that it takes place within the novel's trajectory of two global climatic events—anthropogenic climate change and the onset of glaciation. In other words, the novel's interrogation of shifts in gender dynamics is, when read alongside its two environmental crises, also an interrogation of two very different—and differently gendered—solutions to these crises. That is, the novel first critiques a very masculinist response to *man*-made global warming and then studies an ecomaternalist response to the ice age crisis.

The initial crisis of global warming is readable as a component of a larger whole, as one of the outcomes of a thoughtless, even arrogant, indulgence in a technologically enhanced lifestyle. Once the reader becomes attentive to Saul's unreliability as a narrator, it is possible to read his careless description of these early days as part of a broader ideological context for runaway climate change: his casual jetting around the world for easy, exotic holidays; his soaking up the heat with no anxiety about the rate of temperature increase; his embracing a career in nano-engineering, with no consideration that technology might offer a solution to environmental crisis rather than a path to more affluence. Through it all, Saul's experience—"I felt on the brink of owning the world. I was a man, and human beings ran the planet. . . . I was tall, and strong, and a techie, which qualified me for a lifetime's good money" (24)—is perceptibly gendered.

The onset of the ice age, however, coincides with the rise of an alternative, female political power. Wicca, the women's collective that Sarah joins during one of her many separations from Saul, is, in Saul's words, founded on "a wacky female nature worship, centring on 'the Hidden Goddess,' who apparently 'gave suck' to us all" (117). Wicca successfully wins the national elections on the promise of a "caring revolution" (137), with the tagline "Vote for Wicca. Wicca Cares" (138). This ecomaternalist appropriation of care—effectively rejecting the burden of caring for men but purporting to care for everything else—is expressed in Wicca's promises of "'revaluing nature,' 'nurturing the future'; 'the future is green.' We would 'bloom again' with the 'cooling earth.' We would 'give thanks to the Goddess' for water" (137). When the effects of glaciation become impossible to ignore, however, Wicca's technophobic stance means that it refuses to take seriously the "techfixes" (147) suggested by scientists, and neglects to meet the challenge of securing the necessary international cooperation and funding. In short, Wicca's ecomaternalist revolution, established as an alternative to the anti-nature, pro-technology, globally warmed generation, fails in its attempts to cope with the second environmental crisis. It gets caught up in arguments with its rivals, a men's collective that emerges as a kind of backlash to the backlash. The two sides become bogged down in a macro-version of Saul and Sarah's lifelong argument. Gender relations are exposed as a depressingly insoluble conundrum—where there is difference there is inequity—in both the "old-fashioned" world of domestic squabbles and the "segged" world of political point-scoring. The biosphere suffers collateral damage in the process.

The risks of an ethic of care are here laid bare. Wicca's political campaigning is a reminder of the extent to which ecomaternalist care is an ideological tool rather than an inherent aspect of female identity. To note this, recalling Sandilands, is not to undermine an ethic of care but to subject it to a different kind of assessment: ecomaternalism can be useful as a platform on which to initiate sociopolitical good. In the case of Wicca, however, it becomes not just means but an end, a way of asserting control in order to retain control, particularly over men. Care in this instance becomes a weapon in a gendered power play, with women claiming a monopoly on care and men counterclaiming it as something they can do just as well. This is evident in the controversy that escalates over the domestic robots called "Doves" (87). It is Saul's brand of nanotechnology that is responsible for the Doves; thus, "as a techie, [he] is full of admiration for the basic Dove design" (94). Moreover, the cute, anthropomorphic Doves prove wildly popular with men like Saul, who rely on them not just for domestic chores but for affection and company. Meanwhile, the Wicca government exploits primarily female fears over incidents in which malfunctioning Doves have attacked animals and children, and the robots are banned. To men, the Doves symbolize the successful masculinist appropriation of the traditionally female functions of care; to women, they represent a flawed counterfeit of an authentically feminine trait. In all, the Doves underline the fraught gender politics of care.

The Doves' destructive side also points to the dark side of care itself. *The Ice People* is a sustained reflection on the efficacy of care as a human response. As Tronto reminds us, a relationship of care is actually definable by selfishness, as the decision to care is necessarily about caring for one (or some) over others. Competing priorities of care are not always compatible. Neither Sarah nor Saul could be easily described as uncaring, but their arguments about care have a destructive effect on the person they would seem to care most about—their son. Correspondingly, the wider gender conflict about who cares more proves detrimental to the nonhuman environment, one of the supposed beneficiaries of that debate. (In this implicit link between child and environment, that common slippage between caring for the "environment" and caring for the "future" cannot escape notice.) Of course, this critique is refracted ironically through Saul's first-person narrative, meaning that an understanding of the limitations of care must be gained alongside a compassionate response to this portrayal of fatherly love, for, because Saul cares about his son, the reader cannot help caring about him. As the world enters the ice age in earnest and European society begins to come apart, Saul abducts his son Luke from the Wicca commune. They head for the relative warmth and political stability of Africa (in another ironic comment, this time on the racial politics of environmental justice).[33] However, if Wicca's brand of caring could not save the day and the planet, neither can Saul's. He stops at nothing to save his son, but this means caring for no one else. Not only do they rob fellow refugees; they leave for dead the sympathetic Wicca member Briony who travels with them when they flee attackers in Spain.[34] Here, parental care has become Darwinian survivalism: "I told myself it was all for him. I had even sacrificed Briony" (272). Saul's regrets that Sarah would never acknowledge his love for their son—"She never knew how much I'd loved him. . . . She didn't know how much I'd cared for him" (301)—must coexist with his realization at the end of his life that "I wasn't a hero, or a villain, or any of the things they say in stories—but merely one tiny unit of biology, stopping at nothing to save his genes" (273). Luke, as it turns out, rejects this kind of care; he and many others of his generation run away from their fragile, fighting families and become the Wild Children of the Ice Age.

Yet this novel must not be misunderstood as a preference for one kind of care against another, for it is, if anything, a careful weighing up of care per se. The novel exhibits a deeply ironic interest in care—it cares about care and draws us in on this basis. Still, it reminds us that the dangers of care reside both in its metaphorical and its metonymic slips: it is too easily used as an alibi (that is, a symbol that conceals its status as symbol) for power, and it is also proximal to much less altruistic tendencies such as jealousy, possessiveness, and exceptionalism. Against Saul's selfish, old-fashioned care sits Wicca's failed and vindictive ideology of care, and, against these again, sits the nonsensical affection of the Doves. Then, there is the version of human relations with which the novel ends: the Wild Children and their animalistic pursuit of only the most basic needs. Looking back on his life, which he now spends with an entirely new generation of the ice age, the aging Saul asks: "How can I explain it to these crazy kids, who live for food, and fire, and sex? How love was so important to us. How tiny shades of wants and wishes made us fight, and sob, and part" (63). Saul, in other words, recognizes both the apparent necessity and the shortcomings of love and care in his climate-changed world.

The Ice People is, in common with other climate change dystopias, about an inadequacy in the contemporary human response to the environment. However, unlike these, Maggie Gee's thoughtful vision of the future is no simple account of the inadequacy of the contemporary response in terms of a failure to recognize the necessity of care. What makes this climate change dystopia so poignant is that, first, it is about the inevitability of care in shaping our responsibilities to each other and to the environment, and then it is about the terrible cost of taking care for granted as a way of fulfilling these responsibilities.

Notes

The research leading to this paper was carried out while a Visiting Fellow with the Humanities Research Centre, RSHA, Australian National University.

1. Paolo Bacigalupi, *The Windup Girl* (San Francisco: Night Shade, 2010); Kim Stanley Robinson, *Forty Signs of Rain* (2004; London: HarperCollins, 2005), *Fifty Degrees Below* (2005; London: HarperCollins, 2006), and *Sixty Days and Counting* (London: HarperCollins, 2007). For a comprehensive review of fictional treatments of climate change, see Adam

Trexler and Adeline Johns-Putra, "Climate Change in Literature and Literary Criticism," *Wiley Interdisciplinary Reviews: Climate Change* 2, no. 2 (2011): 185–200.

2. Margaret Atwood, *Oryx and Crake* (2003; London: Virago, 2004), and *The Year of the Flood* (2009; London: Virago, 2010); T. Coraghessan Boyle, *A Friend of the Earth* (2000; London: Bloomsbury, 2001); Cormac McCarthy, *The Road* (2006, London: Picador, 2007); Will Self, *The Book of Dave: A Revelation of the Recent Past and Distant Future* (2006; London: Penguin, 2007); Jeanette Winterson, *The Stone Gods* (London: Penguin, 2008).

3. Doris Lessing, *Mara and Dann* (London: Flamingo, 1999), and *The Story of General Dann and Mara's Daughter, Griot and the Snow Dog* (2006; London: Harper Perennial, 2007).

4. Maggie Gee, *The Ice People* (1998; London: Telegram, 2008). Future references to this novel will be presented in parentheses in the main text.

5. Sheila Jasanoff, "A New Climate for Society," *Theory Culture Society* 27 (2010): 237.

6. Winterson, *Stone Gods*, 83.

7. One could say that Atwood exposes the ethical fine line between environmentalism and misanthropy that characterizes deep green sabotage movements: a similar dilemma on a smaller scale faces eco-warrior Ty Tierwater in Boyle, *Friend of the Earth*.

8. Carolyn Merchant, *Earthcare: Women and the Environment* (London: Routledge, 1995), xix.

9. Ibid., 216.

10. For a brief but effective discussion of the "subjectivation" of nature in environmentalist discourse, see Catriona Sandilands, *The Good-Natured Feminist: Ecofeminism and the Quest for Democracy* (Minneapolis: University of Minnesota Press, 1999), 77–78.

11. John Barry, "Sustainability, Political Judgement and Citizenship: Connecting Green Politics and Democracy," in *Democracy and Green Political Thought: Sustainability, Rights and Citizenship*, ed. Brian Doherty and Marius de Geus (London: Routledge, 1996), 122.

12. Chris J. Cuomo, *Feminism and Ecological Communities: An Ethic of Flourishing* (London: Routledge, 1998), 129.

13. Joan C. Tronto, *Moral Boundaries: A Political Argument for an Ethic of Care* (New York: Routledge, 1993), 170–71. For a more recent critique of the promotion of personal care as a political ideal, see Sherilyn MacGregor, *Beyond Mothering Earth: Ecological Citizenship and the Politics of Care* (Vancouver: University of British Columbia Press, 2006), 57–80.

14. The phrase comes from MacGregor, *Beyond Mothering Earth*, 20.

15. However, McCarthy's *The Road* remains an important exception. The novel, which some have read as a climate change narrative even though the catalyst for the destruction of the biosphere is never named, is a sparse but poignant description of the love between a father and son as they make their way through the devastated landscape. Yet love is carefully sifted here, for it is not clear if the father's steadfast, protective love for his son is really the best way to make sense of one's place in a dying world, compared with the boy's more trusting compassion for others.

16. For the invention of the term *ecoféminisme*, see Françoise d'Eaubonne, *Féminisme ou la mort* (Paris: Femme et Mouvement, 1974); see also Barbara T. Gates, "A Root of Ecofeminism: *Ecoféminisme*," in *Ecofeminist Literary Criticism: Theory, Interpretation,*

Pedagogy, ed. Greta Gaard and Patrick D. Murphy (Urbana: University of Illinois Press, 1998), 15–22.

17. For Andrée Collard, for example, the apparent tendency in matriarchal religions toward respect for nature means that motherhood can be invoked as the essential link between women and the environment. Collard writes of early goddess societies, "Women's skills developed beyond her famed endurance and purveyance of care and wellbeing. She learned the ways of plants. She learned the ways of other creatures of the land, air and sea. She learned them in a spirit of recognition and respect. And with a similar spirit, she partook of them" (11). This allows Collard to state unequivocally, "Pregnancies and child-bearing . . . are a woman's link to the natural world and the hunted animals that are part of that world" (14–15); See Andrée Collard with Joyce Contrucci, *Rape of the Wild: Man's Violence against Animals and the Earth* (London: Women's Press, 1988).

18. See, for example, Mary Mellor's version of ecofeminist political economy: "Feminism is concerned with the way in which women in general have been subordinated to men in general. Ecologists are concerned that human activity is destroying the viability of ecosystems. Ecofeminist political economy argues that the two are linked. This linkage is not seen as stemming from some essentialist female identification with nature, for which some early ecofeminists were criticised, but from women's position in society, particularly in relation to masculine-dominated economic systems." See Mary Mellor, "Ecofeminist Political Economy and the Politics of Money," in *Eco-Sufficiency and Global Justice: Women Write Political Ecology*, ed. Ariel Salleh (London: Pluto Books, 2009), 251.

19. Deborah Slicer, "Toward an Ecofeminist Standpoint Theory: Bodies as Grounds," in *Ecofeminist Literary Criticism: Theory, Interpretation, Pedagogy*, ed. Greta Gaard and Patrick D. Murphy (Urbana: University of Illinois Press, 1998), 49–73.

20. Mellor, *Feminism and Ecology* (London: Polity, 1997), 105–6.

21. The "ethic of care" was first put forward by Carol Gilligan, *In a Different Voice: Psychological Theory and Women's Development* (Cambridge, MA: Harvard University Press, 1982), and further disseminated by Nel Noddings, *Caring: A Feminine Approach to Ethics and Moral Education* (Berkeley: University of California Press, 1984).

22. This is despite the careful historicist work by some ecofeminists in discovering and interrogating a dualistic system of thinking about women and nature at the heart of patriarchal thought. See, for example, Sherry B. Ortner, "Is Female to Male as Nature Is to Culture?" in *Woman, Culture, and Society*, ed. Michelle Zimbalist Rosaldo and Louise Lamphere (Stanford, CA: Stanford University Press, 1974), 67–87; Carolyn Merchant, *The Death of Nature: Women, Ecology, and the Scientific Revolution* (1980; San Francisco: HarperCollins, 1990); and Val Plumwood, *Feminism and the Mastery of Nature* (London: Routledge, 1993).

23. Cuomo, *Feminism and Ecological Communities*, 117.

24. Indeed, as Sandilands reminds us, "social construction and essentialism are not necessarily opposed concepts"; Sandilands, *Good-Natured Feminist*, 71.

25. Ibid., xiii, 209.

26. Ibid., 121.

27. Donna Haraway, "A Cyborg Manifesto: Science, Technology, and Socialist-Feminism

in the Late Twentieth Century," in *Simians, Cyborgs and Women: The Reinvention of Nature* (London: Free Association Books, 1991), 149–81. Material feminist Karen Barad has recently updated such ecofeminist critiques by showing how our relationship with the nonhuman is better understood in terms of agency rather than (gendered) identity, specifically, as what she calls "agential intra-action"; "Posthumanist Performativity: Toward an Understanding of How Matter Comes to Matter," *Signs: Journal of Women in Culture and Society* 28, no. 3 (2003): 801–31.

28. John Sears, "'Making Sorrow Speak': Maggie Gee's Novels," in *Contemporary British Women Writers*, ed. Emma Parker (Cambridge: D. S. Brewer, 2004), 55.

29. Maggie Gee, *The Burning Book* (1983; London: Faber, 1985), and *The Flood* (London: Saqi, 2005).

30. Margaret McKay, "An Interview with Maggie Gee," *Studia Neophilogica* 69, no. 2 (1997): 216.

31. Both *The Flood* (2004) and *Where Are the Snows* (2006) come closest to this, being near-future treatments of environmental crisis; Gee, *Where Are the Snows* (London: Telegram, 2006).

32. According to Gee, the novel was written as a distraction from the disappointment of her publisher's rejection of *The White Family* for, among other things, its controversial race issues: "So I wrote another book, *The Ice People*, which saved me from despair. It dealt with a bi-racial child, but in a very different, light way"; Maya Jaggi, "Maya Jaggi in Conversation with Maggie Gee: *The White Family*," *Wasafiri* 17, no. 39 (2002): 6.

33. That Saul is of mixed race is another aspect of Gee's interrogation of the race politics of environmental crisis and justice, which is, unfortunately, outside the scope of this essay.

34. Saul's survivalist tactics and Luke's compassionate protests against these are echoed by McCarthy's father and son in *The Road*, which, in a comparable way, questions the seemingly unquestionable "good" of parental care as a way of surviving environmental destruction.

Future Ecologies, Current Crisis

Ecological Concern in
South African Speculative Fiction

ELZETTE STEENKAMP

8

In a 2004 essay titled "Science Fiction in South Africa," Deirdre Byrne laments "the regrettable dearth . . . of published science fiction and science fiction readers" in South Africa. Byrne argues that "one cannot expect an advanced awareness of technological or scientific developments" or "even a basic acquaintance with published literature" in a country where the majority of the population live well below the breadline, the spread of HIV/AIDS is rampant, and levels of technological literacy are extremely low.[1] Fast-forward a decade, and the prospects of the South African SF scene seem far less dismal. In 2009, South African–born Neill Blomkamp's Oscar-nominated film *District 9* captured the imagination of audiences worldwide, resulting in an unprecedented boom in local science fiction and fantasy. Add to this the success of Lauren Beukes's Arthur C. Clarke Award–winning SF noir, *Zoo City* (2010), and South African speculative fiction appears to be blipping happily on the international radar.

Aside from comparisons between the sudden international popularity of South African speculative fiction and the meteoric rise of the Scandinavian crime novel,[2] very little has been written in the way of scholarly articles examining the role of science fiction, fantasy, and speculative fiction in South Africa literature. This is partially due to science fiction's association with "pulp" fiction and lowbrow escapism, but can also be attributed to the widely held perception that SF has more to do with shiny machines and spaceships than with actual people. Because of the country's complex history of colonial and apartheid oppression, much attention is paid to the narrative representation of human conflict, and particularly the issues of race and gender, in South African literature; the neglect of SF as an area of critical inquiry in South Africa is based on the mistaken belief that the genre does not address these sorts of "real world" issues. In "Subversive, Undisciplined and Ideologically Unsound or Why Don't South Africans Like Fantasy?" Felicity Wood asks: "Why is there so little fantasy in English South African literature?" Wood attributes this "resistance to fantasy" to the fact that "it's sometimes perceived as being distinct from reality, an escape from it, and thus the way in which fantasy serves as a means of exploring reality has often not been adequately acknowledged."[3] This chapter argues that South African speculative fiction is in fact deeply concerned with the very issue that "serious" South African authors have been examining for many years—alterity.

The notion that SF is more concerned with technology than human lives is explored in Ursula Le Guin's "Science Fiction and Mrs. Brown." Le Guin employs Virginia Woolf's conception of "Mrs. Brown"[4] as representative of a fully rounded, "human" literary character, in order to comment on the apparent lack of "real people" in fantasy and science fiction narratives.[5] Le Guin questions whether there is room for the "too *round*" Mrs. Brown in the "gleaming spaceships" of SF—in short, whether "a science fiction writer [can] write a novel."[6]

Le Guin, inspired by a hobbit named Frodo who looks very much like Mrs. Brown, concludes that SF *is* "worth talking about, because it is a promise of continued life for the imagination, a good tool, an enlargement of consciousness, a possible glimpse, against a vast dark background, of the very frail, very heroic figure of Mrs. Brown."[7] The questions surrounding Le Guin's Mrs. Brown are equally important from a South African perspective. What place does Mrs. Brown's South African counterpart—let's call her Mrs. Khumalo, or Mrs. van der Merwe for that matter[8]—have in a spaceship equipped with ray guns? Surely we cannot dismiss the plight of Mrs. van der Merwe, for she has for too long been restricted to impoverished townships, forcefully displaced, left to die in concentration camps, subjugated, and ignored. The region's legacy of violence demands that the stories told in post-apartheid South Africa should be those of *real* people. But can we successfully write about *real* South Africans who happen to be clones, or genetically engineered donors, or cyborgs?

This chapter argues that the field of South African speculative fiction presents a rich, uncultivated area of study that allows for the exploration of a range of themes relevant to the South African condition, including (but by no means restricted to) issues of gendered and racialized inequity. It examines how South African speculative narratives not only explore the construction of identity in a deeply divided and rapidly changing society, but also the ways in which human beings place themselves in relation to nature and nonhumans and form notions of "ecological" belonging.

These crises of self and place are taken up in South African speculative fiction, most notably through the use of the altered body and the post-apocalyptic wasteland. These tropes are of course well established in Western European and North American SF as well. In the South African speculative texts to be examined in this chapter, the symbolic *novum* of the altered body (in the form of the alien, clone, or cyborg) is utilized in order to comment on racial and gendered relations in South Africa, and related manifestations of alienation and displacement. These texts interrogate the notion of a nuanced and complex identity and its relation to a myriad of hierarchized other(s), proposing afresh the slipperiness of the boundaries between self and seemingly "alien" other.

These encounters with alterity are played out against the backdrop of ecological catastrophe, pointing to an engagement with ecological concerns, particularly the dire threat to Earth's ecosystem as a result of the massive impact of global warming, pollution, the human population's overexploitation of natural resources, and ruthless experimentation with weapons of mass destruction. Identity formation in post-apartheid South Africa is a multifaceted, entangled process, influenced not only by a traumatic history of oppression but also by increased exposure to globalizing supranational factors. In an era of genetic engineering, plastic surgery, and rapid advances in technology and science, questions regarding what constitutes a human being have become ever more complex. What's more, the idea of environmental belonging, the positioning of the self in relation to the natural world, is inevitably problematic for a nation still very much burdened by a violent past characterized by racial segregation, land disputes, forced removals, and the restriction of movement across the land in the form of pass laws. Within a South African context, the notion of belonging to a particular environment or ecosystem is inevitably interwoven with questions regarding the adequate distribution and conservation of natural resources. Lawrence Buell asserts that "for half a century science fiction has taken a keen, if not consistent interest in ecology, in planetary endangerment, in environmental ethics, in humankind's relation to the nonhuman world."[9] Although the trope of an ecologically endangered futuristic landscape is a key feature of post-apartheid South African speculative fiction, the ecological message is often subordinate to the human drama that unfolds on the page. This chapter examines the ways in which the altered bodies presented in Jane Rosenthal's futuristic novel *Souvenir* and Neill Blomkamp's SF film *District 9* attempt to establish a sense of self eroded by dislocation, problematizing the notion of belonging to a specific place or ecology, but ultimately envisioning new and fruitful ways of connecting with both human and nonhuman others.

Set in late twenty-first-century South Africa, Jane Rosenthal's futuristic novel *Souvenir* is primarily concerned with the fragmentary nature of the female experience, a splintering that is expressed through the symbolic *novum* of the clone. Rosenthal's young protagonist, Souvenir Petersen, or Souvie, is a "barbi-clone"—one of "various types cloned from the ideal women of the early years of the century, whether blonde, oriental or dark."[10] Viewed by some as little more than a cloned sex slave and domestic worker, the extraordinarily beautiful, blond Souvenir attempts to escape the discriminatory treatment of others by seeking solitude on a journey across a vastly altered, ecologically threatened Karoo landscape.

Rosenthal draws on scientific postulation, specifically Andy McCaffrey's article "Antarctica's 'Deep Impact' Threat," in order to explore the possible ramifications for South Africa if West Antarctica's ice sheet were to melt.[11] Souvenir's futuristic South Africa is geographically and climatologically altered by storms and tsunamis caused by exactly this ecological catastrophe. The region is plagued by "turbulent weather and heavy rain . . . something that had to be endured while the icebergs passed by, sometimes taking several weeks" (139), and Souvie wryly notes that "the science of weather prediction had long been in disarray, and the only thing that could safely be predicted was that it was hot and would get hotter" (12).

Souvenir can be read as a recasting of the popular genre of the Karoo travelogue. Souvie's expedition is as much a journey of scientific endeavor (she travels with an itinerant lepidopterist) as a quest for self-discovery—not only a means of coming to terms with her own contradictory feelings regarding her clone status, but also an attempt to inscribe herself in the history of her adoptive family, the Petersens. The novel is interspersed with diary entries by Aunt Jem, Souvie's adoptive father's aunt "from the days when everyone had families," a farmer and artist who, seventy years prior to Souvie's tale, made a similar passage across the Karoo (18). A kind of freelance gardener, Aunt Jem traveled the Karoo, leaving behind rosebush hedges and avenues on several farms in the area. Guided by the journal, Souvenir retraces the footsteps of her nonbiological aunt, finding in what remains of Jem's rosebushes and hedges a connection not only to a family, but also to an otherwise hostile and unpredictable landscape.

In "Whales, Clones and Two Ecological Novels," Wendy Woodward suggests that Obed Will Obenbara, the lepidopterist who later becomes Souvenir's husband, "exhibits nostalgia for the days of colonial exploration and scientific amateurism in the best meaning of the word, as one who loves what he does."[12] In Rosenthal's words, "Obed Will sees himself as a gentleman-adventurer of scientific bent. . . . modelled on explorers of the seventeenth and eighteenth centuries, that tribe of Europeans—Dutch, French and English—who came to Africa. He felt he was dressed in the manner of Le Vaillant or Lichtenstein" (35).

Parallels can be drawn between Woodward's reading of Obed Will as intrepid explorer, interested only in the pursuit of knowledge, and the reputation of François Le Vaillant, the eighteenth-century French ornithologist on whom Obed Will Obenbara models himself, as gentlemanly scholar. Le Vaillant undertook two journeys across the Cape Colony between 1781 and 1784, the first of which took him through the Karoo. Large parts of Le Vaillant's accounts of these journeys (published as two volumes in 1790 and 1795 respectively) are considered to be embroidered. Similarly, his magnum opus, the six-volume *Histoire naturelle des oiseaux d'Afrique* (1796–1810) is riddled with inconsistencies and mere fabrications. Stewart Crehan comes to Le Vaillant's defense, arguing that the "insatiable curiosity which we find in Le Vaillant . . . is not the same as a repressive, egocentric desire for control. . . . His visit to South Africa as a student of natural history was motivated not by acquisitiveness but by a desire to discover new information."[13]

In some ways, Le Vaillant's fabulous accounts of the animals and inhabitants of the Cape of Good Hope (and specifically the Karoo) in the late eighteenth century can be seen as the precursor to Rosenthal's fantastic travel narrative. As much as the entertaining nature of Le Vaillant's penchant for exaggeration belies the more sinister expansionist agendas of his colonial counterparts, Rosenthal's account of Obed Will's encounters with fabulous composite creatures such as the "badass" (a genetic mutation that is part donkey and part baboon) is rooted in suspicion regarding modern-day advances in genetic engineering and the possibility of the ruthless exploitation of such technology for profit. Obed Will's mapping of the butterfly population of the Karoo, and Souvenir's retracing of the journey documented in Aunt Jem's botanical journal (an artifact similar to Le Vaillant's illustrated map of his voyages) are indeed attempts at claiming ownership over a place, inscribing the Karoo with their presence. However, much like claims surrounding the intrepid Le Vaillant's benign exploration, these characters' attempts to write themselves into the landscape are presented as a nonthreatening desire to belong. Obed Will's nostalgia for a world still untouched by humankind is reminiscent of Coetzee's Michael K's wish for a piece of land, existing outside the violent grasp of history, where he can live lightly off the land:

> Obed Will knew that this old, almost pre-colonial world was long gone. Yet when-
> ever he thought this he immediately felt a desire to deny or contradict it, arise in
> him. Somewhere there must be pockets, small corners, tops of mountains, difficult
> and inaccessible ravines, dry inhospitable canyons where there were no traces of
> the present, where no one had ever lived or farmed, not even the Khoikhoi. Obed
> Will, suffering from a surfeit of the crowded present in city life, longed for that
> past wilderness. (35–36)

This nonacquisitive approach to belonging to a specific place is proposed in Neil Evernden's "Beyond Ecology." Evernden suggests that the "act of naming" can be a fruitful process through which one may learn to see oneself as imbedded in the physical environment, as part of a complex network of life forms:

> The act of naming may itself be a part of the process of establishing a sense of
> place. This is fairly easy to understand in a personal sense, that is, giving per-
> sonal names to special components of a place, but it also may apply in the case of
> generic names. Perhaps the naturalist, with his penchant for learning the names
> of everything, is establishing a global place, making the world his home, just as the
> "primitive" hunter did on the territory of his tribe.[14]

Rosenthal's nostalgia for the spirit of exploration and scientific endeavor of South Africa's settler past is extended to the character of Souvenir, who is her-self described by her adoptive mother, Mara, as being "in a way . . . a relic of the settler past" (19). As a clone, she represents a scientific frontier, and specifically one that has come to define the twenty-first century as much as the space race defined the twentieth century—what Joan Slonczewski and Michael Levy refer to as "the quest for the genome."[15]

In the case of *Souvenir*, anxieties surrounding the issue of cloning are em-ployed in order to explore, as Adam Roberts puts it, "what it is like to have the label 'different' imposed on a person by some normalising system."[16] Souvenir's femaleness is ultimately the site of her difference. Her blond hair, blue eyes, long legs, and ample breasts mark her not only as female, but as über-female, the per-fect specimen in terms of the Western ideal of feminine beauty. However, these features are also what mark her as a clone, genetically engineered to conform to such an idealized vision of femininity. Souvenir, at once a representation of ideal femaleness and an *unnatural* product of genetic manipulation, recalls Donna Haraway's theories regarding the fragmentary nature of femaleness in "A Cyborg Manifesto"; Rosenthal's barbiclone is the embodiment of Haraway's "fabricated hybrid" or "cyborg."[17] Souvenir is indeed a "postmodern collective," a kind of simulacrum that no longer has an original. She is haunted in her dreams by a mysterious connection to other clones who share her DNA, experiencing memories that she does not recognize as her own.

Throughout the novel, Souvenir must negotiate not only her own unease about her clone status, but also the suspicion and prejudices of others. Although Souvenir is assured that people from the rural areas are more tolerant of cloned individuals, some tension is evident almost immediately after her arrival on the Karoo farm, Springfontein. Here she meets ten-year-old twins Uzi and Clara, whose perfectly formed features cause her to wonder whether they are cloned children or "Dollybabies" (7). The term "dollybaby" is a reference to Dolly the sheep, the first mammal to be cloned from an adult cell, but can also be read as referring to the doll-like features of the children. Here the association with a doll or plaything reinforces the view of barbiclones as submissive sex toys and servants expressed in the novel. The children's mother, Magda, immediately insists that the twins are naturally born children, and Souvenir is disturbed by her defensive attitude.

However, this small confrontation is relatively insignificant in comparison to accounts of other, more vicious, prejudices against Souvenir as barbiclone. It soon becomes apparent that barbiclones are often adopted solely as "indispensable sextoys and household skivvies" (6). In this sense, the barbiclone is representative of not only the fragmented nature of female experience, but by extension also of the sexual exploitation of women. Rosenthal is critical of the ways in which women are held hostage by unattainable versions of feminine beauty perpetuated by Western-centered mass media: that double-edged sword that proclaims a woman unattractive if she does not conform to the pinup ideal, and frivolous, incompetent, unintelligent, and sexually available if she does.

The romance that blossoms between Souvie and Obed Will Obenbara—the two are eventually married, and Souvie becomes pregnant despite the fact that she is a clone—sits uncomfortably given the novel's commitment to the representation of alterity. It may be argued that Souvenir has to relinquish a measure of difference, that is, take on the traditional role of mother and wife, in order to find true contentment. Rosenthal attempts to resolve this tension by drawing on an established trope in South African literature: the Karoo as timeless landscape, which, belonging to no one, belongs to everyone. By establishing the Karoo as the one place that an unorthodox family of hybrids—a barbiclone mother, Nigerian father, and three "café au lait" daughters (triply marked as different through their race, gender, and genetic legacy)—can call home, Rosenthal does not propagate the abdication of difference in order to belong, but rather the desire to belong despite difference (177).

The notion of the Karoo as a primeval landscape, a region that predates human beings and will in all likelihood continue to flourish long after humankind is eradicated from the planet, is articulated in Afrikaans writer Eben Venter's *Brouhaha*, a collection of essays and columns. Venter devises a strategy for living without cynicism in crime-ridden South Africa, what he calls "die land van melk en moorde" (the land of milk and murders). Thinking back to the sense of peace he experienced at a small café in Uniondale, he advises his (presumably white, beleaguered Afrikaans) readers: "With a Fanta in one hand, walk out onto the dusty step of the café and remember: Across those peaks of the Swartberg begins the Great Karoo, ashy and worn from age. There people have been living for as long as a person can remember and it is also yours, no matter what is said. And there you are allowed to go and live forth."[18] *Souvenir's* version of the Karoo landscape, plagued by severe weather and strange, genetically modified creatures, may look vastly different from Venter's, but the sentiment that the Karoo can provide those who feel themselves beleaguered by a hostile dominant system with a safe haven of peace and acceptance remains the same. *Souvenir*, then, like many of the speculative works examined across *Green Planets*, suggests that a sense of self is ultimately (but not unproblematically) rooted in place. The Karoo belongs to Souvenir by virtue of her Aunt Jem's legacy of rosebushes and hedges. She is inscribed in the landscape through a shared history, a legacy.

Rosenthal's futuristic novel is comparable to other speculative South African texts such as Jenny Robson's *Savannah 2116 AD* in the sense that ecological disaster is used as a means of exploring human relationships, and particularly what it means to be different. Such emphasis on humanistic concerns through the lens of the popular SF trope of ecological crisis is not uncommon in South African speculative fiction. Because of the country's violent legacy of human rights violations, South African literature continues to be concerned with questions of alterity and belonging. That the effects of global warming and other ecological crises serve mainly as the backdrop for the human drama in Rosenthal's *Souvenir* does not detract from the ecological message of the novel, which both offers a

dire warning regarding the ecological fragility of our planet and speaks specifically to the impact that environmental decay will have on a South African future.

FAMILIAR ANIMALS: NEILL BLOMKAMP'S *DISTRICT 9*

Like Rosenthal's *Souvenir*, Neill Blomkamp's *District 9* not only highlights the
myriad forms of otherness through the introduction of an altered body or trickster figure, but also turns the gaze inward, exploring moments of self-awareness
of alterity.[19] *D9* explores productive imaginings of hybridity in the form of hu-
man/animal couplings that serve to destabilize hierarchized binary oppositions,
challenging of the kind of anthropocentricism that serves as justification for the
human population's continued dominion over our animal others.

Blomkamp uses conventional sf tropes to express anxieties regarding social,
political, and economic uncertainty within a specifically South African context.
South African audiences in particular (perhaps expecting the sterile glamour of a
typical Hollywood production) may initially be struck by the gritty realism of the
film's depiction of the bustling, dirty streets and shantytowns of Johannesburg,
the commentary by unpolished local "actors," and the authenticity of the various
South African accents and languages. The film maintains a playful attempt at
verisimilitude, presenting its "findings" and interviews in documentary style,
juggling between polished, edited scenes and unsteady handheld footage, and
even featuring a mock television news report in which real-life SABC (South
African Broadcasting Corporation) news anchor Mahendra Raghunath delivers
an update on alien/human conflict. Only after the camera pans out to reveal
a colossal spacecraft hovering over the familiar skyline of Johannesburg, and
the audience is given its first glimpse of the ship's bizarre alien "prawns" (presumably named after the Parktown prawn, a cricketlike insect common to the
Johannesburg area),[20] is the very fantastic nature of the narrative is revealed.

For anyone familiar with the sf genre, and particularly the Hollywood-style
"alien" film, such suspension of disbelief is not difficult. However, this acceptance
of the alien presence takes on a different level of significance in *District 9*. Here,
the alien is accepted not only as a terrifying, unnatural presence that threatens
the lives of the heroic human characters, but as a protagonist with whom the
audience gradually begins to sympathize. The audience's growing empathy with
the plight of the "prawn" is due to the development of a relationship between
the "trickster" protagonist, Wikus van der Merwe, and an alien individual known
as Christopher Johnson. While heading up an Multi-National United operation

to vacate the alien population from District 9, Wikus is accidentally infected by an alien fluid (carefully collected by Christopher from discarded alien devices in order to power the abandoned prawn spacecraft), which causes him to gradually transform into a prawn. Driven by the promise of a reversal of this metamorphosis, Wikus undertakes to help Christopher regain the fluid from MNU headquarters.

It is at this juncture in the film, when Wikus and Christopher storm MNU headquarters with guns blazing and stumble across a torture chamber used to do medical experiments on alien individuals, that Andries Du Toit notes a radical shift in the way both Wikus and the audience respond to the prawn Christopher. He writes:

> By now we are used to anthropomorphising "Christopher," and we can see the horror and the pity—and the rage—that we imagine flowing through him as he looks at the ravaged body of his murdered kin. We can see that he would be entirely within his rights to smear Wikus then and there, and go his own way. But he runs across the passage to join him, and together they crouch behind a bulkhead, the room filling with smoke and the thunder of gunshots, firing madly round corners, covering each other as they dash down the passage. And suddenly we are watching a buddy movie. . . . There are many movies in which the aliens are good guys—but never aliens that look like this. Wikus has crossed over to the other side. And so have we.[21]

Du Toit's suggestion that we can "imagine" the outrage Christopher Johnson experiences when he discovers MNU's gruesome laboratory implies that we can imagine Christopher's revulsion at the sight of such slaughter, because we can think ourselves into the situation. It is the same revulsion we experience when visiting similar sites of torture and captivity at Dachau or Auschwitz or, closer to home, Robben Island and Vorster Square. Despite the strangeness, the complete *alienness* of the prawns, the audience is called on to develop a sympathetic imagination, to *empathize* with the suffering of the extraterrestrial other.

Wikus van der Merwe's Kafkaesque metamorphosis, his process of becoming prawn, allows for some critical reflection on the ways in which the film's human characters, and particularly MNU employees, have treated nonhuman others. Wikus occupies a precarious interstitial position between being human and being prawn, thus taking on the role of the "trickster" and destabilizing distinctions between lawful and unlawful behavior and self and other. In the instant—for "a just decision is always required *immediately*"[22]—that Wikus decides to take up arms and fight alongside Christopher, he is responding to the call of the *wholly* other. This decision to act is made from a position of "undecidability," which Jacques Derrida considers to be the condition for ethical responsibility and hospitality. Thus, Wikus's actions can be considered absolutely just and responsible.

Wikus's unique hybridity and his journey to reclaim his former life, set against the backdrop of a bizarre fictional landscape, also becomes the vehicle for Blomkamp's commentary on contemporary South Africa and its many social and political problems. The film also invokes the country's violent past, while simultaneously succeeding in situating South Africa in relation to a *global* future.

The title of the film clearly references District Six, a former residential area of Cape Town from which the apartheid government forcibly removed tens of thousands of citizens in the 1970s, immediately suggesting that *District 9* can be read as a response to South Africa's policy of institutionalized racism (apartheid) prior to 1994. Casting the alien refugees as representative of the millions of disadvantaged black South Africans who were oppressed by the tyrannical system of apartheid is not by any means a stretch of the imagination: these aliens live in an informal settlement on the outskirts of Johannesburg under the threat of forcible removal, speak a San-like "click" language, and are derogatorily referred to as "prawns" in the same way that offensive, racist terms were used to describe black South Africans in the past and, in some cases, even today.

If *District 9* is a reflection on South Africa's traumatic history of epistemic violence and oppression, it also allows for the imaginative rethinking of present-day concerns, particularly the issues of continued racialized discrimination and xenophobia in South Africa (the film was coincidentally released in the wake of a series of violent xenophobic attacks that spread across the country in 2008). *District 9*'s precursor, *Alive in Joburg*, a 2005 science fiction short film directed by Blomkamp, likewise addresses the issue of xenophobia, with many of the "interviews" about the aliens now living in Johannesburg taken from authentic interviews with South African citizens about their feelings toward Zimbabwean refugees.

District 9's seemingly insensitive treatment of Nigerian nationals is of particular interest in this regard. Blomkamp's depiction of Nigerians as ruthless criminals who exploit the aliens' weakness for tinned cat food in order to amass prawn weapons and technology has been dismissed as discriminatory and offensive by some, including Dora Akunyili, Nigeria's information minister, who requested that the film be banned from cinemas in Abuja. However, the film appears to be lampooning the Nigerian-as-violent-criminal stereotype rather than reinforcing it—suggesting a certain level of self-awareness and ironic distance. The notion of trading cat food for advanced alien weaponry is clearly an exercise in reductio ad absurdum and can thus be seen as a *critique* of such negative stereotyping. In this regard, the film's position as Hollywood blockbuster must also be considered. It appears that Blomkamp is at once lampooning *and* buying into Hollywood's need for "recognizable" villains (mostly Russian, German, South African, or Nigerian). Such mimicking of the American action film, along with the film's neat Hollywood ending, is certainly problematic and threatens to undermine the sociopolitical impact of the film. However, informed viewers (and specifically a South African audience more sensitive to the nuances of the film) will be alerted to the element of playful critique at work here. Those viewers with little or no awareness of South African political history may walk away from the cinema thoroughly entertained, at the very least touched by the "human" drama that has unfolded on the screen.

As suggested earlier, *District 9* not only addresses past and present concerns of racial discrimination and oppression within South Africa, but also seeks to situate the country in relation to a global, technologically advanced future. The sf mode allows for the creation of a dystopic future world in which alien spacecraft and mechanical combat suits (presumably inspired by Japanese anime) are not out of place, and a militant corporation (mnu) can run amuck—a scenario that does not seem too unbelievable in view of increasing globalization, rapid technological advances, and the continued rise of the multinational corporation.

In addition to addressing questions of human injustice in the face of an uncertain future, *District 9* is concerned with human-animal conflict. Thus far, it has been suggested that the alien refugees can be read as representative of disempowered black South Africans. However, the film's use of the word "non-human" to describe the alien other,[23] as well as the term "prawn," also suggests a connection with the *animal* nonhuman (a notion that is strengthened by the a fact that the aliens' main source of nourishment is tinned cat food). In this sense, the torturing of captive prawns raises debates regarding the ethical treatment of animals used for medical experimentation. Once his metamorphosis is uncovered by his colleagues, Wikus is himself subjected to violent experimentation, forced to murder a hapless prawn in order to demonstrate his control over alien weapons. In this way, the boundaries between cold-blooded torture and "necessary" scientific experimentation are blurred. Similarly, human consumption of animal flesh is rendered morally suspect through Wikus's transformation.

As Wikus's body is composed of both human and alien flesh after his exposure to the alien liquid, the Nigerian gang's attempt to consume his alien arm then constitutes a kind of cannibalism.

Wikus is abruptly torn from his human self and forced to occupy the physical and psychological position of a prawn. Despite the violence of this transition, the film suggests that Wikus now occupies a productive and *just* space—and paradoxically a more *human(e)* space. As a human, Wikus is a one-dimensional caricature of the "idiot Afrikaner" or "van der Merwe," but as a prawn he becomes the visual embodiment of the psychological and ethical processes associated with Deleuze and Guattari's "becoming-animal."[24] Wikus occupies the interstitial position of the cyborg or trickster and falls outside the category of "genuine" human, thus exposing its instability.

▶ ▶ ▶

The ecological messages of the speculative texts included for discussion in this chapter are intertwined with an acute awareness of pressing sociopolitical issues in South Africa and the rapidly shifting notion of what it means to be human. South African speculative narratives approach the question of identity formation in South Africa as a complex process, influenced not only by violent legacies of oppression and institutionalized racism, but also by the effects of global technological advances on nature and on the human body. Many contemporary, post-apartheid South African speculative narratives draw on the technological aspect of the SF genre, introducing nonhuman or post-human characters such as clones, genetically engineered donors, extraterrestrial aliens, technologically altered humans, and high-tech equipment such as spaceships and heat-regulating suits.

The South African speculative narratives discussed in this chapter thus have in common not only the representation of a futuristic or alternative South African landscape, but also the expression of an entanglement between self, other, and environment. This is evinced as the need for a sense of responsibility toward and connection with both human and nonhuman others in the face of global ecological disaster and an uncertain technological future. The speculative mode is a useful means of staging such an encounter between self, environment, and human and nonhuman other precisely because the established SF tropes of the apocalyptic wasteland and the altered body allow for the creation of a literary space in which all established boundaries between selves and others can be erased and reestablished in different ways. These tropes highlight the issue of survival and suggest that continued existence of any individual is interdependent with that of the other, be it human, animal, or environment.

Notes

1. Deidre C. Byrne, "Science Fiction in South Africa," *PMLA* 119, no. 3 (May 2004): 522–25 (522).

2. See David Barnett, "Putting South African Fiction on the Map," Guardian.co.uk (May 26, 2011), http://www.guardian.co.uk/books/booksblog/2011/may/26/south-african-science-fiction.

3. Felicity Wood, "Subversive, Undisciplined, and Ideologically Unsound or Why Don't South Africans Like Fantasy?" *Language Projects Review* 6, nos. 3–4 (1991): 32–36.

4. Introduced in Woolf's essay "Mr Bennet and Mrs Brown" (1923).

5. Ursula K. Le Guin, "Science Fiction and Mrs Brown," in *The Language of the Night: Essays on Fantasy and Science Fiction* (London: Women's Press, 1989), 86–102 (90).

6. Ibid., 87–88.

7. Ibid., 102.

8. An apocryphal, dimwitted "Mr. van der Merwe" is the subject of many South African jokes.

9. Lawrence Buell, *The Future of Environmental Criticism: Environmental Crisis and Literary Imagination* (Malden, MA: Blackwell Publishing, 2005), 56.

10. Jane Rosenthal, *Souvenir* (Johannesburg: Bromponie Press, 2004), 4. Additional references to this text are given in parenthetical citation.

11. Andy Caffrey, "Antarctica's Deep Impact Threat," *Earth Island Journal* 13, no. 2 (Summer 1998).

12. Wendy Woodward, "Whales, Clones and Two Ecological Novels: *The Whale Caller* and Jane Rosenthal's *Souvenir*," *Ways of Writing: Critical Essays on Zakes Mda*, ed. David Bell and J. U. Jacobs (Pietermaritzburg: University of KwaZulu-Natal Press, 2009), 142.

13. Stewart Crehan, "Disowning Ownership: 'White Writing' and the Land," *Routes of the Roots: Geography and Literature in the English-Speaking Countries*, ed. Isabelle Maria Zoppi (Rome: Bulzoni, 1998), 41–71 (58–59).

14. Neil Evernden, "Beyond Ecology: Self, Place and the Pathetic Fallacy," in *The Ecocriticism Reader: Landmarks in Literary Ecology*, ed. Cheryll Glotfelty and Harold Fromm (Athens: University of Georgia Press, 1996), 101.

15. Joan Slonczewski and Michael Levy, "Science Fiction and the Life Sciences," in *The Cambridge Companion to Science Fiction*, ed. Edward James and Farah Mendlesohn (Cambridge: Cambridge University Press, 2003), 174–85 (174).

16. Adam Roberts, *Science Fiction* (London: Routledge, 2003), 100.

17. Donna Harraway, "A Cyborg Manifesto: Science, Technology, and Socialist-Feminism in the Late Twentieth Century," in *Simians, Cyborgs and Women: The Reinvention of Nature* (London: Free Association, 1991), 149–81 (150).

18. "Stap Fanta in die hand uit op die stofstoep van die kafee en onthou maar: Oor daardie ruggens van die Swartberge begin die Groot-Karoo, asvaal en gedaan van oudgeid.

Daar bly mense so lank as 'n mens kan onthou en dit is ook joune, dit maak nie saak wat daar gesê word nie. En daar mag jy gaan áánlewe." Eben Venter, *Brouhaha: Verstommings, Naakstudies en Wenresepte* (Cape Town: Tafelberg Publishers, 2010), 57. My translation.

19. *District 9*, dir. Neill Blomkamp (2009; Culver City, CA: Tristar Pictures, 2009), DVD.

20. This aspect of *District 9* evokes Andrew Buckland's play *The Ugly Noo Noo*, first performed in 1988, which depicts the fantastic battle between a man and a Parktown prawn. This conflict between man and insect is representative of Buckland's own struggle against the restrictive apartheid government of the time, but can also be seen as a critique of irrational fear and intolerance of difference.

21. Andries Du Toit, "Becoming the Alien: Apartheid, Racism and *District 9*" (October 1, 2009), http://asubtleknife.wordpress.com/2009/09/04/science-fiction-in-the-ghetto-loving the alien.

22. Jacques Derrida and Maurizio Ferraris, *The Taste for the Secret*, trans. Giacomo Donis, ed. Giacomo Donis and David Webb (Malden, MA: Polity Press/Blackwell Publishers, 2001), 26.

23. This use also echoes the term "nonwhite," which was commonly used in apartheid legislation.

24. See Gilles Deleuze and Felix Guattari, *A Thousand Plateaus: Capitalism and Schizophrenia*, trans. Brian Massumi (London: Continuum, 1988).

Ordinary Catastrophes

Paradoxes and Problems in
Some Recent Post-Apocalypse Fictions

CHRISTOPHER PALMER

Send me, sir, a few trifles to read, but nothing about the prophets:
everything they predicted I assume to have happened already.
Madame du Deffand to Voltaire

In a recent essay, Perry Anderson offers a parable that reflects on the novel as a form. He tells how Franco Moretti and Carlo Ginzburg visited the Metropolitan Museum in New York; Moretti paused before a Vermeer painting with a lucid depiction of everyday life and proclaimed, "That is the beginning of the novel":

> In other words, a narrative of ordinary people in a familiar setting—neither epic nor tragedy. Ginzburg then spun around to a portrait by Rembrandt on the opposite wall, of the disfigured painter Gerard de Lairesse, his nose disfigured by syphilis, and retorted: "No, that is the beginning of the novel." In other words, the anomaly, not the rule.[1]

The implication is that the novel exists in a constant tension and dialogue between the everyday and the anomalous; the present chapter examines a medley of inventive recent post-apocalyptic fiction in the light of this tension. Post-apocalyptic fiction throws both the everyday and the anomalous into uncertainty, but in this uncertainty new ways of controlling or even defeating the fear of apocalypse become available. Apocalypse is by definition exceptional and fearful, yet imagining apocalypse is a pervasive cultural habit; often through its valuing ordinary decency, contemporary post-apocalyptic fiction interrogates the nature of "the ordinary" in a situation in which the ordinary is itself in question and ordinary decency often turns out to be itself anomalous. What is everyday, what is ordinary or normal, is thrown into doubt after the apocalypse, when social forms all have to be reestablished or reimagined. Language struggles to bridge, or paper over, the gap, seeking to normalize the new but often simply banalizing it. And if what is normal is in question, so too is what is anomalous. After a glance at Ursula K. Le Guin's *The Lathe of Heaven*, published in 1971, this chapter traces these considerations through three more recent novels, Douglas Coupland's *Girlfriend in a Coma* (1998), Margaret Atwood's *Oryx and Crake* (2003), and China Miéville's *Kraken* (2010).

In what follows, discussion concentrates on a series of figures who present themselves as ordinary—often in contrast to exceptional figures of power and violence—yet whose ordinariness turns out to be distinctly and even spectacularly extraordinary. It is a tendency that no doubt follows from the democratic desire to find heroism in ordinary people, narratively released when the fiction embraces the comic—but this tension takes a paradoxical and problematic form in the texts under discussion. Narratives of apocalypse form a tradition that frequently degrades into routine. Nuclear disaster and ecological collapse are too important to be ignored—in fact they cannot be ignored because they haunt us in their demand not merely for emotional and imaginative response, but for action. But nuclear disaster and ecological collapse (and their many siblings regarding possible catastrophe) are easily drawn upon through reliable images and appeals. Brian Stableford has argued that the nuclear gloom of the 1950s gave us the sense that the future is "a kind of continuing catastrophe"[2]; if so, recent waves of unease about ecology and about Earth's future will have surely reinforced this. Yet, as Istvan Csicsery-Ronay Jr. notes with regard to SF during the 1950s and 1960s, "the enthusiasm with which sf writers wiped the slate of civilization clean to construct postapocalyptic scenarios struck many as unseemly."[3] Apocalypse threatens to become cliché because we have lived with it too long; its imagery and its impressive effects are too readily available. Textually speaking, we face not "the end," but "the endings," as Miéville explores in *Kraken*, where people have become "endsick."[4] The catastrophe as an event so devastating that it ought to be unique in fact has dozens and dozens of precedents and variants. It is both anticipated and *déjà*. There is, then, some cultural need for skepticism, if not about the real threat of disaster then about our habit of imagining it.

Yet the habit of apocalypse also opens opportunities: if apocalypse is dreamed, then this can give the dreamer power; if apocalypse is repeated, then the repetitions open space for comic excess. The combination of need and opportunity prompts a series of complex and often comic moves in the texts under discussion. The setting of these novels is often local, but when the putatively ordinary is brought into closer focus, its nature and potential tend to be questioned and complicated. What part might ordinary people and ordinary decencies play in narratives of catastrophe and apocalypse? What is the ordinary anyway, in a new world in which social reality has changed, in which, arguably, anomaly has now become normal? A recurrent pattern is one in which ordinary decency is both found to be anomalous and to be locked in a conflict with power and violence that can be resolved only by the action of some third, even more anomalous force, which is not ordinary and sometimes not human. This can be first explored in Le Guin's *The Lathe of Heaven*; in the later novels to be discussed the pattern recurs in a more complicated form, and the questioning of the ordinary and everyday takes in the whole of contemporary society as well as individuals.

In *The Lathe of Heaven* the ordinariness of George Orr is seen as a depth of dignity and integrity, but the series of radical and inadequate rearrangements of reality that his "effective dreaming" brings about cannot simply be blamed on his antagonist/partner, the monstrously egotistic Dr. Haber. Each of the new realities that Haber induces Orr to dream into existence is flawed in a fundamental way. The result is not without comedy; for instance, racial difference is abolished along with racial discrimination in one reality when everyone ends up gray in color. Orr dreams new realities with the literalness characteristic of dreams, and the effect is a series of comic anticlimaxes as well as a series of new demands from Haber, and new unsatisfactory dreams.

Orr stands for being, and its depth, while Haber stands for doing, and its blindness; the moral structure of the novel is clear, as is not so clearly the case in the later novels to be discussed. Haber becomes megalomaniac and all-powerful in the latest world he has had Orr dream into existence, while Orr reacts to the extremity of interference with the grounds of being—an interference in which he feels he is himself participating—by dreaming away the human race. Their relationship has reached deadlock. The deadlock is broken by the accidental introduction of amiable aliens who become Orr's helpers, to the homely tune of "With a Little Help from My Friends." They make a third term that unlocks the impasse between Orr and Haber and brings a halt to the succession of radically rearranged but ironically flawed situations the pair had brought about. Haber is driven mad and reduced to silence, Orr is freed of his ability to have effective dreams, and reality settles into commonplace mess, to which the aliens calmly adapt.[5]

I now turn to three recent novels that are somewhat less easy to schematize than *The Lathe of Heaven*. In Coupland's *Girlfriend in a Coma*, Atwood's *Oryx and Crake*, and Miéville's *Kraken* we can see evidence of the response to the cultural habit of apocalypse in three broad features: catastrophe is repeated; catastrophe is subjective; catastrophe is taken for granted. To expand:

- Catastrophe is repeated: the novel involves a series and variety of catastrophes.
- Catastrophe is subjective: it is dreamed or imagined, often by a given character—this is one reason for the variety of catastrophes just mentioned, but it is also the point at which relations between the dreamer and the universe can be reimagined and some of the terror of apocalypse can be dispelled.
- Catastrophe is taken for granted: the event is not explained in the novel. Given the way humans behave, the event is too predictable to be worth explanation. If it didn't happen this way it would have happened some other way; it is as if the event has already happened, so that, at least potentially, it is reincorporated into the ordinary, and thus available for comic play.

The value of comedy in this context cannot simply be assumed, however. It may be that to make a comic narrative of the way in which catastrophe is a cultural habit is indeed to free us from fear, but the threat of catastrophe remains real, and our situation is often made grimmer by this very habit of imagining catastrophe. *Oryx and Crake* is the case in point, a grim, angry novel in which the ordinary has been corrupted by the banal, by banality of cultural imagination, and catastrophe results. *Girlfriend in a Coma* and *Kraken* are more freely comic, as well as more affectionate in their grasp of the everyday, but both these novels depict worlds in which reality is ungrounded, and the flux of change and crisis threatens to sweep away ordinary values and commitments.

GIRLFRIEND IN A COMA (1998)

Douglas Coupland's *Girlfriend in a Coma*[6] reflects the familiarity of narratives of apocalypse in two main ways. First, it does this by staging the end of life as we know it, annihilating all humans except a group of ordinary thirty-something friends in Vancouver. Then it reveals that this has all been faked, at which point they are returned to the moment before the catastrophe and asked to live as dedicated prophets of change in their restored suburban world. If all fiction of catastrophe is meant to alert us to the dangers of the future and critique how we live in the present, then this one renders the device absolutely naked, running considerable risks in the process, since the revelation that the catastrophe was faked tends to badly strain reader credulity. Second, it refuses a certain kind of dignity and seriousness to both present and future by the way it is written—clever, restless, flippant, mocking the heroic by its vocabulary of brand name and pop culture references.

Girlfriend in a Coma is very concerned to define its narratee; the reader is asked to become that ultra-contemporary person who is both totally saturated in media, pop, and brand-name culture and is also cynically knowing about it, possibly thoroughly sick of it. Given the novel's unfailing, almost relentless cleverness, and the omnipresence of the conditions that supply the novel's range of image and reference, it is not all that difficult to become this inscribed or desired narratee. Easy recognition of reference and allusion enables you to get the jokes but reminds you that your head is just as full of rubbish as are those of the main characters.

Girlfriend in a Coma offers a history of a group of suburban, middle-class friends from high school (1978) to early middle age (1997 or thereabouts). They go from the clever flippancy and aimlessness forgivable or even likable in the young to a more desperate clever flippancy and aimlessness not so attractive in thirty-somethings, knowing themselves that this is no longer attractive. Even though some of their decisions in these years show that they want more meaning and a larger perspective, the language of the novel never gets beyond the immediate-contemporary of consumer and pop culture; this being a point-of-view novel, this is their language, the architecture of their minds. Amazing things happen, and Coupland riskily takes on the challenge of making us believe in them: a girl goes into a coma and awakens seventeen years later, fully alert, having experienced visions of an ominous future while she was in coma; the ghost of one of their friends makes increasingly frequent appearances, and in the last part of the novel directs and changes their lives, speaking almost always, however, as the teenage sports star he was when he died; the world ends and all humans on the planet, except the main characters, fall asleep, die, and rot, to the accompaniment of a great deal of turmoil and mayhem.

Coupland sets himself to convey all this, and subsequent revelations and reversals, in the language of brand-name consumerism, comparisons to the shared currency of pop culture: "'Comas are rare phenomena,' Linus told me once.

'They're a byproduct of modern living, with almost no known coma patients existing prior to World War Two. People simply died. Comas are as modern as polyester, jet travel, and microchips.'[7] It's not exactly that this range of reference is banal or trivial, though it sometimes is, and both characters and author know it; it's that it all has a use-by date, making for an almost painful clash between the global or anomalous events recounted and the way they are described in the currency of that year's rock group or favorite candy, which almost by definition will not be next year's.

Girlfriend in a Coma is a risky and almost brutal exploration of the way in which apocalypse narratives are imagined, done so as to critique the present. This time the end of the world as we know it, though detailed with great vigor and made as effectively real as any we might read or see on screen, is simply faked. It is staged by unknown powers who might well be divine but are never investigated, and who use the teenage ghost Jared as their angel. Its purpose is to teach the main characters a lesson. It is a bit of a shock for the reader. Why violently yoke an effective novel about teen slackers-cum-early-middle-age-slackers to a fantastic story of drastic anomalies (a ghost, a seventeen-year coma) and wholesale catastrophe? Why *these* people? They are characterized and fleshed out, but only as characters in a teen/slacker novel might be, so that their ordinariness and their imprisonment in the culture of their time seems problematic in this different context where we have ghosts, a kind of miraculous rebirth after seventeen years, and the end of the world. Yet they are marked as special in being selected as the (apparent) sole survivors, and then in being chosen as prophets of challenge and questioning when it is abruptly revealed that the life of the world will now resume as normal.

Is this outcome to be seen as the apotheosis of that valuation of the ordinary as anomalous and special that we have been tracing, or a kind of parody of it? It can't be the latter, because the novel makes it plain that nothing and no one else can be relied on. We—ordinary but privileged in our prosperity and freedom[8]—got ourselves in this mess, and so, absurd as it may seem when we look at ourselves (that is, at Linus and Wendy, Ham and Pam, Richard and Karen and Megan), we ourselves will have to get us out of it.

A good deal depends on the novel's analysis of the contemporary condition, which is seen as going beyond mediocre suburban narrowness or tacky consumer waste or slacker narcissism. It is gradually defined as a kind of absence. This diagnosis emerges in Karen's responses to her friends and the society around them when she revives from her long coma and is asked how she finds things now: "Her friends have become who they've become by default" (137); the difference between the world she left and the world she returned to is "a lack" (215). There is an emptiness at the center of people's actions.

At one point Richard meditates on dreams: "Dreams have no negative. This is to say that if, during the day, you think about how much you *don't* want to visit Mexico, your dreams at night will promptly take you to Mexico City" (60). Later, he recalls reading Arthur C. Clarke's *Childhood's End* (1953): "In it, the children of Earth conglomerate to form a master race that dreams together, that collectively moves planets. This made me wonder, what if the children of Earth instead fragmented, checked out, had their dreams erased and became vacant. What if instead of unity there was atomisation and amnesia and comas?" (61).

This must be what Karen, in her coma, has glimpsed: "She saw a picture, however fragmentary, that told her that tomorrow was not a place she wanted to visit—that the future was not a place in which to be" (61). Karen's own version of this, after she revives, is more critically pointed: "It's pretty clear to me that life now isn't what it ought to have become" (155).

The people of the present have had wealth and ease and freedom, and they have squandered the future.[9] Beneath the *umwelt* of brand names and pop culture, offered half nostalgically and half satirically, is an absence; it is figured in Richard's idea of *Childhood's End* flipped to its negative. It follows from this diagnosis that apocalypse, when it comes, is doubly negative: it is a comprehensive end, marked by death, confusion, and degradation, and with no replacement (no post-apocalyptic society, only a group of friends wasting time)—but it's a fake anyway. Like everything else in the novel, it is imaged in the terms of pop culture. Several of the main characters have been working as technical experts providing fake blood and gore for TV and movie producers. Richard, visiting them, opens the wrong door: "Left alone, I wandered round the building and saw a door that was slightly ajar. I opened it, thinking I might find a studio. What I found instead must have been a corpse storage room, a room unlike any I could have imagined—men and women, children and aliens; whole, cut in two, doused in blood; arms and legs stacked like timber; glass bottles of eyes and shelves of noses" (90). Richard could never have imagined this, but his friends did; they even imagined a version of his girlfriend Karen, shrunken and gray-haired in her coma, and Richard stumbles across it. Almost everything has been imagined already, and then turned into cliché, or a pile of grotesque discards in a room, and it is from this that people find themselves perceiving disaster when it comes: "Without warning, the Esso station by the Westview overpass explodes like a jet at an air show—bodies like ventriloquist dolls puked into the sky as though in a cartoon or an action-adventure film" (188) . . . "Below them, the fire on the sloping neighbourhood burns like a million Bic lighters held up in the dark at some vast, cosmic Fleetwood Mac concert" (262).

Because almost everything has been imagined already, and repeated to the point of cliché, the novel reaches for the extreme and implausible. When the extreme and implausible do come, at this climactic point, in the form of catastrophe, they are captured by the already imagined, or are in danger of being captured by it. Of course we have nothing with which to imagine what has not yet happened but what we have already imagined, but Coupland underlines how banal and mediatized this imagination is: the jet at an air show (already something seen on the TV news) becomes something in a cartoon or an action-adventure film. To mention a thing is to mention its brand name, often in our society and always in Coupland; brand names for a second seem so ubiquitous as to be cosmic. A million lighters at a concert (even a Fleetwood Mac concert, even Bic lighters) really would seem grand, but the effect of this is to distract the reader into thoughts about cosmic concerts rather than about the fires of the end of the world.

After he comes across his friends' replica of Karen—"The fallen corpse was now leaning against a wall near an electrical subunit, as though freeze-dried" (91)—Richard drives off: "I wanted to see the real Karen, who only differed slightly from the plastic female replica I'd just seen" (91). It is not so: Karen awakes, becomes a pointed critic of what she sees around her, and, after the crucial revelation that the catastrophe was itself a fake, sacrifices herself and returns to her coma. If everything is to return to what it was before the catastrophe, and life is to resume, then Karen will have to return to her coma—though this doesn't quite follow, since she had revived some time before the catastrophe. Coupland's move here is perhaps gratuitous, but this underlines the lengths he is going to in underlining that our only hope is in the ordinary. Yet this pervasive sense that perception is dogged by what is already known in the form of cliché or familiar pop culture image, and that fakery is at the heart of pop culture, does put the novel under intense pressure. The novel does present a strong social diagnosis: contemporary culture has become hollowed out, a negative, and the future is being squandered. It stages a moral revival that is to be based on the ordinary slackers it centers on. In all this Coupland shares the imaginary of his characters, and makes the reader share it too; he never reaches for some standpoint outside and above the imaginative world of his characters. He accepts that in very important ways contemporary consumer culture has no outside, and the working out of this is what makes *Girlfriend in a Coma* so challenging, precisely because of its flippancy and brand-name allusiveness, which is, after all, a vital part of the imaginary that Coupland shares with his characters. The result, however, is that the diagnosis and the revival can only find expression in the medium of pop culture familiarity and witticism that threatens to undermine them because it is a symptom of the very condition that is being diagnosed. I don't think it does undermine them, but it's a close shave.

ORYX AND CRAKE (2003)

Coupland's *Girlfriend* and Miéville's *Kraken*, as we have seen and will see, engage not so much with the real-world possibility (or likelihood) of catastrophe as with the culture of catastrophe, and they set about freeing us from this by exaggerating it. Margaret Atwood's *Oryx and Crake*, in contrast, is a bitter diagnosis of playfulness, an angry condemnation of taking things lightly that imagines this flippancy as a disease of the imagination to which our own culture is horribly subject. In this context, ordinary decency is more powerless than paradoxically strong, and the narrative structure that was observed earlier, whereby the clash between ordinary decency and its antagonist is resolved by an anomalous third term, is muffled (as will be seen when we come to discuss the role of Oryx in the novel).

Oryx and Crake gives us a dystopia brought to an end by an apocalypse; after the apocalypse the text takes the form of a Last Man story. The dystopian society is divided between luxurious gated communities of the techno-scientific elite and "pleeblands" inhabited by the socially discarded.[10] The Last Man is the point-of-view character Snowman, scabby, his memory going, caretaker of a tribe of Edenic post-humans genetically devised by his friend Crake. Crake, like Snowman a lover of Oryx, released the virus that brutally killed everybody else, in effect replacing humans with amiable, simplified successors. Crake is a brilliant, affectless scientist, highly valued in a world that he eventually destroys without qualms; Snowman in contrast is a graduate of the humanities-centered Martha Graham Academy, where those of the elite who are fit for nothing better end up. He is well-meaning but ineffectual.

We have here banal-cheery brand names, processes, gross transgenic organisms with silly names, nasty computer games also with silly or nasty names. The similarity with Coupland is clear, but the difference is that whereas Coupland, through his characters, admits to a complicity with the language of brand-name banality, Atwood remains fiercely alienated, and her diagnosis is much grimmer. This is a commodified world in which everything is a brand, and the brand names that Atwood invents both furnish it and convey her loathing of it. We have Happicuppa, BlyssPluss, an Internet game called Extinctathon, a live suicide site called niteenite.com, and so on and on. There are pigoons, wolvogs, snats, and the like: coarsely clever portmanteau names for hybrid transgenic inventions. The novel is a lot more interested in the brand names and coinages than in any technical or scientific details, because it is the mentality behind the names and coinages that shapes this society rather than the technical or scientific skill behind the various inventions and practices. In introducing new and sometimes marvelous inventions and practices, a science fiction has to devise names, often colloquial, that express how these inventions and practices have become normal in the novel's *novum*. Here Atwood shears the name away from the thing (there is seldom any explanation of the imagined or extrapolated science behind it) and tilts the name violently toward the coarse and flippant.

The diagnosis is clear. This is an adolescent, game-playing, immature culture that Atwood depicts and loathes, its thinking based on fridge magnets (209). The world is ruined in a fit of "boy genius" superficiality (158), "just kiddie fun" (225). There is no chance that this culture contains within itself the resources to recover, and indeed even in Coupland, where that chance does exist, it requires a series of miracles to be realized. The outcome will be different in *Kraken*, because that novel sets the scene at a greater, more fantastic distance from the confining culture of contemporary consumerism.

Atwood's style is angrily offhand. The decadence of the dystopia, the drugs, sex, and porn of the society that preceded and brought about catastrophe, is not enticing, and we would not expect it to be, but neither is the desolation of the Last Man story that is interwoven in *Oryx and Crake* at all redolent or evocative in the way that many passages of desolation and decay in literature are. These are pleasures and compensations refused. There are irregular gaps and speedings up in the narrative, a refusal of steady consecutiveness, as if this would be false to how things happen or are decided in this world. The tenor of the narrative is marked by "the usual," "another," "the usual strange accidents" (254), "same old stuff" (271); and, of the final annihilating virus, "it looked like the usual melting gumdrop with spines" (341). We are not being told anything new or anything we don't know already. The novel's fierce refusal of readerly pleasure and compensation, its persistence with a dialectic of the banal and

z

167

ORDINARY CATASTROPHES | PALMER

the gross—Happicuppa and a genetically engineered headless chicken with twenty breasts and a mouth ("There's a mouth opening at the top, they dump the nutrients in there" [202])—are the expression of how we are implicated in what it is seeing. Befitting the novel's inverted narrative structure and the anticlimactic "revelation" of the disaster's heavily foreshadowed origins, Atwood is not inventing here so much as provocatively reminding.

Snowman ends up doing the ads for BlyssPluss (a sort of enhanced Viagra, except that Crake has doctored it so that it leaves its users sterile). His feebleness as representative of the world of imagination points to something that is disturbing or maybe enraging this angry novel. It is a variant of what Fredric Jameson points to in his writings on the postmodern: the notion that art no longer has a separate sphere or role, the possibility that culture—the realm of play and critique, of imagination and the refreshed use of language—is now everywhere and so in effect nowhere. Culture is spread so thin as to be a mere veneer. In *Oryx and Crake* everyone is playing games, except that they are pornographic; play with language is widespread in the dozens of brand names that the novel devises, but always both deceptive and infantile. In this context, Crake, the affectless representative of the "socially spastic scientists" (205) at "Asperger's U," is a kind of distraction, a Villain with a capital *V*; the real problem is elsewhere. Snowman is a member of the class of symbolic analysts; he is working in the knowledge industry. It is the imagination that has decayed in the world of the *Oryx and Crake*, more even than the intellect.

Snowman is a mere observer; Snowman and Crake do combine to bring about completing the deaths of Oryx and Crake (Crake stages the event, and Snowman finds himself completing the scene), but the novel is not structured around their complex collaboration as was *The Lathe of Heaven* with Haber and Orr. It's named for Oryx and Crake, not Crake and Snowman. What of Oryx, then? Does she figure as a kind of third term, an anomaly that might resolve the binary blockage between Crake and Snowman, as the aliens do in *The Lathe of Heaven*? It sometimes seems so, but (for this reader) the effect is inconclusive. Oryx is an elusive figure, for all that a child sold from somewhere in Asia into the sex trade and subsequently shy of intimacies and disclosures might seem to fit the grim world of the novel. We can't even be sure that the child and adolescent of her past and the woman who is Crake's possession and whom Snowman pines after are the same person.[11] The two men combine to kill her, but neither really knew her. She slips sideways into her role as the mother of the Crakers, the human who has contact with them and nurtures them, and then after her death becomes their deity. Her elusive course through the novel is in contrast to the gross materiality of the world in which it is set, and to its emphasis on pornography, exploitation, failed marriages (those of Snowman's and Crake's parents), adolescent fumblings and yearnings, and the un-neurotic but purely physical sexuality Crake has bred into the Crakers: a panoply of behaviors in which love has no part. Oryx won't receive or give love. The effect is tantalizing, and enriches the novel's economy as a whole, but baffling. Oryx slips elusively through the novel without participating in it. The story of Oryx, Crake, and Snowman is itself peripheral, after all, because the disaster they precipitate is as if it had already happened. The power of the novel is not in its narrative but in Atwood's powerful and angry analysis of contemporary culture and its destructive banality of imagination.

KRAKEN (2010): AN ANATOMY

China Miéville's *Kraken* is a comedy of apocalypse: a riff on the mood of apocalypse that (while we read the novel) frees us of our fear of it by reconnecting the apocalyptic in the ordinary and everyday and by an anarchic splurge of images and possibilities: "Any moment called *now* is always full of possibles. At times of excess might-bes, London sensitives occasionally had to lie down in the dark."[12] As can be seen in this quotation, the narrating voice of the novel is freely inventive, not tied to the point of view of its usually bewildered characters, or infected by any pervasive banality in its imagined world. Like many of the novels under consideration, *Kraken* multiplies apocalypses—stories, sects, fakes, repetitions. The single overwhelming disaster on which the concept and frisson of apocalypse usually depends is fractured into competing fantasies and sects, and the narrative proliferates crises, all of which threaten to overset reality, only to give way to yet more crises. Further, *Kraken* reimagines the laws of transformation whereby a given state or phase might become something utterly different. These reimagined laws—to be discussed below—involve a literal relation of word and thing; they posit that there are no gaps in nature, not even between life and death; and they posit that the universe is persuadable and may respond to our arguments about its nature by conforming to what those arguments say.

In *Kraken*'s London there is a surplus of accessible and available transformation; transformation is everyday and not usually obtained by great effort or risky evocation of dark powers. This is a novel about London and Londoners; transformation exaggerates ordinary urban conditions:

"The tattoo was *talking*." [Billy, early in the story.]

"Do not start that. Miracles are getting more common, mate. [Dane]

"It's the ends of the world."

"End of the world?"

"Ends." (78)

Marge's problem, when she asked on her bulletin boards where she should go, "as a noob in all this" to learn what London really was, was not too few but too many suggestions. A chaos of them. (248)

There will be a multitude of apocalypses: faked or seeming-ultimate events that threaten ultimate or startlingly fundamental transformations. Banal or very ordinary objects play a powerful role: a phaser (that is, a toy from the world of *Star Trek*), a key that has got mislaid and wedged in the tar of the footpath (247), a flickering lightbulb. Marge, one of the ordinary Londoners who has to stumble through to a solution, is for a while protected by a kind of magic iPod, which she programs with some of her favorite songs. As often in London Gothic,[13] it's scraps of wasteland, forgotten dead-end streets, overlooked courtyards, that are the scenes of the actions and the repositories of mystery or potential; "where the world might end was turpe-industrial": "Scree of rejectamenta. Workshops writing car epitaphs in rust; warehouses staffed in the day by tired teenagers; superstores and self-storage depots of bright colours and cartoon fonts amid bleaching trash. London is an endless skirmish between angles and emptiness. Here was an arena of scrubland, overlooked by suspended roads" (357). Magic is spun out of the ordinary—a kind of origami can fold an ordinary object (in one instance, a cash register) into a new shape, and maybe can fold a man so he can get past barriers; or it can be used to kill, horribly. One of Miéville's best inventions among the cast of habitués of alternative London is Jason Smyle, "the proletarian chameleon": "Jason still plied his knack as he came, and the people he passed were momentarily vaguely sure they knew him, that he worked in the same office a couple of desks along, or carried bricks in the building site, or ground coffee beans like them, though they couldn't remember his name" (234). In similar fashion, much later in the story, Billy and Dane, "hunted by all the violent sects and gangs of alternative London, are 'disguised by how unremarkable they are'" (321).

Billy is an ordinary guy who works in the Natural History Museum, from which at the beginning of the novel the preserved corpse of a giant squid has been stolen. He had once jokingly, in a pub conversation, claimed to be a bottle baby, a product of in vitro fertilization. After repeatedly denying his status as some sort of prophet and thence the way he has been swept to the center of events, he realizes that the universe had taken his claim literally, by a mistaking or perhaps a pun. (The effect resembles what was observed in *The Lathe of Heaven*.) The solution to the mystery and the resolution of the crisis will come not from the giant squid in its huge container but from the glass container itself. Puns, wordplay, and coinages structure the action of the novel as well as its text. The ultimate threat comes from fire, as it happens a kind of time-fire, which, in burning, renders the thing burnt as if it had never been, ever: those swept up in the move to bring about this transformation are named Byrne and Cole.

Literalism is important to the whole project of *Kraken*. The magic potential of the universe (that is, this alternative but grungily grounded universe) doesn't come from the esoteric or from ethereal forces but from transformations of the actual, from takings and mistakings that have the same basis, the same power to change, as puns, wordplay, mishearings. Extraordinary events and transformations happen according to fantastic but definite rules and processes; the anomalous is grounded in nature in *Kraken* as it is not in *Girlfriend* or *Oryx and Crake*. In the fantastic but rule-bound world of *Kraken*, the universe is attending to what we say or enact, is sometimes persuaded by it—"the universe had heard Billy and he had been persuasive" (461)—and sometimes mishears or finds a double meaning. The way the plot will eventually come to rest on words and ink, writings, reflects this metafictionally. There is an emphasis on unexpected, rudimentary, improvised episodes of communication, and on communication as a variety of sympathetic magic. The text mirrors this power of words; each new group or condition will be given a name—not just Teuthists or Chaos Nazis or Londonmancers but also the endsick, the krakenbit.

This literalism follows from Miéville's love of thoroughgoing application, of taking a trope as far as it can be taken. So Wati, originally a model of one of those servants intended to serve the Egyptian upper class in their afterlife who rebelled against that servitude, has gone on in semi-immortality to organize all such beings into revolt or protest. As events unfold in *Kraken* he is leading a strike of the UMA, the Union of Magicked Assistants—a huge variety of those who drudge and are industrially exploited as familiars to magicians: mice, beetles, pigeons, and whatnot. The narrative of the strike—pickets, scabs, strikebreakers—is threaded through the text; meanwhile Wati also helps Billy and Dane in their flights and quests connected with the missing squid and the way in which the squid seems to be precipitating the apocalypse to end all apocalypses. To do this he manifests as a voice and a spirit—not, now, in the original clay model such as one sees in the Egyptian department of a museum, but in anything that is replica or statue-like, banal or dignified. He can go anywhere he can find these things, and Miéville entertains himself with varying them—the insignia on a car, a bronze statue, a crucifix on a necklace, a figure of Captain Kirk from Star Trek:

> "How'd you feel about a Bratz doll?" Dane said.
> "I've been in worse." (177)

The magical rubs up against and is sometimes derived from the everyday, and the everyday comprises not only perennial trash and grunge but also banal contemporary things like Captain Kirk dolls.

Similarly the personage called "the Tattoo" is one of the two crime lords who are masters of the violence of the novel's alternative London. He turns out to be a literal tattoo. He has been imprisoned in the form of a tattoo on the back of an innocent guy named Paul, and from there directs his minions, to Paul's severe discomfort. Later, after a series of adventures, Paul will regain control of his self simply by having a tattooist sew up the mouth of the Tattoo. Earlier Paul and Marge had muffled the Tattoo with tape. The Tattoo, a man able magically to speak and command even though imprisoned as a tattoo on another man's back, is nonetheless subject to ordinary conditions, such that if you plaster tape across his mouth he can't speak. Who imprisoned him? The other crime lord, Grisamentum. Grisamentum is in violent quest of Billy and his allies in order to get hold of the kraken (or more precisely the apparently stolen or disappeared giant squid from the Museum of Natural History). He believes he can restore his own life by combining with the ink of the squid, and can do this by sympathetic magic or magic of literal proximity, whereby if something is near or even concerns another thing, it is on the way to becoming that thing. Grisamentum plans to melt the ink off the writings about the kraken that he has had his minions steal, and blend with that ink too. It all stems from a kind of power in metonymy, or in contiguity.

By this stage we need to invoke another aspect of the world of the novel. This is that there are no gaps in existence, only gradations that may be bridged or used as stepping-stones. It is a Derridean world of slidings and deferred differences, not so much interdependences as overlappings and metamorphoses.

There is no absolute or broad division between death and life. Grisamentum is in process of coming back to life, by way of the ink of the squid and even of the writings about the squid or the kraken, added to his ashes. He utilizes "an interzone closer to life" (that is, closer than his apparent state of being dead), "a threshold-life" (401). Dane comes back to life after being tortured to death. The squid, dead and preserved in the huge glass tank of fluid at the museum, stolen, teleported to a truck, thence to the embassy of the Sea (literally thus: a place at which this vast power may be contacted) and back to the museum, comes to twitching life, dies again in self-sacrifice: transpositions, transformations. The way to spirit (that is, aliveness with more capacities than aliveness has in our world) is through matter, and often the grungiest of matter at that. Familiars or golems may be made out of "a hand-sized clot of mange and clumpy hair" (215) for instance; magicians and esoterics animate and give purpose to a flock of pigeons or a cloud of dead leaves. And even though the plot is largely concerned with keeping the missing squid from a bunch of criminals who are capable of reckless violence and torture, there is a sense in which no distinction exists between good and evil, because both sides are united by a similar kind of manic energy. No one is really in control of the oncoming apocalypse, and both sides have to become manipulators of the forces and factions of alternative London.

The ultimate villain, the one revealed after all the preemptions, fakes, false leads, and inconclusive, supposedly climactic battles, is a certain Vardy, who has no moral character, or at least none that has any kind of manifestation comparable to the highly colored nastiness of characters like Grisamentum and the Tattoo. Vardy is the anomaly among all these personages whose anomalousness is bound into the rules of transformation that otherwise prevail in the novel's apparently anarchic universe, but he is a mere shadow of the resolving third terms we have noted in earlier texts; it is the reimagining of imagined apocalypse as the scene of a dialogue between humans and universe that brings about resolution in this novel.

Each of the novels that have been discussed rethinks and restages the relations of the ordinary and the anomalous in our contemporary, apocalypse-obsessed culture. It is the value of the ordinary, and the threats to it from contemporary culture, that shapes each novel. Each arguably offers a democratic imagination of apocalypse, or apocalypses.

We can observe a shift from *The Lathe of Heaven* through *Girlfriend in a Coma* to *Kraken*, though in each case the governing condition is that reality is the product of human dreams. The struggle against the apprehension of future calamities gives rise to guilt and anxiety in George Orr, the main character in *The Lathe of Heaven*; the universe responds to his effective dreams, often in unexpected ways that give rise to more problems, but otherwise it stands aloof, and help has to come from outer space. Resolution requires an analogous but grander anomaly in Coupland: a teenage ghost, a fake apocalypse. By the time of the carnivalesque *Kraken*, however, we can speak of a release of human fearlessness in the face of apocalypses, and here the universe is "persuadable," though it seems to be only by luck that what persuades it is the version of itself that Darwin advanced, rather than the more violent versions on offer in the world of the novel. The trajectory from *The Lathe of Heaven* to *Kraken* is, then, one that illuminates the issues at stake with contemporary apocalypse, because of the variations played on the relations between the human dream of apocalypse and the universe's responses to it.

These novels further suggest that the ordinary cannot be imagined without being put into relation with the banal and commodified. It is this contemporary condition that challenges Coupland and Atwood, in particular, calling forth their strongest diagnoses. Both Coupland and Atwood give us bizarre and weird worlds, but make us recognize them as our daily and familiar creations, not as alternatives. In the society of *Oryx and Crake* language operates to conceal and trivialize the horribleness of the products of science and commodity culture; Snowman's ordinariness is mediocrity at best, and Oryx, the elusive outsider to the system in this novel, does no more than haunt the aftermath of disaster. Coupland's dealings with the banalities of consumer culture in *Girlfriend* are ambiguous, and incite him to a series of risky narrative moves that only just come off. In this regard Miéville's tactic in *Kraken* is noteworthy in its difference: Miéville seeks instead to redeem and revitalize the banal in ordinary things and to knit them into a thoroughgoing erasure of and play with the blurring of ontological boundaries. *Kraken* thus builds an alternative to our current world not out of extremity or radical difference, but out of its most familiar and most ordinary bits and pieces—and the effect is freeing.

Notes

Javier Marías, *Written Lives*, trans. by Margaret Jull Costa (London: New Directions, 2006), 99.

1. Perry Anderson, "The Force of the Anomaly," *London Review of Books*, April 26, 2012, 3–13 (8).

2. Brian Stableford, "Man-Made Catastrophes," in *The End of the World*, ed. Eric S. Rabkin, Martin H. Greenberg, and Joseph D. Olander (Carbondale: Southern Illinois University Press, 1983), 126.

3. Istvan Csicsery-Ronay Jr., *The Seven Beauties of Science Fiction* (Middletown, CT: Wesleyan University Press, 2008), 160.

4. China Miéville, *Kraken* (London: Pan, 2010), 78.

5. Ursula K. Le Guin, *The Lathe of Heaven* (New York: Avon Books, 1997).

6. Thanks to Rachel Ellis for discussions about Coupland.

7. Douglas Coupland, *Girlfriend in a Coma* (New York: HarperCollins, 1998), 63. Additional references to this work in this section will be provided by parenthetical citation.

8. Ibid., 267–68.

9. Linus asks Richard what is the difference between the afterlife and the future:

> *"The difference," I said, "is that the afterworld is all about infinity; the future is only about changes on this world—fashion and machines and architecture." We were working on a TV movie about angels coming down to Earth to help housewives. (92)*

10. Margaret Atwood, *Oryx and Crake* (London: Bloomsbury, 2003), 27 and throughout. Future references to this work in this section will be given in parenthetical citation.

11. See Veronica Hollinger, "Stories about the Future: From Patterns of Expectation to Pattern Recognition," *Science Fiction Studies* 33, no. 3 (2006): 452–72. Hollinger suggests that it is almost as if Snowman is the only "real character" in the novel (467n.11).

12. Miéville, *Kraken*, 116. Future references to this work in this section will be given in parenthetical citation.

13. A subgenre mixing sf, fantasy, and horror, as discussed by Roger Luckhurst; relevant authors include Peter Ackroyd, Neil Gaiman, Iain Sinclair, and M. John Harrison. See Roger Luckhurst, "The Contemporary London Gothic and the Limits of the 'Spectral Turn,'" *Textual Practice* 16, no. 3 (2002): 526–45.

QUIET EARTHS,

JUNK CITIES, AND

THE CULTURES

OF THE AFTERNOON

3

"The Rain Feels New"

Ecotopian Strategies in the
Short Fiction of Paolo Bacigalupi

ERIC C. OTTO

With many of his stories, Paolo Bacigalupi instigates a reconsideration of dominant ways of thinking in response to ecological degradation and its related social consequences. As such, the author is an environmentalist and a utopian, an ecotopian whose environmental concerns influence his participation in a literary form that articulates "the desire for a better way of being."[1] In utopian literature, the gap between the actual world and the narrative world encourages readers to think about alternatives that would bring about a future better than the present or would prevent a future that is worse than the present. Because the gaps that Bacigalupi highlights are the results of a number of existing and identifiable social and cultural forces, his stories participate in what Tom Moylan calls the critical utopian tradition. As Moylan notes of the revitalization of utopian literature and thought during the oppositional 1960s: "The critical utopias had and still have their place in furthering the processes of ideological critique, consciousness-raising, and social dreaming/planning that necessarily inform the practice of those who are politically committed to producing a social reality better than, and beyond, the one that currently oppresses and destroys humanity and nature."[2]

Bacigalupi mobilizes critical utopianism in the interest of critiquing social and cultural forces that degrade nonhuman nature and the human communities that are imbedded in this nature. As ecotopias, his stories are "efforts to reimagine a sustainable human society," as Kim Stanley Robinson notes of ecotopian efforts in general.[3] In "The People of Sand and Slag" (2004), for example, Bacigalupi "argues for a nature that is not valued merely as a resource for humanity but that is irreplaceably, utterly different from us and valuable for that simple fact."[4] In "Pop Squad" (2006), Bacigalupi works at the nexus of economic and cultural production and biological human reproduction, engaging socialist ecofeminist questions about the tensions between production and reproduction and implicitly arguing for a more ethical relationship between the two.[5] In "Pump Six" (2008), he argues for a revised understanding of the connection between humanity and nonhuman nature as he thinks about the long-term sociocultural consequences of the infrastructural efficiencies we often take for granted—technologies like sewage pumps, which foster misapprehensions about human being and ecological being.

To say Bacigalupi mobilizes utopia to prompt a reconsideration of ethics, economy, thinking, and being in light of ecological and social degradation is not to say his imagined societies are *themselves* utopian. Bacigalupi's fictions are not about future societies that we can assume the author "intended a contemporaneous reader to view as considerably better than the society in which that reader lived."[6] On the contrary, dystopia is Bacigalupi's self-admitted "natural zone."[7] A generic sibling of utopian fiction, dystopian literature "takes what already exists and makes an imaginative leap into the future, following current sociocultural, political, or scientific developments to their potentially devastating conclusions."[8] These developments, for Bacigalupi, are the ethical, economic, and epistemological assumptions and consequent practices that prevail today and structure modern life; the "devastating conclusions" are the rationally extrapolated but imaginatively rendered environmental and social costs of the present. "The People of Sand and Slag," for example, is set in a future when humans have fully transcended the biological world and accept as normal an industrially decimated land and sea, as well as their own post-biological, superhuman, radically atomic being. In "Pop Squad," women who are caught with children are shipped to work camps, their kids murdered by a population-control police force, while complicit citizens wonder what could make women abandon lives of economic and cultural productivity to have kids. In "Pump Six," malfunctioning sewage pumps threaten to flood residents of New York City with their own waste, but apathy among the population prevails as citizens in this polluted future have devolved into thoughtless troglodytes.

Such eco-dystopian representations, while harrowing, are indeed part of the utopian project to imagine and bring about positive social change. Scholars of utopia have long recognized the utopian impulse—the impulse toward hope—in dystopian literature. If, as M. Keith Booker writes, "dystopian societies are generally more or less thinly veiled refigurations of a situation that already exists in reality," then to represent such societies in fiction is an effort to alert readers to elements of social reality that might otherwise be undetectable as a consequence of their ubiquity.[9] Darko Suvin coined the term *cognitive estrangement* to label the utopian literary effort to renew readers' perceptions of normalized, unseen social reality by presenting unfamiliar objects and situations—*nova*—that are nevertheless rationally of this reality. Unlike Victor Shklovsky's *defamiliarization*, which is the artistic attempt to reinvigorate perceptions of the mundane, cognitive estrangement functions with a more political charge. In dystopia, as in all critical utopian fiction, "the real world is made to appear 'strange' in order to challenge the reader's complacency toward accepted views of history and awaken, through the 'truth' of fiction, a new perception of the connections between history and the present world."[10]

By highlighting the connections between fictional *nova*, the present, and historical forces, dystopian fiction operates as "the dark side of hope."[11] As Lyman Tower Sargent notes, "a defining characteristic of the dystopian genre must be a warning to the reader that something must, and, by implication, can be done in the present to avoid the future."[12] With this assertion, Sargent speaks for a critical dystopia that presents dark futures not to background the machinations of characters but instead to foreground the conditions of possibility for these dark futures' emergence. One of Bacigalupi's fundamental ecotopian strategies is to imagine what the future could look like given the full realization of current developments—in short, to prompt ecotopia through ecodystopian storytelling. His "The Tamarisk Hunter" (2006), for example, is about water—how societies use, abuse, and unfairly apportion it to the detriment of politically and economically disadvantaged citizens. By the third decade of the twenty-first century, rampant suburban development within the Colorado River Basin, careless water use, and the thirsty, invasive tamarisk tree have depleted the water table enough to prompt California to secure its allotment with lawsuits. No one on the river, including the protagonist, Lolo, and his wife, Annie, can touch the water without the threat of punishment, leaving Lolo to reflect on a past when "football fields still had green grass and sprinklers sprayed their water straight into the air."[13] Of course, this past is our now; the story's dystopian *nova* draw our attention to the present and cue us to think about this present as having a role in bringing about a certain kind of future.

Bacigalupi's "The Calorie Man" (2005) and "Yellow Card Man" (2006), both of which take place in the same literary universe as his Nebula- and Hugo-Award-winning novel *The Windup Girl* (2009), likewise extrapolate dystopian futures from specific present developments. These stories envision the inevitable end of the fossil fuel economy as a monopolistic business opportunity for global corporations who modify and patent food crop genetics. The world economy has run out of oil calories to power its machinery, but it has not run out of food calories to do so. With full legal rights to these food calories, biotech firms such as "AgriGen" and "PurCal" employ intellectual property police to crack down violently on people transporting, growing, and eating pirated food or using such food to nourish the genetically modified animals whose calorie-fed movements power spring winders and computers. The calorie companies have more than IP police, however: "What makes [AgriGen's patented grain] SuperFlavor so perfect from a CEO's perspective" is its *sterility*.[14] Monsanto's terminator technology has been perfected, and its consequences realized in this imagined future. As the protagonist of "The Calorie Man" has learned through childhood experience, planting seeds obtained from crops originally grown from calorie monopoly seeds is futile. They will not germinate—radically reconfiguring the relationship between farmers, corporations, and the natural world.

As Dale Knickerbocker argues, "it is possible to see dystopia as a call to pursue its opposite."[15] Bacigalupi's fiction calls us to pursue modes of thinking and social being that would prevent, for example, the unjust privatization of "a privilege that nature once provided willingly"—the automatic reproduction of plant life.[16] Of course, such natural resources as water and food are *already* unjustly politicized and privatized, and Bacigalupi's fiction is of a piece with nonfictional modes of social commentary like critical journalism and documentary film that expose why, how, and to what effects. If we take Bacigalupi at his word, he creatively represents future consequences of current developments to raise in readers the question "Does that seem like something we want to be going toward?"[17] Bacigalupi has a clear ecotopian motivation for writing ecodystopias. He wants first to place readers in worlds where the negative consequences of present ways of thinking and being are distressingly palpable and second to use these possible worlds to influence readers to take action. In addition to imagining possible futures, another one of Bacigalupi's ecotopian strategies is thus analogous to philosopher Jean-Pierre Dupuy's strategy for social change. Dupuy, Slavoj Žižek notes, proposes to confront dystopian disaster like this:

> We should first perceive it as our fate, as unavoidable, and then, projecting
> ourselves into it, adopting its standpoint, we should retroactively insert into its
> past (the past of the future) counterfactual possibilities ("If we had done this and
> that, the calamity that we are now experiencing would not have occurred!") upon

which we then act today. We have to accept that, at the level of possibilities, our future is doomed, that the catastrophe will take place, that it is our destiny—and then, against the background of this acceptance, mobilize ourselves to perform the act which will change destiny itself and thereby insert a new possibility into the past.[18]

Ultimately, Bacigalupi's ecodystopian fiction displays "some critical awareness of the present," as Peter Fitting notes of critical dystopia in general, and it attempts "to explain how this dystopia came about" in an effort to get readers to think about and act in the world differently.[19]

"The People of Sand and Slag," "Pop Squad," and "Pump Six" make readers aware of the present and its connection to ecodystopian futures, but in these stories Bacigalupi employs an additional strategy to instigate critical reflection on better ways of being in the world. This strategy is in line with that of hopeful ecotopian fiction, as it encourages three key questions, addressing (1) protagonists' new ways of thinking about the world after their experiences of something that gets them to reflect on the dominant worldview, (2) their abilities to act on this thinking, and, importantly, (3) our abilities as readers to institute similar transformations. In literary ecotopias—ecological utopias—such as Ernest Callenbach's *Ecotopia* (1975) and Marge Piercy's *Woman on the Edge of Time* (1976), protagonists who visit ecotopian societies initially reject the changes they see. William Weston of Callenbach's book expresses many prejudices against the culture and society he experiences in Ecotopia. Connie Ramos of Piercy's book finds the future ecotopian world she visits—Mattapoisett—to be too backward, too pastoral, for her liking. In both books, ecotopia has the immediate effect of making the main characters uncomfortable, of radically destabilizing their conceptions about how the world operates. After spending time in ecotopia, however, the main characters of these narratives embrace it. Weston stays in Ecotopia, and Ramos wishes her daughter could grow up in Mattapoisett. A fundamental strategy of ecotopia is thus to prompt this question: What led the protagonist to reject their previous worldview and embrace a different one? In Ecotopia and Mattapoisett, Weston and Ramos, respectively, experience a quality of life and life-in-environment that far exceeds what they experience outside these ecotopian places. Among many reasons, they embrace ecotopian thinking because it has generated societies that are physically and psychologically healthier for them, and while in these societies they feel a deep sense of connection to community—human and nonhuman.

Literary ecotopia explores alternatives that its protagonists embrace, and it confirms the structural possibility of its protagonists' transformations. But ecotopian fiction must be measured by its ability to affect us. As utopian scholar Lucy Sargisson writes, "The exploration of alternatives is a necessary part of the process of transformation. It creates changes in the ways we think about the world and is an integral part of sustainably changing the way that we behave."[20] A final question in ecotopia's political strategy is about whether the protagonists' new ways of ecotopian thinking and being are inside the realm of possibility for us. This is not a question about representing progress, about imagining the future, which Fredric Jameson has pointed out our inability to do as a consequence of "the systemic, cultural and ideological closure of which we are all in one way or another prisoners."[21] Rather, this is a question about living the present in a different way, not with an unimaginable utopian blueprint as our guide, but instead with a commitment to ecological sustainability and environmental and social justice. In a way, then, ecotopian fiction is not really about ecological utopia; it is about drawing our attention to the possibility of different ways of being now. To co-opt Jameson's language on the future orientation of SF in general, literary ecotopia's represented futures serve the function of "transforming our own present into the determinate past of something yet to come."[22] That "something yet to come" is indeed an unknowable something, but its becoming at least a better something (that is, ecologically responsive, socially just) is contingent upon the existence or creation of supportive structures in the present moment.

Weston's and Ramos's new ways of ecotopian thinking and being are inside the realm of possibility for us, who have a certain degree of agency over how we live our personal and community lives. While there are many existing challenges to sustainability and justice (for example, the fossil fuel economy, agribusiness, the capitalist subsumption of "all natural and social relationships to the drive to accumulate capital"), these challenges are not beyond being contested by individual behavior and collective action.[23] This is not to imply, simply, that *us* is consumer society and that agency equals purchasing decisions. Such an equation fits the dominant narrative of neoliberal capital, which subjects the world's peoples and ecosystems to market whim and (against ethics and science) deems this subjection rational. Ecosocialists John Bellamy Foster and Brett Clark speak against the consumer sovereignty thesis, "or the notion that all economic decisions are driven by the demands of consumers, who then become responsible for the entire direction of the economy."[24] Environmental sustainability and social justice are not merely votes we can cast with our wallets. They require, as Foster and Clark argue, "finding new ways of building an economy and interacting with nature, based on socialist and indigenous principles, in which we 'accumulate no more,' while at the same time improving the human condition."[25] Living ecotopia, as *Ecotopia* and *Woman on the Edge of Time* make clear, is about *being* differently, and this different being is both an individual and community possibility that—while it often seems unlikely to get a foothold in production-driven, consumer society—has yet to be shut out completely by the existing hegemony.

If we apply the strategic questions reviewed above to Bacigalupi's "The People of Sand and Slag," "Pop Squad," and "Pump Six," we see main characters who are firmly of the culture and society that "the author intended a contemporaneous reader to view as considerably worse than the society in which that reader lived."[26] Then, as with the ecotopias, we see these characters reconsidering this culture and society in response to a lived experience, demonstrating the malleability of mind-set even within determining contexts. The first ecotopian question applies here: What led the protagonists to think against the grain of the dominant culture?

In "The People of Sand and Slag" the entire globe seems to be a zone of hyper-industrial activity, as implied by the razed Montana landscape and the oil-black, flammable waves of Hawaii. Amid this degradation the only way humans can survive is by using a biotechnology called "weeviltech" that allows them to metabolize inorganic material such as sand and mine waste. The world imagined in the story emerges from a value system that, as Christy Tidwell observes, sees the land and nonhuman animals as "nothing more than resources to be profited from or destroyed," as "objects or tools."[27] Chen, the protagonist and narrator of "The People of Sand and Slag," is a guard for a mining company and a complicit participant in the objectification of the world. When Chen and his fellow guards find an "unmodified organism"—a real dog—wandering in the mining fields, and then take it in because it is "cool" and "Old-timey," they are inconvenienced by its defecation, its slow-healing injuries, and the cost of its food.[28] But then Chen shakes hands with the dog, its eyes staring up at him and watching him walk away. After this moment—and against his peers, who want to eat the dog—Chen begins to reflect deeply on the nonhuman animal and on what humans have become. Prompted to consider making an animal from "building blocks" if he really wants to have one around, Chen responds, "That dog's different from a bio-job. It looks at us, and there's something there, and it's not us. I mean, take any bio-job out there, and it's basically us, poured into another shape, but not that dog."[29]

Tidwell notes that the objectification of the dog "is undercut as Chen begins to see the dog as a creature in its own right, a consciousness separate from his own, a material presence that has not been biologically modified or constructed to serve his needs."[30] The handshake, the dog's amber eyes, the morning face lick, the warmth, the "something" that is friendly about the dog—these experiences of the nonhuman, which are novel for Chen and anyone living in this future (a biologist in the story is only interested in a sample of the dog's DNA)—lead Chen to question whether humans are even human anymore.[31] Chen lives in a world where "we have transcended the animal kingdom"; when he asks "If someone came from the past, to meet us here and now, what do you think they'd say about us? Would they even call us human?" he inherently questions this transcendence and, for a little while at least, challenges the dominant worldview of his society.[32]

By the end of Bacigalupi's "Pop Squad" the story's protagonist and narrator is also thinking against his society, which condemns motherhood and reproduction while it exalts immortality and economic and cultural production. As the story begins, the narrator is executing children and imprisoning their mothers, and throughout the piece he questions women who choose to defy the law and reproduce: "It amazes me that women can end up like this, seduced so far down into gutter life that they arrive here, fugitives from everyone who would have kept them and held them and loved them and let them see the world outside."[33] Mothers have given up their lives, according to the narrator, and judging by what is socially valued in the story, we can assume that the accepted life in this future is one in which the person first maintains regular immortality, or "rejoo," treatments, and is also actively engaged in producing economic and cultural artifacts, not in reproducing life. In one scene, the narrator follows a suspected, law-breaking mother into an antique shop—a toy shop, really—and speculates on the career she might have had before quitting rejoo because it has a contraceptive in it, and then becoming a mother. She might have been an actress, a financial adviser, a code engineer, a biologist, or a waitress.[34] Earlier, moments after killing three sibling children and arresting their mother, the narrator of "Pop Squad" attends his girlfriend Alice's viola performance, where she is later grandly celebrated for her unmatched virtuosity. As these scenes demonstrate, this future society values economically and culturally productive activity while at the same time grossly devaluing human biological reproduction.

The narrator's attitude toward human reproduction changes when, face to face with a breast-feeding mother whose baby he is professionally obligated to execute, he becomes "curious about what you breeders are thinking." The woman's response: "I'm thinking we need something new. I've been alive for one hundred and eighteen years and I'm thinking that it's not just about me. I'm thinking I want a baby and I want to see what she does today when she wakes up and what she'll find and see that I've never seen before because that's new. Finally, something new. I love seeing things through her little eyes and not through dead eyes like yours."[35] Together with feeling his own suppressed reproductive urges at the sight of the woman's exemplified fertility, as well as his playful experience with the cute child—once an "it" to him, but to whom he eventually and significantly attaches the correct pronoun, "she"—the woman's reasoning and accusation work on the narrator to get him to walk away without fulfilling the mission that his society requires of him. He does not kill the girl, and as he walks out into the rainy jungle, "for the first time in a long time, the rain feels new."[36]

Finally, in "Pump Six," Bacigalupi imagines the intellectual and biological devolution of the human species as a consequence of environmental pollutants and the infrastructural efficiencies of modern society. Polychlorinated biphenyls, heptachlor, and other harmful compounds contaminate New York City's drinking water, contributing to reproductive disorders and mental deficiencies in the story's twenty-second-century humans, as well as the birth of hermaphroditic troglodytes, or in the narrator's words, "mash-faced monkey people shambling around with bright yellow eyes and big pink tongues and not nearly enough fur to survive in the wild."[37] The plot of "Pump Six" centers on a malfunctioning sewage pump that previously operated for over one hundred years without needing service, its existence therefore "forgotten by everyone in the city above."[38] The story thus stages the collision of toxicity-induced human intellectual defects with an efficiently mechanized infrastructure that likewise has contributed to a sense of unknowing among the human species, unknowing about where drinking water comes from and unknowing about what happens to human waste once it is flushed. When the pump goes silent, no one can fix it, and no one but the story's protagonist, Alvarez, seems to care.

Prior to the pump breaking down, however, Alvarez never wondered about the trogs, the crumbling buildings of the city, or the reproductive disorders, so he was a complicit participant in this decaying society. But as the one responsible for keeping the pumps working, Alvarez must figure out how to fix them. This leads him to seek advice at Columbia University's engineering department, which turns out to be over twenty years defunct. The library at the university is empty but for an "old faculty wife" who initially waves Alvarez away with a pistol but then, upon learning that the broken pump serves Columbia, invites Alvarez to browse the stacks and learn whatever he needs to learn to fix the pump.[39] She leaves him not only with the key to the library, but also with a new awareness of his society's decay. As he leaves the library, he narrates,

> A crash of concrete rain echoed from a couple blocks away. I couldn't help shivering. Everything had turned creepy. It felt like the old lady was leaning over my shoulder and pointing out broken things everywhere. Empty autovendors. Cars that hadn't moved in years. Cracks in the sidewalk. Piss in the gutters.
> What was normal supposed to look like?[40]

In asking "What was normal supposed to look like?" while at the same time making an effort to learn how to fix the pump, Alvarez steps outside his society's constraints to try to become a different person.

We must question whether the protagonists of these stories are able to make real or carry out their new ways of thinking and being within their societies' determining contexts. In "The People of Sand and Slag," "Pop Squad," and "Pump Six," as in many dystopias, it is indeed the protagonists' "desires and hope for a better present or future that distinguish [them] from the rest of the population and additionally bring [them] into conflict with the dystopian establishment."[41] But as Ruth Levitas argues, "The transformation of ways of thinking and of being ... depends on an alternative *structure* within which another logic of action and understanding makes sense."[42] Unfortunately for the main characters of Bacigalupi's stories, such alternative structures do not exist. In "The People of Sand and Slag," Chen does not "ultimately change his value system and become willing to pay for [the dog's] upkeep at the cost of his other pleasures," because there is no support for the care of nonhuman life.[43] It is expensive to feed the dog, it is inconvenient to tend to the wounds that it will inevitably receive in the ubiquitously polluted and toxic world, and commercial society has triumphed so much that Chen would rather use his money for a new pair of virtual reality goggles. In the end, he and his friends eat the dog. "Pop Squad" concludes with its protagonist newly aware of the value of human reproduction against the desire among most in his society to live forever as productive citizens. The rain feels new to him, but as Levitas notes about the energies of utopian transformation, "the personal is not political enough."[44] The ending of "Pop Squad" is indeed left open, but the protagonist's "micro-changes" seem unlikely to find enough, if any, support to become "macro-changes" in the thinking and being of his culture.[45] Open-ended, too, is "Pump Six," with Alvarez reading a book at random as the story closes. But Alvarez's society is one in which pollutants saturate the bodies of everyone, buildings are beyond repair, and, perhaps most notably, the normally engaged and activist students of an Ivy League university have become apathetic and indolent. Within these contexts, Alvarez's personal change seems unlikely to become anything more than short-lived.

The end of a structure that supports utopian action does not mar our contemporary reality as it does the reality for the characters in Bacigalupi's stories. The new ways of thinking and being that Bacigalupi's characters adopt are inside the realm of possibility for us. Ecotopian fiction such as Callenbach's and Piercy's works on us by placing its characters within the social contexts that structure the possibility of better ways of being, and then leading us to see that such structuring remains imaginable and attainable for us. In contrast, Bacigalupi's ecodystopian stories work—that is, instigate ecotopian transformation—by staging a productive tension between what is (im)possible for their protagonists and what is still possible for us. There are social, political, economic, and cultural forces that work against the realization of ecologically and socially better ways of being today. But these forces have not fully interrupted our ability to care for nonhuman species ("The People of Sand and Slag"), to balance economic and cultural production with reproduction rather than subordinate the latter to the former ("Pop Squad"), and to disseminate the understanding that the human body, like all other species' bodies, is always in ecosystems and will therefore always absorb industrial pollutants ("Pump Six"). Bacigalupi's fiction reminds us that, "we have not yet crossed the threshold of the unthinkable."[46] If we wake up tomorrow, and the rain feels new, this profound personal change can still become political.

Notes

1. Lucy Sargisson, "The Curious Relationship between Politics and Utopia," in *Utopia Method Vision: The Use Value of Social Dreaming*, ed. Tom Moylan and Raffaella Baccolini (Oxford: Peter Lang, 2007), 26. For Bacigalupi's perspective on his role as an environmentalist writer, see Michelle Nijhuis, "A Sci-Fi Writer and an Environmental Journalist Explore Their Overlapping Worlds" (2008), http://grist.org/article/bacigalupi/.

2. Tom Moylan, *Scraps of the Untainted Sky: Science Fiction, Utopia, Dystopia* (Boulder, CO: Westview, 2000), 82.

3. Kim Stanley Robinson, introduction to *Future Primitive: The New Ecotopias*, ed. Kim Stanley Robinson (New York: Tor, 1994), 11.

4. Christy Tidwell, "The Problem of Materiality in Paolo Bacigalupi's 'The People of Sand and Slag,'" *Extrapolation* 52, no. 1 (2011): 94–109 (95).

5. For more on socialist ecofeminism see Carolyn Merchant, *Radical Ecology: The Search for a Livable World* (New York: Routledge, 2005), 208–12.

6. Lyman Tower Sargent, "The Three Faces of Utopianism Revisited," *Utopian Studies* 5, no. 1 (1994): 1–37 (9).

7. Nijhuis, "Sci Fi Writer," no page.

8. Katherine V. Snyder, "'Time To Go': The Post-apocalyptic and the Post-traumatic in Margaret Atwood's *Oryx and Crake*," *Studies in the Novel* 43, no. 4 (2011): 470–89 (470).

9. M. Keith Booker, *The Dystopian Impulse in Modern Literature: Fiction as Social Criticism* (Westport, CT: Greenwood Press, 1994), 15.

10. Maria Varsam, "Concrete Dystopia: Slavery and Its Others," in *Dark Horizons: Science Fiction and the Dystopian Imagination*, ed. Raffaella Baccolini and Tom Moylan (New York: Routledge, 2003), 206–7.

11. Ruth Levitas and Lucy Sargisson, "Utopia in Dark Times: Optimism/Pessimism and Utopia/Dystopia," in *Dark Horizons: Science Fiction and the Dystopian Imagination*, ed. Raffaella Baccolini and Tom Moylan (New York: Routledge, 2003), 26.

12. Lyman Tower Sargent, "The Necessity of Utopian Thinking: A Cross-National Perspective," in *Thinking Utopia: Steps into Other Worlds*, ed. Jorn Rusen, Michael Fehr, and Thomas W. Reiger (New York: Berghahn, 2005), 3.

13. Paolo Bacigalupi, "The Tamarisk Hunter," in *Pump Six and Other Stories*, by Paolo Bacigalupi (San Francisco: Night Shade, 2008), 132.

14. Paolo Bacigalupi, "The Calorie Man," ibid., 114.

15. Dale Knickerbocker, "Apocalypse, Utopia, and Dystopia: Old Paradigms Meet a New Millennium," *Extrapolation* 51, no. 3 (2010): 345–57 (349).

16. Bacigalupi, "Calorie Man," 114.

17. Nijhuis, "Sci-Fi Writer."

18. Slavoj Žižek, *First as Tragedy, Then as Farce* (London: Verso, 2009), 151.

19. Peter Fitting, "Beyond This Horizon: Utopian Visions and Utopian Practice," in Moylan and Baccolini, *Utopia Method Vision*, 261–62.

20. Levitas and Sargisson, "Utopia in Dark Times," 17.

21. Fredric Jameson, *Archaeologies of the Future: The Desire Called Utopia and Other Science Fictions* (London: Verso, 2005), 289.

22. Ibid., 288.

23. John Bellamy Foster, Brett Clark, and Richard York, *The Ecological Rift: Capitalism's War on the Earth* (New York: Monthly Review, 2010), 75.

24. John Bellamy Foster and Brett Clark, "The Ecology of Consumption: A Critique of Economic Malthusianism," *Polygraph* 22, ed. Gerry Canavan, Lisa Klarr, and Ryan Vu (2010): 117.

25. Ibid., 127.

26. Sargent, "Three Faces of Utopianism Revisited," 9.

27. Tidwell, "Problem of Materiality," 100–102.

28. Paolo Bacigalupi, "The People of Sand and Slag," in Bacigalupi, *Pump Six and Other Stories*, 60.

29. Ibid., 63–64.

30. Tidwell, "Problem of Materiality," 104.

31. Bacigalupi, "People of Sand and Slag," 64.

32. Ibid., 66.

33. Paolo Bacigalupi, "Pop Squad," in Bacigalupi, *Pump Six and Other Stories*, 138.

34. Ibid., 153.

35. Ibid.

36. Ibid., 161.

37. Bacigalupi, "Pump Six," in Bacigalupi, *Pump Six and Other Stories*, 219 and 215.

38. Ibid., 229.

39. Ibid., 236.

40. Ibid., 238.

41. Varsam, "Concrete Dystopia," 205.

42. Levitas and Sargisson, "Utopia in Dark Times," 19.

43. Tidwell, "Problem of Materiality," 105.

44. Levitas and Sargisson, "Utopia in Dark Times," 23.

45. Ibid., 23.

46. Snyder, "'Time to Go,'" 473.

Life after People

Science Faction and Ecological Futures

BRENT BELLAMY AND IMRE SZEMAN

In a May 9, 2012, *New York Times* article, James Hansen, head of the NASA Goddard Institute for Space Studies and a leading environmental critic, made a startling and blunt declaration about Canadian oil extraction and climate change: "If Canada proceeds [in the tar sands], and we do nothing, it will be game over for the climate."[1] In a flash, the stakes on Hansen's now thirty-year-old warning about climate change and the necessity of action on the environment have been raised precipitously. The intent of his article is all too clear: to convince us of the fact that the time for human beings to modify their life activity in a manner that will significantly offset their impact on the planet's environment is *now*, as we have reached the point when the continued development of a single oil field (however large it may be) will push us over the ecological edge. He summarizes his predictions about the dire long- *and* short-term effects of collective ecological neglect with a strident declaration: "If this sounds apocalyptic, it is."

What strikes us about Hansen's interventions in the politics of climate—both his 1981 *Science* article about the speed of global warming due to CO2 production and this most recent piece in the *Times*—is his propensity to project and to extrapolate.[2] Ecological thinking here remains inseparable from some form of thinking about the future; indeed, ecology in general has become so closely linked to narratives of the future that to even draw attention to this link between the environment and what-is-yet-to-come can seem beside the point or even tautological. It is the presumed effect of this link that interests us here as much as the presence of the connection itself. Hansen's gambit, a play at the heart of ecological writing, is that this form of extrapolative writing can spur action—that depicting a future wracked by devastating weather patterns, rising ocean levels, species loss, crop failure and soil erosion, and so on, would of necessity result in the required political intervention, whether on a governmental or grassroots level or as some combination of the two, at the scale required by a problem that encapsulates and affects the whole globe.

All manner of assumptions are built into this narrative demand for action, including a continuing faith and belief in the drama of Enlightenment maturity outlined by Kant (in which we get smarter and better as we trundle along through history), the presumed power of scientific inquiry to guide political decision making, and the possibility of narrative to generate change (a longstanding dream of writers across the political spectrum)—and a hope, too, that latent species survival impulses still persist in human beings and can be activated by appeals to reason. Recently, no less a figure than leading environmentalist Dr. David Suzuki has suggested that such appeals to action have all been for naught: "Quite frankly, as far as I'm concerned, I feel all the effort that I've been involved in has really failed. We're going backward."[3] Is there another way of naming the ecological crisis of the future that could generate the outcome that we are so desperately in need of—one that might marry scientific insight with political action in a way that would prevent the eco-apocalyptic outcomes identified by Hansen and others? As a way of probing the importance of form for ecological politics, we want to focus here on the problematic insights raised by a book that represents the ecological future in a narrative mode distinct from prevalent ways of imagining the future as either more of the same or post-catastrophe: Alan Weisman's best seller *The World Without Us* (2007). This form—what we call "science faction"—has become increasingly prominent over the past decade, appearing not only in book form but in documentaries such as National Geographic's *Aftermath*, the History Channel's *Life after People*, and the BBC show *The Future Is Wild*. Such quasi-scientific, quasi-science-fictional texts depict the world after the final collapse of civilization and the extinction of the human race, often at hyperbolic geologic time scales extending millions of years. In addition to identifying the nature and function of this form, we want to critically examine what it tells us about narrative and political limits at the present time, and to consider what the problems of science faction tell us about what we might need to do to overcome such limits.

THE WORLD WITHOUT US

Weisman's book unfolds around a thought experiment: If humans were to suddenly vanish from Earth today, what would happen to the world in our absence? He tells the story of a world without people by springboarding from a particular ecological context and its associations to another context of damaged nature and another zone of analysis and exploration, and so on throughout the book.[4] Weisman attempts to chart the complicated web of relations that characterize the ecological history of the present even as he struggles to simplify these relations by removing humanity from the picture. The pleasure of the text comes from its patient and thorough investigation of the extent of human impact on the planet through thought experiments that imagine how long it would take nature to recover from the various damages we have inflicted upon it. *The World Without Us* is simultaneously a primer in environmental studies and a text that—like so many texts about the environment—identifies the need for rapid changes in the mode of human activity on the planet.

The book opens in the Amazon among the Zápara people, a scene that crystallizes one of the major internal contradictions of *The World Without Us*: thinking nature as the other of humanity. Weisman connects the demand for rubber trees created by Henry Ford's mass-production of automobiles with the decimation of the Zápara. The point is straightforward enough: by draining Earth of its resources, we have become our own worst enemies, a fact once felt only on the (post)colonial peripheries of the planet but now a feature of daily life all over the world. Recognizing the position of human beings *within* nature—as opposed to the outsider status that many critics imagine humans occupy with respect to the environment—Weisman asks whether it is "possible that, instead of heaving a huge biological sigh of relief, the world without us would miss us?"[5] He poses this type of unanswerable question with frequency, as a reminder that the book aims to produce change in human activity with the insights produced from its attempt to "narrate the unnarratable."[6] The only reason to think of a world without us is to use the knowledge generated through such a narrative experiment to reimagine a world *with* us.

Weisman narrates what might happen after our disappearance by looking for evidence at sites that have already been left behind, performing an archaeology of abandonment, loss, and forgotten space. For instance, in the chapter "What Falls Apart," he traces out what happens in Varosha, Cypress, a newly built tourist city that was forced to close in 1974 because of the ongoing border dispute between Greece and Turkey. Just six years after the city of twenty thousand had shut down, Metin Münir, a Turkish journalist who visits Varosha, is struck not by the absence of life in the city but by "its vibrant presence." Münir reflects: "With the humans who built Varosha gone, nature was recouping it. . . . Tiny seeds of wild Cyprus cyclamen had wedged into cracks, germinated, and heaved aside entire slabs of cement. Streets now rippled with white cyclamen combs and their pretty, variegated leaves."[7] While these enclaves emerge, in most cases, as the result of a spatial contradiction between politics and economics, the nation-state and global capital, Weisman's narrative strategy posits them as representative examples of a world devoid of humans by treating them as if they were outside humanity altogether—a telling lack of attention to or interest in the place of politics in shaping the environment.

If such enclaves highlight the speed with which nature is likely to make a return to spaces previously occupied by humans, Weisman shows that elsewhere on the planet evidence of humanity's presence and environmental impact will persist for much longer. The North Pacific garbage gyre—an immense "trash vortex" in the Pacific Ocean now said to be as large as the United States—marks the accumulative effects of the use of plastic polymers, a human legacy not set to disappear from Earth for one million years. We would be remiss if we failed to mention New York City—ever the apocalyptic metonym for the destruction or decay of humanity and urbanism. Weisman projects that within thousands of years, "what's left of New York City [will be] scraped clean by glaciers. Only some tunnels and other underground structures [will] remain."[8] Weisman's project, dialing back and forth from the massified minutiae of polymers to the destruction of the great cities to the reclamation of farmland by fast-growing plant species, maps out an imagined ecological future that is at the same time intensely informed and constructed by the contradictions and impasses of the present.

SCIENCE FACTION

The World Without Us has been dubbed an "eco-thriller" and a "thought experiment" by critics, and as a "love letter" to the planet and to the human race in an interview given by Weisman.[9] We prefer to read it, and other works in this strange new subgenre, in relation to science fiction, but argue that it could be better described as "a fiction of science fact," or *science faction*. Science faction represents a landscape devoid of people, an emptiness that bizarrely and of necessity generates an immediate challenge to narrative logic (that is, that narrative can persist even in a world without either narrators or audience). It is perhaps this founding antagonism that is one of the reasons why these fictions take the form of a didactic teaching of fact, science, and environmental politics, adopting a documentary form dominated by its presumed immediate relation to the real.

As in science documentary, the "fact" of the narrated developments tends to displace questions about narrator, addressee, or audience. And yet, the fiction of the yet-to-be facts of texts like the *World Without Us* place them outside of documentary and closer to the mode of typical science fictions.

Indeed, there are characteristically SF elements to the book. On the one hand, at times it imagines the evolution of humanlike intelligence all over again: "One hundred thousand years hence," Weisman writes, "the intellectual development of whatever creature digs them up might be kicked abruptly to a higher evolutionary plane by the discovery of ready-made tools. Then again, lack of knowledge of how to duplicate them could be a demoralizing frustration—or an awe-arousing mystery that ignites religious consciousness."[10] On the other, it pictures the discovery of the post-human Earth by aliens who are then tested by the remaining objects of human civilization. Do they recognize us, in spite of our disappearance?

> Supposing, however, that before such entropic vandalism occurs, the collection is discovered by visiting alien scientists who happen upon our now-quiet planet, bereft of voracious, but colorful, human life. Suppose they find the Rothamsted archive, its repository of more than 300,000 specimens still sealed in thick glass and tins. Clever enough to find their way to Earth, they would doubtless soon figure out that the graceful loops and symbols penned on the labels were a numbering system. Recognizing soil and preserved plant matter, they might realize that they had the equivalent of a time-lapse record of the final century-and-a-half of human history.[11]

In this sense, like SF, science faction encodes what appears to be a temporal displacement of contradictions from the present onto a narrative future in order to explore their full significance and consequences.

But the differences between the two genres are significant. Science faction makes an aesthetic-epistemological gambit toward solving or seeking the resolution of historical problems through its unusual, hybrid narrative form. In SF, this well-recognized process has been described by Darko Suvin as "cognitive estrangement."[12] Carl Freedman has rearticulated Suvin's thesis about cognitive estrangement as a dialectic between the two elements, arguing that "the first term refers to the creation of an alternative fictional world that, by refusing to take our mundane environment for granted, implicitly or explicitly performs an estranging critical interrogation of the latter. But the *critical* character of the interrogation is guaranteed by the operation of cognition, which enables the sf text to account rationally for its imagined world and for the connections as well as the disconnections of the latter to our own empirical world."[13] The estrangement element of Weisman's book is that humanity is simply gone. Weisman's self-described aesthetic strategy was to dissipate the anxiety that typically attends ecological issues by killing off humans at the outset. He says, "You can take your time and really look at all this stuff, because we're already out of the picture."[14] For a critic of sf like Suvin, this type of admission marks the book's historical nature in a double sense: first, that Weisman's science faction could only appear at a particular moment in history, and second, that from moment to moment its estrangement (the disappearance of humans) will have different meanings (think, for instance, of the difference between post–World War II and Cold War anxieties about the atomic bomb compared to ecological anxiety today).

For Freedman, the "cognition effect" can be produced whether or not a text adheres strictly to a set of scientifically or empirically determined facts, as long as it bears out the logic of its science-fictional propositions immanently, with internal consistency. The key distinction between science faction and sf is that the former suspends the need to secure this cognition effect by relying on a future that is the same as the present, in so far as it is shaped by known scientific principles and data. The cognitive element, the *fact* of science faction in the case of *The World Without Us*, is secured through the expert testimony of architects, maintenance workers, climate change experts, and many, varied scientific researchers. The sole site at which Weisman's book mimics the operations of sf is thus in its absence of people. But rather than being a site at which the cognition effect can play out, generating a social or political allegory based on the believability of the world that the book has crafted, it is here that the genre of science faction instead produces one of its primary contradictions. The answer to the central question of the book can't help but betray itself by making it clear that a world without us is still intensely bound up *with us*. And Weisman knows it; he says, "And yet there's a kind of paradox there too, isn't there? It's supposed to be a world without us, but the book is filled with people, too."[15]

The aim of science faction is to mobilize some of the formal and imaginative energies produced by the tensions and contradictions of its form—not quite science documentary, not quite sf—to generate the kinds of political outcomes longed for by those concerned about human impacts on the environment. However, science faction tends to make at least two connected, problematic assumptions that impede or block such a politics: first, that humanity *can* disappear without impacting or altering nature in some significant way, and second, that nature would flourish in the absence of humans. Taken together, even given the potential effects of the text's formal inventiveness, these two assumptions render a deeply conservative message about ecology—the opposite of what Weisman and the form of science faction more generally intend. In the first case, positioning humans as in some deep way external to nature—as outside nature to such a degree that their disappearance produces no tangible effect of its own—reinforces existing views of the divide between humanity and nature that have made the latter a mere instrument of the former. In a very real sense, from this perspective the world is always already without us, which is why nature need only address the consequences of human activity and need not try to manage the sudden disappearance of its largest mammalian species and the most dominant predator in the ecosystem.

The second assumption is equally problematic. According to Weisman's thought experiment, the elimination of humans from the picture can't help but lead to a situation in which nature rapidly recovers from the impacts of human activity; even a million years is insignificant in geological time, and Weisman discovers that much of the recovery would take place in only a few hundred. The ability of nature to recover in the absence of humanity leads to two additional and equally problematic conclusions. First, the fact that nature can recover—and indeed, do so relatively quickly—undermines ecological narratives about the threat of human activity to the environment's health and sustainability. And even if we were to concede that humans have made a significant impact on the planet, Weisman's thought experiment suggests that nothing can be done. If the only way by which the environment can be ameliorated is by bringing about the end *of* humanity (or, at a minimum, producing a massive, unprecedented reduction of humans' environmental footprint) then there is nothing that can be done *by* humanity, much less *for* humanity. It is perhaps because he recognizes these limits to the narrative form he employs that Weisman repeatedly invokes the need to "dream of a way for nature to prosper that doesn't depend on our demise"[16]—a dream that SF might be able to outline for us through its rich allegories of the future consequences of present contradictions, but which science faction, in its reconfiguration of SF's cognitive estrangement function, cannot.

Commenting on the fiction of E. L. Doctorow, Fredric Jameson writes: "If there is any realism left here, it is a 'realism' that is . . . of slowly becoming aware of a new and original historical situation in which we are condemned to seek History by way of our own pop images and simulacra of that history, which itself remains forever out of reach."[17] Science faction exceeds the limits of this kind of realism, if falsely, by using the crutch of its scientific explanation as something like an extra-historical justification for the present as what *is*—a present that "doesn't need any explanation," historical or otherwise, because of the simple fact of its existence. To put this somewhat differently: the fact of science factions means that these texts cannot engage in an analysis of what is, after all, the most significant factor in thinking about the ecological future: politics—the messy reality of human social configurations and their deleterious impact on the environment that is at the heart of the problems that necessitate the production of science factions in the first place.

ECOLOGICAL THINKING IN THE INTERREGNUM

What can be done to push and prod us into addressing the ecological crisis that we have generated for ourselves—into, that is, taking up the political challenges that necessitate the narrative appeals of Hansen, Suzuki, Weisman, and other environmentalists? The capacity (or rather, incapacity) of collective social amelioration lies at the heart of the endeavor called critical theory, which has since its inauguration in the work of the Frankfurt School been nothing if not an elaboration of the characteristics of late modernity that have blocked or impeded political possibility. One of the founding limits of narratives like Weisman's—above and beyond those already listed above—is that while they attend to consequences of the dark side of the Enlightenment, they remain enraptured by the capacities of reason and fact to generate collective action; they see environmental destruction as a misstep in a story of progress rather than as a necessary outcome of that self-same science that is so apt at diagnosing the problem if not generating any solution (other than the elimination of humanity *tout court*).

Lauren Berlant's analysis of the affective dynamics of "cruel optimism" generates an explanation for the above impasse. The very way in which contemporary life is lived out points to the affective limits of science faction and, indeed, of other dominant modes of environmental narrative, in generating the change they so desire. For Berlant, contemporary narratives of future change open up the optimistic "possibility that the habits of a history might *not* be reproduced."[18] They do so, however, in a way that, instead of pushing toward a historical break, generates a desire for a "reanchoring in the symptom's predictability."[19] Despite the fact that ordinary life constitutes a slow wearing out of the subject, the tendency is for contemporary subjects to "choose to ride the wave of the system of attachment that they are used to," instead of leaping into a new social mode that might well no longer wear them out, but whose precise form and nature is necessarily uncertain and unknown.[20]

Berlant intends "cruel optimism" to describe the form of contemporary politics in general. The suspension of politics and the reaffirmation of the inevitability of the present even in critiques of it are, however, especially powerful in narratives of environmental futures. Though there might initially seem to be little that is optimistic about tales of future environmental destruction premised on humanity continuing in its ways, the generation of the possibility of a new historical trajectory is optimistic in precisely the sense Berlant identifies. Even at the risk of collective destruction, in the case of such narratives the cruel "retreat to the ordinariness of suffering, the violence of normativity" is understandable: the trauma of ecological crisis never arrives as a determinate event but remains a relatively abstract component of a quotidian reality in which (for example) even the most extreme meteorological events are read simply as evidence of the usual vagaries of weather in any given year.[21] The optimism of science faction is of a different and even less effective sort. If the cruel optimism of typical environmental narratives generates a potential political opening that is then shoved aside because of the demands of our exuberant attachments to the mechanics of daily life, the optimism of Weisman's science faction merely affirms the already given: *The World Without Us* suggests that, in the end, our impact will have been seen to be inconsequential and easily remedied, and that since the planet can recover in our absence, then our presence can't have been as bad as we may have feared.

The limited operations of science faction within our protracted political interregnum are also highlighted in Slavoj Žižek's attempts to unsettle the shape and character of dominant forms of ecological analysis. In *The World Without Us*, nature is the "good other" of humanity; in the wake of the latter's disappearance, nature would gradually and smoothly reclaim cities and sites of human development with little impact or consequence. Žižek counters how science faction imagines the changing face of the planet, understanding humanity's relation to ecological balance in a precisely opposite way: "The lesson to be fully endorsed is that of an environmental scientist who concluded that while we cannot be sure what the ultimate result of humanity's interventions into the geosphere will be, one thing is sure: if humanity were to abruptly cease its immense industrial activity and let nature on Earth take its balanced course, the result would be a total breakdown, an imaginable catastrophe."[22] For Weisman, the catastrophe is only speculative—either humanity avoids such a catastrophe via action, or the environment (and as a result humanity) suffers a fatal downfall (though neither scenario is spelled out or described in the book). Žižek's assertion that the cessation of human activity would necessarily produce a catastrophe illustrates the *inadequacy* of any narrative that would separate humans from nature and write them out of the future. If it is our future *inactivity* (just as much as our current activity) that spells catastrophic doom, how can we argue that we are somehow separate from nature, that our lives are somehow not complexly knotted and entwined with the fate of the planet?[23] For Žižek, the configurations of "nature" with which science faction and other environmental narratives operate have to be seen as an ideological crutch that manages a problem rather than resolves it. He writes: "With the latest developments, the discontent shifts from culture to nature itself: nature is no longer 'natural,' the reliable 'dense' background of our lives; it now appears as a fragile mechanism which, at any point, can explode in a catastrophic direction."[24]

Žižek characterizes this moment's version of ecology as an ecology of fear—as a "fear of a catastrophe (human-made or natural) that may deeply perturb or even destroy human civilization; fear that pushes us to plan measures that would protect our safety."[25] Science faction is an example par excellence of such fear, generating a mode of pessimism about the present that has to be read as suspect about its true inclinations and desires. Citing Hans-Georg Gadamer, Žižek reads such forms of ecological pessimism as simulated: "'The pessimist is disingenuous because he is trying to trick himself with his own grumbling. Precisely while acting the pessimist, he secretly hopes that everything will not turn out as bad as he fears.' Doesn't the same tension between the enunciated and the position of enunciation characterize today's ecological pessimism: the more those who predict a catastrophe insist on it, the more they secretly hope the catastrophe will not occur."[26] In the secret heart of the pessimist, then, is an optimistic core, a small piece of hope that grows in intensity with the insistence on the inevitability of imminent destruction. This optimism is not that described by Berlant but, once again, a less political form of hope for the future, which projects, extrapolates, and predicts the dangers of ecological change, in order to affirm the desirability of keeping everything else—liberal, democratic capitalism—the same as ever.

One of the implicit political claims of those who would imagine a world without people is that there is no necessity of addressing the fourth antagonism of contemporary capitalism that Žižek describes: the population explosion of global slum dwellers.[27] Žižek observes that today "the needy people in society are no longer the workers."[28] Science faction depicts the discontented negatively, representing the absence of the worker in the world as a perverse solution to global slums and the ever-increasing surplus armies of the global South, armies that are blamed (by developed countries) for many of the environmental problems detailed by Weisman. Ironically, science faction's dream of a world without people, a perfect nature able to move unhindered by a human presence on Earth, is only fully realized through the fictional genocide of indigent and slum populations: they are truly the only humans wiped from the face of the earth, while the so-called "symbolic class" is retained to describe the events of the supposedly peopleless world. The problem of (the lack of) narrator and audience that we described earlier reappears here in another guise, in the contrast between the *presence* of the talking heads and interviewees and the perverse *absence* of global slums and the unemployed—a problematic intimately related to the very ecological questions Weisman and others had set out to address. Once again, here, we detect through the absence of one of the major contradictions of global capitalism—massive, epidemic unemployment and underemployment—a lack of any consideration of the political in the unfolding of the future narratives of science faction. Indeed, one has to conclude that this absence of the political, which emerges in the celebration of the cleanliness of expertise in contradistinction to the filth, problems, and drama of human social life, is necessarily constitutive of the genre as a whole: the latter is wiped away so that the former can do its work.[29]

There is a desperate need to produce a response to environmental change. The difficulties in doing so have little to do with our understanding of or our belief in human impacts on the environment and much more to do with the broader limits of political discourse at the present moment. Generating new forms of narrative that might unsettle or undo these limits is essential. Rather than opening possibilities, Mark Jendrysik has suggested that those texts we have described here as science factions are anti-utopian, since the consequence of texts such as Weisman's is that they "reject the possibility of human action to perfect or save the ecosphere."[30] But perhaps even more problematic, however, is the manner in which these texts position themselves *as utopian* through their affirmation of the desirability and inevitability of a political present even as they draw attention to the problems of the environmental future—a utopia in the mode not of novel political possibilities but of Francis Fukuyama's infamous end of history. The challenges posed to ecological writing by thinkers such as Berlant and Žižek demand a far more powerful narrative intervention than thinking of a life after people; they demand a negative, rather than an affirmative or positive, utopian impulse. Such an approach to the impasse would necessarily take more than the strictly ecological into its scope, accounting for the social relations of capital (labor, underemployment, and unemployment) as well as the petroculture that fuels such relations. Dipesh Chakrabarty has recently written of the inseparability of fossil fuels from the Enlightenment project as a whole, noting that, "the mansion of modern freedoms stands on an ever-expanding base of fossil-fuel use. Most of our freedoms so far have been energy-intensive."[31] What remains certain is that ecological narratives that fail to make such direct connections between the dreams and nightmares of the Enlightenment do little more than comfort us with the belief that we can change everything without having to change anything. *The World Without Us* and texts like it provide good fodder for NPR interviews and dinner-table speculations about the future-to-come, but do nothing to solve the political problem of how to make this future different from the present.

Notes

1. James Hansen, "Game Over for the Climate," *New York Times*, May 9, 2012, http://www.nytimes.com/2012/05/10/opinion/game-over-for-the-climate.html?src=me&ref=general.

2. See J. Hansen, D. Johnson, A. Lacis, S. Lebedeff, P. Lee, D. Rind, and G. Russell, "Climate Impact of Increasing Atmospheric Carbon Dioxide," Science 213 (1981): 957–66.

3. David Suzuki in Guy Dixon, "The Bottom Line? He Has Some Regrets," *Globe and Mail,* June 30, 2010, R2.

4. One such image that begins chapter 2 is that of nature clearing houses "off the face of the Earth." This wouldn't seem noteworthy if it wasn't oddly prescient of the housing crisis in the United States—an instance where we could see Weisman's world without us in the cleared out, emptied homes of the racialized and gendered victims of housing foreclosures who bore the brunt of the financial recession. With this in mind, Weisman's words take on a cruel irony: "If you're a homeowner, you already knew it was only a matter of time for yours, but you've resisted admitting it, even as erosion callously attacked, starting with your savings. Back when they told you what your house would cost, nobody mentioned what you'd also be paying so that nature wouldn't repossess it long before the bank." Alan Weisman, *The World Without Us* (New York: Picador, 2007), 17.

5. Ibid., 6.

6. See Gerry Canavan, Lisa Klarr, and Ryan Vu, "Ecology and Ideology: An Introduction,"

Polygraph 22 (2010): 21. Canavan, Klarr, and Vu indicate that both aesthetic directions one could take in order to solve this puzzle—that of defaulting to a "higher omniscience" or to "project our consciousness into non-human entities"—are "equally implausible." They are discussing the television documentary series *Life after People*, but the characterization of a "post-human *non*-perspective" applies here as well.

7. Weisman, *World Without Us*, 119.

8. Alan Weisman, "Interview: Alan Weisman," *Tricycle* 17, no. 2, with Clark Strand (2007): 62.

9. Ibid., 60, 67.

10. Weisman, *World Without Us*, 21.

11. Ibid., 196.

12. See Darko Suvin, *Metamorphoses of Science Fiction: Poetics of a Genre* (New Haven, CT: Yale University Press, 1979).

13. Carl Freedman, *Critical Theory and Science Fiction* (Middletown, CT: Wesleyan University Press, 2000), 16–17.

14. Weisman, "Interview," 61.

15. Clark Stand responds, "True. The biologists and physicists and environmentalists and artists you interviewed are all right there on nearly every page of the book, speaking in their own voices about what would happen if we suddenly disappeared. In that respect, it's a very densely populated book." Weisman continues, "The whole book is really a way of getting people to imagine, first of all, how amazing the world would be without us, and second, how we might add ourselves back into this equation. We could still be a part of it. But then, there are a lot of things that we should do now in order to make sure that happens." Weisman, "Interview," 63.

16. Weisman, *World Without Us*, 6.

17. Fredric Jameson, *Postmodernism, or, the Cultural Logic of Late Capitalism* (Durham, NC: Duke University Press, 1991), 24.

18. Lauren Berlant, "Cruel Optimism," *Differences: A Journal of Feminist Cultural Studies* 17, no. 3 (2006): 31.

19. Ibid.

20. Ibid., 23.

21. Ibid.

22. Slavoj Žižek, "Nature and Its Discontents," *SubStance* 37, no. 3 (2008): 56.

23. Ibid., 50.

24. Ibid., 50.

25. Ibid., 53.

26. Ibid.

27. "Although their population is composed of marginalized laborers, redundant civil servants and ex-peasants, they are not simply a redundant surplus: they are incorporated into the global economy in numerous ways, many of them working as informal wage workers or self-employed entrepreneurs, with no adequate health or social security coverage. (The main source of their rise is the inclusion of the Third World countries in

the global economy, with cheap food imports from the First World countries ruining local agriculture.) They are the true 'symptom' of slogans like 'Development,' 'Modernization,' and 'World Market': not an unfortunate accident, but a necessary product of the innermost logic of global capitalism." Ibid., 40.

28. Ibid., 37.

29. See Jasper Bernes, "The Double Barricade and the Glass Floor," in *Communization and Its Discontents*, ed. Benjamin Noys (New York: Minor Compositions, 2011), 157–72. Bernes takes up the questions that motivates Žižek's piece, arguing for political response to the increasing tendency of capital to generate groups and people who appear outside of the system but remain deeply a part of its operations: "Examining capitalism in this way, as a process of production that contains moments both inside and outside of the workplace, allows us to expand our notion of antagonistic agents, to expand our notion of the proletariat—so that it includes the unemployed, students, unwaged house workers and prisoners." Bernes, "Double Barricade," 164. See also Aaron Benanav and *Endnotes*, "Misery and Debt: On the Logic and History of Surplus Populations and Surplus Capital," *Endnotes* 2 (June 27, 2012), http://endnotes.org.uk/articles/1, where Benanav, with *Endnotes*, makes a cogent argument for a reconsideration of Marx's general law of capital accumulation (that increasing amounts of surplus capital always and of necessity generate growing populations of surplus labor beyond the amount required by capital to keep employment rates and wages low) in light of the current historical conjuncture. For a discussion of unemployment, see also Fredric Jameson, "Political Conclusions," in *Representing Capital* (London: Verso, 2011), 139–51.

30. Mark S. Jendrysik, "Back to the Garden: New Visions of Posthuman Futures," *Utopian Studies* 22, no. 1 (2011): 36.

31. Dipesh Chakrabarty, "The Climate of History: Four Theses," *Critical Inquiry* 35 (Winter 2009): 208.

Pandora's Box

Avatar, *Ecology, Thought*

TIMOTHY MORTON

The movie *Avatar* was so successful because it speaks, and fails to speak, about issues related to ecology, environment, and world, some of the most pressing issues of our age.[1] And yet, despite the surface-level anticapitalist and anticolonialist appearance of *Avatar*, the picture is more complex. *Avatar* acknowledges the philosophical and political dilemma we face around ecological thought while failing to resolve it. This dilemma is precisely to do with *thought* and *thinking* at the very moment at which humans have begun to deposit a thin layer of carbon in Earth's crust, thus opening the intersection of human history and geological time now known as the Anthropocene. In this essay, I shall argue that *Avatar* performs a kind of chiasmic figure-of-eight: on the one hand, it gives us a sense of being-in-a-world that I argue is strictly untenable in an era of ecological emergency; on the other hand, *Avatar* dissolves this very sense of "being-in"—taking with one hand what it gives with the other. What the Kantian revolution in philosophy opened was, to use a pun that I shall use perhaps too often here, a Pandora's box that allowed both for the ultimate expression thus far of human nihilism and instrumental reason and for the very ecological awareness that brings this nihilism not so much to an end but to its logical conclusion: reason as both poison and cure, as homeopathic medicine. In so doing, I show that *Avatar* is not the total assault on modernity it seems to be but holds out, rather, the possibility of a *logical conclusion* to modernity.

Environmental philosophy often claims to be Heideggerian, but what does this mean? It usually amounts to asserting, without much substantiation, that humans are embedded in a *world*. A careful reading of Heidegger, however, demonstrates that this view could not be less Heideggerian. On the contrary, as I shall argue in this essay, the fully Heideggerian view is the feeling that the world has suddenly disappeared. This feeling is highly congruent with contemporary developments in the cultural imaginary of the Anthropocene. The Anthropocene is that geological period defined by the deposition of a fine layer of carbon in Earth's crust as a result of human activity, starting around 1790. What is called the *Great Acceleration* logarithmically sped up the processes of the Anthropocene when the Gadget (Trinity test), Little Boy (Hiroshima), and Fat Boy (Nagasaki) began to deposit radioactive materials in Earth's crust in 1945. The precision with which geology measures this date (against the incomprehensible vastness of geological time) is itself a symptom of the profound disorientation of habitual views of *world*. These views depend for their coherence on a stable enough contrast between a foreground and a background—but in an era of global warming, no such contrast is available to us.

This chapter shall therefore argue that the notion of "planetary awareness," then, far from being a utopian upgrade of normative embeddedness ideology, is instead an uncanny realization of coexistence with a plenum of ungraspable hyperobjects—entities such as *climate* and *evolution* that can be computed but that cannot directly be seen or touched (unlike *weather* or *this rabbit*, respectively)—and nonhuman beings. Moreover, the sense of being "in" a world itself is, in Heideggerian terms, a covering over of the very being that it endeavors to assert. The anthem of the current era, instead, is "We *Aren't* the World." As we shall see, *Avatar* dramatizes this perilous ambiguity. On one hand, its stunningly immersive graphics and sentimental suction make us feel as if we are practically enveloped by its world. On the other hand, the disorientating scales and strange luminous aesthetics of the Pandoran forest and its inhabitants promise something much more disturbing, and, I shall argue, much more ecological.

OF PLANET-SENSE

One of the key charms of *Avatar* is its dramatization of a fantasy about distributed interaction (where action takes place in multiple places and times at once, owing to devices such as internet technology), a fantasy that one can't help seeing as a displacement of human hopes and fears about online activity and identity; the very term *avatar*, it is well known, denotes an immaterial "skin" for an online space. The Na'vi are connected to their planet, Pandora, via a kind of organic Internet, a "living," breathing "good" version of the "bad" interconnection of the humans. The plot is essentially that the protagonist, Jake Sully, gradually identifies with, then fully pours himself into, his Na'vi avatar. It is more desirable to be one of the Na'vi, because they are not dislocated from their planet as humans are. In part, this is because the planet Pandora itself provides them with a palpable communal awareness, a thrilling mirror play of feedback: the planet's entire biosphere is a brain–mind. I shall be calling this feedback awareness *planet-sense.*

In this section I play on the possibility that the phrase "sense of planet"—as in Ursula Heise's book *Sense of Place and Sense of Planet*—is in fact a subjective genitive, which is to say that "sense of planet" means that the planet itself can "sense."[2] Even if humans are the only "persons" on Earth, which now seems astonishingly unlikely, they act as the planet's sense organs insofar as they are its direct outgrowths, and insofar as sentience just is an "interobjective" system's emergence as information-for some "perceiver." That is to say, sentience is somewhat in the eye of the beholder: as we now know, for instance, plants are in some respects sentient, though they lack the hardware that animals have. But Earth senses us in a far deeper and more disturbing way, since environmental awareness is predicated on an always-already. Our fear as to whether global warming has started or not is directly correlated to our uncertainty as to what the weather is telling us. This fear and uncertainty is an ironic product of the fact that *global warming has indeed started.* Unable to see it directly, we assess global warming insofar as it takes the measure of us. A tsunami assesses the fragility of a Japanese town. An earthquake probes the ability of humans and their equipment to resist the liquefaction of crust. A heat wave scans us with ultraviolet rays. These largely harmful measurements direct our attention to human coexistence with other life-forms inside a gigantic object that just is, yet is not reducible to, these life-forms and ourselves. The Anthropocene—the term for human intervention on a scale recognizable in geological time—is the ironic name for a moment at which the nonhuman is discerned to be inextricable from the human, a variation of the noir plot of the Oedipus story in which the measurer turns out to be the measured. To understand the contemporary age, then, is to understand the form of the Oedipus story—namely, how we still remain within the confines of agricultural ritual, a plot that plots the world as graspable, technical object and horizon, a plot that eventually leads nowhere but to what I shall define precisely as a specific kind of *doom.* What underlies sense of planet, then, is *planet-sense,* experienced by humans as physical enmeshment in a trap that is by no means free, pleasant, or utopian, precisely to the extent that it is a "global" awareness—but cognitively liberating nonetheless.

This is not the political affect of planet-sense in *Avatar.* Indeed, the movie seems designed quite specifically to thwart this weird, "evil" loop, the Möbius strip that defines the contours of ecological awareness. Evil indeed is a banned category in the movie, which seems rather to operate with a Spinozan (that is to say, Californian) logic of health and pathology. One way to understand the work movies do is to imagine that they embody forms of thinking.

Let's do a thought experiment and wonder what it would be like if the universe were structured according to the logic of the film. It makes sense sometimes to look at movies this way—as pictures of the world, just like philosophy. One way to understand such pictures is to magnify them by imagining what reality would be like if the picture were wildly, totally successful. We shall see that the reality of *Avatar* is one in which things like planets can have thoughts and feelings. We will also see that it is a reality in which evil is a banned category. There is one word for such a picture, and that word is Spinoza.

There is but one substance—symbolized by the planet and its sentient sprouts, one of which is the Na'vi—in which mind and body are indistinguishable, a plane of immanence with no ontological gaps. There is a smooth continuum between what on Earth is called *body* and what is called *mind*. Thus, via the organic internet, the Na'vi are able to reincarnate by titrating their essence into another body, just as at the end of the film the human protagonist Jake Sully is able to become one of them, in a seamless manner. The humans with their militaristic science are simply confused or perhaps mentally ill, not evil. They blunder around violently: there is no evil, only inadequately expressed *conatus*, the will-to-exist that takes joy in imposing itself on the rest of the planet-substance. It wasn't that the humans were evil to rob the planet of its unobtainium—they were confused. If the humans had only read the government health warning embedded in the unobtainium, as it were, they would never have tried mining for this mineral. This view edits out something very powerful: why have the humans even wanted unobtainium in the first place? Were their reasons really rational, only confused? Or is unobtainium something like (to quote another movie) an "obscure object of desire"? There is no way, in the logic of the movie, to see what the humans are doing as fundamentally *wrong* or *evil*. This is self-defeating, since according to this view, the Na'vi are simply more successful at playing the game humans are playing. They are upgraded humans—or we are downgraded Na'vi. By wishing for and consuming the right things, we will create a just society; we just have to change our ways a bit. Isn't this the dominant environmentalist paradigm of our age?

There is no fundamental difference between humans and the Na'vi. This raises a deeper issue. There is no *nothing*, no *nothingness*, in a reality that contains no ontological gaps—for instance, the gap between brain and mind, filled by the suggestiveness of cinematic imagery to render the planet of *Avatar* a sentient world. There is *not even nothing*, for Spinoza's substance is everything. For Spinoza, the entity *nothing* is *oukontic*, that is, not even nothing: substance is everywhere, without lack. But what was opened up from the time of Kant—that is, from the opening of the Anthropocene—was indeed a *nothingness* that is better described as *meontic*. This is a weirdly "positive" nothing that is not absolutely nothing at all, but rather a kind of flickering nothing, or a quality of nothing-*ness*. This is the nothingness that Hegel banishes to the outer reaches of his philosophical system, a pure self-reference that he describes as "the night in which all cows are black."[3]

Hegel's nothingness was a reaction to Kant, whose *Critique of Pure Reason* had discerned a threatening gap in the real. Measurement, understanding, calculating, are predicated on reason, but this reason is an abyss that I cannot directly access. I can count and measure, but I can't display the concept of number itself, even to myself—I must rely on indexical signs, such as pointing to my fingers and counting "One, two, three . . ." But these signs are precisely not *number* as such. Yet I can think *number*. There is thus a gap, a crack, in reality, a crack that allows me to think reason not as playing with preestablished pieces of thought, but as thinking in itself. It is as if I have discovered a gigantic, empty ocean just behind my head, an ocean that I can't understand, but which I can think. An abyss of reason. This abyss might, indeed, not be quite human—it is as if there is an alien, impersonal presence at my core, a void that is not oukontic but meontic.

Does the planet Pandora not evoke this abyss? The film's audience first plunges into it on board Jake Sully's transport ship. As a Na'vi, Sully then dives from a floating island atop his winged reptilian mount, in a blissful ballet that evokes the pure freedom amid vertiginous terror we discover in the experience of the Kantian sublime. This is indeed *science fiction*—the thrill of science as such, the aesthetic plunge into the abyss of reason, evoked by the Yes-album-like architecture of floating islands and arches (Yes being a progressive rock band whose appeal also lies in a fusion of science and a world-saving, hippie aesthetic).

What has happened to our thought experiment? We have discovered something weird—*Avatar*'s "world without gaps" depends on *reason*, which *implies gaps*. The very attempt to produce a gapless, immersive world depends on dynamiting the world into a vast and threatening abyss—the gigantic realm where number is never the same as counting. This isn't just an implicit message in the movie. This realm of reason is the condition of the movie's physical reality, the fact that we can see it at all, since to produce it, an immense amount of computation (counting and other forms of calculating) was required. An immense battery of machines evokes the world of *Avatar*, implying a vast transcendental abyss, namely, an abyss we can't see or touch—the abyss of reason.

I can access something like a virtual reality version of the ocean of reason through the aesthetic, in particular through this experience of the sublime. I can at least glimpse the vertigo of reason's abyss when I try to count to infinity, and realize that I can't—which realization precisely is how infinity must be thought.[4] I have discovered a part of reality (the noumenal, in Kant's terms) that *transcends* what I can understand (the phenomenal, again in his terms). This transcendence is the mortal philosophical enemy of immanence, the trademark of Spinozism. On this view, there is an ontological break between the physical biosphere-brain and the mind assembled by its neural connections between its trees and other life-forms. The abyss of Pandora, our thrill ride between its floating islands, threaten the Spinozan continuum, destabilizing any fantasy of uncomplicated embeddedness. This means that the viewer's attempt to resolve the movie contains an inevitable gap.

Idealism is one way to close the gap in the real. This is Hegel's solution—and in a sense many viewers of *Avatar* have done a Hegel by taking it simply as fantasy. Another solution is to collapse again the gap in the real into some modified version of materialism—Deleuze, Bergson, Whitehead: to paper over the crack with the spackle of matter. Surely this is one reason for the appeal of Spinozism in modernity—it allows for a pantheism that is not so different from atheism, since everything is of one substance and thus God. This spackling approach is rather like what this essay has described as the more sophisticated approach to viewing *Avatar*. But for all its visions of oneness, *Avatar* also invites us to see twos: humans and Na'vi, Earth and Pandora, floating islands and abysses, planets and space, modernity and ecology. These twos are mashed together in the person of Sully, whose very name suggests a dirtiness that seems excluded from the pristine world of Pandora, a dirtiness associated with an excess of thinking over its physical conditions: "Oh that this too too sullied flesh would melt" moans Hamlet, first voyager in the ocean of reason ("I could be bounded in a nutshell, and count myself a king of infinite space, were it not that I have bad dreams").[5] It is virtual reality that enables this mash-up to take place—virtual reality that is perhaps the analogue within the space of the movie for the viewer, who exists within a video-game culture where movies are part of a larger ludic space. This mash-up is a basis for the fantasy work that *Avatar* asks us to do. There is the possibility that human virtual technology could be replicated in the nonhuman world, and that the two could then communicate. But another aspect of the fantasy is that one of the communicators and one of the communication media must "win." Thus under the possibility that humans and nonhumans can communicate is a darker fantasy—the idea that the nonhuman media are simply more efficient and powerful versions of the human one. Human technology is a debased version of Na'vi technology, and if we could only harness it, make our technology more harmonious with "nature". . . Underneath the idea of humans and nonhumans communicating is another idea, which just is what is called *modernity*—the idea that we can do things better, stronger, faster, with less "noise" (such as social hierarchy) getting in the way. Modernity is what generated the environmental emergency that gives rise to movies such as *Avatar* in the first place. Thus to replicate the Na'vi media system is really to progress along the same path that brought directors such as James Cameron to make gigantic movies about how modernity is flawed. We seem to be caught in a loop.

The movie speaks about its nonsynthesis of these dualities in the person of the dying Jake Sully, who must finally be uploaded from the human virtual computer into the Na'vi natural world-system rather than continue to live a double life. Both/and is not possible in a world of unique and discrete beings. A radical choice must be made, akin to love, in which I select one being from all the others. This choice is, as Slavoj Žižek puts it, synonymous with evil, a radical imbalance. The scene in which Neytiri cradles the gasping Jake, infant-small in comparison, shows us this asymmetry in an extreme way: the love of a mother for an infant is excessive, "evil" in its hostility to other beings that might threaten it. For a magical moment, it is as if the movie is able to show that condition for the harmony between Jake and Neytiri is this pre-Oedipal asymmetry, in which the beautiful luminous being admires the ugly, dirty, sullied tiny one.

We must now take a short detour through the abyss of reason, which is precisely what *Avatar* hopes we can avoid. I shall try to shoot some threads back toward the movie as we go.

Accepting transcendence means diving into the cold abyssal ocean of reason to see what it might contain: Husserlian phenomenology discovers all kinds of "intentional objects" there, floating like shoals of fish. Far lower down, Heidegger's U-boat patrols the depths, sliding through the opaque darkness of angst. Far above, on the surface of the ocean of reason, float the islands of "facts"—in other words, regions of preestablished pieces of calcified reason that were taken before Kant to be real things: the notion, for instance, that everything must have a cause, without understanding what causality as such might be. These islands are what scholasticism took to be truth, so that Kant's discovery of the abyss of reason is like the discovery of a third dimension in a world inhabited by stick people. Fleshing out Hume, Kant realizes that it just is impossible to establish causality without diving into the abyss of reason. Scientific facts are beings that are correlated to events in a statistical way. This is what allows cigarette companies to assert, quite correctly, that the causal link between smoking and cancer cannot be proved, since scientific facts just are statistical correlations. Science is Humean: in other words, science is based on statistics rather than on metaphysical "certainties."[6] This is what allows global warming deniers to assert, also quite correctly, that the causal link between human fossil fuel burning and climate change can't be proved. Indeed, this problem is more existentially and politically urgent than the smoking problem—since by the time it might be proved beyond doubt, global warming will be catastrophically irreversible.[7] The world of ecological awareness is a world of *anxiety*, because there is a fundamental gap between the empirical data and what they mean, and ecological entities such as *biosphere* and *climate* are huge enough to make us painfully aware of this gap.

Pandora—it's the name of the ever-giving planet the humans fantasize about in *Avatar*. But it's also the name for a box in which all the evils of the world are kept. It is not so difficult to see that what Hume and Kant did—and subsequently "gigantic" science that discovered things like *biosphere* and *evolution*—was to open up a Pandora's box in the second sense. The plenitude of data evokes anxiety. If everything is equally real and unique, there is no hierarchy, no reality-confirming world that allows me to differentiate between things in advance. To see the universe as a weird, structurally incomplete set of discrete beings necessarily pushes us toward anxiety, an affect in which things become flat since they do not match my inner space, another unique being in itself. Modern philosophy is the confrontation with nothingness—and so is modern consumer-ism, in which there is no good reason (given in advance by a king or a priest or whoever) why I should buy this particular bottle of shampoo. Or indeed why I should be fascinated with this unobtainium, whose very name is a punning circularity: part of why I need it is simply because I can't obtain it (easily). This self-swallowing serpent of a syndrome is precisely what *Avatar* is designed to make us think we can circumvent. But it appears that since the nothingness is what this chapter has called the *logical conclusion* of modernity, we must in the end pass through the nothingness as a necessary phase of thinking and coexist-ing, to see what might lie on the other side.

Avatar is not alone in trying to leap over nothingness. Dominant forms of nihilism itself, for instance, could be viewed as a reaction-formation against the disturbance of meontic angst: this is Heidegger's view, which I share. What is required for thinking is not to wish away the ocean that provides the reason for the problems identified by Hume, as if we could unthink the fact that we are three-dimensional beings. Heidegger correctly saw that the task was to voyage beneath nihilism, not to take flight above it or to try to circumvent it. The ocean of reason seeps through the cracks in the pavement of prepackaged facts, a metaphor I choose deliberately in an age in which the ocean is beginning to inundate Pacific islands, precisely because of the Anthropocene that is the flip side of the Kantian "Copernican turn." For Kant had decided that the human–world correlate was what gave reality to things: the ocean of reason is human, or at any rate an aspect of my (human) mind. But what if the ocean went deeper than the human, in spite of it, outside of it. This is a frightening thought if you are an anthropocentrist. But don't gigantic computational machines—the ones that made *Avatar* possible—prove that every day, every time we switch them on? This thought, that reason isn't really human, has preoccupied us mightily since the late eighteenth century—since the invention of the steam engine and the march toward all kinds of unobtainium. Consider how contemporary "speculative realist" philosophy deals with it. These philosophies understand that Kant and his Pandora's box cannot be rejected, and that one could see the last two hundred years of philosophy as a struggle to restrict what had happened in the late eighteenth century.[8] Yet some of these very philosophies continue to make humans the special openers of Pandora's box. They are trying to contain what lies inside. Yet what if my (human) ocean of reason was just one such transcendental gap in the world? What if the same kind of gap exists between a slice of pineapple and a cereal bowl? Or between a slice of pineapple and itself? This possibility is what inspired Graham Harman to discover, at a depth unheard of in the Heideggerian U-boat, below Heidegger and implied by him in the tool-analysis, but never explicitly spoken, a gigantic coral reef of what he calls "objects," by which he means any entity whatsoever: a human, an iPhone, the movie *Avatar*, the fiction of the Na'vi, spoons, leather, and tornadoes. A truly animist view, the view the Na'vi hold, in which everything is a "person," is not a world of smoothness, but a riot of anxiety in which I confront the full uncanniness of things. Astonishingly, this view is the logical end-point of reason itself.

Yet at the end of *Avatar*, the "alien" humans must return to a poisoned Earth, and we must exit the cinema. What did we really see in there? Did we really see that modern humans have fallen from a state of nature in which there were better, stronger media, taller, healthier bodies and more integrated minds, and a sense of being part of something bigger than us? Or did we see a brief, somewhat disturbing glimpse of *our future selves*—people who had made friends with the nothingness that erupts out of Pandora's box, the philosophy and science of the modern age, people coexisting with other people who are not the same as us, uncanny people with four legs, wings, scales, and fur?

WE AREN'T THE WORLD

Kant's project was the first in a rather long series of "end of metaphysics" arguments in continental philosophy. Pre-Kantian metaphysics had, he argued, relied on prepackaged concepts that floated around unexamined. What were the conditions of possibility of these concepts, these facts? Supposed facts, he argued, were just projections, in the same way that we think the sun is rising and setting, whereas we are in fact hurtling through space on a planet revolving around the sun, spinning on its axis. From the bottom of the ocean, we undergo another Copernican turn, as we realize that the abyss of reason that Kant opens up, the third dimension that bisects the stick-figure world of scholastic metaphysics, is only the *human–world* gap. There is an iPhone–world gap, a pineapple–world gap, a galaxy–world gap. A Pandora's boxful of gaps. Indeed, what is really proclaimed, from the bottom of the ocean, beneath nihilism, is that *there is no world*.

   Why? Because there is no top-level box, no set of sets, into which everything fits, of which everything is a part. This lack of a top level is totally obscured in *Avatar*, whose vision is of holistic oneness, a vision that depends upon the idea of a top level—the biosphere itself. A hundred years into the Anthropocene, Husserl had discovered shoals of factical fish darting around in what Kant took to be the unified, singular containers of time and space, fish such as hoping, asserting, hating. These intentional objects are units that are not simply symptoms of the mind that produces them: they have some kind of autonomy, which marks the difference between psychologistic logic, which sees logic as a symptom of the (human) mind (or rather, brain), and phenomenology, which understands logic as ontologically prior to psychology. Each intentional fish in the ocean is discrete.[9] In the same way, and at roughly the same time, Cantor discovered discrete *transfinite sets*, sets that seemed to lack a definite or smooth bridge between them: the set of real numbers contains the set of rational numbers, but is separated from it infinitely. What Cantor discovered were beings that could be members of a set that radically transcended them, giving rise to the irksome Russell set paradox, the set of all sets that are not members of themselves. Another way of saying the same thing would be to suppose that a mind is not simply an emergent product of neurons and brain activity.

Thus if we think about it, there is a way in which the logic of a world full of gaps contradicts the aesthetic logic of *Avatar*, a contradiction that has a salient political resonance. Despite the dominant message of the movie, the biosphere of Pandora is not reducible to its components. If it were, we would confront a purely mechanistic holism of interlocking parts, a contexture in which one thing matters the same as—which is to say as little as—anything else. Nor, however, is the whole greater than the sum of its parts, for the whole is simply another being, another entity with an unbridgeable ontological chasm between it and the beings that are its members. If we were to accept this holism, *Avatar*'s biosphere would simply be a more efficient machine than the human mechanisms that exploit it. On this view, the final confrontation between Miles Quaritch, in his alien-killing cyborgian outfit, and Neytiri on her leopard-like mount, is one between equally matched pieces of machinery. If Pandoran society is not simply a more efficient form of Western modernity, it must take the form of a Pandora's box—that is, a being that contains an infinitude of other beings that cannot be reduced to it: a set whose members are not members of themselves. Pandora's box, a paradox.

What Cantor did was precisely to have opened Pandora's box. He discovered that there might not be an integral top level that bestowed smoothness to reality, at least the region of reality associated with logic. If thought is a reflex of reality in some sense, then reality is profoundly disjointed, riddled with gaps, voids, wormholes to other universes. To think is to open Pandora's box, an image whose instrumental yet ecological resonance *Avatar* expresses fully, like two halves of a torn whole that, in Adorno's words, do not add up together. This fractured quality of the movie might explain its massive popularity—like a myth, it is an attempt to compute a problem that we have not yet fully thought out.

In the world of Pandora's box, there are meontic nothings everywhere, between, for instance, the set of real and the set of rational numbers. Trying to find a smooth bridge between these sets (the "Continuum Hypothesis") drove first Cantor, then Gödel, insane, as if reason was indeed toxic to humans, an obsessive plunge into the Kantian abyss that could easily result in fatality. Trying to turn nothingness into a thing, into something given—forgetting precisely that at this depth, there are no factical islands, no stand-out "truths," no solid pre-given mounds of metaphysical dirt. It is indeed, as Deleuze and Guattari point out, not the sleep of reason that breeds monsters, but rather the hypervigilance of an overactive rationality.[10]

This is why Zermelo and Fraenkel smoothed out Cantor's sets with a simple fix: they were not sets, but rather "classes." This is somewhat the same as the logician Alfred Tarski smoothing out the sentence "This sentence is false" by ruling that it isn't a sentence. The trouble with this procedure, which was the early twentieth-century direct response to the monsters of reason discovered by Cantor, is that one could construct an ever-escalating series of "viral" sentences to get around the rule. Consider for instance the following:

This is not a sentence.

And so on.[11] It appears that, as Lacan later observed, *there is no metalanguage*: no vantage point outside of sentences—or sets, or for that matter spoons—from which to pronounce with perfect authority the rules of sentences, spoons, or sets. One finds oneself phenomenologically glued to whatever one is thinking, saying, physically or mentally grasping, and so on. Like the mirror that sticks to Neo in *The Matrix*, reality can't be peeled away. Isn't this one of the deeply structural layers of *Avatar* itself? If something happens to your virtual body, your Na'vi avatar, you are hurt or die. The virtual experience of "being in" the Na'vi world is not totally vicarious. You can bleed. And vice versa: if Miles Quaritch pulls the plug in the human world, your Na'vi avatar collapses. This lack of a true and rigid separation between virtual and actual is why the Na'vi think of the human avatars as evil spirits—a thought that Neytiri and others do their best to dispel. But in a sense, it is quite a significant thought. What ecological awareness is like is very much a kind of coexistence with weird spirits, zombies, half-physical, half-psychic entities, in a non-thin, non-rigidly defined zone. This is what happens when we choose to let go of a rigid difference between human and nonhuman, not some back-to-nature happy stupidity.

What Heidegger means by *world* is precisely this inability to peel myself out of my own skin. This is precisely the opposite of what is meant by *world* in the common way: a top-level container into which everything meaningfully fits. This meaningfulness itself depends upon some further rather fishy criteria. Worlds require, for instance, a single stable correlator to make sense of them: my world, which revolves around the stable reference point of myself, appears as a series of backgrounds and foregrounds. Worlds depend upon the notion of *away*, and in a time of ecological awareness, what is shattered is precisely this illusion of *away*, because now we know that the waste we flush goes into the wastewater treatment plant, or the Pacific Ocean, and so on. If there is no *away*, there can be no foreground–background distinction; thus there can be no world, because my correlation to the world depends upon my ability to establish such a distinction. In this sense, the worlding of Pandora is a desperate attempt to put the uncanny beings back inside Pandora's box and close it. To be convinced of a foreground–background distinction now requires thousands of gigabytes of graphics processing, incredible, immersive art reminiscent of the massive gatefold album sleeves of the 1970s, and so on. It is this gigantic, industrial-scale desperation that the movie works with—and in the very attempt, it undermines the world, because it must rely on (literally) globally distributed computational systems to achieve the illusion.

Since there are as many correlators as there are beings, and since all these beings have a world in some trivial sense, there is no (one) world, and the concept of world is severely weakened. Yet as we have just seen, the problem is much more severe than that. This is because *world* is the meaningful and coherent set of things that surround me, correlated to me, and we have just shown that there can be no such set, only a non-totalizable, not-all plenum of discrete beings. There is no reason why some of these beings can't be countries or football teams or unions, but this proves the point in another way. Lithuania isn't reducible to its borders or its roads or its people or its boundaries on a map, or its grasses or its sand. It is not the sum of, or greater than the sum of, these components added together (the latter idea is organicism). Strangely, then, ecological awareness implies *the end of the world*. It would be better, as Brecht would have said, to start with the bad news that "We Aren't the World," as Michael Jackson didn't put it. And we see this only in negative in our viewership of the film and its (failed) attempt to depict that kind of wholeness in which we are actually the world.

Those passages of *Being and Time* that address the notion of angst have to do precisely with a sense of the loss of a world. In the experience of anxiety everything becomes horribly flat and meaningless.[12] Angst strips away the metaphysics of presence that seems to guarantee that I am "in" a world, ruthlessly revealing that to be a mere convenient fiction. I am, rather, suspended in a nothingness. It is as if instead of trees and flowers and birds I encounter a strange ethereal mist that appears to have no depth, or is perhaps of infinite depth—there is no way to tell.

This chapter's understanding of Heidegger must then be juxtaposed against the supposed "Heideggerian" environmentalist discourse of world and embeddedness. Consider the concept of *worlding* in Haraway. This somewhat user-friendly version of "world" is far from adequate as a basis for the ethics and politics that Haraway derives from it. Consider only the "world" of witch-dunking in the Middle Ages, or the "world" of lynching in the segregated American South. Just because something constitutes a world is no reason to preserve it. But there is a more serious problem—*there is no such thing as a world*, or "world" is so diluted—since it applies equally to thumbtacks, bottlenose dolphins, and packets of chips—that it ceases to be significant.

The idea that everything is interconnected is usually a more "rational," less drastic-seeming version of "we are the world" thinking. Interconnectedness fits well with modernity on many levels—just consider many advertisements, not exactly for products, but for globalization, especially the ones that were broadcast on TV in the United States in the 1990s. It sounds so "right," and of course it sounds very "ecological." And yet, another way to close Pandora's box is to emphasize that everything is interconnected. Why on earth would a sensible ecological philosopher want to deny the primacy of that fact? Yet interconnectedness-speak blocks us from thinking Pandora as a set of unique beings that cannot ever be regarded as totally complete and consistent, which is what I have been arguing is the recipe for a more cogent ecological thought.

The rise of global interconnectedness has been reflected in contemporary philosophy. Recent philosophy has witnessed a rise of relationist ontologies that stress the notion of embeddedness and interconnection—the turn to Whitehead and to Spinoza. These ontologies are in effect attempts to erase the memory of deconstruction, behind which lurks the (genuine) threat of the Heideggerian uncanny, which in turn was a "destructuring" (*Destruktion*) of the sclerotic certainties of Western metaphysics. Why? Because relationism forgets Kant, grandfather of the "end of metaphysics"—forgets the fundamental ontological cut between phenomena (things we understand and observe) and noumena (things-in-themselves). The difference between relationism and deconstruction can be observed in the history of deconstruction's engagement with structuralism, which just is relationism applied to linguistics, and very successfully. Derrida showed how meaning, for instance, depends upon language, which depends upon the opacity of the signifier, the technical supplements of signifiers such as ink, paper, pixels, or iPads, and so on. Not everything is quite contained in a relational system—something always escapes, in order for the system to function as a system. Sets of relations, then, float on top of uncanny, alien beings that are not subject to these relations, and yet they try to include such aliens even as they exclude them, thus resulting in aporia and paradox.

The easiest way to link this to *Avatar* is to think about how the movie depends upon a massive technological apparatus—and yet it cannot speak about this layer directly, for fear of destroying its message. In the movie, powerful technology enables the humans to interact with the Na'vi. "Outside" the movie, powerful technology enables us to imagine an alien world. Without the technology—which depends on the kinds of "rare earth" that just is unobtanium to structure the silicon wafers that physically support the software—there would be no movie, no back-to-nature fantasy, no we-are-the-world.

Avatar is unable to speak the technologies that enable it. *Avatar* was produced because of gigantic cloud-based computing systems that enabled a worldwide distribution of artists and other technicians to work in sync. This worldwide distribution precisely announces the end of the world as such, as *world* depends on distances that these technologies have abolished. James Cameron waited precisely for such cloud-based systems to emerge before making *Avatar*. The piercingly psychedelic world of *Avatar*, like some fluorescent Yes album by Roger Dean, depends upon the world-destroying (because time and space collapsing) technological apparatus of cloud computing. This is perhaps reflected in the film, in which, as in the Yes art of Roger Dean, floating pieces of world hover like jagged islands. The movie seems thus to suggest that we are looking at how things stand after the end of the world—the point is, should we be trying to put the pieces back together again?

The hypnotic intensity of *Avatar*'s graphic design grips us on a sub-Kantian aesthetic level, a level dismissed as kitsch, that is, the bad taste of the other, a realm of disgust that one must learn how to spit out in order to perform true taste.[13] In order to have the attunement of beauty, in order to have the aesthetic experience that calibrates us to the Kantian ocean of reason, there must already be, always already, this hypnotic, magnetic field of compulsion between me and something else, some not-me, some alien being. Just as the realm of *objects* subtends the dark waters of angst and nihilism, so a bejeweled, scintillating sparkle of kitsch subtends the straitlaced cleanliness of beauty—it is this hypnotic, magnetic level that philosophy has habitually labeled a realm of evil, because precisely of its agency. Thus, while watching *Avatar*, it is as if we are seeing naturalistic pastoral, but on acid, where trees and fungi have become huge, luminous, Day-Glo, radiant as if they were made of some dangerous isotope.

FIGURE 1 *Les Fleurs du Mal*: Night in *Avatar*

The movie is unable to contain this preternatural, glowingly "evil" dimension, which just is the transcendental realm of aliens, of objects, rearing its irreducibly ugly head, in the face of the smoothed-out Spinozan metaphysics that is the film's official ideological frame. Seeing this is not the privilege of a specially gifted viewer—the phenomena are there in plain sight, so that our experience of *Avatar* is fascinatingly fractured, in a way that makes the movie compelling. The very attempt to force viewers to accept an ecological view of interconnectedness results in pushing humans to accept the proximity of a more-than-human non-world of uncanny strangers. And indeed, this non-world is already populated by technological devices whose cloud-being outstrips their localizable, physical embodiment for us as desktop machines or handheld devices. A gigantic non-world of technology, lying just to the side of the world of *Avatar*, reflected within it as the asymmetrically doubled "bad" internet of the humans and the "good" internet of the Na'vi. It is tempting indeed to see these with Melanie Klein as the "good breast" and "bad breast" of the necessarily psychotic infant—in which case, when it comes to ecological awareness, humans have a lot of growing up to do.[14]

Thus when, in the climactic battle between humans and Na'vi, Sully as a Na'vi summons by telepathy ferociously toothy psychedelic beasts to rip apart the cyborgian humans in their body-extension armor, we are compelled to experience a thrill, a sadistic thrill that without doubt goes all the way back to Kant—the thrill of a reason unleashed, a reason that is beyond the human, that might lurch into the human stick-figure world and annihilate it with the flick of a switch or, in this case, the snap of fluorescent jaws. We are placed on the side of the inhuman, not simply of the marginalized or victimized Other, but of a technologically weaponized, distributed reason, a planet-sense that overrides our need for tasteful aesthetic distance, sentimentally overwhelming us, jerking tears and laughter. (It is truly frightening the extent to which this movie can force one to cry.) Yet this is no regression to some metaphysical paradise island. It is rather a sentimentality that is far from regressive but instead absolutely futural, post-Romantic, post-Kantian, the overwhelming flood of an ocean of reason inundating the islands of fact, of metaphysics. The call of nonhumans below the resonance of *Da-sein*, below the dark icy waters of angst, the nothingness Heidegger thought was the precious property of humans, but which has turned out to be the fissure in anything—a teacup, a jar of Marmite, a meteor—between its withdrawn essence (its in-itself) and its appearance (the phenomenal). The human who brings this on, Sully, himself dies in his summoning of these beings, his avatar mortally wounded recursively eliminates him, and he is swept up into the gigantic arms of his lover, into the good breast, which nourishes him and "restores" him to life—a life without the human, not a restoration so much as an evacuation, a download.

What *Avatar* gestures toward, then, is a genuine "postmodernity," a historical moment after modernity, in which humans have incorporated the nothingness that leaks out of Pandora's box into a new way of being and thinking ecologically. It gestures toward this future moment, without ever quite being able to tell us to go there, or even wanting with all its heart to push us there. This new moment is available directly on and in front of the surface of the film, not in some esoteric depth, as I hope now to show.

Ecological awareness is indeed as it goes in the film. Ecological awareness is not a return to innocence, but rather a joyful Oedipus who blinds himself with horrified pleasure, knowing he is the evil he was seeking, the cause of the environmental disaster (Greek *miasma*, plague)—Oedipus, answerer of the riddle of the Sphinx, whose question concerned the human and its strangely dislocated embodiment (four legs at dawn, two legs at noon, three legs at eve). Oedipus, figure for a self-destructive tendency within reason itself, which is revealed not as entirely on the side of humans, through the very processes of Enlightenment, of self-outstripping, that Kant himself bankrolled.[15] *Avatar* directly makes this into a theme with its depictions of humans bent on destruction in a self-destructive way. The reduction of thinking to the human–world correlate is part and parcel of the instrumentality that created the Anthropocene. At the very moment at which thinking decides it can only talk about talking about

FIGURE 2 Tyger! Tyger! Burning Bright!

access to things, humans are directly intervening in Earth's crust, facts that are two sides of the same coin. The promise of a cozy familiarity with nonhumans, a handshake or finger-touch across the reaches of space, is bought at the price of a reason that churns up Earth in its blind refusal to see its own complicity, its inability to attain metalinguistic escape velocity from what it is thinking and what it is churning.

Thus there arise true aliens, strange strangers, products of reason's reach into life as such—the beings revealed by evolution are non-chimps, nonhumans, non-insects, non-species, the joke of Darwin's title *The Origin of Species* being that this is a book that argues that *there are no species and they have no origin*.[16] The very attempt to exit Earth ends the world, not by allowing us to float free in space, but by gluing us every more tightly to the viscous gravitational pull of the aesthetic dimension, which is now discovered to emanate from all things, not only from things humans want to hang in art galleries, a dimension that Plato was quite accurate to describe as an evil realm of demonic magnetism.[17] The "death of god" and the long march of eliminative materialism go hand in hand with the rebirth of evil and of radically transcendental realms, realms that are now found to inhabit plastic bottles, pellets of Plutonium 239, and tree frogs, but which can be located nowhere in ontically given, phenomenal space. The crack in the real discovered by Kant multiplies everywhere, like crazy paving. The disenchantment of the world gives rise to the reenchantment of the world! But not as a benevolent world, not as a *world* at all—but rather as the threatening proximity of aliens, aliens wherever we tread, flashing their compelling webs of illusion, a non-total crowd of leering clowns. This is the non-world that ecological awareness glimpses, not in spite of nihilism but through it, underneath it. The void is the meontic nothing of a pair of cat's eyes (Figure 12.2).[18]

This is the dark ecological truth that *Avatar* tries to peel away from the ostensible "message," but which it simply can't help but reveal in every luminescent tendril of color, every glowing resonance, the very filmstock that seems to gaze at us with night eyes:

Tyger Tyger, burning bright
In the forests of the night;
What immortal hand or eye,
Could frame thy fearful symmetry?[19]

Notes

1. *Avatar*, directed by James Cameron (2009; Los Angeles: Twentieth Century Fox, 2010), DVD.

2. Ursula Heise, *Sense of Place and Sense of Planet: The Environmental Imagination of the Global* (New York: Colombia University Press, 1982).

3. Georg Wilhelm Friedrich Hegel, *Hegel's Phenomenology of Spirit*, trans. A. V. Miller, analysis and foreword by J. N. Findlay (Oxford: Oxford University Press, 1977), 9.

4. Immanuel Kant, *Critique of Judgment: Including the First Introduction*, trans. Werner Pluhar (Indianapolis: Hackett, 1987), 103–17.

5. William Shakespeare, *Hamlet*, ed. Philip Edwards (Cambridge: Cambridge University Press, 2003), 2.2.243 (141).

6. Judea Pearl, *Causality: Models, Reasoning, and Inference* (Cambridge: Cambridge University Press, 2010), 78–85.

7. Wendy Chun, "Crisis, Crisis, Crisis, or Sovereignty and Networks," *Theory, Culture and Society* 28, no. 6 (2011): 91–112 (106–7).

8. Quentin Meillassoux, *After Finitude: An Essay on the Necessity of Contingency*, trans. Ray Brassier (New York: Continuum, 2009), 112–28.

9. Edmund Husserl, *Logical Investigations*, trans. J. N. Findlay, ed. Dermot Moran (London: Routledge, 2006), 1:275–76.

10. Gilles Deleuze and Félix Guattari, *Anti-Oedipus: Capitalism and Schizophrenia*, trans. R. Hurley, M. Seem, and H. Lane (Minneapolis: University of Minnesota Press, 1983).

11. See Graham Priest, *In Contradiction: A Study of the Transconsistent* (Oxford: Oxford University Press, 2006), passim: the most notable recent quarantine officers have been Tarski, Russell, and Frege.

12. Martin Heidegger, *Being and Time*, trans. Joan Stambaugh (Albany: SUNY Press, 1996), 131–34, 171–72, and esp. Section 40 (172–78).

13. See Jacques Derrida, "Economimesis," *Diacritics* 11, no. 2 (Summer 1981): 2–25.

14. Melanie Klein, *Envy and Gratitude and Other Works, 1946–1963* (New York: Simon & Schuster, 1975), 61–64.

15. Immanuel Kant, "An Answer to the Question: What Is Enlightenment?" in *Kant: Political Writings*, ed. H. S. Reiss (Cambridge: Cambridge University Press, 1991), 54–60.

16. A full explication of the *strange stranger* can be found in Timothy Morton, *The Ecological Thought* (Cambridge, MA: Harvard University Press, 2010), 14–15, 17–19, 38–50. See also Jacques Derrida, "Hospitality," trans. Barry Stocker with Forbes Matlock, *Angelaki* 5, no. 3 (December 2000): 3–18.

17. Plato, *Ion*, trans. Benjamin Jowett, available at http://classics.mit.edu/Plato/ion.html (accessed May 27, 2012).

18. I am of course referencing Jacques Derrida, *The Animal That Therefore I Am*, ed. Marie-Louise Mallet, trans. David Wills (New York: Fordham University Press, 2008), 3–11.

19. William Blake, "The Tyger," in *The Complete Poetry and Prose of William Blake*, ed. David V. Erdman (New York: Doubleday, 1965; rev. 1988).

Churning Up the Depths

Nonhuman Ecologies of Metaphor
in Solaris and "Oceanic"

MELODY JUE

The first time I watched the BBC's *Blue Planet* documentary series, I was fascinated by deep-sea footage of a dark, calm pool of water whose surface was carpeted by a bed of mussels. How could there be a second surface of water—underwater? David Attenborough's voice patiently explained that this was in fact a deepwater brine lake: "During the Jurassic period, the water here was shallow and became cut off from the ocean. The area soon dried out, leaving a thick layer of salt and other minerals up to 8 km thick. When the ocean water returned after the region rifted apart, the super-saline layer at the bottom of the Gulf became an underwater lake. Now brine, which is continually released from a rift in the ocean floor, feeds the lake."[1] Seeing this underwater lake, I began to rethink my spatial intuition. The ocean, for us, is commonly conceptualized as a Cartesian volume that can be gridded and measured, with a surface only at the top.[2] This dominant metaphorical sense of "depth" as the below and "surface" on top is based on the normal position of a human observer. By surprising us with a counterexample of a unique "surface" *within* the depths, *Blue Planet* reveals both the pervasiveness of our land-based perspective of surface and depth and how it colors the terrestrial metaphors we live by. We expect a surface on top and depth underneath in both reality and in figurative language, but there may be other possible senses of these terms.[3] The underwater lake example suggests a stigmatism, or misalignment of the figurative and the literal figures, which produces a kind of cognitive estrangement similar to what we experience in science fiction about oceans and aquatic beings.

This chapter discusses how the cognitively estranged environments of SF challenge our terrestrial senses of surface and depth. As case studies, I focus on two texts: Polish writer Stanislaw Lem's seminal 1961 novel *Solaris* and Greg

Egan's novella "Oceanic." *Solaris* imagines a sentient ocean and its responses to scientific investigation, while "Oceanic" imagines smaller-scale ocean microbes whose chemical excretions produce religious feeling. In both texts, oceans disrupt human practices of symptomatic reading and valuation of depth. Gender and sexuality also play key roles, for in both texts a feminized "nature" no longer accommodates the kind of scientific penetration that would accompany a deep reading. Instead the feminine—as a character, and the element of water—disorients male protagonists in both texts, such that they rethink their relation to transcendental or "deep" knowledge and epistemological limits. In the following analysis, I hope to churn up the "clean" model of surface versus depth through science fictional estrangements, using *Solaris* as a diagnosis of habitual figurations of depth, and "Oceanic" as the story that imagines how the mutual relations of human and nonhuman suggest alternative relations to depth and interpretive practices. Rather than considering depth as a single definable concept, both stories introduce other possibilities through the participation of nonhumans to suggest an ecological and participatory sense of figurative meaning.

SOLARIS

Stanislaw Lem's *Solaris* (1961) dramatizes scientific attempts to penetrate and understand the ocean-planet Solaris according to the classic model of surface/depth, provoking a crisis that is jointly scientific, masculine, colonial, and terrestrial. The novel begins with psychologist Kris Kelvin, an expert on "Solaris studies," moving from a transport ship to the space station above Solaris in a kind of embryonic pod. The space station, hovering from an Archimedean standpoint above the planet, would seem to offer the scientists an ideally objective location from which to study Solaris. Yet Solaris has long been suspected of sentience on a planet-wide scale: it may be altering its own orbit in space, and it routinely throws up radiant, geometrically complex structures from its surface. In one early description, Kelvin calls the Solaris ocean "a monstrous entity endowed with reason, a protoplasmic ocean-brain enveloping the entire planet and idling its time away in extravagant theoretical cogitation about the nature of the universe. Our instruments had intercepted minute random fragments of a prodigious and everlasting monologue unfolding in the depths of this colossal brain, which was inevitably beyond our understanding."[4] Here, Kelvin draws an analogy between psychological and oceanic "depths," reading the ocean planet as both a geological and psychological text where visible currents and large three-dimensional surface structures might be seen as evidence of "thinking"—a sort of distributed cognition throughout the planetary body. Yet the legibility of the planet-as-text proves elusive, for the planet-ocean Solaris enacts an insistent *détournement* against scientific legibility, psychoanalysis, and symptomatic reading, deflecting human attempts to understand the Solaris ocean as either a physical environment or a colossal brain. Solaris modifies the instruments scientists submerge into its ocean, producing "a profusion of signals—fragmentary indications of some outlandish activity, which in fact defeated all attempts at analysis."[5] Lem's fantastic ocean resists both physical and epistemic human penetration, an impervious mirror surface with depths that remain cognitively out of reach to whatever extent they even exist at all. Fredric Jameson calls this Lem's "Unknowability Thesis," in which Solaris "resists scientific inquiry with all the serene tenacity of the godhead itself."[6]

Yet what we miss if we see only the resistance of Solaris is the depth reading *that it practices* on Kris Kelvin and the other scientists from the very beginning of the novel. The clearest example of this involves the arrival of unexpected visitors on the space station. After scientists bombard the ocean's surface with X-rays during one test, the ocean begins to read the brain waves of the human scientists while they sleep, producing physical "phantoms"—also described as "simulacra" or "phi-creatures"—which are intimately tied to each individual's unconscious. Kris Kelvin's uncanny visitor is Rheya, a simulacrum of his deceased wife on Earth who had committed suicide. Although she looks and speaks like the Rheya from Earth, the hyper-real Rheya has no calluses on her feet, perfect skin, and also possesses superhuman strength. "Born" amnesiac, she does not know she is a copy, her own memory based on what Kelvin remembers of Earth's Rheya.[7] While on Solaris, every scientist gets such a visitor, projected from the depths of each scientist's own repressed memories. We could say that Solaris gives the scientists access to a different register of depth—their *own* psychological depths—by turning the mirror on them. Is this not a classic example of symptomatic reading? In their critique of a hermeneutics of suspicion, Best and Marcus define symptomatic reading as "a mode of interpretation that assumes that a text's truest meaning lies in what it does not say, describes textual surfaces as superfluous, and seeks to unmask hidden meanings. For symptomatic readers, texts possess meanings that are veiled, latent, all but absent if it were not for their irrepressible and recurring symptoms."[8] The questions here are: What is Rheya's ontological status? Does she embody a kind of depth "reading" that Solaris performs on Kelvin? Is she a memory, an individual, an extension of the Solaris ocean, or an interpretation of Kelvin's unconscious?

Both the failure of symptomatic readings and the possibility of other kinds of depth reading hinge on Rheya. Ann Weinstone's insight that Rheya "occupies a gap" can extend further.[9] Rheya occupies not only the gap between Kelvin's memories and Solaris's materiality, but also a gap in scale between macro and micro, life and death, object and subject, environment and organism. One scene that specifically addresses Rheya's ontological suspense occurs in chapter 7, where Kelvin decides to give Rheya a medical examination and takes a sample of her blood to analyze under a powerful neutron microscope. It is a moment when Rheya becomes, for him, a landscape. Part of what compels me to look at the microscope scene is the way that Rheya's body is rendered as a surface (literally placed on a slide) for the benefit of a male observer. Bending over a microscope, Kelvin says: "I could hear Rheya's voice, but without taking in what she was saying. Beneath my gaze, sharply foreshortened, was a vast desert flooded with silvery light, and strewn with rounded boulders—red corpuscles—which trembled and wriggled behind a veil of mist. I focused the eye-piece and penetrated further into the depths of the silvery landscape."[10] The fact that Kelvin cannot "hear" Rheya or take in what she is saying privileges the visual and objective over the aural and subjective; he also ignores her as a legitimate subject worthy of response. His comment also draws on the long history of equating women's bodies with landscapes, of forcefully penetrating into the secrets of a feminized "nature"—a silvery, ethereal one at that. Yet like Solaris itself, Rheya's blood resists Kelvin's total comprehension. Looking further, Kelvin notices an anomaly: a deformed erythrocyte, "sunken in the centre, whose uneven edges projected sharp shadows over the depths of a circular crater. The crater, bristling with silver ion deposits, extended beyond the microscope's field of vision." Curious, Kelvin enlarges the resolution, expecting that "at any moment, I should reach the limit of this exploration of the depths; the shadow of a molecule occupied the whole of the space; then the image became fuzzy. There was nothing to be seen. There should have been the ferment of a quivering cloud of atoms, but I saw nothing."[11] In attempting to gaze into Rheya's physical structure, to know what makes phi-creatures different, Kelvin gets simply nothing.

Incredulous as to what he is *not* seeing, Kelvin performs another test to examine the materiality of Rheya's blood. He drops congealed acid onto the "coral tinted pearl" of blood; it turns gray, "a dirty foam rose to the surface,"[12] and then the blood surprisingly re-creates itself. Kelvin's attempt to disintegrate the blood sample only results in a stubborn reintegration, a reterritorialization of its structure. Kelvin then answers the call to be part of a three-way teleconference with the other two male scientists on board—forming a kind of triangular solidarity between them, exclusive of Rheya. During this conversation, Kelvin proposes that the blood is in fact "a camouflage. A cover, in a way, it's a super-copy, a reproduction which is superior to the original. I'll explain what I mean: there exists, in man, an absolute limit—a term to structural divisibility—whereas here, the frontiers have been pushed back. We are dealing with a sub-atomic structure."[13] The subatomic structure Kelvin infers—from not being able to see a structure beyond the erythrocyte—is the neutrino. Importantly, Rheya's ontological difference does not appear through visual signs, but only the absence of known signs. Rheya—and by metonymic association, Solaris—continues to resist scientific depth reading, her concreteness only inferred. That Kelvin only sees human blood cells suggests that he can only relate her difference in terms of what he knows. In a telling line earlier in the novel, one of the other scientists, Dr. Snow, tells Kelvin, "We are only seeking Man. We have no need of other worlds. We need mirrors."[14] This line resonates with a central crisis of the novel: that human beings can only know what is other through existing frameworks of cognition and linguistic means.

While this interpretation would be sympathetic to Jameson's thesis that Lem's ocean is ultimately unknowable, suggesting a kind of asymptotic limit to what the human can understand, such a reading misses the entire affect of the scene. The scene is particularly difficult to bear reading if one's sympathies lie with Rheya rather than the scientists—to endure a kind of isolating scrutiny and scopic vivisection by scientists whose aim is to tell you what you are, what you are made of. If one sympathizes with Rheya, it becomes clear that the version of depth reading performed here fails not because Rheya is entirely unknowable, but because the entirely wrong questions are being asked of her without regard to the relational nature of knowledge. Earlier in the novel, we learn that Rheya's phantom-like existence depends upon Kelvin and his memories; she finds it physically painful to leave his presence, and violently breaks down barriers between them if restrained by objects like doors. Kelvin even considers if she might be a projection from his mind, for it is clear that her existence depends on physical proximity to him. However, Kelvin entirely neglects his own role in Rheya's existence when he looks through the microscope into the silvery landscape of her blood cells, with the intention of investigating what she is made of—not what she is in relation to himself. The critical problem that *Solaris* dramatizes is the cul-de-sac of scientific investigation that brackets the observer out of the dynamic relation between phenomena/other and self.

At this point, I want to distinguish between symptomatic and depth reading, and suggest that *Solaris* introduces the possibility of other kinds of "deep" reading, where depth ceases to be synonymous with penetration, mastery, and vision, but instead shifts into a register of experience based on curiosity, tactility, and the production of meaning in a particular moment. Depth understood this way—as bi-directional, heading to the waters and the sky—unfolds in the last scene of the novel where Kelvin interacts with an ocean wave. Although throughout the text Kris Kelvin never visits the surface of Solaris—which should be surprising, considering that he is an expert in Solaris studies—he finally decides to make a trip down to the surface after Rheya dies.[15] After descending to the surface and exploring a Mimoid (a large surface structure with a finite life span), Kelvin realizes that "I had flown here not to explore the formation but to acquaint myself with the ocean."[16] Kelvin continues on to describe his encounter with a wave at the edge of the Mimoid:

> When the next wave came I held out my hand. What followed was a faithful reproduction of a phenomenon which had been analyzed a century before: the wave hesitated, recoiled, then enveloped my hand without touching it, so that a thin covering of "air" separated my glove inside a cavity which had been fluid a moment previously, and now had a fleshy consistency. I raised my hand slowly, and the wave, or rather an outcrop of the wave, rose at the same time, enfolding my hand in a translucent cyst with greenish reflections. I stood up, so as to raise my hand still higher, and the gelatinous substance stretched like a rope, but did not break. . . . A flower had grown out of the ocean, and its calyx was molded to my fingers.[17]

Kelvin's approach to Solaris studies shifts dramatically from positioning himself as a distant observer to becoming a participant in mutual exploration and experimentation. Although Kelvin calls it a "faithful reproduction of a phenomenon" observed before, his description suggests that the wave acts in the moment, according to its curiosity: "the wave hesitated, recoiled, then enveloped my hand." Kelvin's observations show the wave as active and agential through these verbs, rather that as passive, as object; it exhibits "cautious but feral alertness, a curiosity avid for quick apprehension of a new, unexpected form."[18] That the wave envelops Kelvin's hand, rather than the other way around, suggests that the wave is partially in control of the situation and literally grasps/apprehends Kelvin by itself.

Kelvin notes that none of the accounts of Solaris he had read "prepared me for the experience as I had lived it, and I felt somehow changed." We see a distinct shift in his descriptions of Solaris that relate to the singularity and affect of lived experience. This leads into a brief moment of identification: "The contrast was inexpressible between that lively curiosity [of the wave] and the shimmering immensity of the ocean. . . . I sat unseeing, glided down an irresistible slope and identified myself with the dumb, fluid colossus."[19] Kelvin no longer brackets himself out of the experimental situation; his experience with the wave leads him to momentarily identify with the larger Solaris ocean—an ocean silent (dumb) but expressively tactile. Although we might doubt Kelvin's success in doing this, the moment is significant as the only time in the entire novel that Kelvin feels compelled to identify with any form of an other, or imagine that other's point of view.

Thus at the "surface" of the planet, we see the possibility of knowledge production that takes place at the interface between beings that share mutual curiosity. Yet the interface is by no means flat; it too can take on a sense of depth, of dimensional relation. Departing from a model of depth reading that we saw throughout most of the novel, which involved the interpretive efforts of a distant observer seeking to uncover secrets of a reticent subject (Rheya, Solaris), the narrative ends with the possibility of a new practice of gathering knowledge that shifts from an aerial/visual sense to a liquid/tactile one. Whereas the aerial/visual method of investigation allowed Kelvin to bracket himself out of the observed phenomena, such as with his studies of Rheya's blood, the liquid/tactile method of investigation at the end of the novel implicates Kelvin in the coproduction of knowledge. The wave encircling his hand responds directly to his movements, such that what Kelvin observes is entirely contingent on his own participation—and ecology of knowledge production. Kelvin's question shifts away from "What is it?" or "What are you?" to, rather, "What are you in relation to me when I am here?" The Solaris ocean opens the possibility of depth reading as the unfolding of a dimensional relation between two or more entities who mutually respond to each other.

"OCEANIC"

If "depth reading" in Solaris ends on the possibility of the unfolding of a dimensional relation, "Oceanic" offers yet another alternative for understanding "depth" in relation to both a terrestrial and oceanic point of view. Just as Solaris trained us to look for the way "depth reading" could change from a one-way to a relational process, "Oceanic" suggests that we investigate how the figurative meanings of depth—religious, gendered—also find their meaning in relation between ocean and land. Egan's novella takes place on a planet called Covenant, set at an unspecified date in the future after human beings achieve both space travel and the ability to live forever without material bodies. The mythic "crossing" had taken place long enough ago that the people of Covenant no longer know why the "Angels" chose to incarnate into material bodies again, nor why there was a significant decrease in technology soon after they terraformed Covenant. The title "Oceanic" transparently alludes to the "oceanic feeling" coined by Romain Rolland and popularized by Sigmund Freud in *Civilization and Its Discontents*. Freud begins with a friend's description of the feeling of transcendent limitlessness, which he does not feel himself, and goes on to relate it to the ego's original unity with nature and the maternal body.[20] Egan both literalizes and fictionalizes Freud's oceanic feeling, imagining a religion in which a drowned and resurrected Beatrice figures as Jesus, and in which religious feeling is experienced most intensely during and after a brief baptism in the depths of the ocean. "Oceanic" dramatizes the religious crisis that occurs when the ocean depths cease to signify a holy, mysterious connection to Beatrice and instead become knowable through the pharmacological effects of indigenous microbes. This ultimately suggests an ecology of metaphoric meaning in which depth ceases to be legible as a stable concept, but evolves in relation to multiple factors that include science, gender, religion, myth, the ocean, and its microbes.

The story begins with the protagonist Martin slowly falling asleep on a boat to the rhythm of the waves. Martin's brother Daniel suddenly asks him if he believes in God, admitting that he has joined the Deep Church and taken literally the following piece of scripture: "'Unless you are willing to drown in My blood, you will never look upon the face of My Mother.' So they bound each other hand and foot, and weighted themselves down with rocks." The way to acquire true faith, Daniel insists, is through immersion deep in the ocean, for "In the water, you're alone with God."[21] In Daniel's view, a literal baptism enables real, spiritual faith. Martin's induction into the church through consensual drowning repeats the language of Freud's oceanic feeling: "Suddenly, everything was seared with light . . . as if I was an infant again and my mother had wrapped her arms around me tightly. It was like basking in sunlight, listening to laughter, dreaming of music too beautiful to be real."[22] This moment of oceanic feeling merges the spiritual and the physical, taking the ocean as the site or wellspring of religious feeling and faith. The Mother (God) and the mother ocean are taken as one, where Martin is able to both feel the immenseness of the universe and, ecstatically, experience himself as inseparable from it.

The main conflict of the story revolves around Martin's disenchantment with the Deep Church once he begins studying science. His work on Covenant's pre-Angelic fauna, or life before the arrival of human colonists, threatens to demystify the "true" cause of the oceanic feeling by pinning it on microbes rather than a relationship with holy Beatrice. Martin finds that "rather than rain bringing new life from above, an ocean-dwelling species from a much greater depth had moved steadily closer to the surface, as the Angels' creations drained oxygen from the water." In other words, the process of what the story calls "ecopoiesis"—or the terraforming that made Covenant hospitable to human colonists—creates conditions that end up being favorable to a specific kind of benthic microbe:

> Zooytes that had spent a billion years confined to the depths had suddenly been able to survive (and reproduce, and mutate) closer to the surface than ever before, and when they'd stumbled on a mutation that let them thrive in the presence of oxygen, they'd finally been in a position to make use of it. The ecopoiesis might have driven other native organisms into extinction, but the invasion from Earth had enabled this ancient benthic species to mount a long overdue invasion of its own. Unwittingly or not, the Angels had set in motion the sequence of events that had released it from the ocean to colonize the planet.[23]

Covenant's human modifications lead to a parallel set of planetary changes put into effect by the benthic microbes. Martin doesn't push the potential implications of this further, until he attends a conference and notices one of the paper titles: "Carla Reggia: 'Euphoric Effects of $Z/12/80$ Excretions.'" All at once, it hits him: this microbe could be responsible for religious feeling: "$Z/12/80$, Carla explained, excreted among its waste products an amine that was able to bind to receptors in our Angel-crafted brains. Since it had been shown by other workers (no one recognized me; no one gave me so much as a glance) that $Z/12/80$ hadn't existed at the time of the ecopoiesis, this interaction was almost certainly unde-signed, and unanticipated."[24] In this passage, Martin suggests that the religious experience of drowning has a material basis in waste products of the microbes. To put it crudely, Martin wasn't simply drowning in the holy love of Beatrice, he was drowning in the potent drug of $Z/12/80$ excrement. Religious feeling moves from the sacred to the profane, a matter of absorbing abject products from ocean microbes.

This disturbing conclusion shakes Martin's faith in the reality of Beatrice, and in order to see if *Z/12/80* really does produce a sense of religious love, he travels to a holy bay of water known to have particularly high concentrations of the microbes. He pushes past local stewards guarding the sacred waters and lays down flat in the water, covering his face: "The love of Beatrice flooded into me, and nothing had changed: Her presence was as palpable as ever, as undeniable as ever. I *knew* that I was loved, accepted, forgiven." Yet as he confirms the material cause of this feeling of love, he comes to the conclusion that "it said no more about my place in the world than the warmth of sunlight on skin. I'd never mistake that touch for a real hand again."[25] Beatrice, now a physical phenomenon like the warmth of sunlight on skin, is nothing mystical but the name given to an explainable, physical quality of Covenant's microbes. The *Z/12/80* microbes, understood as a source of "oceanic feeling" and spirituality, have in fact been at the surface—literal and figurative—all along. The potential readings have inverted: that which had been symptomatically read (religious feeling, transcendence) is now accessible for being read at the surface (level of observable scientific phenomena). That which was read as surface (the physical traits of microbes) can now be experienced as depth (feeling of religious love).

It would be easy to view this story as a straightforward narrative about science explaining away religious feeling. However, an important detail about sexuality, easy to forget after the revelation of the microbes, is key to understanding the changing conception of depth. Early on, Egan drops hints that sexual intercourse means not simply inserting but *exchanging* the phallus, which the people of Covenant call a "bridge." When the Angels incarnated into new bodies, they designed the bodies with a bridge that could be passed between people. When a man had sex with a woman, she would take the bridge and he would grow a new vagina. Our first introduction to this is just prior to Daniel's wedding, when Martin meets another teenager named Lena. She proposes sexual intercourse and coaches him through it, clearly the more experienced partner. During the experience, Martin reflects: "It wasn't any better than my Drowning, but it was so much like it that it had to be blessed by Beatrice."[26] Martin's observation draws a clear parallel between sexual union, oceanic immersion, and spiritual connection with Beatrice. It also relates vaginal depth and oceanic depth, which immerses Martin as a male subject. Reading sexuality in "Oceanic" alongside its religious, scientific, and aquatic dimensions suggests a conception of "depth" as female, as capable of receiving a bridge.

While the characterization of water as a feminine element has ancient roots, what is new is Martin's postcoital anxiety that ties together feminine depth, chemical penetration by microbes, and loss of his original phallus.[27] After Martin and Lena both reach orgasm, Egan graphically describes the withdrawal where Martin's bridge breaks off and passes to Lena. Martin proposes marriage, but Lena declines and tries to assuage his feelings:

> Lena said, "What do you think, you can never get married now? How many
> marriages do you imagine involve the bridge one of the partners was born with?"
>   "Nine out of ten. Unless they're both women."
> Lena gave me a look that hovered between tenderness and incredulity. "My
> estimate is about one in five."
>   I shook my head. "I don't care. We've exchanged the bridge, we have to be
> together." Lena's expression hardened, then so did my resolve. "Or I have
> to get it back."[28]

Lena's comment suggests that the people of Covenant are—sexually—similar to microbes: just as microbes laterally transfer genes,[29] the people of Covenant pass the "bridge" from person to person, in what we might read as a queer act no matter which sexes it involves. In fact the whole concept of stable sexes falls apart at the notion of passing bridges and the widespread practice of male pregnancy. Marriage, then, becomes a way of tethering and securing a single "bridge" between two people, preventing it from wandering within larger networks. While it would be fair to question whether or not Freudian/Lacanian psychoanalysis—theorized on the relations of distinctly male and female bodies—would or should apply to the people of Covenant and their phallus-exchanging bodies, Martin's resolve to get back his original bridge is clearly a response to castration, the literal as well as symbolic loss of the phallus.

Much more could be said about sexuality and Egan's *novum* of a phallus-exchanging society in which men and women can equally bear children, but one conclusion we may draw involves the relation of depth to loss of the phallus, where feminine depth implies masculine vulnerability, castration, and existential crisis. We see this in a very physical way when Martin regains his bridge from Lena through intercourse, where she takes on the male role. The ocean microbes, symbolically allied with the feminine, also parallel Lena's role: they too penetrate through Martin's skin chemically and spiritually through their excretions. Thus, the ocean depths are not only a place where one penetrates, but a place where one is subject to chemical penetration by the drug-like excretions of microbes. Martin's discovery of the effects of *Z/12/80* microbes fractures not only his relation to Beatrice and the Deep Church, but to the feminine that Beatrice, now aligned with microbes, symbolizes. Whereas Martin's initial sense of depth (joining the "Deep Church") implied unity with Beatrice and the deepening of sacred knowledge, by the end of the story, the sacred "depths" have been rendered "surface" (the known, accessible, literal, secular), as Martin realizes there is nothing spiritual or transcendental beyond the physical ocean, only microbes producing their all-too-material excretions. To quote playwright Bertolt Brecht out of context, the ocean turns out to be "just depth" after all, the wellspring not of a mystical religious feeling, but only of microbes.[30] For Martin, depth as "just depth" forestalls curiosity about any spiritual beyond. The ocean, no longer the sacred place of transcendence, becomes mundane, explainable.

Despite these revisions of depth as a place and a concept, I want to end on a final scene from "Oceanic" that recuperates the "oceanic feeling" as sense of unity and connection. "Oceanic" challenges us further to consider concepts of surface and depth not as anthropocentric, but as trans-species in origin. After the incident at the bay of concentrated microbes, Martin wanders over to the steps of a church to sit down in despair. A church member calls out to him and asks, "Do you need a room? I can let you into the Church if you want." Martin declines, but as the man walks away, Martin asks him, "Do you believe in God?" The man hesitates before replying,

"As a child I did. Not anymore. It was a nice idea . . . but it made no sense." He eyed me skeptically, still unsure of my motives.

I said, "Then isn't life unbearable?"

He laughed. "Not all the time."[31]

The man's offer of shelter is key. Because "Oceanic" ends on this extension of hospitality, we could say it offers an alternative possibility that an oceanic feeling doesn't have to be guaranteed by a divine being such as Beatrice. Instead, the oceanic feeling might be generated by human relations, a sense of home, of being together, anchored by human community, a situation where life isn't unbearable all the time. Although the source may change, the feeling might remain. However, since Martin declines the church member's invitation and extension of hospitality, it seems that the secular oceanic feeling is not a precondition of existence, but a conscious choice to develop community.

Another reading would be more radically ecological: the discovery that religious faith is the product of microbial excretions chemically affecting humans suggests that spiritual depth depends on microbes; it is a relational, trans-species phenomenon that literally *does* connect Martin with his home planet in a physical and intimate way through a chemical that he takes out of the environment into his body. What oceanic feeling indicates then is not the holy presence of Beatrice, but the sublime presence of microbes as they affect human beings. Furthermore, the new ecological basis for oceanic feeling is fundamentally *unnatural*, since Covenant's *Z/12/80* bloom only happened as a response to human terraforming of the planet. In this way, "Oceanic" dramatizes a shift from an anthropogenic view of embodied metaphor to a more expansive sense of how nonhuman others might influence the way that human subjects experience embodiment and depth.[32] Going beyond Lakoff and Johnson's thesis that human embodiment informs the metaphors we use to cognize our world, Egan's fiction opens the door to thinking about ways that nonhumans (microbes) might influence—or might already be influencing—human figurations and metaphors of depth. In this way, both science fiction and metaphor theory relate to the provocations of S. Eben Kirksey and Stefan Helmreich's article "The Emergence of Multispecies Ethnography," which calls on anthropologists and other humanists alike to consider how the lives and deaths of nonhuman organisms affect human social worlds. I read *Solaris* and "Oceanic" as narratives that suggest a practice of literary criticism that opens to multispecies relations, particularly sensitive to the ways that the metaphors we use depend on particular framings of ecological interconnection. If we take Egan's microbes seriously as coproducers of the depth, then we need to think about the trans-species creation of metaphorical meaning. This perspective suggests that the nonhuman already inheres in the human, where metaphor is not only informed by vertebrate embodiment but also by a multitude of other beings that live, die, and become with us in the world.

DEPTH AND ECOLOGIES OF METAPHOR

In this chapter, we looked at how *Solaris* moved away from a hermeneutics of suspicion (as practiced on Rheya), a model of reading that probes for the hidden or masked meanings of a text, and instead explored the possibility of "depth reading" as the co-creation of meaning practiced by two aware participants in a moment of mutual curiosity. This repositioned Kris Kelvin from being a distant observer on the surface looking down to being an immersed participant in the process of deepening a relational knowledge between himself and the curious ocean wave he interacted with. "Oceanic" also built on this relational sense of meaning, continuing to move us away from a sense of the depths as a site of transcendent knowledge. Once Martin discovered the *Z/12/80* microbes and linked their pharmacological effects with the deep-water baptism he experienced as an adolescent, he lost faith in holy Beatrice. That which was deep (oceanic/religious feeling/sexual awakening) was exposed as surface (knowable, not transcendent, secular). Yet the ending of the story suggests that despite being knowable scientifically, Covenant's microbes still play a role as coproducers of "oceanic feeling"—the immanent ecological relation of members of a community.

Solaris and "Oceanic" share a similar methodology: through the medium of science fiction, they denaturalize the relationship between literal and figurative depths. By experiencing relationships to the ocean depths other than that presumed by the "depth reading" metaphor (with the interpreter on top, and meaning hidden below), these texts offer alternative spatialities of interpretation by putting fictive protagonists and the reader in a different relationship with water. Note that both narratives end in the liminal space of the coastline, between solid ground and ocean: *Solaris* next to ocean waves, "Oceanic" at the site of a sacred bay. Ending in such a space of dynamic change and negotiation, these new relationships with water move us away from a hermeneutic practice that brackets out the observer and instead toward considering the relationality of knowledge production. A model of interpretation based on the terrestrial observer above is not inevitable just because it is in our way of speaking; these science fiction stories ask us to rethink the way that we position ourselves in relation to the waters, to others, and how the dynamic tidal space of contact might offer an alternate and more mutualistic space for interpretive practice and sensing ecologies of metaphor.[33]

Notes

1. *The Blue Planet: Seas of Life*, nar. David Attenborough (2001; London: BBC, 2002), DVD.

2. Philip Steinberg's *Social Construction of Ocean Space* (Cambridge: Cambridge University Press, 2001) discusses more historically specific conceptions of ocean space in relation to culture and economy.

3. George Lakoff and Mark Johnson, *Metaphors We Live By* (Chicago: University of Chicago Press, 1980).

4. Stanislaw Lem, *Solaris* (New York: Walker, 1970), 22.

5. Ibid., 21.

6. Fredric Jameson, *Archaeologies of the Future: The Desire Called Utopia and Other Science Fictions* (New York: Verso, 2007), 108.

7. She also cannot be permanently killed. When Kelvin panics at her first appearance, he tricks her into entering a space shuttle alone, and then remotely programs the shuttle to launch into space, a clean death. Yet after his next sleep cycle, a new simulacrum-Rheya returns with no memory of having arrived before.

8. Stephen Best and Sharon Marcus, "Surface Reading: An Introduction," *Representations* 108, no. 1 (Fall 2009): 1–21 (1). Clearly in response to Fredrick Jameson's *Political Unconscious* and strategies of reading for ideology, Best and Marcus aim to broaden "the scope of critique to include the kinds of interpretive activity that seek to understand the complexity of literary surfaces—surfaces that have been rendered invisible by symptomatic reading."

9. Quoted in Ann Weinstone, "Resisting Monsters: Notes on 'Solaris,'" in *Science Fiction Studies* 21, no. 2 (July 1994): 173–90.

10. Lem, *Solaris*, 98.

11. Ibid.

12. Ibid., 99.

13. Ibid., 101.

14. Ibid., 72.

15. Specifically, I mean the second simulacrum Rheya.

16. Lem, *Solaris*, 202.

17. Ibid., 203.

18. Ibid.

19. Ibid.

20. Relating a friend's description, Freud writes, "it is a feeling which he would like to call a sensation of 'eternity,' a feeling as of something limitless, unbounded—as it were, 'oceanic.' This feeling, he adds, is purely subjective fact, not an article of faith; it brings with it no assurance of personal immortality, but it is the source of the religious energy which is seized upon by the various Churches and religious systems, directed by them into particular channels, and doubtless exhausted by them. One may, he thinks, rightly call oneself religious on the ground of this oceanic feeling alone, even if one rejects every belief and every illusion. . . . I cannot discover this 'oceanic' feeling in myself." See Sigmund Freud, *Civilization and Its Discontents*, trans. James Strachey (New York: W. W. Norton, 1961), 11–12.

21. Greg Egan, "Oceanic," in *The Year's Best Science Fiction, 16th Annual Collection*, ed. Gardner Dozois (New York: St. Martin's Press, 1999), 1–36 (4).

22. Ibid., 8.

23. Ibid., 28–29.

24. Ibid., 30.

25. Ibid., 35.

26. Ibid., 20–22.

27. I could give many examples. Gaston Bachelard's *Water and Dreams: The Imagination of Matter*, trans. Edith R. Farrell (Dallas: Pegasus Foundation, 1983) has a detailed chapter

on the poetics of maternal waters. In critical theory, Luce Irigaray allies the ontological difference of the feminine with water in *The Sex That Is Not One*, and also in *Marine Lover of Friedrich Nietzsche*, where she reads and critiques Nietzsche from the perspective of water. In Chinese medicine, women are associated with the "yin," which is dark, cool, and associated with water. See Luce Irigaray, *Marine Lover of Friedrich Nietzsche* (New York: Columbia University Press, 1991).

28. Egan, "Oceanic," 22.

29. Lateral gene transfer refers to the condition in which genes are not only passed from parent to offspring, but parent to other parents, within the same lifetime.

30. "You've got to look around in Kafka's writings as you might in such a wood. Then you'll find a whole lot of very useful things. The images are good, of course. But the rest is pure mystification. It's nonsense. You have to ignore it. Depth doesn't get you anywhere at all. Depth is a separate dimension, it's just depth—and there's nothing whatsoever to be seen in it." Quoted by Walter Benjamin in *Understanding Brecht* (London: New Left Books, 1973), 110.

31. Egan, "Oceanic," 36.

32. I want to qualify my use of "human" here by reminding the reader that the people of "Oceanic" are biologically different from Earth's humans, because males can give birth, and the phallus can be passed between any couple.

33. Although from a different literary and critical tradition, Kamau Brathwaite's "tidal dialectic" and Elizabeth Deloughrey's elucidation of the concept in *Routes and Roots: Navigating Pacific and Caribbean Island Literatures* (Honolulu: University of Hawai'i Press, 2010) also offer valuable perspectives on figurations of the tides.

Afterword

Still, I'm Reluctant to Call This Pessimism

GERRY CANAVAN & KIM STANLEY ROBINSON

GC ▶ *What is the relationship between ecological science fiction and crisis? Are there other categories beyond "crisis" available to us in* SF *today? Or is crisis the only relevant category if we want to think seriously about the future we are creating for the planet?*

KSR ▶ The coming century will bring to one degree or another a global eco-logical crisis, but it will be playing out at planetary scales of space and time, and it's possible that except in big storms, or food shortages, things won't happen at the right scales to be subjectively experienced as crisis. Of course it's possible to focus on moments of dramatic breakdown that may come, because they are narratizable, but if we do that we're no longer imagining the peculiar kinds of ordinary life that will precede and follow them. Maybe to find appropriate forms for the situation we should be looking to archaic modes where the seasons were the subject, or to Hayden White's nineteenth-century historians, whose sum-marized analytical narratives were structured by older literary modes, turning them into philosophical positions or prose poems or Stapledonian novels.

I think even the phrase "climate change" is an attempt to narrate the ecologi-cal situation. We use the term now as a synecdoche to stand for the totality of our damage to the biosphere, which is much bigger than mere climate change, more like a potential mass extinction event. I don't think it's a coincidence that we are representing the whole by the part most amenable to human cor-rection. We're thinking in terms of thermostats, and how we turn them up or down in a building. That image suggests "climate change" has the possibility of a fix, maybe even a silver bullet of a fix. No such fix will be possible for a mass extinction event.

Lots of words and phrases are being applied to this unprecedented situation: global warming, climate change, sustainable development, decarbonization, permaculture, emergency century, climate adaptation, cruel optimism, climate mitigation, hopeless hope, the sixth mass extinction event, and so on. But maybe sentences are the minimum unit that can begin to suggest the situation in full. "This coming century looks like the moment in human history when we will either invent a civilization that nurtures the biosphere while it supports us, or else we will damage it quite badly, perhaps even to the point of causing a mass extinction event and endangering ourselves." A narrative rather than words or labels.

GC ▸ *Is it a problem, then, that our narrative forms (both fictional and political) seem to rely on "crisis" for their internal energy?* SF, *especially ecological* SF, *seems to trend toward sudden, apocalyptic breaks that may not reflect the glacial pace of environmental change. Even in your* Science in the Capital *series (to take one example) you turn to "abrupt climate change" as a way of narrativizing, on human spatial and temporal scales, a complex network of feedback loops that in actuality is almost impossible to perceive at the level of day-to-day perception. Are there other models for thinking about change, and where do you see these at work in your work?*

KSR ▸ It's true that I puzzled over how to narrate a story about climate change, which I got interested in when I went to Antarctica and listened to scientists down there talking about it. That was in 1995, and I could not think of a plot for such a story. Then in 2000 the results from the Greenland ice coring project showed that the Younger Dryas had begun in only three years, meaning the global climate had changed from warm and wet to dry and cold that quickly. That finding was a big part of the impetus behind the coining of the term "abrupt climate change." By 2002 the National Academies Press had published a book exploring this new term and assembling a good explanation for the drop into the Younger Dryas; it appeared that the Gulf Stream had stalled, because the North Atlantic had gotten much less salty very quickly as the result of one of the massive outflows of fresh meltwater that were occasionally pouring off the melting top of the great Arctic ice cap. These same studies pointed out that the North Atlantic was now freshening again, because of the rapid melting of the Arctic sea ice and the Greenland ice cap.

Major climate change in three years: that was a story that could be told, I thought. But while writing the novel I found that even in this crisis, abrupt on geological scales, events still resolved to individual humans living variants of ordinary life. There would be storms and freezes, power outages, and the threat of food shortages; these would make those years expensive and inconvenient, and give them a tinge of dread, it seemed (like now); but doing something about it was going to consist mostly of political action in Washington and elsewhere, and in geo-engineering projects of doubtful effectiveness and safety, which would be executed by some people, but not everyone. Beyond that, it would be daily life of a slightly different sort, and seldom more. I still wasn't finding the crisis. And the movie *The Day after Tomorrow* showed me what can happen if you choose to represent climate change only as crisis. I wanted something better than that.

So in *Science in the Capital*, and again in *2312*, I kept coming up against the lack of a break to something radically different. It seemed as if the story of climate change was going to have to be told as some kind of daily life, which in narrative terms meant it could not be a thriller. Thrillers live in crisis mode, and anything extraneous is a category error. A review calling *Science in the Capital* "a slow-motion thriller" made me smile, because there can be no such thing. If a thriller stops to portray the protagonist frolicking in the snow with his toddler son, or changing his diapers, that's a blatant genre break. It's true I wanted those, and wrote in as many as I could. At the time I thought of it as just fooling around, giving the novel surprises, but maybe it was also a stab at representing how it might feel to live during climate change. The biggest crisis in the story is thus not any weather event, but the scientist Frank going through a change of consciousness. For any of us that is always a big crisis.

Now I think that the novel proper has the flexibility and capaciousness to depict any human situation, including ordinary life. That's what the modern novel was created to do, and that capacity never leaves it. It's only when you shrink the novel to the thriller that you run into problems in representing ordinary realities.

GC ▶ *It seems to me that the dystopian or apocalyptic side of your work has increased in importance since* Pacific Edge *and the* Mars *trilogy, especially in your most recent novels. In the* Science in the Capital *trilogy our relationship to ecological crisis is much more contingent and haphazard, almost just-in-time. In* Galileo's Dream—*though we don't find out all that much about the transition between the present and humanity's future on the moons of Saturn—the strong implication is that this has been a terrible, even tragic history, with great losses. And in your most recent novel,* 2312, *we return to something very much like the Accelerando of the* Mars *trilogy, only now the environmental problems of Earth have not been dealt with at all—leaving Earth a "planet of sadness," home to starving billions. Does this reflect an increasing pessimism about the possibilities of the future? Or is something else at work?*

KSR ▶ I try to give my novels whatever attitude I think will help them work best. The bleak history sketched in *Galileo's Dream*, for instance, is there because

I needed a reason for people from the far future to be interfering in Galileo's life, and what I came up with was a history so bad that some future people would want to erase and rewrite if they could. I'm always working like that, so I don't feel my own sense of the future is well expressed by my books. Indeed in *Green Mars* I had the West Antarctic Ice Sheet slip off into the sea, just in order to create so much chaos that it would seem more plausible that Mars could successfully secede from Terran rule. That's not pessimism, but just a somewhat brutal focus on making plots seem realistic.

I do have a constantly shifting sense of what the future will "most likely bring," like everyone else. And I am still very interested in writing about utopian futures. How to express that interest changes over time, and in the wake of previous efforts.

GC ▸ *2312 in particular seems like a direct attempt to rewrite the situation of your Mars trilogy with significantly more pessimism, at least in terms of the Accelerando's uneven distribution over class and species lines. One character suggests that even post-scarcity won't be enough to end the problem of human suffering at all, and that in fact true "evil" might be possible only after scarcity: "Before [post-scarcity], it could always be put down to want or fear. It was possible to believe, as apparently you did, that when fear and want went away, bad deeds would too. Humanity would be revealed as some kind of bonobo, altruistic, cooperative, a lover of all. . . . However you explain it, people do bad things. Believe me." Another chapter contains a long list of reasons why utopia is impossible, from original sin to greed to "because it probably wouldn't work" to "because we can get away with it."*

KSR ▸ For me that list is not a list of reasons why utopia is impossible, but rather a list of the shabby excuses we make for not making improvements when they are technically achievable. It was a pretty long list, and yet not comprehensive.

It's true that the situation on Earth in *2312* is presented as somewhat dire. It's very much like the situation we are in now. The exaggeration of three extra centuries of damage merely heightens the representation of now. It's a kind of surrealism, and it could mean that the book describes an impossible future history, in that if things were to go that badly for three hundred more years, they might long before the year 2312 have necessarily spiraled down into something very much worse than what the book depicts. But the way that we live now, in a mixed situation, with some in misery and some in luxury, suggested that we might limp along in a degraded manner for quite a long time. In any case the book's scenario is a distorted image of present reality, in the usual metaphorical way of science fiction.

Given that SF novels are always images of the times they were written in, maybe *2312* is somewhat more pessimistic than my earlier novels, even if I myself am not. In other words, it's just the difference between 1990 and 2010. In those twenty years there's been a lot of dithering, and that might seep into the text in unexpected ways. Still, I'm reluctant to call this pessimism.

GC ▸ *2312 does point to the continued possibility of utopia as you define it in* Pacific Edge*, "struggle forever." The characters do make an improvement in the situation of the solar system, and the logic of the novel's encyclopedia-like interstitial chapters suggest that, in retrospect, a genuine historical break of some kind has been initiated.*

KSR ▸ Yes, that part of *2312* suggests humanity will have the means to repair damage to Earth, and also to make a more just society, and that the two efforts are parts of each other. Having started with a metaphorical description of our own time, there is then a prescription for action in the plot, again presented in surreal or symbolic form. Anything we do in reality will surely be messy and protracted, and the "we" will never be a unanimity. What I wanted to suggest is that because we have the ability to do better, our situation eventually will get so dangerous it will force us to do better. The desire will be there, and the tools are there (science and politics and culture), so the struggle is on, starting now and going on for some centuries at least. We don't have to wait until the year 2312 to act, obviously, and it would be terrible if we did. Since we know now that we can greatly improve the situation by what we do, we should start now, and shoulder the frustrations of how long it will take without too much whining or quitting.

GC ▸ *You've said that there won't be a sequel to* 2312—*no* 2313, *no* 2412. *Does this speak to the ultimate unrepresentability of utopia? Would it be possible to set an artistically successful novel in a "civilization that nurtures the biosphere"—or, to paraphrase Tolstoy, are all happy civilizations alike?*

KSR ▸ Well, as we have not yet seen any happy civilizations, the first one to come along should be interesting as a novelty at least. So yes, it should be possible to write an artistically successful novel set in a happy civilization. I would like to try one myself, but if I did, it would not be a sequel to *2312*, as really it should be set much closer to now. It would be a new try at the subject that would follow on my earlier books, but in the way that a train of thought is followed (or not). I think it's well worth coming back to the problem from time to time, as our current situation and its potentiality keep changing. So there is an opportunity to try something different.

The problems that will remain even in utopian futures are big, like death,

247
STILL, I'M RELUCTANT… | CANAVAN & ROBINSON

or heartbreak; others could be added without straining anyone's imagination. If these big problems still occur in a social context of equality and well-being, might they not become even more acutely felt, as clearly unavoidable losses and sorrows? Doesn't our inescapable biological fate mean the utopia should always shade into tragedy?

GC ▸ *A chapter in* 2312 *emphasizes the impossibility of a classic science fictional subgenre in which you've never participated: the galactic empire of the space opera, with human beings zipping between stars at supra–light speeds. You note that everything we currently know about physical reality tells us this is simply an impossibility—and further note that if it is an impossibility, Earth becomes tremendously important, the single best place we'll ever know.*

KSR ▸ The only place we'll ever know. I firmly believe this point made in 2312, that our solar system exists at human distances and constitutes our home, or our potential home—Earth our home, the solar system a potential home—while the universe beyond the solar system exists beyond human distances and will forever remain a backdrop only, to be observed but not visited.

Clearly there is one exception in terms of stories engaged in real possibilities, which is the story of the generational starship. This is a really interesting science fiction subgenre, full of excellent work already, but it is almost always saying a variant of what I said above; we can't get out to other stars and stay sane, as they are all too far away.

GC ▸ *I'm curious, though, as a thought experiment: if we could get beyond the solar system—if relativity were revised tomorrow—would that really change significantly your commitment to environmentalist thinking? Does ecological thought depend in some sense on a recognition of a limited futurological horizon for mankind, or, alternatively, does it draw from other modes of thinking besides the imperial-economic question of how far we can go and how much stuff we can bring back? Given how capitalism has acted on a planet it knows to be finite and limited, one can scarcely imagine how it would act if it genuinely had the entire universe to spread across. It seems to me from this perspective that ecological thinking may become more important, not less, when mankind faces no limitations on its endless expansion. The wall of the solar system almost makes this too easy a problem, by shifting the register from morality to self-interest; we have to protect our environment to keep ourselves alive, not because it's right.*

KSR ▸ If we had the galaxy within reach . . . but this is something like the land of Cockaigne, which I'm not sure is science fiction. In any case it's not a thought I can follow. I guess the way I come at it is to ask myself: What kind of story could I tell using this device of the galactic setting, that I couldn't tell by way of a more realistic device? And when I don't find any, as usually happens to me when I think about any fantasy devices, I can't see the point of trying them, or at least, I can't find my own way into them. If a good idea for a galactic story did come to me, I would immediately get much more interested. It doesn't feel like that's going to happen, but you never know. I enjoy reading some writers' space operas, and I've written a time travel novel, a reincarnation novel, a shape-shifter novella; I don't stick to realism on principle, it's just a tendency.

As for having to protect our environment to keep ourselves alive, rather than because it's morally right, that's fine by me; it's probably better that way. I suppose if we had entire galaxies to play in, we could be more careless about housekeeping without killing ourselves. That would shift ecological thinking and morality both, I'm sure. But it is too much of a hypothetical.

GC ▸ *The moment from your work that frames this question for me most directly is the radicalism of the Red Martians from the Mars books, who insist on protecting Mars* simply for its own sake*, even though it has no persons on it at all. Part of the dystopian character of 2312, in fact, descends precisely from the fact that in that timeline Mars was settled quickly and maximally, with no regard to preservation, and with something like a seventh of the planet being permanently scorched in the process.*

KSR ▸ This brings up the question of intrinsic value, whether places have value in themselves independent of our use of them or even our regard for them. It's a question in environmental ethics, but as Chris McKay pointed out in "Should Rocks Have Standing?"—echoing Christopher Stone's famous essay "Should Trees Have Standing?"—when we speak of "nature" we tend to mean "life," so that the lifeless rocky bodies of our solar system are not "nature" as we usually mean it. There's slippages all over in our words of course, but this problem of nature's intrinsic value became in my Mars books a way to discuss the possibility of Mars as it is now having a value for us that was greater than its use value; and that if we felt that strongly enough, it would make sense to live there with as little impact on the place as possible, as a visitor almost, or at least an inhabitant that changes almost nothing. It seems like an extreme position, and yet desert lovers on Earth might already feel something like that. Greening a desert might have utilitarian value, but if you love deserts for their look and feel, then an aesthetic is being harmed if you green that desert. In the Mars books the Red position was analogous to that situation, with the added element of Mars's exoticism and otherness, the way it is a very gorgeous rock right now with its own history inscribed on it. It's a very odd special case in environmental thinking, if you think of it as a lifeless rock (as it may not be), and I'm not even sure it is much use to us in thinking about more general cases.

GC ▸ *In* 2312 *something similar happens with the animals—the final utopian reversal of the threatened "mass extinction event" with which our conversation began. So much of debates over animals both in and outside* SF *seems to hinge on the question of whether animals exist as beings in their own right or as something more like that desert, existing (or not) purely to satisfy human needs. I'm struck by Christina Alt's essay on Wells that begins this volume, which finds Wells taking the deliberate extermination of animal life as a marker of utopian achievement. So much supposedly ecological thinking seems predicated on an anthropocentrism that denies the possibility of nonhuman values.*

KSR ▸ Nonhuman values I take to mean human values in support of the non-human. In the case of animals, it's very clear, I think; they exist as beings in their own right, they do not exist to serve us. We predate on them as food, but that is a violation of their existence. We are such powerful animals that we have even domesticated some other animals to make our predation on them easier, but they still live their own lives, whether enslaved to us or not. I think it's best to consider all our fellow mammals as direct cousins, with mental lives much like ours. I've been learning to think similarly about birds, though these are much more distant relatives; fish even more so. I still feel it's all right to eat them, because animals eat other animals, but that doesn't mean the eaten animals were not existences in their own right, and should be treated respectfully and humanely. I think Temple Grandin's position in these matters is impressive and persuasive.

I think what ecological thinking brings us here is the ability to see better how much we are interrelated to all the other species in our biosphere. If we drive them to extinction we are damaging ourselves too, because we are all part of a functioning network of organisms. There can be an anthropocentrism that acknowledges this physical reality and then goes on from there, continuing to value humanity first, but realizing every other living thing is part of us in a quite literal sense. Also, valuing humanity means valuing sentience, and that exists in other living creatures. So as a matter of self-regard and as a matter of respect for others, we need to care about all living creatures and act accordingly.

GC ▸ *You once told me that you see part of your job as a science fiction writer as speaking on behalf of the people of the future—to ensure they have a voice in a present that is robbing them blind. Do you think much about the people of the future as readers of your novels? What might the people of* 2100*, or* 2200*, think about a* *culture that consumed stories of their radically transformed world as entertainment, while simultaneously refusing to act in the material realm?*

KSR ▸ "Speaking for future generations" is a narrative mode or a rhetorical stance. It's similar to the stance of writing as if from the future; in other words, a fictional position. Both can help to create an effect that Roger Luckhurst called "proleptic realism."

As for people in the future reading my work, hopefully it would be like reading any literature from older times. Books are a window back into previous minds and their thoughts. Old science fiction inevitably looks creaky and dated, but in revealing ways, and hopefully despite the datedness, some of the ordinary pleasures of the novel will remain, if they were there in the first place. It is a worry, that SF becomes wrong in ways that obscure everything else about it. But when I was reading for *Galileo's Dream*, I learned about the genre you could call renaissance fantasia, which includes works like the *Hypnerotomachia*, or Bruno's *The Expulsion of the Triumphant Beast*, or *Somnium* by Kepler. These are strange texts, but they have an inventiveness and linguistic energy that reminded me of science fiction. Maybe they were the science fiction of their time, when science was still natural philosophy. In the future people may judge our science to be almost as unformed and primitive as natural philosophy (our science not yet ruling the world, after all, as it might in the year 3000), but hopefully our science fiction will still hold some pleasure as a kind of fantasia.

I don't think people in the future will judge science fiction readers of our time as being especially hypocritical, just because we were reading science fiction while not acting on its lessons in the real world. We will be complicit with all the rest of our time, whatever happens, and it may be that science fiction readers will be judged to be among the secret agents of whatever good comes out of our time. It will be very hard to untangle all that and assign culpability or praise.

By and large I think science fiction has been fulfilling its role as a tool of human thought, while at the same time striving to entertain enough people to make money in the current economy. That's the usual odd combination of requirements that art deals with.

GC ▸ *How do you evaluate the influence of* SF *on ecological and environmentalist discourse? For every* Silent Spring *that uses science fictional imagery to mobilize people, there is a* Star Trek *that persuades us that we just have to sit back and wait for cold fusion to fix everything. Does* SF *generally steer us right, or wrong?*

KSR ▸ Science fiction is a genre, and can hold many different kinds of content, across a wide ideological range.

It probably does have certain generic attributes that constitute its "content of the form." For instance, as it is composed of stories set in the future, or in alternative histories, or in prehistory—thus, all the histories that we can never know—it does seem to indicate a commitment to history. It's a strange version of that commitment, focusing as it does on the histories we can't know; a kind of realism of the absent, made of thought experiments that use the counter-factual or the unknowable.

Another kind of content of the form comes from the genre's focus on the future; this seems to be saying that there will be a future, and maybe a human future. And because future histories are sketched out to explain these fictional futures, there's also usually the implication of causality, even an explanatory causality. Most stories have that, however.

Beyond these contents of the form, many different messages can be conveyed, some helpful, others harmful. Some thought experiments are so badly designed that their results (the contents of the form) are "not even wrong."

Still, pretty prominent in science fiction is a body of work that concerns itself with planets and how humans live on them, and these stories are always ecological in some loose sense. And a subset of this group of stories is about Earth as a planet. One basic message they all convey goes something like, "We live on a planet, and planets are therefore interesting." This is a good thing to remember and think about, as being inescapably ecological. So again, my feeling is that science fiction has by and large done its job as a form, and helped us to think ecologically.

GC ▸ *How does this concern impact your own practice as a writer? What sort of research do you do when you set out to write? How do you square a commitment to the facts to your commitment to the art?*

KSR ▸ Facts are stories, and often the raw material for my stories, so really it is just one single commitment. Most of my stories are realist stories in some sense.

One recent exception that might help illustrate my attitude toward these matters: *Galileo's Dream* is a time travel novel, so I felt more comfortable writing that as a fantasia. Time travel does regularly get defined as a science fictional idea, of course, but I think it is unreal enough to be best presented as a fantasia, so that's what I did. But more often I'm trying for science fiction with a strong reality effect, so the physical facts of the world are very much part of those projects.

My research consists mostly of a lot of reading, augmented by conversations with scientists, historians, and others. I generally sketch out a story in my mind and then start researching it, and what I learn often greatly alters the initial idea. I keep researching right to the end of the writing, so often the later parts of a book (especially the multivolume ones) will seem to know things that the earlier parts didn't, and this is indeed the case.

Because I am trying to create a strong reality effect for variously unreal situations, research is important. It is always bringing me more stories, and many of these are at least as interesting as my initial idea, and they all seem to be woven together and lead off in all directions. It can become a problem finding where the appropriate edge of the spreading network of interesting stories should be cut. It's like cutting a patterned fabric when you love all the patterns. Thus the length of my novels, and the crowded feeling they often have. But I am seeing better now that cut stories can be interesting in their cuts, and that's been helping me to shape the latest novels.

GC ▶ *Did earlier ecological* SF *provide examples or inspiration to you?*

KSR ▶ Yes, my very first attraction to science fiction had a lot to do with the strand in the genre that could be called the planetary romance. What I got was often simply the joy of exploration, something I had already found as a young reader in Jules Verne, but now that joy extended to a romantic feeling about visiting other planets, and regarding them as places or landscapes. My discovery of science fiction happened in the same years I was discovering the Sierra Nevada on foot, also the years I was first reading Gary Snyder and then Buddhist texts, so the three interests were wrapped together for me, they became parts of a single pursuit.

I particularly enjoyed books like Edgar Pangborn's early novels (*West of the Sun*, etc.) and many of the planetary adventures of Jack Vance, who had a very evocative way with landscapes, no doubt because of the way he lived and sailed around Earth during his working life. I also enjoyed Clifford Simak, who managed to make Wisconsin a mysterious planetary surface, connected to places all over the cosmos. Then the first four novels of Ursula K. Le Guin cast a very strong spell, and in *City of Illusions* the exotic planet to be traversed was a far future Earth, which was nice as well. After that I read Herbert's *Dune* as a planetary romance, but also an ecological primer on desert survival.

All these together won me over. It was then I read John Brunner's *Stand on Zanzibar* quartet, which made a very different impact, a somber corrective: planets were great, but we were wrecking ours. Quite a few of Brunner's earlier novels had been planetary romances in the old joyful style, so for him to put the Dos Passos lens on the damage we were doing to Earth was powerful. This for me marked the moment when ecology was added to the original romance.

That allowed me to resituate Ballard as more than a psychological novelist, and *The Crystal World* became a great novel of our alienation from a wrecked Earth.

Since then I have continued to enjoy novels about other planets, everything from Lem's *Solaris* to Molly Gloss's *The Dazzle of Day*. I'm sure this strand in science fiction is what led me to my work on Mars. There exists a kind of canon of planetary science fiction by now, and ecological science fiction is either a subset of that, or vice versa.

GC ▸ *Do any particularly bad stories spring to mind from your early reading? Stories with ridiculous or repugnant premises that point us in a completely wrong direction?*

KSR ▸ Oh, yes, there are several types of bad stories. One that points us in a completely wrong direction is this commonly expressed notion that Earth is humanity's cradle. I know this story began with Tsiolkovsky, but it became a commonplace in American science fiction, and I still hear it a lot in discussions about inhabiting Mars or space more generally, both in the science fiction community and in the space advocacy community. The assumption in that phrase and the future history it suggests is that humanity can survive apart from Earth, which is completely unproven and is likely to be wrong. It further suggests that, as humanity has a destiny to colonize the universe, the "cradle" is of only momentary importance, a thing to be used in infancy and then discarded, or at most revered as "Old Earth." This story therefore carries within it terrible mistakes in thinking about our reliance on our planet, and it rightly causes an instinctive revulsion against the space project on the part of people who are a little more grounded. It is much more accurate, considering that only 10 percent of the DNA inside us is human DNA, to recall Flora Thompson's line from *Lark Rise to Candleford*, which is quoted in John Crowley's *Little, Big*: "We are bubbles of Earth! Bubbles of Earth!"

Another bad story is the one about "the Singularity," which is also connected, though it is not exactly the same idea, to the notion of uploading human minds into computers. These both point us in wrong directions, as being disguised versions of immortality or transcendence—the rapture of the nerds, as Ken MacLeod put it. They are religious stories, misunderstanding or misrepresenting the brain, computers, consciousness, and history. And again they encourage carelessness toward Earth as our indispensable home, and even toward our own bodies, and our historical project as a species.

GC ▸ *It's interesting that you bring up religion, as in addition to denigrating climate change as a science fiction, the denialist Right has frequently insisted it is a "religion." I think we'd both feel comfortable criticizing these characterizations in fairly strident terms—and yet it seems to me one must admit that reality has been taking on the aura of a biblical apocalypse of late. If science fiction is the realism of our time, as you have often said, what to do with the fact that it frequently seems to be the opening crawl for some B-movie dystopia?*

KSR ▸ What I've said is that we are now living in a science fiction novel that we are all writing together. That doesn't necessarily mean we are writing realistic science fiction. If our imaginations are crawling with B-movie dystopias, it may mark that in some Ballardian symbolic way we are hoping for these, rather than fearing them. The underlying feeling may be that anything would be better than now, and that only a big break will free us from the chains we have forged and wrapped around ourselves. But this is mostly hoping for an easy way out, an alternative to revolution where we don't have to do anything. These dystopian scenarios would break the hold of the present order, yes, but they would also make things even worse. We would be freed of some constraints, but worse ones would replace them. This is where Ballard's apocalyptic fantasies, depicting disaster as a flight to freedom, are wrong, because in the chaos he describes so lovingly (I'm thinking of the end of *The Drowned World*) we would be much less free than we are now. I think Ballard himself recognizes and says something like this in *The Crystal World*, the last and most beautiful of his planetary disaster series. The painfully ironic thing is that the kind of freedoms he seemed to crave, which were psychological and personal, can be had by merely walking outdoors, or by hanging out with people you love. It doesn't take the collapse of civilization to defeat suburban alienation. In this project the Dalai Lama is a better guide to happiness than J. G. Ballard. I guess that should be immediately obvious, but I mean that focusing on present reality, and what you can do in it to better things for yourself and everyone, is better than the imaginary freedom expressed in the apocalyptic strain in our science fiction.

Maybe we can say that we need to see the real situation more imaginatively, while imagining what we want more realistically.

GC ▸ *Along the same lines: Is utopia a religion? Or, perhaps it would be better to say: Is there continuity between the vision of utopia you set out and the (happy) end of history figured by something like the Christian kingdom of heaven?*

KSR ▸ Is science a religion? I have trouble grasping exactly what a religion is, once you take it out of church. It's a big word. I think the Christian kingdom of heaven is meant to be an end state, where the operating rules are fixed for good, and the inhabitants are immortal souls. That seems to me very different from an idea that we could try to make a more just society, which is my notion of utopia. That will always be a receding horizon ahead of us, which we can at best approach asymptotically, and will never reach. So it's the difference between a desired end state (but what do they do there?) and a set of means to operate in a process that will never end.

good, and the inhabitants are immortal souls. That seems to me very different from an idea that we could try to make a more just society, which is my notion of utopia. That will always be a receding horizon ahead of us, which we can at best approach asymptotically, and will never reach. So it's the difference between a desired end state (but what do they do there?) and a set of means to operate in a process that will never end.

GC ▶ *Is there a fundamental conflict between mystical and scientific ways of thinking the environment that is registered in your work, or across* SF *generally? Is narrative* SF *on some level incompatible with eco-religion, deep ecology, and other attempts to derive reliably transcendent categories out of "Nature"?*

KSR ▶ My principal criterion for science fiction is that it be set in the future, so if you depict a future in which some kind of eco-religion became widely believed, or was somehow revealed to be true, that's just another science fiction scenario to me, which will work or not as a story, but still be an example of science fiction. So I don't think there is a fundamental conflict.

For myself, I often regard the environment, meaning the planet but also the universe, as a miracle. I have mystical feelings for the Earth and the universe, but feel these can be joined to the most minute investigations of science; nor am I off-put by human attempts to manipulate the Earth or physical reality for human purposes. So science as investigation, and technology as manipulation, are both fine by me in principle, and not an impingement on my mystical feelings. We study and thus worship a sacred reality, which we manipulate in order to survive. This is an emotional state. It seems to me science is already the best eco-religion, in other words, therefore the one I adhere to, but as a lay person.

Deep ecology seemed to be suggesting that humanity was a planetary disease that would run its course and then die back or die out. This did considerable harm to the environmental cause, thus ultimately to the environment. To me deep ecology made it clear why environmentalism needs Marxist critical theory. That said, Marxism could often use a major infusion of ecological thinking, maybe even from the deep end of the pool, if not the drowned stuff. Quite a few of the original observations of Arne Naess were scientifically valid, or admirable in their values. But adding the adjective "deep" was a mistake. The point should have been that plain old ecology was already at the right depth to be very helpful.

GC: I'm reminded here of Gib Prettyman's observations in his chapter on Le Guin, which suggests the ways in which Marxism, ecology, and Eastern religion sit in somewhat uneasy relation with one another. You yourself have frequently taken up non-Western ways of thinking in your novels, for instance your use of non-Christian religion in the Mars books and Tibetan religion specifically in both Years of Rice and Salt *and the climate trilogy. Is this an attempt at crafting a synthesis, or more of an attempt to think the problem?*

KSR ▸ It's just thinking the problem. I'm not capable of a synthesis of those three. Maybe something more like a bricolage. I am interested in all three, and have tried plotting stories by putting them together in various combinations, and tracing what happens. I tend to use Marxist critical theory when thinking about history, ecology when thinking about the biosphere, and Buddhism when thinking cosmically or personally, although immediately when I say that I realize I often use all three in a slurry. My narrators often take "the most scientific view" of everything, even metaphysics, because that leads to funny sentences. And thinking of science as a critical utopian leftist political action from its very beginning—something like the best Marxist praxis so far performed in the real world—is very provocative and stimulating. Likewise thinking of science as a devotional practice, in which the universe is the sacred object of study. It can be almost a scissors-rock-paper thing among the three. The enjambments have been good for my books.

GC ▸ *Do you feel like these kinds of experimental enjambments are more successful than attempts to found "new" eco-religions, as Octavia Butler suggests in her Parables series and Margaret Atwood does in her MaddAddam books, especially* The Year of the Flood? *Perhaps this is really a question about historical continuity versus radical break, and the retention of old forms in the new.*

KSR ▸ I don't know. My inclination is to trying mixing elements we already have rather than invent something new, especially any kind of religion. We have the elements of a good eco-religion already, in science and Buddhism. So, possibly this new mongrel religion should be named, and its pedigree given, in order to impress it more clearly on the mind. As the exercise would hopefully be a thought experiment only (thinking of how several cults have come out of various books' fictional religions), it could be a way to reformulate the concepts of ecology into new and revealing stories. On the whole, I don't see any problem in trying both methods and seeing what kind of stories come.

GC ▸ *You've spoken recently about the ways scientists have become politically engaged, even radicalized, and in some ways this is a major theme of both* Science in the Capital *and* 2312. *Do you find* SF *(of the kind you write, or even* SF *more generally) has a role to play in that? Do the scientists you meet still read science fiction? Does science fiction provide a framework through which scientists can begin to understand themselves as political agents?*

KSR ▶ I think science fiction can help scientists, yes. I hope for that, and try to write some of my novels with that goal in mind.

Now it has to be said, many scientists do not read fiction of any kind; they're like everyone else in that regard. Fiction readers are a subculture, maybe a big one, maybe a minority of the population and growing smaller; it's very hard to say, especially in this stage of technological change, where so many people are very engaged with computers and therefore perhaps reading a lot. And it seems to me that as we are all addicted to stories, there is bound to be a certain draw to the best stories, and written fiction has almost all the best stories. So as we are a species of story addicts, there is always going to be a place for fiction, as being the best stories.

But scientists are busy, and the scientists who read fiction may be a minority among scientists. Still, these are the ones who tend to have philosophical interests in what they do, and to realize that doing science is by no means a natural or self-evident activity. In their curiosity they read, and of course science fiction comes up as a possible source of good stories about science, even illuminating stories. So, many scientists will give science fiction a try. Many used to read it when they were young, then gave it up when they got too busy, or when they came to realize that it did not seem to know much about real science, that it was naïve, a collection of power fantasies for younger readers. It's hard to over-come that judgment and get those people reading SF again. It depends on their level of curiosity, but one very common personality trait of scientists is a lot of curiosity. So there is always the possibility that word of mouth will bring them to some interesting book that they will then check out; and if it pleases them, or even if it irritates them in a stimulating way, they may go on and read more.

I've seen scientists react very strongly against my assertion that science is a form of politics and that scientists should get more involved as scientists in policy making. That breaks what for them was a dichotomy, in which science was clear and good and pure, while politics was dirty and bad and corrupt. They say to me, "But if we spoke politically as scientists it wouldn't be science anymore, and what is good in science would get wrecked." There is some truth to that objection, and yet I still think it's good to irritate them in that way. Subsequently they may see things from a different angle. There is a lot of "dirty politics" inside science, as they know better than anyone; they have to struggle to keep science "scientific." Part of that struggle involves precisely diving into funding, policy, and politics. So it is a good problem to bring up in their minds. Really, scientists need science fiction, or could use it; but it needs to be good on science, or they will see that it isn't, and it won't work for them.

GC ▸ *A recent slogan of yours—again echoed by one of your characters in 2312—has been that social justice is a survival technology. You've also recently discussed the ways in which scientific praxis (at least in some idealized form) reflects a kind of actually existing communism—cooperative, collaborative, rewarding work done outside a market logic. And yet in the bleakest of our dystopian fictions—John Brunner's* The Sheep Look Up*, for instance, to choose one book you have been influenced by—we find reflected the ways in which science and scientific progress seem to be hurling us faster and faster toward final cataclysmic disaster. Where is the intervention point, or the Archimedean lever, for science to reorient itself toward survival and justice as ultimate goals? If story and narrative have power here, why don't they seem to be working?*

KSR ▸ But let's imagine that they are working, just slowly, and against resistance from countervailing forces. This is how I imagine it to be happening. Also, you said "scientific praxis (at least in some idealized form)": no, I mean to say that actually existing science is already working, not just outside market logic, but against market logic. This is my point, and it can be stated in different ways, one of them being that economics should become a subset of ecology, which already measures and values things that economics mismeasures and does not value.

Brunner is a good example of how stories can help here, and have. He did often represent science in a mode of reckless hubris, making the environmental situation worse; but he was writing in the era of the atomic bomb and thalidomide and DDT being sprayed in the streets. There was a postwar moment, in other words, when the scientific community was painfully overconfident in its ability to manipulate the world for human good. In essence they were being unscientific in this attitude, because they were acting on a belief not based on enough evidence to justify it. Their confidence was an arrogance, but having just won the biggest war in history (by way of radar, penicillin, and the atom bomb), as a community they lost their head and thought "We can do anything!"

But the scientific community is very self-regarding and reiterative; it is always trying to make a better scientific method, it is explicitly an unfinished project at all times, and implicitly, maybe even unconsciously, it is a utopian project trying to push history in directions that will reduce suffering and increase justice. So now the 1950s moment of hubris looks embarrassing to the scientific community, and in general there is a much more careful attitude and methodology.

Science is better than it was in the 1950s, in ways that can be demonstrated; here too we have to historicize, to be aware of change and progress. In that longer account, Brunner's books were one part of the corrective to the 1950s moment of hubris, joining the stories of Rachel Carson and many other sources of critique from all directions.

There's always going to be the need for this kind of self-examination and corrective action. We are better now at doing science, partly because we're better at doing theory, and partly because science fiction retold all the old stories about pride going before a fall. However, we're still allowing capitalism to shape our actions and wreck the Earth, meaning our bio-infrastructure, meaning ourselves. So our culture is not yet scientific enough; when it becomes so, we will be making more rapid progress toward both justice and sustainability, as the two are stranded parts of the same project. At least this is the story I'm trying to tell.

Of Further Interest

GERRY CANAVAN

What follows is an annotated list of selected sf works (very broadly defined) that stake out some position on questions of ecological futurity and the environment. Not all of the authors and creators listed necessarily understood themselves to be producing "ecological sf," and by no means are all of these texts equally recommended from either a political or an aesthetic perspective. All, however, are at least potentially of interest to readers interested in the way sf has both drawn from and influenced ecological thinking and environmentalist politics.

Literature and Nonfiction

Douglas Adams, *The Hitchhiker's Guide to the Galaxy*. Earth is demolished to build an interstellar highway in this timeless satire of progress, technology, capitalism, bureaucracy, life, the universe, and everything. Adams's concern for the environment is also evident in his elegiac *Last Chance to See* (1989), cowritten with Mark Carwadine, on endangered species across the globe.

Richard Adams, *Watership Down* (1972). Rabbits are people, too.

Chris Adrian, *The Children's Hospital* (2006). A hospital must shut its doors and become a completely self-sustaining entity following a global flood in this American magical realist novel.

Brian Aldiss, *Non-Stop* (1958; *Starship* in the United States). The novel explores life inside the artificial environment of a generational starship that has lost all memory of its mission or even that it is a spaceship at all. Aldiss fans might also be interested in *Hothouse* (1962), set on a hot future Earth whose new temperature has caused the entire planet to be completely overrun with plant life, as well as *White Mars, or, the Mind Set Free* (1999), his quasi-reply to Kim Stanley Robinson's *Mars* trilogy.

Ibn al-Nafis, *Theologus Autodidactus* (c. 1268–77). One of the earliest sf texts ends with an apocalyptic vision of radical climate change.

M. T. Anderson, *Feed* (2002). Dystopian cyberpunk novel set amid widespread pollution, ocean acidification, mass infertility, and even the replacement of natural clouds (which can no longer form) with artificial Clouds™.

Isaac Asimov, *The Gods Themselves* (1972). One of Asimov's most technically sophisticated novels; the narrative concerns a free energy machine called the Electron Pump, which, alas, is too good to be true. Although he is not commonly thought of as an ecological writer, ecological themes appear across Asimov's work in such texts as *Foundation's Edge* (1982) and *Robots and Empire* (1985), discussed in the introduction, as well as in such texts as *The Caves of Steel* (1953), which converts Asimov's lifelong struggle with agoraphobia into a vision of immense domed cities in which no one would *ever* have to go outside. In the Foundation series we also have the city-planet Trantor, a fully urbanized planet with no natural spaces left to speak of; only in later entries in the series do we begin to get a sense of the unimaginable influx of food and fuel that would be required, on a daily basis, to make such a situation possible.

Margaret Atwood, *Oryx and Crake* (2003). The first entry in Atwood's MaddAddam series finds a mad scientist crunching the numbers and determining that it would be best to eliminate *Homo sapiens* in favor of an upgraded and improved Humanity 2.0. After reciting a cavalcade of long horrors both historical and futuristic, the novel more or less dares us to agree with him.

Paolo Bacigalupi, *The Windup Girl* (2009). Set in Thailand after a cascading series of global calamities including Peak Oil, climate change, and plagues and food shortages caused by genetically modified foods; the Western multinationals are finally ready to start global capitalism up again by raiding the independent kingdom's seed bank. Also of definite interest: Bacigalupi's short fiction (collected in *Pump Six and Other Stories* [2006]) and *Ship Breaker* (2010).

J. G. Ballard, *The Drowned World* (1962). Really, one could start with almost any of the apocalyptic and entropic disasters that appear across the early Ballard—*The Wind from Nowhere* (1961), *The Burning World* (1964), *The Crystal World* (1966), etc.—but this novel's rise of the sea levels and the spreading of the tropical zone as far north as England perhaps speaks most directly to our contemporary concerns about the future. Another noteworthy Ballard novel for students of ecological SF is *High Rise* (1975), which sees civilization utterly break down and all historical progress reverse in a modern apartment building once the lights go out.

Iain M. Banks, *Excession* (1996). The novel offers an extended rumination on what Banks called the "Outside Context Problem," in which a society encounters something so wildly outside its historical-cultural-ideological assumptions that it is barely able to contemplate the situation in the first place. This is, to say the least, a very useful frame for thinking of the way modernity encounters ecological crises like climate change.

John Barnes, *Mother of Storms* (1994). A massive hurricane, caused by runaway climate change after methane release, breaks down into a series of even-more catastrophic global storms.

Greg Bear, *Blood Music* (1985). The nanobots get out.

Edward Bellamy, *Looking Backward* (1888). One of the key improvements in the Boston of one hundred years hence is the elimination of smokestacks and smog, as well as pollution from the Charles River.

J. D. Beresford, "The Man Who Hated Flies" (1929). A perfect insecticide isn't all it's cracked up to be.

Alfred Bester, "Adam and No Eve" (1941). In this remarkable Quiet Earth fantasy, an inventor's novel rocket fuel causes a chain reaction during the test flight that kills all life on Earth. Now the last man, the inventor commits suicide in the ocean so that the bacteria in his body can jumpstart a new cycle of life.

Lauren Beukes, *Zoo City* (2010). The inseparability of the human and the animal is staged in this inventive response to Philip Pullman's *His Dark Materials* trilogy, which sees human beings receive a mystical animal "familiar" whenever they commit a sufficiently grievous sin.

James Blish, "Surface Tension" (1952). Microscopic humans, descended from a crashed colony ship from Earth, befriend paramecia and battle predators under the ocean of an aquatic alien world.

T. C. Boyle, *A Friend of the Earth* (2000). Novel following a convicted ecoterrorist, split between before (1980s) and after (2020s) an ecological collapse.

Ray Bradbury, *The Martian Chronicles* (1950). Bradbury's epic of Martian colonization includes within itself a strongly elegiac sense of what has been lost in the process. Few stories in the book (or anywhere else, for that matter) are as powerful as "There Will Come Soft Rains," which depicts the automatic functioning and ultimate breakdown of a computerized house years after a nuclear war has killed off all the people.

David Brin, *Earth* (1990). The novel—focused on an experiment with black holes that goes awry and threatens all life on the planet—depicts human civilization at an inflection point between growth and final catastrophe, as ecological disaster and energy crisis reach their shared climax. Also of interest is Brin's long-running *Uplift* series (1980s–1990s), which concerns great apes and dolphins raised to sapience by human beings.

Max Brooks, *World War Z* (2006). One of the more innovative entries in the zombie craze of the 2000s, Brooks's novel depicts the catastrophic consequences of a zombie outbreak on both governments and ecosystems.

John Brunner, *The Sheep Look Up* (1972). Formally modeled on John Dos Passos's *U.S.A.* trilogy, this innovative but utterly devastating work excoriates the denialism with which U.S. capitalism encounters the consequences of its own poisonous methods of production. *Stand on Zanzibar* (1968), about overpopulation, is also excellent.

Tobias S. Bucknell, *Arctic Rising* (2012). International intrigue amid rising sea levels and global warming.

Louis McMaster Bujold, *Barrayar* (1991). Harsh environmental conditions and lingering radiation from a nuclear war have led to a social tradition of killing "mutie" babies born with birth defects.

Kenneth Burke, "Towards Helhaven: Three Stages of a Vision" (1971). Burke's scathing indictment of the logic of progress deploys science fictional tropes about pollution, sustainability, and lunar colonization: "When you find that, within forty years, a great and almost miraculously handsome lake has been transformed into a cesspool, don't ask how such destruction might be undone. That would be to turn back—and we must fare ever forward. Hence, with your eyes fixed on the beacon of the future, rather ask yourselves how, if you but polluted the lake ten times as much, you might convert it into some new source of energy. Thus, conceivably, you might end up by using the rotted waters as a new fuel. Or, even better, they might be made to serve as raw material for some new kind of poison, usable either as a pesticide or to protect against unwholesome political ideals."

Octavia E. Butler, *Parable of the Sower* (1994). In Butler's near-future America nearly everything has gone wrong, from the disastrous neoliberal privatization of necessary governmental functions to global warming to widespread poverty. The protagonist, Lauren Olamina, puts her hope in that great science fictional dream, the colonization of the stars, founding a religion based upon this supposed destiny for humankind. The sequel, *Parable of the Talents* (1998) significantly complicates this ambition by revealing it as a kind of apolitical (perhaps even antipolitical) quietism. Also of interest is Butler's wonderfully ambiguous *Xenogenesis* series from the 1980s, in which an advanced alien race from the stars intervenes, following a nuclear war, to both interbreed with humanity and convert the entire Earth into one of their spaceships.

Samuel Butler, *Erewhon* (1872). Pastoral utopia in which all machines have been destroyed.

Ernest Callenbach, *Ecotopia* (1975). The novel that coined the term, *Ecotopia* imagines an alternative to U.S. social and environmental collapse located in a politically separatist Pacific Northwest, whose revolutionary institutions have been inspired both by ecological science and by Native American cultural practices.

Karel apek, *War with the Newts* (1936). Čapek's satire of imperialism and labor exploitation takes an apocalyptic turn in its final third, as the Newts transform the planet to their liking, sinking the continents so they have room to expand.

Orson Scott Card, *Ender's Game* series (1985–). While the first book in the novel takes place almost exclusively within an anthropocentric context, later entries imagine alternative environments and ecologies, as well as the sorts of subjectivities that might be produced under radically different modes of life (such as hive consciousness). Ender's crime rises even above the level of genocide: he exterminates the biosphere of an entire planet.

Terry Carr (ed.), *Dream's Edge* (1980). Anthology of ecological SF including Herbert, Le Guin, Niven, and Sturgeon, among others.

Rachel Carson, *Silent Spring* (1962). Carson notably chooses to begin her work not with scientific data nor with political polemic but a science fictional "Fable for Tomorrow."

Angela Carter, *The Passion of New Eve* (1977). Race war, sadomasochism, and rape culture in a decadent, disintegrating United States.

Suzy McKee Charnas, *The Vampire Tapestry* (1980). Charnas's translation of the classic horror genre into a science fictional register imagines the vampire as a highly specialized predator operating in the very particular ecosystem that is human culture. Also of interest: her *Holdfast Chronicles* (1974–99).

Ted Chiang, "Exhalation" (2008). Transcendent novella in which a race of argon-breathing artificial life forms, living in some sort of sealed canister, confront the inevitable and tragic end of their civilization.

John Christopher, *The Death of Grass* (1956). A virus kills off a huge swath of Earth's plant biomass, including varieties of grass (like wheat and barley), leading to massive upheaval and starvation.

Arthur C. Clarke, "The Forgotten Enemy" (1949). A new ice age comes to London. Clarke's famous 2001 series of novels may also be of note, given its interests in space colonization and in evolution.

J. M. Coetzee, *The Lives of Animals* (2001). Philosophical-ethical treatise on vegetarianism and justice for animals premised on the cognitively estranging notion that animals—despite the way we treat then—have a self-evident right to life and safety.

Suzanne Collins, *The Hunger Games* (2008). Teenagers are forced to fight each other to the death in gladiatorial games in a post-apocalyptic America.

John M. Corbett, "The Black River" (1934). A massive oil spill destroys Los Angeles.

Michael Crichton, *Jurassic Park* (1990). Science brings back the dinosaurs for an amusement park. What could possibly go wrong?

Daniel DeFoe, *Robinson Crusoe* (1719). This is the unacknowledged template for any number of future post-apocalyptic narratives of survival after the collapse of civilization, beginning with the truly prodigious amount of material Crusoe is able to salvage from his wrecked ship.

Samuel R. Delany, "The Star Pit" (1967). An extended mediation on the confrontation with limit, this novella takes as its central metaphor an "ecologarium"—the outsized, space operatic answer to a child's ant farm. Apocalyptic themes—both ecological and cultural—are also quite important in *Dhalgren* (1975), *Triton* (1976), and *Stars in My Pocket Like Grains of Sand* (1984).

Don DeLillo, *White Noise* (1985). Airborne toxic event.

Jared Diamond, "The Worst Mistake in the History of the Human Race" (1987). Agriculture.

Philip K. Dick, *Do Androids Dream of Electric Sheep?* (1968). Largely left out of the novel's adaptation as *Blade Runner* in 1982 is its intense focus on animals as an object of both empathy and desire. Among Dick's less-known novels can also be found *The Crack in Space* (1966), which depicts the first black president's attempt to save his badly overpopulated, economically depressed Earth by invading the apparently empty one in the universe next door.

Grace Dillon (ed.), *Walking the Clouds: An Anthology of Indigenous Science Fiction* (2012). This collection of "Native slipstream" speaks directly to debates over indigenous science and sustainable culture practice, as well as to native visions of the apocalypse—an apocalypse which, as Dillon notes in her introduction, is commonly thought of as having already taken place at the moment of North America's disastrous first contact with Europe.

Thomas Disch, *334* (1972). Overpopulation has caused shortages and made birth control compulsory in this novel of 2020s New York. See also *The Genocides* (1965), discussed in this volume, and the ecologically themed anthology Disch edited, *The Ruins of Earth* (1971), which includes stories from Dick, Vonnegut, Ballard, and du Maurier.

Harold Donitz, "A Visitor from the Twentieth Century" (1928). A lack of cars makes the future a utopia after oil runs out around 1975.

W. E. B. Du Bois, "The Comet" (1920). The end of the world briefly seems like it will, at least, include an end to white supremacy. Briefly.

Daphne du Maurier, "The Birds" (1952). The inspiration for the Hitchcock film is, if anything, even more stark and apocalyptic.

Jeanne DuPrau, *The City of Ember* (2003). An underground city, founded after the surface became uninhabitable, faces an impending energy crisis.

Harlan Ellison, "A Boy and His Dog" (1969). The ultimate in post-nuclear horror.

Harlan Ellison (ed.), *Again, Dangerous Visions* (1972). This sequel to the original American New Wave anthology from 1968 marks the sea change in environmental consciousness that happened in those years; the first collection contains basically no stories about the environment, while the second contains multiple ecological stories, including the novella version of Le Guin's *The Word for World Is Forest*.

Roger Elwood and Virginia Kidd (eds.), *The Wounded Planet* (1974). Only one of a dozen anthologies Elwood put out with ecological and apocalyptic thematic focuses during the period, among them *The Other Side of Tomorrow* (1973), *Omega* (1973), *Crisis* (1974), and *Dystopian Visions* (1975).

E. M. Forster, "The Machine Stops" (1909). An ur-text for the next century of stories about technological collapse. The people inhabiting Forster's dystopia are hopelessly alienated from the natural world on which, they come to discover, their lives still depend.

Pat Frank, *Alas, Babylon* (1959). Life in Florida at the dawn of the "thousand year night," after a one-day nuclear war.

Buckminster Fuller, *Operating Manual for Spaceship Earth* (1969). Still the best known of the "Spaceship Earth" texts that combine a call for better technocratic management of Earth's resources with a science-fictional reimagining of the planetary ecosystem as a starship.

Sally Miller Gearheart, *The Wanderground: Stories of the Hill Women* (1980). Ecofeminist lesbian utopian fantasy that takes place after men (and patriarchy) have been confined to the cities.

David Gerrold, *The War against the Chtorr* (1983). Alien invaders seek to terraform Earth for settlement, while we're still on it.

Amitav Ghosh, *The Calcutta Chromosome* (1996). Medicine meets indigenous knowledge practices in this postcolonial critique of Western science.

William Gibson, "The Gernsback Continuum" (1981). The story marks the shift away from (or perhaps the final grave site of) the glittering techno-utopias of the Golden Age, which appear within the story as ghosts quite literally haunting a grittier, dirtier future much more like the Junk City we've actually come to inhabit.

Charlotte Perkins Gilman, *Herland* (1914). Among the innovations in this influential feminist utopia text is the willingness of the Herlanders to rationally control their population growth. The increased importance of explicitly eugenic themes in the sequel, *With Her in Ourland* (1916), makes it uncomfortable reading today.

Molly Gloss, *The Dazzle of Day* (1997). Quakers in space. Interconnected stories set before, during, and after the voyage of a generational starship to a harsh new planet.

Nicola Griffith, *Slow River* (1995). Biopunk noir with large narrative interest in water purity and treatment.

Martin Harry Greenberg and Joseph D. Olander (eds.), *Tomorrow, Inc.: SF Stories about Big Business* (1976). The overarching attitude of this anthology of stories about capitalism run amuck is nicely suggested by the dedication the book bears: "To Fred Pohl, who tried to warn us."

Harry Harrison, *Make Room! Make Room!* (1966). The novel that brought us *Soylent Green* (1973).

Jean Hegland, *Into the Forest* (1998). Teenage girls living alone in an isolated forest home try to ride out the collapse of civilization.

Robert A. Heinlein, *The Moon Is a Harsh Mistress* (1966). The quintessential novel of interplanetary settlement and revolution gives us the ecological proverb TANSTAAFL: There ain't no such thing as a free lunch.

Frank Herbert, *Dune* (1965). In addition to its ambitious depiction of a wholly alien ecosystem, *Dune* ranks among the best allegorizations of U.S. energy policy and Middle

East imperialism ever achieved in SF. Also of interest: *The Green Brain* (1966), which has the human race seeking to exterminate insect life.

Arthur Herzog, *Heat* (1977). A scientist discovers that the imminent release of the ocean's CO_2 reserves will trigger abrupt, catastrophic climate change, but the government doesn't want to tell anyone before the next election.

Nalo Hopkinson, "A Habit of Waste" (1999). The anti-ecological practices of modern capitalism reach their apotheosis when people can simply discard their own body and select a new one.

W. H. Hudson, *The Crystal Age* (1887). Another classic late-nineteenth-century pastoral ambiguous utopia, notable for its near-total rejection of technology and its anticipatory gender politics.

Aldous Huxley, *Brave New World* (1931). The nightmare of the future retains a "Savage Reservation" as an internal release valve.

Kazuo Ishiguro, *Never Let Me Go* (2005). Critically acclaimed alternate-history narrative of biopolitical exploitation run amuck through the harvesting of human clones for organs—in a world than seems to be in no other way different from ours.

Richard Jefferies, *After London, or, Wild England* (1885). England returns to the wild after a catastrophe destroys civilization.

Gwyneth Jones, *White Queen* (1991). Postcolonial reversal of the white, male alien invader narrative template set amid a future of ecological and economic collapse.

Janet Kagan, *Mirabile* (1991). Environmental troubleshooting on an off-world human colony stocked with genetically engineered life.

Stephen King, *Under the Dome* (2009). The sudden, inexplicable imposition of an impenetrable dome around a small Maine town—a story King had been trying to make work since the 1970s—highlights questions of sustainability and resource scarcity that have global implications. After all, the atmosphere may be much larger, but the sky is still a dome.

Paul Kingsnorth and Dougald Hine, "The Dark Mountain Manifesto" (2009). The joyful apocalypse contained in these "Eight Principles of Uncivilization" is posited as the only possible response to our ongoing "age of ecocide."

C. M. Kornbluth and Frederik Pohl, *The Space Merchants* (1958). Wonderful novel, recently rereleased, which pits a capitalist world run by advertising execs against Greens with other plans.

James Howard Kunstler, *World Made by Hand* (2008). America's premier Peak Oil doomsayer—see his 2005 predictive nonfiction *The Long Emergency*—imagines capitalism returning to a mid-1800s craft economy following the age of cheap oil.

Ray Kurzweil, *The Singularity Is Near* (2005). The handbook for anti-ecological fantasies of technological Singularity. Technology got us into this mess, now it'll get us out. . . .

Kurd Lasswitz, *Two Planets* (1897). German novel of a Martian base at the North Pole that likely inspired one of the founding fathers of American SF, Hugo Gernsback.

Ursula K. Le Guin, *The Dispossessed* (1973). Le Guin's "ambiguous utopia" pits a utopia of abundance (rich, fertile Urras) against a utopia of scarcity (its barren moon, Anarres). Near the end of the novel a new possibility is introduced when the ambassador at an interplanetary embassy describes her home world: the ruined planet Earth, whose inhabitants could not adjust their destructive cultural practices until it was far too late. Le Guin's interest in ecosystem and in the environment extends across her work, playing crucial roles in the development of such works as *The Word for World Is Forest* (novella 1972, novel 1976) and the earthbound *Always Coming Home* (1985), set in a future, post-technological California.

Stanislaw Lem, *Solaris* (1961). Made into very different films by Andrei Tarkovsky (1972) and Steven Soderbergh (2002), the novel depicts an encounter with absolute, radical otherness, a living ocean. Also of interest: *Eden* (1959) and *The Invincible* (1964), in which spaceship crews likewise encounter strange alien species and bizarre ecosystems—even necrosystems—while exploring truly alien worlds.

Edward Lerner, *Energized* (2012). Solar satellites are our only hope for energy after catastrophic and permanent oil shortage.

Ira Levin, *This Perfect Day* (1970). Anti-utopian treatment of a society of total technocratic control.

C. S. Lewis, *Out of the Silent Planet* (1938). The first book in Lewis's *Space Trilogy* sees first contact with a Martian civilization that doesn't have the vocabulary to think in the selfish, wasteful manner of humans.

Laurence Manning, *The Man Who Awoke* (1933). A man from the twentieth century travels into the future by means of prolonged sleep, exploring future civilizations in crisis that are sometimes not happy to see a man from "the height of the false civilization of Waste." The inevitable spirit of progress toward utopia, however, happily wins out.

D. Keith Mano, *The Bridge* (1973). Ecodystopia in which the absolute legal equality of all life has left civilization stagnant.

Gabriel García Márquez, *One Hundred Years of Solitude* (1967). SF published under the cover of magic realism, the novel (whose review in the *New York Times Book Review* famously declared it "the first piece of literature since the Book of Genesis that should be required reading for the entire human race") explores the destructive influence of the introduction of foreign technology and global trade on the once-isolated, once-Edenic town of Macondo.

George R. R. Martin, *Tuf Voyaging* (1986). Interconnected stories about a space trader who winds up in charge of *Ark*, a "seedship" with terraforming and planetary engineering capabilities.

Cormac McCarthy, *The Road* (2006). Father and son wander the blasted ruins of America scavenging for food after an unspecified apocalypse in what is surely the most depressing book ever to be chosen for Oprah's Book Club.

Will McCarthy, *Bloom* (1998). Humanity has retreated to the asteroid belt after a gray goo disaster consumes Earth.

Maureen McHugh, *After the Apocalypse* (2011). Short story collection that includes catastrophes of all kinds, from ecological to pandemic to zombie.

Vonda McIntyre, *Dreamsnake* (1978). In a post-apocalyptic (but also radically bioengineered) desert America, the bite of the dreamsnake produces drug-like hallucinations in humans.

Bill McKibben, *Eaarth* (2010). The environmental activist argues that we have already so altered Earth's natural systems and climate that it would be best to begin thinking of it as another planet altogether.

Judith Merrill, "That Only a Mother" (1948). Nightmarish exploration of the effects of radiation on pregnancy and motherhood.

China Miéville, *Embassytown* (2011). Miéville's first foray into space opera, set on a human colony on an alien world at the margins of known space. See also the surreal, dark-comedic *Kraken* (2010).

Walter M. Miller, *A Canticle for Leibowitz* (1959). Monks attempt to retain modern knowledge in the catastrophic dark age centuries following a nuclear war.

Walter M. Miller and Martin H. Greenberg (eds.), *Beyond Armageddon* (1985). Bracing collection of stories of what happens after the end. Also of interest to students of the apocalypse: *Wastelands: Stories of the Apocalypse* (edited by John Joseph Adams, 2008) and *The Apocalypse Reader* (edited by Justin Taylor, 2007).

David Mitchell, *Cloud Atlas* (2004). Multiple futures populate the middle sections of this formally innovative novel: cloned human fabricants in a dystopic Brave New World, and then tribal hunters and gatherers in Hawaii in a post-apocalyptic, post-technological future a little further down the line.

Naomi Mitchison, *Memoirs of a Spacewoman* (1962). This early feminist SF novel, anticipating later developments of the 1970s a decade in advance, is also noteworthy for its imagination of alternative biologies and ecosystems.

L. E. Modesitt Jr., *The Forever Hero* trilogy (1987–88). Superhero story set after ecological collapse that has its nearly immortal hero seeking to salvage a devastated Earth.

Judith Moffett, *The Ragged World* (1991). Aliens come and demand we clean up our mess.

Ward Moore, "Lot" (1953) and "Lot's Daughter" (1954). Deeply disturbing visions of life after nuclear catastrophe in which we will, Moore suggests, finally be free to be the monsters we always were.

Sir Thomas More, *Utopia* (1516). More's imaginary island remains the template for utopian form to this day.

William Morris, "News from Nowhere" (1890). Socialist utopia that is both anticapitalist and anti-progress, functioning instead as a primarily agrarian society in tune with nature.

James Morrow, *This Is the Way the World Ends* (1985). Survivors of a nuclear war are put on trial by the Unadmitted—the time-traveling spirits of the people of the future who will now never exist.

Larry Niven and Jerry Pournelle, *The Mote in God's Eye* (1974). Overpopulation novel in which a space-faring humanity encounters an alien culture whose bioforms must either reproduce or die, leading to inevitable cycles of population explosion followed by total civilizational collapse. The Moties (as they are called) have a social archetype called Crazy Eddie who believes that there must be some solution to this cycle of boom and bust; the humans realize with horror that if the Moties were able to get off their home world, "Crazy Eddie" would be right, and furthermore their rapid population cycle would help the Moties quickly overrun the galaxy. Fans of the fantasy genre will also be interested in Niven's "The Magic Goes Away" (1976), which imagines a magic fantasy world experiencing the shock of Peak Mana.

George Orwell, *1984*. Shortage, fascism, and misery after an atomic war.

Dexter Palmer, *The Dream of Perpetual Motion* (2010). One of the more interesting entries in the steampunk subgenre from an ecological perspective, as it begins with the fantasy of advanced machinery without the horrors and limits of the twentieth century, only to have the machines all fail in the end anyway.

Edgar Pangborn, *Davy* (1965). Science is suppressed centuries after an atomic war. Also recommended: *West of the Sun* (1953).

Marge Piercy, *Woman on the Edge of Time* (1976). In this classic work of 1970s ecofeminist SF, a woman incarcerated in a contemporary mental institution travels to two possible futures—a pastoral ecotopia and an urban, technologized dystopia—and comes to realize her actions in the present will determine which one becomes real. Piercy's excellent *He, She, and It* (1991) is also notable for its biopunk-inflected exploration of a post-apocalyptic America following an ecological collapse.

Frederik Pohl, *The Cool War* (1981). "Power piggery" is outlawed in world facing crisis at the end of the fossil fuel age. Pohl also edited an anthology called *Nightmare Age* (1970), which included work from Paul Ehrlich alongside C. M. Kornbluth, Mack Reynolds, Fritz Leiber, and Robert Heinlein, among others.

Christopher Priest, *The Inverted World* (1974). Sublime novel in which a city on rails (called "Earth") must continually move forward in advance of a singularity that has inverted the categories of time and space, wonderfully allegorizing on the levels of both form and content the absolute dependence of civilization on resource management and the natural environment.

Daniel Quinn, *Ishmael* (1992). In this cult classic continually being rediscovered on college campuses, a talking ape metaphorizes agricultural civilization as an outlandish nineteenth-century flying contraption rolled off a cliff; we think it's working only because we haven't crashed yet.

Mack Reynolds, *Lagrange 5* (1979). Socialism in a closed environment in high orbit.

Adam Roberts, *The Snow* (2004). It starts snowing and just won't stop.

Keith Roberts, *The Chalk Giants* (1974). Linked stories set in a dark age after the bomb.

Kim Stanley Robinson, the *Mars* trilogy (1990s). While one could explore ecological themes almost anywhere in Robinson's work, from his *Three Californias* trilogy (1980s) to his *Science in the Capital* trilogy (2000s), the incomparable *Mars* trilogy stages these questions in particularly unforgettable form. As the colonization of Mars gets under way, the colonists find themselves in two camps—the Green Martians, progressives who want to develop the planet, and the Red Martians, ecologists and aesthetes who wish to preserve Mars in its original state for its own sake. Robinson's latest novel, *2312* (2012), is set in a kind of parallel history to the Mars books; here, Mars was maximally terraformed immediately upon settlement, bespeaking in miniature the crisis of a solar system where the problems posed by the Mars books never got solved.

Kim Stanley Robinson (ed.), *Future Primitive: The New Ecotopias* (1994). Short-story anthology, collecting visions of primitivist and anarchist ecotopias.

Joanna Russ, *The Female Man* (1975). Much of this novel is set on the beautiful ecotopia of Whileaway, a planet populated by only women centuries after a plague has killed off all the men—or, at least, that's how they remember it.

Mary Doria Russell, *The Sparrow* (1996) and *Children of God* (1998). Jesuits in space. First-contact novel that depicts a planet with two sapient races: one a predator, and one their prey.

José Saramago, *Death with Interruptions* (2005). Death takes a holiday, leading to the catastrophic breakdown of all human institutions. Saramago's *Blindness* (1995), while not focused on the environment per se, is nonetheless a riveting depiction of apocalyptic urban breakdown and radical scarcity following a city-wide epidemic of blindness.

Nat Schachner, "The Revolt of the Scientists II—the Great Oil War" (1933). Heroic scientists invent a device capable of transforming the world's oil into useless jelly if their anti-monopolistic demands for oil industry reform are not met.

Mary Shelley, *Frankenstein* (1818). First published anonymously the same year as her husband Percy's poem "Ozymandias" (below), *Frankenstein*, widely acknowledged as the first SF novel, dramatizes man's overstepping of his natural bounds in a manner that would become paradigmatic for the genre.

Percy Bysshe Shelley, "Ozymandias" (1818). As discussed in the introduction, this poem templates a thousand visions of decadence and ruin that would follow both in and outside the science fiction genre.

Nevil Shute, *On the Beach* (1957). The last survivors of mankind, living in Australia, await salvation or death, depending on the winds that may or may not blow radioactive fallout from the destroyed Northern Hemisphere southward after the last war.

Robert Silverberg, *The World Inside* (1971). Overpopulation pressures have forced massive changes to U.S. society.

Clifford Simak, *City* series (1940s). Earth goes to the dogs.

Dan Simmons, *Hyperion* series (1989–1999). Space opera detailing a human diaspora following the destruction of Earth during the "Big Mistake," which frequently touches on ecological themes.

Joan Slonczewski, *A Door into Ocean* (1986). Feminist ecotopia set among a community of "Sharers" on an ocean planet.

Olaf Stapledon, *Star Maker* (1937). Alongside Stapledon's career-long fascination with the cosmic drama of life, the universe, and everything, we find here created dozens of alternative forms of sentient life as adapted to alternative planetary niches, from Insectoid Men and Echinoderm Men to Plant Men and intelligent flocks of birds. Also of significance: Stapledon's *Last and First Men* (1930), which details the repeated collapse of human civilization across millions of years and eighteen evolutions of *Homo sapiens*, and his inventive, tragicomic *Sirius* (1944), which borrows from *Frankenstein* to imagine the life of a dog raised to human intelligence.

Starhawk, *The Fifth Sacred Thing* (1993). Life in an ecotopia, following the apocalyptic crash of the United States, is threatened by invasion from a dystopian theocracy.

Neal Stephenson, *Zodiac* (1988). Trash, toxic waste, and conspiracy in Boston Harbor.

George Stewart, *Earth Abides* (1949). After a plague kills nearly everyone in the United States, survivors band together to survive. The years-later final third depicts the old age of our protagonist, who has managed to build a new tribe but who is not of it; to his descendants, the word "American" connotes the time of myth, not real or relatable history.

Charles Stross, *Accelerando* (2005). Contact with interstellar civilizations means the introduction of Capitalism 2.0, in which corporations no longer require human beings for their smooth operation and can begin consuming the Earth directly. The last humans flee out into the far reaches of the solar system looking for refuge. Stross's dystopian Singularity is thus not the moment computers become self-aware—it's the moment *corporations* do.

Boris and Arkady Strugatsky, *Beetle in the Anthill* (1979). The title derives from the possibility that aliens interfering with Earth's people and ecosystem might be akin to the human child who puts a beetle in an anthill just to see what will happen. Aliens are similarly thoughtless and incautious in *Roadside Picnic* (1972), the loose inspiration for Tarkovsky's cinematic *Stalker* (1979), which suggests that the bizarre artifacts left behind after an alien Visitation might simply be the discarded trash from their lunch.

Theodore Sturgeon, "Thunder and Roses" (1947). Definitive staging of that central moral recognition of the Cold War—that there would be no point in firing back, even if the other side launched first. Our hero chooses life over universal death, even if he has to kill to ensure that the future gets its chance.

Leo Szilard, "The Voice of the Dolphins" (1961). Once we learn to speak with the dolphins, they ask us to please not destroy the planet with our bombs.

Sherri S. Tepper, *The Gate to Women's Country* (1988). Another secessionist ecotopia set in the Pacific Northwest, this one with more radical gender politics than Callenbach's.

Sheree R. Thomas (ed.), *Dark Matter* (2000) and *Dark Matter: Reading the Bones* (2004). Afro-futurist anthologies that each contain stories of ecological crisis, environmental justice, and environmental racism.

Lavie Tidhar (ed.), *The Apex Book of World* SF (2009) and *The Apex Book of World* SF 2 (2012). Stories across both collections of global SF suggest the increasing indistinguishability between postcolonial theory, anticapitalism, antiglobalization, and ecocritique. Also strongly recommended along these same lines: *So Long Been Dreaming* (edited by Nalo Hopkinson and Uppinder Mehan, 2004).

James Tiptree Jr. (Alice Sheldon), "The Last Flight of Dr. Ain" (1969). Another mad scientist decides the only answer to the ecological crisis is to destroy the human race through a virus. "Houston, Houston, Do You Read?" (1976) is also noteworthy for its refreshingly straightforward articulation of the premise of much 1970s feminist and ecofeminist works of SF—"First, let's kill all the men."

J. R. R. Tolkien, *The Lord of the Rings* (1954). Another fantasy entry, *The Lord of the Rings* depicts a clash between the Brave New World of the orcs and the Arcadia of the hobbits, culminating with a snake-in-the-garden moment of attempted industrialization within Hobbiton itself.

Karen Traviss, *City of Pearl* (2004). The first book in Traviss's *Wess'har Wars* series of novels details competition between colonizing groups with very different cultural assumptions on the alien world Cavanaugh's Star.

George Turner, *The Sea and Summer* (1987). A future historian looks back on the society whose collapse (ours) created his own. A new edition has just been released from Gollancz.

Jack Vance, *The Dying Earth* (1950). Seminal fantasy series deals with an Earth near the end of time, with a transformed climate and biosphere.

Gordon Van Gelder (ed.), *Welcome to the Greenhouse* (2011). An anthology of previously unpublished stories about climate change from well-known authors across the genre.

Jules Verne, *Invasion from the Sea* (1905). Verne's last novel concerns the possibility of terraforming Africa by flooding the Sahara.

Kurt Vonnegut, *Galápagos* (1985). Vonnegut's evolutionary novel sees the last fertile human beings on the planet shipwrecked on the Galápagos Islands and evolving, over millennia, into creatures much like dolphins. The next evolution of man has much-diminished cognitive capacity, but for the darkly comic Vonnegut that's just another argument in its favor. Also of note is Vonnegut's *Cat's Cradle* (1963), which has civilization end as a result of man's propensity to invent insane, destructive, and totally unnecessary devices without ever stopping to ask first if it *should*.

David Foster Wallace, *Infinite Jest* (1996). Ecological disasters abound in this important novel of the near future, which also memorably treats consumer capitalism, nuclear war, and the porousness of the human-animal boundary.

Ian Watson, *The Jonah Kit* (1975). This strange but intriguing novel includes frequent trips inside the minds of whales. Fans of Watson will also enjoy his "Slow Birds" (1983), about an idyllic pastoral world that is periodically invaded by strange, metal cylinders, nuclear missiles from another dimension (ours).

Peter Watts, *Starfish* (1999). Grim novel finds bioengineered humans working power stations at thermal vents deep underwater.

Alan Weisman, *The World Without Us* (2007). Speculative nonfiction concerning what would happen to human infrastructure following the disappearance of the human race, from the near term (days, weeks, months) to geologic time (hundreds of millions of years). Draws in part from Weisman's journalistic work in the Chernobyl zone, a "world without us" that already exists in the present.

H. G. Wells, *The Island of Doctor Moreau* (1896). Vivisection horror. Environmental themes actually characterize most of Wells's early fiction, from the pseudo-pastoral of *The Time Machine* (1895) to the near-miss asteroid collision of "The Star" (1897) to the climate change that causes the Martians to invade Earth in *The War of the Worlds* (1898). 1914's *The World Set Free* depicts a human race saved from its plunderous waste of fossil fuels by the invention of atomic energy; Leo Szilard credits the book as his inspiration for the initial theorization of the nuclear bomb.

Scott Westerfield, *Uglies* (2005). The occasion for the formation of this Young Adult dystopia is a social collapse brought about by energy scarcity.

Kate Wilhelm, *Where Late the Sweet Birds Sang* (1976). Environmental panics collide when, in a collapsing world of pollution, climate change, and overpopulation, an isolated planned community seeking to weather the storm discovers it is universally infertile and must turn to cloning for reproduction.

Robert Charles Wilson, *Julian Comstock: A Story of 22nd-Century America* (2009). Set against a U.S. war in Canada with an emerging Dutch superpower over control of the thawed Northwest Passage, this inventive novel finds the people of a post-oil, post-climate-change future looking back on our era as "the Efflorescence of Oil"—the word "efflores-cence" describing an evaporating of water that leaves behind a thin layer of salty detritus.

Jeanette Winterson, *The Stone Gods* (1997). Thematically intertwined, self-referential stories about the historical repetition of human-caused ecological disasters, in both the past and the future.

Gene Wolfe, *The Book of the Long Sun* (1993–96). Four-book series set on a generational starship in the Dying Earth setting of Wolfe's even larger *Book of the New Sun* series.

Austin Tappan Wright, *Islandia* (1942). Arcadian utopia located in the South Pacific.

Ronald Wright, *A Scientific Romance* (1996). The sudden, inexplicable appearance of H. G. Wells's *Time Machine* in a London flat facilitates a trip into a depopulated future.

Philip Wylie, *The End of the Dream* (1972). Ecological catastrophe comes to America. Also noteworthy is *When Worlds Collide* (1933) and its sequel, *After Worlds Collide* (1933), in which a small number of humans flee Earth, before it is destroyed by collision with a rogue planet, to settle on Bronson Beta.

John Wyndham, *The Day of the Triffids* (1951). Walking, intelligent plants take over the world. Also of interest: *The Chrysalids* (1955), set after an apparent nuclear holocaust that has altered the climate and mutated the biosphere.

Karen Tei Yamashita, *Through the Arc of the Rain Forest* (1990). Surreal and comic magical realist novel depicting a network of ecological and capitalist disasters centering on the threatened Brazilian rain forest.

Pamela Zoline, "The Heat Death of the Universe" (1967). In the end, alas, time and entropy only run the one way.

Film and Television

A.I. (Steven Spielberg, 2001). Decline and extinction for the human race, with only our robots left behind to succeed us.

Alien (Ridley Scott, 1979). Invasive species wrecks havoc on prey lacking natural defenses.

The Atomic Café (Jayne Loader, Kevin Rafferty, and Pierce Rafferty, 1982). Compilation and creative reframing of U.S. nuclear propaganda.

Avatar (James Cameron, 2009). A human race desperate for energy sources to sustain their dying civilization attempts to steal unobtainium from the Pandora, only to be forced off the planet by a Gaia-like global consciousness uniting plants, animals, and the indigenous Na'vi.

Battlestar Galactica (Ronald D. Moore, 2003). Humans and their robot servants are locked within a cosmic cycle of destruction.

The Birds (Alfred Hitchcock, 1963). Sublime allegory of our absolute dependence upon nature, as well as its radical alterity and unknowability.

Children of Men (Alfonso Cuarón, 2006). Outstripping its source material, this adaptation of the P. D. James novel depicts the human race eighteen years after it has been spontaneously struck infertile.

The Colony (Beers and Segal, 2005). Reality TV series about people living in a simulated post-apocalyptic environment.

The Dark Knight Rises (Christopher Nolan, 2012). The conclusion of Nolan's Batman trilogy sees billionaire Bruce Wayne mothballing a cold fusion device that would end class struggle and usher in universal global prosperity out of fear that it might be turned into a bomb. The series started, of course, with *Batman Begins* (2005), in which the main villain is deep-ecological ecoterrorist Ra's al Ghul.

Dawn of the Dead (George Romero, 1978). U.S. consumer culture literally consumes itself.

The Day after Tomorrow (Roland Emmerlich, 2004). Abrupt climate change brings an instant ice age to New York City, convincing even a sinister Dick Cheney analogue of the seriousness of the problem.

Daybreakers (Michael Spierig and Peter Spierig, 2009). Ten years after a viral epidemic has turned most of the global elite into vampires, humanity's successors now face critical shortages after hitting Peak Blood.

The Day the Earth Caught Fire (Val Guest, 1961). Nuclear testing throws Earth off its axis, hurtling it toward the sun.

The Day the Earth Stood Still (Scott Derrickson, 2008). Updated remake of the Robert Wise–directed 1951 original has Klaatu (Keanu Reeves) issuing a grim warning about humanity's failure to protect its ecosystem.

District 9 (Neill Blomkamp, 2009). An alien spaceship arrives over Johannesburg, bringing not the untold riches of the future but an even more wretched version of the present: miserable, starving insectoids called "prawns," who are promptly housed in a concentration camp until some more permanent solution can be found.

Doctor Who: "The Green Death" (Michael E. Briant, 1973). The Third Doctor confronts the mad computer running Global Chemicals, which is hell-bent on polluting the planet. See also (among others) the Tenth Doctor's "The Sontaran Stratagem/The Poison Sky" (Douglas Mackinnon, 2008) in which carbon-dioxide-free cars turn out to be poisoning the atmosphere even faster.

Dr. Strangelove or: How I Learned to Stop Worrying and Love the Bomb (Stanley Kubrick, 1964). U.S. Cold War militarism absurdly reaches its logical conclusion.

The End of Suburbia (Gregory Greene, 2004). Documentary depicting the coming collapse of fossil-fuel-intensive infrastructure in the United States.

Fail-Safe (Sidney Lumet, 1964). U.S. Cold War militarism logically reaches its absurd conclusion.

Firefly (Joss Whedon, 2002). The backstory for the Western-cum-space-opera has the "Earth-that-was" being "all used up" before the remnants of humanity takes to the stars in search of a new home.

Fringe (J. J. Abrams, 2008). Contact between parallel universes causes the environment of one to catastrophically degrade.

Godzilla (Ishirō Honda, 1954). Monster awoken by undersea nuclear testing ravages Tokyo.

The Happening (M. Night Shyamalan, 2008). In an effort to protect itself from destruction, Nature generates a disease that triggers mass suicide in humans.

Idaho Transfer (Peter Fonda, 1973). Time travel allows a small group of teenagers to skip over the ecological catastrophe that will soon wipe out humanity and start civilization anew fifty-six years in the future.

Ilha de Flores / Island of Flowers (Jorge Furtado, 1989). A narrative voice reminiscent of the *Hitchhiker's Guide to the Galaxy* traces wealth, power, and waste through the networks of contemporary global capitalism.

I Live in Fear (Akira Kurosawa, 1955). A man paranoid about nuclear war is desperate to relocate his family from Japan to Brazil. The Cold War as itself a nightmarish science fiction.

An Inconvenient Truth (Davis Guggenheim, 2006). Al Gore tries to mobilize Americans toward climate action through an extended PowerPoint presentation.

Invasion of the Body Snatchers (Philip Kaufman, 1978). Spore-like aliens invade San Francisco, replacing human beings whose gray, shriveled corpses are removed by ubiquitous sanitation trucks. As with the 1956 original, the implication is that these replacements may be better at being us than we are.

Lessons of Darkness (Werner Herzog, 1992). An unknown intelligence unfamiliar with human society visits the apocalyptic site of burning oil fields following the first Gulf War.

Life after People (2008). This paradigmatic example of the Quiet Earth subgenre of books and documentaries concerned a world emptied of people, frequently drawing on footage of *present-day* postindustrial cities for its supposedly futuristic visuals.

Logan's Run (Michael Anderson, 1976). Based on the book by William F. Nolan and George Clayton Johnson, a future civilization has struck a sustainable balance for consumer capitalism by executing people the day they turn thirty.

Lost in Space (Irwin Allen, 1965). Both the lighthearted original television series and the darker 1998 "reboot" film see the Space Family Robinson escape an ecologically threatened Earth.

Mad Max (George Miller, 1979). Life isn't easy in Australia after the end of cheap oil.

The Man in the White Suit (Alexander MacKendrick, 1951). Capitalism requires a logic of planned obsolescence and egregious waste for its continuance.

The Matrix (Andy Wachowski and Lana Wachowski, 1999). The battle between man and machine takes a turn when humans black out the sky in an effort to stop their solar-powered creations from taking over. Later editions in the series make clear that humanity really can't leave the Matrix, even if they'd like to; the environment they've ruined could not possibly sustain their numbers.

Metropolis (Fritz Lang, 1926). This seminal film of class division between a pastoral leisure class and a brutally exploited industrial class still speaks to us.

Moon (Duncan Jones, 2009). Humanity has finally solved its energy problems through helium-3 mining on the moon. There's only one problem: someone's got to run the facility.

Planet of the Apes (Franklin J. Schaffner, 1968). Catastrophic climate change following a nuclear war has scorched the United States, transforming New York into Arizona. Later films in the series reveal that the mass extinction of both cats and dogs is responsible for the very importation of great apes first as pets and then, quickly thereafter, as servants, which is what started the whole mess in the first place.

"Plastic Bag" (Ramin Bahrani, 2010). Solitary inner monologue of a plastic bag (unforgettably voiced by Werner Herzog) that survives the human race by millions of years, wishing only that his creators had manufactured him so he could die.

Pumzi (Wanuri Kahiu, 2010). Spellbinding Kenyan short film depicts a dystopian future for Africa in which all life on the surface has died.

The Quiet Earth (Geoff Murphy, 1985). An experiment to create a new global energy grid goes horribly wrong, causing nearly everyone on Earth to vanish.

Quintet (Robert Altman, 1979). Almost excruciatingly slow film about high-stakes gambling after a new ice age.

Revolution (J. J. Abrams, 2012). What happens when all the lights go out.

Silent Running (Douglas Trumbull, 1972). All planet life is extinct, save for those housed in a threatened orbital nature preserve.

Sleep Dealer (Alex Rivera, 2008). Among the many deprivations of this post-apocalyptic future is the privatization of water.

Soylent Green (Richard Fleischer, 1973). A wildly overpopulated globe is fed by Soylent Green, a tofu-like food substitute that is absolutely derived from high-energy plankton, not from ground-up human corpses.

Stalker (Andrei Tarkovsky, 1979). Surreal film loosely based on the Strugatsky's *Roadside*

Picnic, whose depiction of a dangerous depopulated "Zone" eerily anticipates the Chernobyl disaster seven years in advance.

Star Trek IV: The Voyage Home (Leonard Nimoy, 1986). Facing certain destruction at the hands of a whale-friendly alien probe, the crew of the *Enterprise* travels back in time for a madcap romp in twentieth-century San Francisco as they try to save the whales.

Star Trek: The Next Generation: "Force of Nature" (Robert Lederman, 1993). The Federation discovers that their overuse of warp drive is slowly destroying the fabric of the galaxy. A galactic speed limit is imposed, but the imposition of even this slim reality check so disrupts the series's cornucopian, expansionist fantasy that it is essentially never mentioned again.

Terra Nova (Brannon Braga and Steven Spielberg, 2011). Settlers from a dying future seek to colonize the Cretaceous.

Things to Come (William Cameron Menzies, 1936). Based on a novel by H. G. Wells, the film depicts a human race that repeatedly destroys itself through violence and blunt stupidity. The film's final lines argue that unless mankind is ultimately able to conquer the stars, it might as well have never existed at all.

Threads (Mick Jackson, 1984). Incredibly bleak BBC miniseries about life in a blighted England following a nuclear war.

The Time Machine (Simon Wells, 2002). Accidental overdevelopment of the moon destroys technology civilization, ushering in the familiar Eloi and the Morlocks of Wells's 1895 novel. Almost entirely forgettable aside from its sublime, time-lapsed vision of Earth's destruction and renewal after the loss of the moon.

Time of the Wolf (Michael Haneke, 2003). A family seeks clean water and safe food after an ecological catastrophe has destroyed civilization.

Torchwood: Miracle Day (Russell T. Davies, 2011). Everybody living forever is not as great as you'd think.

Twelve Monkeys (Terry Gilliam, 1996). A virologist deliberately releases a supergerm to kill off the human race in the name of protecting the environment.

The Twilight Zone: "The Midnight Sun" (Anton Leader, 1961). Rod Serling's vision of an Earth growing ever hotter takes on new relevance in an era of climate change. See also "Two" (Montgomery Pittman, 1961), in which a post-apocalyptic landscape is revealed to be a new Garden of Eden in one of the series's few happy endings.

Waterworld (Kevin Reynolds, 1995). Catastrophic sea level rise after the ice caps melt.

Weekend (Jean-Luc Godard, 1967). This New Wave apocalyptic masterpiece is required viewing for the long tracking shot of an endless traffic jam alone.

Zardoz (John Boorman, 1974). Surreal Sean Connery fantasy film that begins with the proposition that "The gun is good. The penis is evil."

ZPG: Zero Population Growth (Michael Campus, 1972). An overpopulated, environmentally degraded Earth installs a thirty-year-ban on procreation.

Comics, Animation, Music, Games, and Other Media

"Big Yellow Taxi" (Joni Mitchell, 1970). Song. They paved paradise, and put up a parking lot.

Captain Planet and the Planeteers (Barbara Pyle and Ted Turner, 1990). The Spirit of Earth, desperate for a solution to the ecological crisis, entrusts five teenagers from around the world with element-themed magic rings capable of summoning an ecological superhero. The power is yours.

Civilization (MicroProse, 1991). Long-running computer game series includes both fallout zones and global warming in later stages. Ecological themes are extended in the sequel, *Sid Meier's Alpha Centauri* (1999).

Cowboy Bepop (Shinichirō Watanabe, 1998). Anime space opera in which Earth is a marginally habitable, ruined backwater as a result of both an apocalyptic scientific accident and everyday industrial degradation.

Dungeons and Dragons: Dark Sun (TSR, 1991). Dungeons and Dragons campaign setting in which the release of wild, uncontrolled magic has laid waste to the world.

Fallout (Interplay, 1997). Satirical series of post-apocalyptic video games, parodying 1950s and 1960s fantasies of post-nuclear-war survival.

Ferngully: The Last Rainforest (Bill Kroyer, 1992). Didactic coproduction between animation studios in Australia and the United States on the need to save the rain forests.

Fraggle Rock (Jim Henson, 1983). Children's television series about an underground ecological niche where all life forms have a necessary role to play. Another Jim Henson Productions project, the ABC sitcom *Dinosaurs* (1991–94), frequently focused on ecological themes, culminating in a highly unusual series finale that sees these anthropomorphic dinosaurs cause the ice age that leads to their extinction through excess capitalist development.

Futurama (Matt Groening, 1999). Episodes of this long-running animated series frequently lampoon the excesses of consumer capitalism from an ecological perspective.

H. M. Hoover, *Children of Morrow* (1976). Another children's book series set after the end of the civilization, this once caused by pollution.

"In the Year 2525" (Zager and Evans, 1969). Song. In the year 9595, I'm kinda wonderin' if Man is gonna be alive; he's taken everything this old Earth can give, and he ain't put back nothing in. . . .

The Jetsons (Hanna and Barbara, 1962). Futuristic cartoon look at the world of tomorrow depicts a humanity that lives entirely in domed skyscrapers. Occasional references to the natural environment in follow-on movies darkly hint that the air below their homes is hopelessly polluted by smog, and that grass is recognizable only from history textbooks.

Katamari Damacy (Namco, 2004). In this delightful and ecologically minded video game, the ceaseless accumulation of our disposable junk progresses on larger and larger scales until it ultimately rolls up the entire Earth.

Jack Kirby, *Kamandi: The Last Boy on Earth* (1972). A young human boy emerges from a nuclear shelter (Command D) into a post-apocalyptic wasteland populated by mutants and talking animals. Later issues of the comic book suggest this is, in fact, the actual future of the canonical DC Universe of Batman and Superman. Even stranger are the Atomic Knights created by John Broome and Murphy Anderson in 1960, with whom Kamandi shares a universe; the Atomic Knights wander a post-nuclear-holocaust (but surprisingly stable) America in medieval suits of armor, riding giant mutated dalmatians.

Robert Kirkman, *The Walking Dead* (2003–). Alongside *World War Z*, the best of the current zombie fictions depicting a bleak already-dead world, in which hardened bands of survivors struggle both to survive and retain their human decency.

The Land before Time (Don Bluth, 1988). Perhaps the best children's film ever made about mass extinction.

Dr. Seuss, *The Lorax* (1971). Capitalism's ruthless exploitation of the environment inevitably destroys the conditions required for its own continuation, unless.

"Mercy Mercy Me (the Ecology)" (Marvin Gaye, 1971). Song. Things ain't what they used to be.

Alan Moore, *The Saga of the Swamp Thing* (1982). While the character technically predates Moore, his take on the inhuman living swamp (who fights on behalf of Earth, either for or against the Justice League) is definitive. Current storylines have Swamp Thing (as the avatar of the Gaia-like "Green") fighting alongside Buddy Baker, a.k.a. Animal Man (avatar of the "Red"), against the "Black" (the embodiment of death, decay, and rot). In Moore's *V for Vendetta* (1982) floods and crop failures are a major cause of the dystopian government in power in future Britain, while his seminal superhero comic *Watchmen* (1985) takes place against a backdrop of looming nuclear war and inevitable ecological disaster.

9 (Shane Acker, 2009). Insidious "Fabrication Machine" technology has destroyed the environment in this animated film, leaving nine self-aware rag-dolls the only conscious life in a ruined world.

"(Nothing but) Flowers" (Talking Heads, 1981). Song. There was a factory; now there are mountains and rivers. If this is paradise, I wish I had a lawnmower.

Portal and *Portal 2* (Valve Corporation, 2007, 2011). The madness of science. Apeture Science's slogan is the cracked motto of the American century: "We do what we must, because we can."

Princess Mononoke (Hayao Miyazaki, 1997). The most strident articulation of the ecological themes operative across Miyazaki's work, also evident in *Nausicaä of the Valley of the Wind* (1984) and *Spirited Away* (2001).

Settlers of Catan (Klaus Teuber, 1995). The iPad "app" version of the game features a single-player "story mode" that culminates in a climate-change-inspired rules modification in which overdevelopment of Catan leads to total desertification of the island.

SimEarth (Maxis, 1990). Early "god game" from Will Wright, the creator of SimCity, allows players to fiddle with the variables of the environment. *Spore* (Maxis, 2008), also designed by Wright, has a similar feel, but is dedicated primarily to biological evolution.

WALL-E (Andrew Stanton, 2008). Let Disney sell you a critique of its own ecologically destructive practices, nicely packaged in an environmentally friendly cardboard DVD case never used again for any subsequent film releases. And yet the film has an unexpected utopian streak that somehow manages to transcend its troubled origins. Pixar similarly explores tough ecological questions in its 2001 film *Monsters, Inc.* (Peter Docter, 2001), which subtly and smartly allegorizes resource imperialism and the economics of scarcity in late capitalism.

Brian K. Vaughan, *Y: The Last Man* (2002). Killing off all the men is once again the necessary first step toward a rational and sustainable ecotopia.

ABOUT THE CONTRIBUTORS

CHRISTINA ALT is a postdoctoral fellow at the University of Sydney, currently researching intersections between early ecology and literary modernism. She will be taking up a lectureship at the University of St Andrews in 2013.

BRENT BELLAMY is a PhD candidate in English and Film Studies at the University of Alberta, writing a dissertation on contemporary U.S. post-apocalyptic fiction.

GERRY CANAVAN is an assistant professor in the Department of English at Marquette University, teaching twentieth- and twenty-first-century literature. He is currently at work on two book projects: one on SF and totality, and the other on the work of Octavia Butler. He is also (with Eric Carl Link) the editor of *The Cambridge Companion to American Science Fiction*.

SABINE HÖHLER is an Associate Professor of Science and Technology Studies at KTH Royal Institute of Technology in Stockholm. Recently she has finished a book-length study titled *Spaceship Earth: Envisioning Human Habitats in the Environmental Age* that explores ecological discourses on the Earth's "life support systems" between 1960 and 1990.

ADELINE JOHNS-PUTRA is Reader in English Literature at the University of Surrey. Her books include *The History of the Epic* (2006) and, edited with Catherine Brace, *Landscape: Process and Text* (2010). She is currently editing a special issue on climate change for the journal *symplokē*.

MELODY JUE is a PhD candidate in the Program in Literature at Duke University, writing her dissertation on intersections between ecological thinking and oceanic literatures, with particular interest in oceanic SF.

ROB LATHAM is Professor of English at the University of California, Riverside. A senior editor of *Science Fiction Studies*, he is the author of *Consuming Youth: Vampires, Cyborgs, and the Culture of Consumption* (2002) and coeditor of *The Wesleyan Anthology of Science Fiction* (2010). He is currently editing *The Oxford Handbook of Science Fiction*.

ANDREW MILNER is Professor of English and Comparative Literature at Monash University in Melbourne, Honorary Research Fellow in the School of English at the University of Liverpool, and the Ludwig Hirschfeld Mack Visiting Professor of Australian Studies for 2013 in the Institut für Englische Philologie at the Freie Universität Berlin. His recent published work includes *Tenses of Imagination* (2010) and *Locating Science Fiction* (2012).

TIMOTHY MORTON holds the Rita Shea Guffey Chair in English at Rice University, where he lectures on literature, ecology, and critical theory. He is the author of *Ecology without Nature* (2007) and *The Ecological Thought* (2010), as well as the forthcoming *Realist Magic: Objects, Ontology, Causality*.

ERIC C. OTTO is Associate Professor of Environmental Humanities at Florida Gulf Coast

University. He is the author of *Green Speculations: Science Fiction and Transformative Environmentalism* (2012).

MICHAEL PAGE teaches English at the University of Nebraska–Lincoln. He is currently working on two book projects, *Views of the Land: Romanticism, Agriculture, Landscape, and Ecology* and *Ecology and Science Fiction*.

CHRISTOPHER PALMER is an Associate Professor in the School of Communication, Arts, and Critical Enquiry at Australia's La Trobe University. He is the author of multiple investigations into SF and related genres, including *Philip K. Dick: Exhilaration and Terror of the Postmodern* (2003).

GIB PRETTYMAN is Associate Professor of English at Penn State Fayette. His recent work focuses on the role of Eastern religions in SF and utopia, with an emphasis on the work of Aldous Huxley, Ursula Le Guin, and Kim Stanley Robinson. He also serves as associate editor of *Resources for American Literary Study*.

KIM STANLEY ROBINSON is the Hugo-, Nebula-, and Locus-Award-winning author of myriad SF novels and stories, including most recently *Galileo's Dream* (2009) and *2312* (2012).

ELZETTE STEENKAMP recently completed a PhD in English at Rhodes University in Grahamstown, South Africa. Her research focuses on the treatment of ecological crisis in South African speculative fiction. She is currently working as the production manager of *LitNet Akademies*, an online academic journal based in Stellenbosch, South Africa.

IMRE SZEMAN is Canada Research Chair in Cultural Studies and Professor of English and Film Studies at the University of Alberta. He is the author, coauthor, or coeditor of ten books to date, including most recently *Cultural Theory: An Anthology* (2010, coeditor) and *Contemporary Literary and Cultural Theory: The Johns Hopkins Guide* (2012, coeditor). He is currently working on a book on the cultural politics of oil.

INDEX

Alaimo, Stacey, 41

Aldiss, Brian, 7, 47, 77, 81

alien encounters: advanced extraterrestrials in H. G. Wells, 25–28; alien other in South African SF, 145, 149; alien susceptibility to bacteria in *War of the Worlds*, 27; in *Avatar*, 220–24; British "cosy catastrophe" narratives, 79–80; colonized earth in *The Genocides*, 81; cyborgs, 145, 149, 155, 221; empathy emergence in *War of the Worlds*, 29–30; "first contact" narratives, 77; human/ animal couplings in *District 9*, 151, 154–55; human simulacra/phantoms in *Solaris*, 228–30; indigenous Other in *Avatar*, 13, 19; Martians in *City*, 46; 1950s alien menace narratives, 78–79; sympathetic prawns in *District 9*, 151–52, 154–55, 157n20. *See also* human beings; robots

Amazing Stories, 2, 42

Anderson, Perry, 158

animals: animal objectification in Bacigalupi, 185–86, 188; animal rights movement, 89–90; dog paradise in *City*, 47; human-animal analogy in H. G. Wells, 27–28, 36–37, 250; human-animal couplings in *District 9*, 151, 154–55; nonhuman values and, 250; primitivist conceptions of, xi. *See also* human beings; mass extinction; multispecies relations; nature

Anker, Peder, 30–31

Anthropocene: defiant rationality in *Avatar* and, 221–23; Enlightenment philosophy and, 210; overview, 206–8; scientific provenance of, x, 4–5; SF as interpretation of, 16. *See also* climate change; mass extinction

anthropocentrism. *See* human beings

apocalypse: ancient ruins as projected future, 11–12; apocalyptic capitalism, 12–14; apocalyptic religious discourse, 254–55; class difference in apocalyptic worlds, 201–2, 204n27; early development of, 48–49; in Kim Stanley Robinson, 245–46; Last Man theme, 48, 166; natural catastrophe themes, 50–51; nuclear catastrophe themes, 4, 116; ordinariness and anomaly in, 158–161, 170–74; parodies of, 161–66, 169–170; pastoral new-beginning mode, 49; post-apocalyptic theme types, 3; radical potential of doom, 12–13; retained agency in, 4; staged apocalypse in *Girlfriend in a Coma*, 161–66; survival of lasting catastrophe, 10–11; transformation of humanity, 13–14, 169–73. *See also* climate change; dystopian fiction; eco-catastrophe narratives; nuclear weapons/ nuclear war; scarcity

Arata, Stephen, 77

Asimov, Isaac: ecological limits in, 7, 20n17. Works: *Foundation and Earth*, 20n17; *Foundation's Edge*, 20n17; *Before the Golden Age*, 40; *Robots and Empire*, 7

Astounding Science Fiction Stories, 42, 78. See also *City* series

Atwood, Margaret: climate change themes in, 128, 131; cultural alienation as theme in, 166–69, 174; eco-religion in, 257; environmentalist ethics in, 140n7; Quiet Earth theme in, 11; reversal of historical expansion in, 15. Works: *The Handmaid's Tale*, 117; *MaddAddam* series, 257; *Oryx and Crake*, 11, 18, 128, 166–69, 171, 173–74; "Time Capsule Found on the Dead